Praise for Jason Mott and *The Returned*

"Intriguing.... *The Returned* pulses with life."
—*Entertainment Weekly*

"Mott's haunting debut...is a crackling page-turner."
—*People*

"An impressive debut novel."
—*USA TODAY*

"*The Returned* transforms a brilliant premise into
an extraordinary and beautifully realized novel. My spine is
still shivering from the memory of this haunting story. Wow."
—Douglas Preston, #1 *New York Times* bestselling author
of *The Monster of Florence*

"In his exceptional debut novel, poet Mott brings drama,
pathos, joy, horror, and redemption to a riveting tale."
—*Publishers Weekly* (starred review)

"Flawless.... One of the best novels this reviewer
has encountered this year."
—*Sci Fi* magazine

"Beautifully written and emotionally astute.... A breathtaking novel
that navigates emotional minefields with realism and grace."
—*Kirkus Reviews* (starred review)

"Mott brings a singularly eloquent voice to this elegiac novel, which
not only fearlessly tackles larger questions about mortality but also
insightfully captures life's simpler moments.... A beautiful meditation
on what it means to be human."
—*Booklist* (starred review)

"A masterly first novel.... It speaks to many aspects
of the human condition.... Highly recommended for those who
love a strong story that makes them think."
—*Library Journal* (starred review)

THE
RETURNED

jason mott

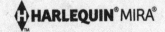

Recycling programs
for this product may
not exist in your area.

ISBN-13: 978-0-7783-1707-4

THE RETURNED

For questions and comments about the quality of this book, please contact us at CustomerService@Harlequin.com.

www.Harlequin.com

For my mother and father

THE
RETURNED

ONE

Harold opened the door that day to find a dark-skinned man in a well-cut suit smiling at him. At first he thought of reaching for his shotgun, but then he remembered that Lucille had made him sell it years ago on account of an incident involving a traveling preacher and an argument having to do with hunting dogs.

"Can I help you?" Harold said, squinting in the sunlight— light which only made the dark-skinned man in the suit look darker.

"Mr. Hargrave?" the man said.

"I suppose," Harold replied.

"Who is it, Harold?" Lucille called. She was in the living room being vexed by the television. The news announcer was talking about Edmund Blithe, the first of the Returned, and how his life had changed now that he was alive again.

"Better the second time around?" the announcer on the television asked, speaking directly into the camera, laying the burden of answering squarely on the shoulders of his viewers.

The wind rustled through the oak tree in the yard near the house, but the sun was low enough that it drove horizontally beneath the branches and into Harold's eyes. He held a hand over his eyes like a visor, but still, the dark-skinned man and the boy were little more than silhouettes plastered against a green-and-blue backdrop of pine trees beyond the open yard and cloudless sky out past the trees. The man was thin, but square-framed in his manicured suit. The boy was small for what Harold estimated to be about the age of eight or nine.

Harold blinked. His eyes adjusted more.

"Who is it, Harold?" Lucille called a second time, after realizing that no reply had come to her first inquiry.

Harold only stood in the doorway, blinking like a hazard light, looking down at the boy, who consumed more and more of his attention. Synapses kicked on in the recesses of his brain. They crackled to life and told him who the boy was standing next to the dark-skinned stranger. But Harold was sure his brain was wrong. He made his mind to do the math again, but it still came up with the same answer.

In the living room the television camera cut away to a cluster of waving fists and yelling mouths, people holding signs and shouting, then soldiers with guns standing statuesque as only men laden with authority and ammunition can. In the center was the small semidetached house of Edmund Blithe, the curtains drawn. That he was somewhere inside was all that was known.

Lucille shook her head. "Can you imagine it?" she said. Then: "Who is it at the door, Harold?"

Harold stood in the doorway taking in the sight of the boy: short, pale, freckled, with a shaggy mop of brown hair. He wore an old-style T-shirt, a pair of jeans and a great look of relief in his eyes—eyes that were not still and frozen, but trembling with life and rimmed with tears.

"What has four legs and goes 'Boooo'?" the boy asked in a shaky voice.

Harold cleared his throat—not certain just then of even that. "I don't know," he said.

"A cow with a cold!"

Then the child had the old man by the waist, sobbing, "Daddy! Daddy!" before Harold could confirm or deny. Harold fell against the door frame—very nearly bowled over—and patted the child's head out of some long-dormant paternal instinct. "Shush," he whispered. "Shush."

"Harold?" Lucille called, finally looking away from the television, certain that some terror had darkened her door. "Harold, what's going on? Who is it?"

Harold licked his lips. "It's...it's..."

He wanted to say "Joseph."

"It's Jacob," he said, finally.

Thankfully for Lucille, the couch was there to catch her when she fainted.

Jacob William Hargrave died on August 15, 1966. On his eighth birthday, in fact. In the years that followed, townsfolk would talk about his death in the late hours of the night when they could not sleep. They would roll over to wake their spouses and begin whispered conversations about the uncertainty of the world and how blessings needed to be counted. Sometimes they would rise together from the bed to stand in the doorway of their children's bedroom to watch them sleep and to ponder silently on the nature of a God that would take a child so soon from this world. They were Southerners in a small town, after all: How could such a tragedy not lead them to God?

After Jacob's death, his mother, Lucille, would say that she'd known something terrible was going to happen that day on account of what had happened just the night before.

That night Lucille dreamed of her teeth falling out. Something her mother had told her long ago was an omen of death.

All throughout Jacob's birthday party Lucille had made a point to keep an eye on not only her son and the other children, but on all the other guests, as well. She flitted about like a nervous sparrow, asking how everyone was doing and if they'd had enough to eat and commenting on how much they'd slimmed down since last time she'd seen them or on how tall their children had gotten and, now and again, how beautiful the weather was. The sun was everywhere and everything was green that day.

Her unease made her a wonderful hostess. No child went unfed. No guest found themselves lacking conversation. She'd even managed to talk Mary Green into singing for them later in the evening. The woman had a voice silkier than sugar, and Jacob, if he was old enough to have a crush on someone, had a thing for her, something that Mary's husband, Fred, often ribbed the boy about. It was a good day, that day. A good day, until Jacob disappeared.

He slipped away unnoticed the way only children and other small mysteries can. It was sometime between three and three-thirty—as Harold and Lucille would later tell the police—when, for reasons only the boy and the earth itself knew, Jacob made his way over the south side of the yard, down past the pines, through the forest and on down to the river, where, without permission or apology, he drowned.

Just days before the man from the Bureau showed up at their door Harold and Lucille had been discussing what they might do if Jacob "turned up Returned."

"They're not people," Lucille said, wringing her hands. They were on the porch. All important happenings occurred on the porch.

"We couldn't just turn him away," Harold told his wife. He stamped his foot. The argument had turned very loud very quickly.

"They're just not people," she repeated.

"Well, if they're not people, then what are they? Vegetable? Mineral?" Harold's lips itched for a cigarette. Smoking always helped him get the upper hand in an argument with his wife which, he suspected, was the real reason she made such a fuss about the habit.

"Don't be flippant with me, Harold Nathaniel Hargrave. This is serious."

"Flippant?"

"Yes, flippant! You're always flippant! Always prone to flippancy!"

"I swear. Yesterday it was, what, 'loquacious'? So today it's 'flippant,' huh?"

"Don't mock me for trying to better myself. My mind is still as sharp as it always was, maybe even sharper. And don't you go trying to get off subject."

"Flippant." Harold smacked the word, hammering the final *t* at the end so hard a glistening bead of spittle cleared the porch railing. "Hmph."

Lucille let it pass. "I don't know what they are," she continued. She stood. Then sat again. "All I know is they're not like you and me. They're…they're…" She paused. She prepared the word in her mouth, putting it together carefully, brick by brick. "They're devils," she finally said. Then she recoiled, as if the word might turn and bite her. "They've just come here to kill us. Or tempt us! These are the end days. 'When the dead shall walk the earth.' It's in the Bible!"

Harold snorted, still hung up on "flippant." His hand went to his pocket. "Devils?" he said, his mind finding its train of thought as his hand found his cigarette lighter. "Devils are superstitions. Products of small minds and even smaller imaginations. There's one word that should be banned from the dictionary— *devils*. Ha! Now there's a flippant word. It's got nothing to do with the way things really are, nothing to do with these 'Returned' folks—and make no mistake about it, Lucille Abigail Daniels Hargrave, they are people. They can walk over and kiss you. I ain't never met a devil that could do that…although, before we were married, there was this one blonde girl over in Tulsa one Saturday night. Yeah, now she might have been the devil, or a devil at least."

"Hush up!" Lucille barked, so loudly she seemed to surprise herself. "I won't sit here and listen to you talk that way."

"Talk what way?"

"It wouldn't be our boy," she said, her words slowing as the seriousness of things came drifting back to her, like the memory of a lost son, perhaps. "Jacob's gone on to God," she said. Her hands had become thin, white fists in her lap.

A silence came.

Then it passed.

"Where is it?" Harold asked.

"What?"

"In the Bible, where is it?"

"Where's what?"

"Where does it say 'the dead will walk the earth'?"

"Revelations!" Lucille opened her arms as she said the word, as if the question could not be any more addle-brained, as if she'd been asked about the flight patterns of pine trees. "It's right there in Revelations! 'The dead shall walk the earth'!" She was glad to see that her hands were still fists. She waved them at no one, the way people in movies sometimes did.

Harold laughed. "What part of Revelations? What chapter? What verse?"

"You hush up," she said. "That it's in there is all that matters. Now hush!"

"Yes, ma'am," Harold said. "Wouldn't want to be flippant."

But when the devil actually showed up at the front door—their own particular devil—small and wondrous as he had been all those years ago, his brown eyes slick with tears, joy and the sudden relief of a child who has been too long away from his parents, too long of a time spent in the company of strangers…well…Lucille, after she recovered from her fainting episode, melted like candle wax right there in front of the clean-cut, well-suited man from the Bureau. For his part, the Bureau man took it well enough. He smiled a practiced smile, no doubt having witnessed this exact scene more than a few times in recent weeks.

"There are support groups," the Bureau man said. "Support groups for the Returned. And support groups for the families of the Returned." He smiled.

"He was found," the man continued—he'd given them his name but both Harold and Lucille were already terrible at remembering people's names and having been reunited with their dead son didn't do much to help now, so they thought of him simply as the Man from the Bureau "—in a small fishing village outside Beijing, China. He was kneeling at the edge of a river, trying to catch fish or some such from what I've been told. The local people, none of whom spoke English well enough for him to understand, asked him his name in Mandarin, how he'd gotten there, where he was from, all those questions you ask when coming upon a lost child.

"When it was clear that language was something of a barrier, a group of women were able to calm him. He'd started crying—and why wouldn't he?" The man smiled again. "After all, he wasn't in Kansas anymore. But they settled him down.

Then they found an English-speaking official and, well…"
He shrugged his shoulders beneath his dark suit, indicating
the insignificance of the rest of the story. Then he added, "It's
happening like this all over."

He paused again. He watched with a smile that was not dis-
ingenuous as Lucille fawned over the son who was suddenly
no longer dead. She clutched him to her chest and kissed the
crown of his head, then cupped his face in her hands and
showered it with kisses and laughter and tears.

Jacob replied in kind, giggling and laughing, but not wiping away his mother's kisses even though he was at that particular point in youth when wiping away a mother's kisses was
what seemed most appropriate to him.

"It's a unique time for everyone," the man from the Bureau said.

The brass bell chimed lightly as he entered the convenience store. Outside someone was just pulling away from the gas pump and did not see him. Behind the counter a plump, red-faced man halted his conversation with a tall, lanky man and the two of them stared. The only sound was the low hum of the freezers. Kamui bowed low, the brass bell chiming a second time as the door closed behind him.

The men behind the counter still did not speak.

He bowed a second time, smiling. "Forgive me," he said, and the men jumped. "I surrender." He held his hands in the air.

The red-faced man said something that Kamui could not understand. He looked at the lanky man and the two of them spoke at length, glancing sideways as they did. Then the red-faced man pointed at the door. Kamui turned, but saw only the empty street and the rising sun behind him. "I surrender," he said a second time.

He'd left his pistol buried next to a tree at the edge of the woods in which he'd found himself only a few hours ago, just as the other men had. He had even removed the jacket of his uniform and his hat and left them, as well, so that, now, he stood *in the small gas station at the break of day in his undershirt, pants and well-shined boots. All this to avoid being killed by the Americans. "Yamamoto desu," he said. Then: "I surrender."*

The red-faced man spoke again, louder this time. Then the second man joined him, both of them yelling and motioning in the direction of the door. "I surrender," Kamui said yet again, fearing the way their voices were rising. The lanky man grabbed a soda can from the counter and threw it at him. It missed, and the man yelled again and pointed toward the door again and began searching for something else to throw.

"Thank you," Kamui managed, though he knew it was not what he wanted to say. His English vocabulary was limited to very few words. He backed toward the door. The red-faced man reached beneath the counter and found a can of something. He threw it with a grunt. The can struck Kamui above the left temple. He fell back against the door. The brass bell rang.

The red-faced man threw more cans while the lanky man yelled and searched for objects of his own to throw until, stumbling, Kamui fled the gas station, his hands above him, proving that he was not armed and meant to do nothing other than turn himself in. His heart beat in his ears.

Outside, the sun had risen and the city was cast a soft orange. It looked peaceful.

With a trickle of blood running down the side of his head, he raised his hands into the air and walked down the street. "I surrender!" he yelled, waking the town, hoping the people he found would let him live.

TWO

Of course, even for people returning from the dead, there was paperwork. The International Bureau of the Returned was receiving funding faster than it could spend it. And there wasn't a single country on the planet that wasn't willing to dig into treasury reserves or go into debt to try and secure whatever "in" they could with the Bureau due to the fact that it was the only organization on the planet that was able to coordinate everything and everyone.

The irony was that no one within the Bureau knew more than anyone else. All they were really doing were counting people and giving them directions home. That was it.

When the emotion had died down and the hugging and all stopped in the doorway of the Hargraves' little house—nearly a half hour later—Jacob was moved into the kitchen where he could sit at the table and catch up on all the eating he'd missed in his absence. The Bureau man sat in the living room with Harold and Lucille, took his stacks of paperwork from a brown, leather briefcase and got down to business.

"When did the returning individual originally die?" asked

the Bureau man, who—for a second time—revealed his name as Agent Martin Bellamy.

"Do we have to say that?" Lucille asked. She inhaled and sat straighter in her seat, suddenly looking very regal and discriminating, having finally straightened her long, silver hair that had come undone while fawning over her son.

"Say what?" Harold replied.

"She means 'die,'" Agent Bellamy said.

Lucille nodded.

"What's wrong with saying he died?" Harold asked, his voice louder than he'd planned. Jacob was still within eyesight, if mostly out of earshot.

"Shush!"

"He died," Harold said. "No sense in pretending he didn't." He didn't notice, but his voice was lower now.

"Martin Bellamy knows what I mean," Lucille said. She wrung her hands in her lap, looking for Jacob every few seconds, as if he were a candle in a house of drafts.

Agent Bellamy smiled. "It's okay," he said. "This is pretty common, actually. I should have been more considerate. Let's start again, shall we?" He looked down at his questionnaire. "When did the returning individual—"

"Where are you from?"

"Sir?"

"Where are you from?" Harold was standing by the window looking out at the blue sky.

"You sound like a New Yorker," Harold said.

"Is that good or bad?" Agent Bellamy asked, pretending he had not been asked about his accent a dozen times since being assigned to the Returned of southern North Carolina.

"It's horrible," Harold said. "But I'm a forgiving man."

"Jacob," Lucille interrupted. "Call him Jacob, please. His name is Jacob."

"Yes, ma'am," Agent Bellamy said. "I'm sorry. I should know better by now."

"Thank you, Martin Bellamy," Lucille said. Again, somehow, her hands were fists in her lap. She breathed deeply and, with concentration, unfolded them. "Thank you, Martin Bellamy," she said again.

"When did Jacob leave?" Agent Bellamy asked again softly.

"August 15, 1966," Harold said. He moved into the doorway, looking unsettled. He licked his lips. His hands took turns moving from the pockets of his worn, old pants up to his worn, old lips, finding no peace—or cigarette—on either side of the journey.

Agent Bellamy made notes.

"How did it happen?"

The word *Jacob* became an incantation that day as the searchers looked for the boy. At regular intervals the call went up. "Jacob! Jacob Hargrave!" And then another voice lifted the name and passed it down the line. "Jacob! Jacob!"

In the beginning their voices trampled upon one another in a cacophony of fear and desperation. But then the boy was not quickly found and, to save their throats, the men and women of the search party took turns shouting out as the sun turned gold and dripped down the horizon and was swallowed first by the tall trees and then by the low brush.

Then they were all trudging drunkenly—exhausted from high-stepping through the dense bramble, wrung out from worry. Fred Green was there with Harold. "We'll find him," Fred said again and again. "Did you see that look in his eyes when he unwrapped that BB gun I gave him? You ever seen a boy so excited?" Fred huffed, his legs burning from fatigue. "We'll find him." He nodded. "We'll find him."

Then it was full-on night and the bushy, pine-laden land-scape of Arcadia sparkled with the glow of flashlights.

When they neared the river Harold was glad he'd talked Lucille into staying back at the house—"He might come back," he had said, "and he'll want his mama"—because he knew, by whatever means such things are known, that he would find his son in the river.

Harold sloshed knee-deep in the shallows—slowly, taking a step, calling the boy's name, pausing to listen out in case he should be somewhere nearby, calling back, taking another step, calling the boy's name again, and on and on.

When he finally came upon the body, the moonlight and the water had shone the boy to a haunting and beautiful silver, the same color as the glimmering water.

"Dear God," Harold said. And that was the last time he would ever say it.

Harold told the story, hearing suddenly all the years in his voice. He sounded like an old man, hardened and rough. Now and again as he spoke, he would reach a thick, wrinkled hand to run over the few thin, gray strands still clinging to his scalp. His hands were decorated with liver spots and his knuckles were swollen from the arthritis that sometimes bothered him. It didn't bother him as badly as it did some other people his age, but it did just enough to remind him of the wealth of youth that was not his anymore. Even as he spoke, his lower back jolted with a small twinge of pain.

Hardly any hair. Mottled skin. His large, round head. His wrinkled, wide ears. Clothes that seemed to swallow him up no matter how hard Lucille tried to find something that fit him better. No doubt about it: he was an old man now.

Something about having Jacob back—still young and vibrant—made Harold Hargrave realize his age.

Lucille, just as old and gray as her husband, only looked away as he spoke, only watched her eight-year-old son sit at the kitchen table eating a slice of pecan pie as if, just now, it were 1966 again and nothing was wrong and nothing would ever be wrong again. Sometimes she would clear a silver strand of hair from her face, but if she caught sight of her thin, liver-spotted hands, they did not seem to bother her.

They were a pair of thin, wiry birds, Harold and Lucille. She outgrew him in these later years. Or, rather, he shrank faster than she so that, now, he had to look up at her when they argued. And Lucille also had the benefit of not wasting away quite as much as he had—something she blamed upon his years of cigarette smoking. Her dresses still fit her. Her thin, long arms were nimble and articulate where his, hidden beneath the puffiness of shirts that fit him too loosely, made him look a bit more vulnerable than he used to. Which was giving her an edge these days.

Lucille took pride in that, and did not feel quite so guilty about it, even though she sometimes thought she should.

Agent Bellamy wrote until his hand cramped and then he wrote more. He'd had the forethought to record the interview, but he still found it good policy to write things down, as well. People seemed offended if they met with a government man and nothing was written down. This worked for Agent Bellamy. His brain was the type that preferred to see things rather than hear them. If he didn't write it all down now he'd just be stuck doing it later.

Bellamy wrote from the time the birthday party began that day in 1966. He wrote through the recounting of Lucille's weeping and guilt—she'd been the last one to see Jacob alive; she only remembered a brief image of one of his pale arms as he darted around a corner, chasing one of the other children.

Bellamy wrote that there were almost more people at the funeral than the church could hold.

But there were parts of the interview that he did not write. Details that, out of respect, he committed only to memory rather than to bureaucratic documentation.

Harold and Lucille had survived the boy's death, but only just. The next fifty-odd years became infected with a peculiar type of loneliness, a tactless loneliness that showed up unbidden and began inappropriate conversations over Sunday dinner. It was a loneliness they never named and seldom talked about. They only shuffled around it with their breaths held, day in and day out, as if it were an atom smasher—reduced in scale but not in complexity or splendor—suddenly shown up in the center of the living room and dead set on affirming all the most ominous and far-fetched speculations of the harsh way the universe genuinely worked.

In its own way, that was a truth of sorts.

Over the years they not only became accustomed to hiding from their loneliness, they became skilled at it. It was a game, almost: don't talk about the Strawberry Festival, because he had loved it; don't stare too long at buildings you admire because they will remind you of the time you said he would grow into an architect one day; ignore the children in whose face you see him.

When Jacob's birthday came around each year they would spend the day being somber and having difficulty making conversation. Lucille might take to weeping with no explanation, or Harold might smoke a little more that day than he had the day before.

But that was only in the beginning. Only in those first, sad years.

They grew older.

Doors closed.

Harold and Lucille had become so far removed from the tragedy of Jacob's death that when the boy reappeared at their front door—smiling, still perfectly assembled and unaged, still their blessed son, still only eight years old—all of it was so far away that Harold had forgotten the boy's name.

Then Harold and Lucille were done talking and there was silence. But despite its solemnity, it was short-lived. Because there was the sound of Jacob sitting at the kitchen table raking his fork across his plate, gulping down his lemonade and burping with great satisfaction. "Excuse me," the boy yelled to his parents.

Lucille smiled.

"Forgive me for asking this," Agent Bellamy began. "And please, don't take this as any type of accusation. It's simply something we have to ask in order to better understand these... unique circumstances."

"Here it comes," Harold said. His hands had finally stopped foraging for phantom cigarettes and settled into his pockets. Lucille waved her hand dismissively.

"What were things like between you and Jacob *before?*" Agent Bellamy asked.

Harold snorted. His body finally decided his right leg would better hold his weight than his left. He looked at Lucille. "This is the part where we're supposed to say we drove him off or something. Like they do on TV. We're supposed to say that we'd had a fight with him, denied him supper, or some kind of abuse like you see on TV. Something like that." Harold walked over to a small table that stood in the hallway facing the front door. In the top drawer was a fresh pack of cigarettes.

Before he'd even made his way back to the living room Lucille opened fire. "You will not!"

Harold opened the wrapper with mechanical precision, as

if his hands were not his own. He placed a cigarette, unlit, between his lips and scratched his wrinkled face and exhaled, long and slow. "That's all I needed," he said. "That's all."

Agent Bellamy spoke softly. "I'm not trying to say that you or anyone else caused your son's...well, I'm running out of euphemisms." He smiled. "I'm only asking. The Bureau is trying hard to make heads or tails of this, just like everyone else. We might be in charge of helping to connect people up with one another, but that doesn't mean we have any inside knowledge into how any of this is working. Or why it's happening." He shrugged his shoulders. "The big questions are still big, still untouchable. But our hope is that by finding out everything we can, by asking the questions that everyone might not necessarily be comfortable answering, we can touch some of these big questions. Get a handle on them, before they get out of hand."

Lucille leaned forward on the old couch. "And how might they get out of hand? Are things getting out of hand?"

"They will," Harold said. "Bet your Bible on that."

Agent Bellamy only shook his head in an even, professional manner and returned to his original question. "What were things like between you and Jacob before he left?"

Lucille could feel Harold coming up with an answer, so she answered to keep him silent. "Things were fine," she said. "Just fine. Nothing strange whatsoever. He was our boy and we loved him just like any parent should. And he loved us back. And that's all that it was. That's all it still is. We love him and he loves us and now, by the grace of God, we're back together again." She rubbed her neck and lifted her hands. "It's a miracle," she said.

Martin Bellamy took notes.

"And you?" he asked Harold.

Harold only took his unlit cigarette from his mouth and rubbed his head and nodded. "She said it all."

More note-taking.

"I'm going to ask a silly question now, but are either of you very religious?"

"Yes!" Lucille said, sitting suddenly erect. "Fan and friend of Jesus! And proud of it. Amen." She nodded in Harold's direction. "That one there, he's the heathen. Dependent wholly on the grace of God. I keep telling him to repent, but he's stubborn as a mule."

Harold chuckled like an old lawn mower. "We take religion in turns," he said. "Fifty-some years later, it's still not my turn, thankfully."

Lucille waved her hands.

"Denomination?" Agent Bellamy asked, writing.

"Baptist," Lucille answered.

"For how long?"

"All my life."

Notes.

"Well, that ain't exactly right," Lucille added.

Agent Bellamy paused.

"For a while there I was a Methodist. But me and the pastor couldn't see eye to eye on certain points in the Word. I tried one of them Holiness churches, too, but I just couldn't keep up with them. Too much hollering and singing and dancing. Felt like I was at a party first and in the house of the Lord second. And that ain't no way for a Christian to be." Lucille leaned to see that Jacob was still where he was supposed to be—he was half nodding at the table, just as he had always been apt to—then she continued. "And then there was a while when I tried being—"

"The man doesn't need all of this," Harold interrupted.

"You hush up! He asked me! Ain't that right, Martin Bellamy?"

The agent nodded. "Yes, ma'am, you're right. All of this may prove very important. In my experience, it's the little details that matter. Especially with something this big."

"Just how big is it?" Lucille asked quickly, as if she had been waiting for the opening.

"Do you mean how many?" Bellamy asked.

Lucille nodded.

"Not terribly many," Bellamy said in a measured voice. "I'm not allowed to give any specific numbers, but it's only a small phenomenon, a modest number."

"Hundreds?" Lucille pressed. "Thousands? What's 'modest'?"

"Not enough to be concerned about, Mrs. Hargrave," Bellamy replied, shaking his head. "Only enough to remain miraculous."

Harold chuckled. "He's got your number," he said.

Lucille only smiled.

By the time the details were all handed over to Agent Bellamy the sun had sighed into the darkness of the earth and there were crickets singing outside the window and Jacob lay quietly in the middle of Harold and Lucille's bed. Lucille had taken great pleasure in lifting the boy from the kitchen table and carrying him up to the bedroom. She never would have believed that, at her age, with her hip the way it was, that she had the strength to carry him by herself.

But when the time came, when she bent quietly at the table and placed her arms beneath the boy and called her body into action, Jacob rose, almost weightlessly, to meet her. It was as if she were in her twenties again. Young and nimble. It was as if time and pain were but rumors.

She carried him uneventfully up the stairs and, when she had tucked him beneath the covers, she settled onto the bed beside him and hummed gently the way she used to. He did not fall asleep just then, but that was okay, she felt.

He had slept long enough.

Lucille sat for a while only watching him, watching his chest rise and fall, afraid to take her eyes away, afraid that the magic—or the miracle—might suddenly end. But it did not, and she thanked the Lord.

When she came back into the living room Harold and Agent Bellamy were entangled in an awkward silence. Harold stood in the doorway, taking sharp puffs of a lit cigarette and throwing the smoke through the screen door into the night. Agent Bellamy stood next to the chair where he'd been sitting. He looked thirsty and tired all of a sudden. Lucille realized then that she hadn't offered him a drink since he'd arrived, and that made her hurt in an unusual way. But, from Harold and Agent Bellamy's behavior, she knew, somehow, that they were about to hurt her in a different way.

"He's got something to ask you, Lucille," Harold said. His hand trembled as he put the cigarette to his mouth. Because of this she made the decision to let him smoke unharassed.

"What is it?"

"Maybe you'll want to sit down," Agent Bellamy said, making a motion to come and help her sit.

Lucille took a step back. "What is it?"

"It's a sensitive question."

"I can tell. But it can't be as bad as all that, now can it?"

Harold gave her his back and puffed silently on his cigarette with his head hung.

"For everyone," Agent Bellamy began, "this is a question that can seem simple at first but, believe me, it is a very complex and serious matter. And I hope that you would take a moment to consider it thoroughly before you answer. Which isn't to say that you only have one chance to answer. But only to say that I just want you to be sure that you've given the question its proper consideration before you make a decision. It'll be difficult but, if possible, try not to let your emotions get the better of you."

Lucille went red. "Why, Mr. Martin Bellamy! I never would have figured you for one of those sexist types. Just because I'm a woman doesn't mean I'm going to go all to pieces."

"Dammit, Lucille," Harold barked, though his voice seemed to have trouble finding its legs. "Just listen to the man." He coughed then. Or perhaps he sobbed.

Lucille sat.

Martin Bellamy sat, as well. He brushed some invisible something from the front of his pants and examined his hands for a moment.

"Well," Lucille said, "get on with it. All this buildup is killing me."

"This is the last question I'll be asking you this evening. And it's not necessarily a question you have to answer just now, but the sooner you answer it, the better. It just makes things less complicated when the answer comes quickly."

"What is it?" Lucille pleaded.

Martin Bellamy inhaled. "Do you want to keep Jacob?"

That was two weeks ago.

Jacob was home now. Irrevocably. The spare room had been converted back into his bedroom and the boy had settled into his life as if it had never ended to begin with. He was young. He had a mother. He had a father. His universe ended there.

Harold, for reasons he could not quite put together in his head, had been painfully unsettled since the boy's return. He'd taken to smoking like a chimney. So much so that he spent most of his time outside on the porch, hiding from Lucille's lectures about his dirty habit.

Everything had changed so quickly. How could he not take up a bad habit or two?

"They're devils!" Harold heard Lucille's voice repeat inside his head.

The rain was spilling down. The day was old. Just behind the trees, darkness was coming on. The house had quieted. Just above the sound of the rain was the light huffing of an old woman who'd spent too much time chasing a child. She came through the screen door, dabbing sweat from her brow, and crumpled into her rocking chair.

"Lord!" Lucille said. "That child's gonna run me to death."

Harold put out his cigarette and cleared his throat—which he always did before trying to get Lucille's goat. "You mean that devil?"

She waved her hand at him. "Shush!" she said. "Don't you call him that!"

"You called him that. You said that's what they all were, remember?"

She was still short of breath from chasing the boy. Her words came staggered. "That was before," she huffed. "I was wrong. I see that now." She smiled and leaned back in exhaustion. "They're a blessing. A blessing from the Lord. That's what they are. A second chance!"

They sat for a while in silence, listening to Lucille's breath find itself. She was an old woman now, in spite of being a mother of an eight-year-old. She tired easily.

"And you should spend more time with him," Lucille said. "He knows you're keeping your distance. He can tell it. He knows you're treating him differently than you used to. When he was here before." She smiled, liking that description.

Harold shook his head. "And what will you do when he leaves?"

Lucille's face tightened. "Hush up!" she said. "'Keep your tongue from evil and your lips from speaking lies.' Psalm 34:13."

"Don't you Psalm at me. You know what they've been saying, Lucille. You know just as well as I do. How sometimes they just up and leave and nobody ever hears from them again, like the other side finally called them back."

Lucille shook her head. "I don't have time for such nonsense," she said, standing in spite of the heaviness of fatigue that hung in her limbs like sacks of flour. "Just rumors and nonsense. I'm going to start dinner. Don't you sit out here and catch pneumonia. This rain will kill you."

"I'll just come back," Harold said.

"Psalm 34:13!"

She closed and locked the screen door behind her.

From the kitchen came the clattering of pots and pans. Cabinet doors opening, closing. The scent of meat, flour, spices, all of it drenched in the perfume of May and rain. Harold was almost asleep when he heard the boy's voice. "Can I come outside, Daddy?" Harold shook off the drowsiness. "What?" He had heard the question perfectly well.

"Can I come outside? Please?"

For all the gaps in Harold's old memory, he remembered how defenseless he'd always been when "Please" was laid out just so before him.

"Your mama'll have a fit," he said.

"Just a little one, though."

Harold swallowed to keep from laughing.

He fumbled for a cigarette and failed—he'd sworn he'd had at least one more. He groped his pockets. In his pocket,

where there was no cigarette, he found a small, silver cross—
a gift from someone, though the place in his mind where the
details of that particular memory should have been stored was
empty. He hardly even remembered carrying it, but couldn't
help looking down at it as if it were a murder weapon.

The words *God Loves You,* once, had been etched in the
place where Christ belonged. But now the words were all
but gone. Only an *O* and half a *Y* remained. He stared at the
cross, then, as if his hand belonged to someone else, his thumb
began rubbing back and forth at the crux.

Jacob stood in the kitchen behind the screen door. He leaned
against the door frame with his hands behind his back and his
legs crossed, looking contemplative. His eyes scanned back
and forth over the horizon, watching the rain and the wind
and, then, his father. He exhaled heavily. Then he cleared his
throat. "Sure would be nice to come outside," he said with
flourish and drama.

Harold chuckled.

In the kitchen something was frying. Lucille was humming.

"Come on out," Harold said.

Jacob came and sat at Harold's feet and, as if in reply, the
rain became angry. Rather than falling from the sky, it leaped
to the earth. It whipped over the porch railing, splashing them
both, not that they paid it any heed. For a very long time the
old man and the once-dead boy sat looking at each other.
The boy was sandy-haired and freckled, his face as round and
smooth as it always had been. His arms were unusually long,
just as they had been, as his body was beginning its shift into
an adolescence denied him fifty years ago. He looked healthy,
Harold suddenly thought.

Harold licked his lips compulsively, his thumb working the
center of the cross. The boy did not move at all. If he hadn't
blinked now and again, he might as well have been dead.

* * *

"Do you want to keep him?"

It was Agent Bellamy's voice inside Harold's head this time.

"It's not my decision," Harold said. "It's Lucille's. You'll have to ask her. Whatever she says, I'll abide by."

Agent Bellamy nodded. "I can understand that, Mr. Hargrave. But I still have to ask you. I have to know your answer. It will stay between us, just you and me. I can even turn off the recorder if you want. But I have to have your answer. I have to know what you want. I have to know if you want to keep him."

"No," Harold said. "Not for all the world. But what choice do I have?"

Lewis and Suzanne Holt

He awoke in Ontario; she outside Phoenix. He had been an accountant. She taught piano.

The world was different, but still the same. Cars were quieter. Buildings were taller and seemed to glimmer in the night more than they used to. Everyone seemed busier. But that was all. And it did not matter.

He went south, hopping trains in a way that had not been done in years. He kept clear of the Bureau only by fortune or fate. She had started northeast—nothing more than a notion she felt possessed to follow—but it was not long before she was picked up and moved to just outside Salt Lake City, to what was quickly becoming a major processing facility for the region. Not long after that he was picked up somewhere along the border of Nebraska and Wyoming.

Ninety years after their deaths, they were together again.

She had not changed at all. He had grown a shade thinner than he had been, but only on account of his long journey. Behind fencing and uncertainty, they were not as afraid as others.

There is a music that forms sometimes, from the pairing of two people. An inescapable cadence that continues on.

THREE

The town of Arcadia was situated along the countryside in that way that many small, Southern towns were. It began with small, one-story wooden houses asleep in the middle of wide, flat yards along the sides of a two-lane blacktop that winded among dense pines, cedars and white oaks. Here and there, fields of corn or soybeans were found in the spring and summer. Only bare earth in the winter.

After a couple of miles the fields became smaller, the houses more frequent. Once one entered the town proper they found only two streetlights, a clunky organization of roads and streets and dead ends cluttered with old, exhausted homes. The only new houses in Arcadia were those that had been rebuilt after hurricanes. They glimmered in fresh paint and new wood and made a person imagine that, perhaps, something new could actually happen in this old town.

But new things did not come to this town. Not until the Returned.

The streets were not many and neither were the houses. In the center of town stood the school: an old, brick affair with small windows and small doors and retrofitted air-conditioning that did not work.

Off to the north, atop a small hill just beyond the limits of town, stood the church. It was built from wood and clapboard and sat like a lighthouse, reminding the people of Arcadia that there was always someone above them.

Not since '72 when the Sainted Soul Stirrers of Solomon—that traveling gospel band with the Jewish bassist from Arkansas—came to town had the church been so full. Just people atop people. Cars and trucks scattered about the church lawn. Someone's rust-covered pickup loaded down with lumber was parked against the crucifix in the center of the lawn, as if Jesus had gotten down off the cross and decided to make a run to the hardware store. A cluster of taillights covered up the small sign on the church lawn that read Jesus Loves You—Fish Fry May 31. Cars were stacked along the shoulder of the highway the way they had been that time back in '63—or was it '64?—at the funeral of those three Benson boys who'd all died in one horrible car crash and were mourned over the course of one long, dark day of lamentation.

"You need to come with us," Lucille said as Harold parked the old truck on the shoulder of the road and pawed his shirt pocket for his cigarettes. "What are folks going to think when you're not there?" She unfastened Jacob's seat belt and straightened his hair.

"They'll think, 'Harold Hargrave won't come in the church? Glory be! In these times of madness at least something is as it always has been!'"

"It's not like there's a service going on, you heathen. It's just a town meeting. No reason why you shouldn't come in."

Lucille stepped out of the truck and straightened her dress. It was her favorite dress, the one she wore to important things, the one that picked up dirt from every surface imaginable—a cotton/polyester blend colored in a pastel shade of green with small flowers stitched along the collar and patterned around the end of the thin sleeves. "I don't know why I bother some-times. I hate this truck," she said, wiping the back of her dress.

"You've hated every truck I've ever owned."

"But still you keep buying them."

"Can I stay here?" Jacob asked, fiddling with a button on the collar of his shirt. Buttons exercised a mysterious hold over the boy. "Daddy and me could—"

"Daddy and I could," Lucille corrected.

"No," Harold said, almost laughing. "You go with your mama." He put a cigarette to his lips and stroked his chin. "Smoke's bad for you. Gives you wrinkles and bad breath and makes you hairy."

"Makes you stubborn, too," Lucille added, helping Jacob from the cab.

"I don't think they want me in there," Jacob said.

"Go with your mama," Harold said in a hard voice. Then he lit his cigarette and took in as much nicotine as his tired old lungs could manage.

When his wife and the thing that might or might not be his son—he was still not sure of his stance on that exactly—were gone, Harold took one more pull on his cigarette and blew the smoke out through the open window. Then he sat with the cigarette burning down between his fingers. He stroked his chin and watched the church.

The church needed to be painted. It was peeling here and there and it was hard to put a finger on exactly what color the building was supposed to be, but a person could tell that it had once been much grander than it was now. He tried to think back to what color the church had been when the paint was fresh—he'd most certainly been around to see it painted. He even could almost remember who had done the job—some outfit from up around Southport—the name escaped him, as did the original paint color. All he could see in his mind was the current faded exterior.

But isn't that the way it is with memory? Give it enough time and it will become worn down and covered in a patina of self-serving omissions.

But what else could we trust?

Jacob had been a firecracker. A live wire. Harold remembered all the times the boy had gotten in trouble for not coming home before sunset or for running in church. One time he'd even come close to having Lucille in hysterics because he'd climbed to the top of Henrietta Williams's pear tree. Everybody was calling after him and the boy just sat there up in the shaded branches of the tree among ripe pears and dappled sunlight. Probably having himself a good old laugh about things.

In the glow of the streetlights Harold caught sight of a small creature darting from the steeple of the church—a flash of movement and wings. It rose for a second and glowed like snow in the dark night as car headlights flashed upon it.

And then it was gone and, Harold knew, not to return.

"It's not him," Harold said. He flicked his cigarette on the ground and leaned back against the musty old seat. He lolled his head and asked only of his body that it should go to sleep and be plagued by neither dream nor memory. "It's not."

Lucille held tightly to Jacob's hand as she made her way through the crowd cluttered around the front of the church as best as her bad hip would let her.

"Excuse me. Hi, there, Macon, how are you tonight? Pardon us. You doing okay tonight, Lute? That's good. Excuse me. Excuse us. Well, hello, Vaniece! Ain't seen you in ages. How you been? Good! That's good to hear! Amen. You take care now. Excuse me. Excuse us. Hey, there. Excuse us."

The crowd parted as she hoped they would, leaving Lucille unsure as to whether it was a sign that there was still decency and manners in the world, or a sign that she had, finally, become an old woman.

Or, perhaps they moved aside on account of the boy who walked beside her. There weren't supposed to be any Returned here tonight. But Jacob was her son, first and foremost, and nothing or no one—not even death or its sudden lack thereof—was going to cause her to treat him as anything other than that.

The mother and son found room in a front pew next to Helen Hayes. Lucille seated Jacob beside her and proceeded to join the cloud of murmuring that was like a morning fog clinging to everything. "So many people," she said, folding her hands across her chest and shaking her head.

"Ain't seen most of them in a month of Sundays," Helen Hayes said. Mostly everyone in and around Arcadia had some degree of relation; Helen and Lucille were cousins. Lucille had the long, angular look of the Daniels family: she was tall with thin wrists and small hands, a nose that made a sharp, straight line below her brown eyes. Helen, on the other hand, was all roundness and circles, thick wrists and a wide, round face. Only their hair, silver and straight now where it had once been as dark as creosote, showed that the two women were indeed related.

Helen was frighteningly pale, and she spoke through pursed lips, which gave her a very serious and upset appearance. "And you'd think that when this many people finally came to church, they'd come for the Lord. Jesus was the first one to come back from the dead, but do any of these heathens care?"

"Mama?" Jacob said, still fascinated by the loose button on his shirt.

"Do they come here for Jesus?" Helen continued. "Do

they come to pray? When's the last time they paid their tithes? When's the last revival they came to? Tell me that. That Thompson boy there…" She pointed a plump finger at a clump of teenagers huddled near the back corner of the church. "When's the last time you seen that boy in church?" She grunted. "Been so long, I thought he was dead."

"He was," Lucille said in a low voice. "You know that as well as anyone else that sets eyes on him."

"I thought this meeting was supposed to be just for, well, you know?"

"Anybody with common sense knows that wasn't going to happen," Lucille said. "And, frankly, it shouldn't happen. This meeting is all about them. Why shouldn't they be here?"

"I hear Jim and Connie are living here," Helen said. "Can you believe it?"

"Really?" Lucille replied. "I hadn't heard. But why shouldn't they? They're a part of this town."

"They were," Helen corrected, offering no sympathy in her tone.

"Mama?" Jacob interrupted.

"Yes?" Lucille replied. "What is it?"

"I'm hungry."

Lucille laughed. The notion that she had a son who was alive and who wanted food still made her very happy. "But you just ate!"

Jacob finally succeeded in popping the loose button from his shirt. He held it in his small, white hands, turned it over and studied it the way one studies a proposal of theoretical math. "But I'm hungry."

"Amen," Lucille said. She patted his leg and kissed his forehead. "We'll get you something when we get back home."

"Peaches?"

"If you want."

"Glazed?"

"If you want."

"I want," Jacob said, smiling. "Daddy and me—"

"Daddy and *I*," Lucille corrected again.

It was only May, but the old church was already boiling. It had never had decent air-conditioning, and with so many people crowded in one atop the other, like sediment, the air would not move and there was the feeling that, at any moment, something very dramatic might occur.

The feeling made Lucille uneasy. She remembered reading newspapers or seeing things on the television about some terrible tragedy that began with too many people crowded together in too small of a space. Nobody would have anywhere to run, Lucille thought. She looked around the room—as best she could on account of all the people cluttering up her eye line—and counted the exits, just in case. There was the main doorway at the back of the church, but that was full up with people. Seemed like almost everybody in Arcadia was there, all six hundred of them. A wall of bodies.

Now and again she would notice the mass of people ripple forward as someone else forced entry into the church and into the body of the crowd. There came a low grumbling of "Hello" and "I'm sorry" and "Excuse me." If this were all a prelude to some tragic stampede death, at least it was cordial, Lucille thought.

Lucille licked her lips and shook her head. The air grew stiffer. There was no room for a body to move but, still, people were coming into the church. She could feel it. Probably, they were coming from Buckhead or Waccamaw or Riegelwood. The Bureau was trying to hold these town hall meetings in every town they could and there were some folks who'd become something akin to groupies—the kind you hear about that go around following famous musicians from one show to another. These people would follow the agents from the Bureau from one town hall meeting to another, looking for inconsistencies and a chance to start a fight.

Lucille even noticed a man and a woman that looked like they might have been a reporter and a photographer. The man looked like the kind she saw in magazines or read about in books: with his disheveled hair and five-o-clock shadow. Lucille imagined him smelling of split wood and the ocean.

The woman was sharply dressed, with her hair pulled back in a ponytail and her makeup flawlessly applied. "I wonder if there's a news van out there," Lucille said, but her words were lost in the clamor of the crowd.

As if cued by a stage director, Pastor Peters appeared from the cloistered door at the corner of the pulpit. His wife came after, looking as small and frail as she always did. She wore a plain black dress that made her look all the smaller. Already she was sweating, dabbing her brow in a delicate way. Lucille had trouble remembering the woman's first name. It was a small, frail thing, her name, something that people tended to overlook, just like the woman to whom it belonged.

In a type of biblical contradiction to his wife, Pastor Robert Peters was a tall, wide-bodied man with dark hair and a perpetually tanned-looking complexion. He was solid as stone. The kind of man who looked born, bred, propagated and cultivated for a way of life that hinged upon violence. Though, for as long as Lucille had known the young preacher, she'd never known him to so much as raise his voice—not counting the voice raising that came at the climax of certain sermons, but that was no more a sign of a violent soul than thunder was the sign of an angry god. Thunder in the voice of pastors was just the way God got your attention, Lucille knew.

"It's a taste of hell, Reverend," Lucille said with a grin when the pastor and his wife had come near enough.

"Yes, ma'am, Mrs. Lucille," Pastor Peters replied. His large, square head swung on his large, square neck. "We might have to see about getting a few people to exit quietly out the back. Don't think I've ever seen it this full. Maybe we ought to pass the plate around before we get rid of them, though. I need new tires."

"Oh, hush!"

"How are you tonight, Mrs. Hargrave?" The pastor's wife put her small hand to her small mouth, covering a small cough. "You look good," she said in a small voice.

"Poor thing," Lucille said, stroking Jacob's hair, "are you all right? You look like you're falling apart."

"I'm fine," the woman said. "Just a little under the weather. It's awfully hot in here."

"We may need to see about asking some of these people to stand outside," the pastor said again. He raised a thick, square hand, as if the sun were in his eyes. "Never have been enough exits in here."

"Won't be no exits in hell!" Helen added.

Pastor Peters only smiled and reached over the pew to shake her hand. "And how's this young fellow?" he said, aiming a bright smile at Jacob.

"I'm fine."

Lucille tapped him on the leg.

"I'm fine, sir," he corrected.

"What do you make of all this?" the pastor asked, chuckling. Beads of sweat glistened on his brow. "What are we going to do with all these people, Jacob?"

The boy shrugged and received another tap on the thigh.

"I don't know, sir."

"Maybe we could send them all home? Or maybe we could just get a water hose and hose them all down."

Jacob smiled. "A preacher can't do stuff like that."

"Says who?"

"The Bible."

"The Bible? Are you sure?"

Jacob nodded. "Want to hear a joke? Daddy teaches me the best jokes."

"Does he?"

"Mmm-hmm."

Pastor Peters kneeled, much to Lucille's embarrassment. She hated the notion of the pastor dirtying his suit on account of some two-bit joke that Harold had taught Jacob. Lord knows Harold knew some jokes that weren't meant for the light of holiness.

She held her breath.

"What did the math book tell the pencil?"

"Hmm." Pastor Peters rubbed his hairless chin, looking very deep in thought. "I don't know," he said finally. "What did the math book tell the pencil?"

"I've got a lot of problems," Jacob said. Then he laughed. To some, it was only the sound of a child laughing. Others, knowing that this boy had been dead only a few weeks prior, did not know how to feel.

The pastor laughed with the boy. Lucille, too—thanking God that the joke hadn't been the one about the pencil and the beaver.

Pastor Peters reached into the breast pocket of his coat and, with considerable flourish, conjured a small piece of foil-wrapped candy. "You like cinnamon?"

"Yes, sir! Thank you!"

"He's so well mannered," Helen Hayes added. She shifted

in her seat, her eyes following the pastor's frail wife, whose name Helen could not remember for the life of her.

"Anyone as well mannered as him deserves some candy," the pastor's wife said. She stood behind her husband, gently patting the center of his back—even that seemed a great feat for her, with him being so large and her being so small. "It's hard to find well-behaved children these days, what with things being the way they are." She paused to dab her brow. She folded her handkerchief and covered her mouth and coughed into it mouselike. "Oh, my."

"You're just about the sickest thing I've ever seen," Helen said.

The pastor's wife smiled and politely said, "Yes, ma'am."

Pastor Peters patted Jacob's head. Then he whispered to Lucille, "Whatever they say, don't let it bother him…or you. Okay?"

"Yes, Pastor," Lucille said.

"Yes, sir," Jacob said.

"Remember," the pastor said to the boy, "you're a miracle. All life is a miracle."

Angela Johnson

The floors of the guest bedroom in which she had been locked for the past three days were hardwood and beautiful. When they brought her meals, she tried not to spill anything, not wanting to ruin the floor and compound her punishment for whatever she had done wrong. Sometimes, just to be safe, she would eat her meals in the bathtub of the adjoining bathroom, listening to her parents speaking in the bedroom on the other side of the wall.

"Why haven't they come to take it back yet?" her father said.

"We never should have let them bring her...it to begin with," her mother replied. "That was your idea. What if the neighbors find out?"

"I think Tim already knows."

"How could he? It was so late when they brought it. He couldn't have been awake at that time of night, could he?"

A moment of silence came between them.

"Imagine what will happen if the firm finds out. This is your fault."

"I just had to know," he said, his voice softening. "It looks so much like h—"

"No. Don't start that again, Mitchell. Not again! I'm calling them again. They need to come and take it away tonight!"

She sat in the corner with her knees pulled to her chest, crying just a little, sorry for whatever she had done, not understanding any of this.

She wondered where they had taken her dresser, her clothes,
the posters she had plastered around the room over the years. The
walls were painted a soft pastel—something all at once red and
pink. The holes left by pushpins, the marks left by tape, the
pencil marks on the door frame indicating each year of growth...
all of them were gone. Simply painted over.

FOUR

when there were so many people and so little air in the room that everyone began to consider the likelihood of tragedy, the noise of the crowd began to grow silent. The silence began at the front doors of the church and marched through the crowd like a virus.

Pastor Peters stood erect—looking as tall and wide as Mount Sinai, Lucille thought—and folded both hands meekly at his waist and waited, with his wife huddled in the shelter of his shadow. Lucille craned her neck to see what was happening. Maybe the devil had finally grown tired of waiting.

"Hello. Hello. Pardon me. Excuse me. Hello. How are you? Excuse me. Pardon me."

It came like an incantation through the crowd, each word driving back the masses.

"Excuse me. Hello. How are you? Excuse me. Hello…" It was a smooth, dark voice, full of manners and implication. The voice grew louder—or perhaps the silence grew—until there was only the rhythm of the words moving over everything, like a mantra. "Excuse me. Hi, how are you? Pardon me. Hello…"

Without a doubt, it was the well-practiced voice of a government man.

"Good evening, Pastor," Agent Bellamy said gently, finally breaching the ocean of people.

Lucille sighed, letting go of a breath she did not know she had been holding.

"Ma'am?"

He wore a dark, well-cut gray suit very similar to the one he was wearing on the day he came with Jacob. It wasn't the kind of suit you see many government men wearing. It was a suit worthy of Hollywood and talk shows and other glamorous things, Lucille mused. "And how's our boy?" he asked, nodding at Jacob, his smile still as even and square as fresh-cut marble.

"I'm fine, sir," Jacob said, candy clicking against his teeth.

"That's good to hear." He straightened his tie, though it had not been crooked. "That's very good to hear."

The soldiers were there then. A pair of boys so young they seemed to be only playing at soldiering. At any moment Lucille expected them to start chasing each other around the pulpit, the way Jacob and the Thompson boy had once done. But the guns asleep at their hips were not toys.

"Thank you for coming," Pastor Peters said, shaking Agent Bellamy's hand.

"Wouldn't have missed it. Thank you for waiting for me. Quite the crowd you've got here."

"They're just curious," Pastor Peters said. "We all are. Do you…or, rather, does the Bureau or the government as a whole have anything to say?"

"The government as a whole?" Agent Bellamy asked, not breaking his smile. "You overestimate me. I'm just a poor civil servant. A little black boy from—" he lowered his voice "—New York," he said, as if everyone in the church, everyone in the town, hadn't already heard it all in his accent. Still, there was no sense in him wearing it on his sleeve any more than he had to. The South was a strange place.

The meeting began.

"As you all know," Pastor Peters began from the front of the church, "we are living in what can only be called interesting times. We are so blessed, to be able to...to witness such miracles and wonders. And make no mistake, that's what they are—miracles and wonders." He paced as he spoke, which he always did when he was uncertain about what he was saying. "This is a time worthy of the Old Testament. Not only has Lazarus risen from the grave, but it looks like he's brought everyone with him!" Pastor Peters stopped and wiped the sweat from the back of his neck.

His wife coughed.

"Something has happened," he belted out, startling the church. "Something—the cause of which we have not yet been made privy—has happened." He spread his arms. "And what are we to do? How are we to react? Should we be afraid? These are uncertain times, and it's only natural to be frightened of uncertain things. But what do we do with that fear?" He walked to the front pew where Lucille and Jacob were sitting, his hard-soled shoes sliding silently over the old burgundy carpet. He took the handkerchief from his pocket and wiped his brow, smiling down at Jacob.

"We temper our fear with patience," he said. "That is what we do."

It was very important to mention patience, the pastor reminded himself. He took Jacob's hand, being sure that even those in the back of the church, those who could not see, had time enough to be told what he was doing, how he was speaking of patience as he held the hand of the boy who had been dead for half a century and who was now, suddenly, peacefully sucking candy in the front of the church, in the very shadow of the cross. The pastor's eyes moved around the room and the crowd followed him. One by one he looked at the other Returned who were there, so that everyone might see how large the situation already was. In spite of the fact that, initially, they were not supposed to be there. They were real, not imagined. Undeniable. Even that was important for people to understand.

Patience was one of the hardest things for anyone to understand, Pastor Peters knew. And it was even harder to practice. He felt that he himself was the least patient of all. Not one word he said seemed to matter or make sense, but he had his flock to tend to, he had his part to play. And he needed to keep her off his mind.

He finally planted his feet and pushed the image of her face from his mind. "There is a lot of potential and, worse yet, there is a lot of opportunity for rash thoughts and rash behavior in these times of uncertainty. You only need to turn on the television to see how frightened everyone is, to see how some people are behaving, the things they're doing out of fear.

"I hate to say that we are afraid, but we are. I hate to say that we can be rash, but we can. I hate to say that we want to do things we know we should not do, but it's the truth."

In his mind, she was sprawled out on the thick, low-hung bough of an oak tree like a predatory cat. He stood on the ground, just a boy then, looking up at her as she dangled one arm down toward him. He was so very afraid. Afraid of heights. Afraid of her and the way she made him feel. Afraid of himself, as all children are. Afraid of...

"Pastor?"

It was Lucille.

The great oak tree, the sun bubbling through the canopy, the wet, green grass, the young girl—all of them disappeared. Pastor Peters sighed, holding his empty hands in front of him.

"What are we gonna do with 'em?" Fred Green barked from the center of the church. Everyone turned to face him. He removed his tattered cap and straightened his khaki-colored work shirt. "They ain't right!" he continued, his mouth pulled tight as a rusty letterbox. His hair had long since abandoned him, and his nose was large, his eyes small—all of which conspired together over the years to give him sharp, cruel features. "What are we gonna do with 'em?"

"We're going to be patient," Pastor Peters said. He thought of mentioning the Wilson family in back of the church. But that family had a special meaning for the town of Arcadia and, for now, it was best to keep them out of sight.

"Be patient?" Fred's eyes went wide. A tremble ran over him. "When the Devil himself shows up at our front door you want us to be patient? You want us to be patient, here and now, in the End Times!" Fred looked not at Pastor Peters as he spoke, but at the audience. He turned in a small circle, pulling the crowd into himself, making sure that each of them could see what was in his eyes. "He wants patience at a time like this!"

"Now, now," Pastor Peters said. "Let's not start up about the 'End Times.' And let's not go into calling these poor people devils. They're mysteries, that's for certain. They may even be miracles. But right now, it's too soon for anyone to get a handle on anything. There's too much we don't know and the last thing we need is to start a panic here. You heard about what happened in Dallas, all those people hurt—Returned and regular people, as well. All of them gone. We can't have something like that happen here. Not in Arcadia."

"If you ask me, them folks in Dallas did what needed to be done."

The church was alive. In the pews, along the walls, at the back of the church, everyone was grumbling in agreement with Fred or, at the very least, in agreement with his passion.

Pastor Peters lifted his hands and motioned for the crowd to calm. It dulled for a moment, only to rise again.

Lucille wrapped an arm around Jacob and pulled him closer, shuddering at the sudden recollection of the image of Returned—grown folks and children alike—laid out, bloodied and bruised, on the sun-warmed streets of Dallas.

She stroked Jacob's head and hummed some tune she could not name. She felt the eyes of the townspeople on Jacob. The longer they looked, the harder their faces became. Lips sneered and brows fell into outright scowls. All the while the boy only went about the business of resting in the curve of his mother's arm, where he pondered nothing more important than glazed peaches.

Things wouldn't be so complex, Lucille thought, if she could hide the fact of him being one of the Returned. If only he could pass for just another child. But even if the entirety of the town didn't know her personal history, didn't know about the tragedy that befell her and Harold on August 15, 1966, there was no way to hide what Jacob was. The living always knew the Returned.

Fred Green went on about the temptation of the Returned, about how they weren't to be trusted.

In Pastor Peters's mind were all manner of scripture and proverb and canonical anecdote to serve as counterargument, but this wasn't the church congregation. This wasn't Sunday morning service. This was a town meeting for a town that had become disoriented in the midst of a global epidemic. An epidemic that, if there were any justice in the world, would have passed this town by, would have swept through the civilized world, through the larger cities, through New York, Los Angeles, Tokyo, London, Paris. All the places where large, important things were supposed to happen.

"I say we round them all up somewhere," Fred said, shaking a square, wrinkled fist at the air as a crowd of younger men huddled around him, nodding and grunting in agreement. "Maybe in the schoolhouse. Or maybe in this church here since, to hear the pastor tell it, God ain't got no gripe with them."

Pastor Peters did something then which was rare for him. He yelled. He yelled so loud the church shrank into silence and his small, frail wife took several small steps back.

"And then what?" he asked. "And then what happens to them? We lock them up in a building somewhere, and then what? What's next?

"How long do we hold them? A couple of days? A week? Two weeks? A month? Until this ends? And when will that be? When will the dead stop returning? And when will Arcadia be full up? When will everyone who has ever lived here come back? This little community of ours is, what, a hundred and fifty? A hundred and seventy years old? How many people is that? How many can we hold? How many can we feed and for how long?

"And what happens when the Returned aren't just our own anymore? You all know what's happening. When they come back, it's hardly ever to the place that they lived in life. So not only will we find ourselves opening our doors to those for whom this event is a homecoming, but also for those who are simply lost and in need of direction. The lonely. The ones untethered, even among the Returned. Remember the Japanese fellow over in Bladen County? Where is he now? Not in Japan, but still in Bladen County. Living with a family that was kind enough to take him in. And why? Simply because he didn't want to go home. Whatever his life was when he died, he wanted something else. And, by the graces of good people willing to show kindness, he's got a chance to get it back.

"I'd pay you good money, Fred Green, to explain that one! And don't you dare start going on about how 'a Chinaman's mind ain't like ours,' you racist old fool!"

He could see the spark of reason and consideration—the possibility for patience—in their eyes. "So what happens when there isn't anywhere else for them to go? What happens when the dead outnumber the living?"

"That's exactly what I'm talking about," Fred Green said. "What happens when the dead outnumber the living? What'll they do with us? What happens when we're at their mercy?"

"If that happens, and there's no promise that it will, but if it does, we'll hope that they'll have been shown a good example of what mercy is…by us."

"That's a goddamn fool answer! And Lord forgive me for saying that right here in the church. But it's the truth. It's a goddamn fool answer!"

The volume in the church rose again. Yammering and grumbling and blind presupposing. Pastor Peters looked over at Agent Bellamy. Where God was failing, the government should pick up the slack.

"All right! All right!" Martin Bellamy said, standing to face the crowd. He ran a hand down the front of his immaculate gray suit. Of all the people in the church, he seemed to be the only one not sweating, not suffering in the tight air and heavy heat. That was a calming thing.

"I wouldn't doubt if this was all the government's fault to start with!" Fred Green said. "It wouldn't surprise me one bit if we find out the government had a hand in all of this once it all washes out. Maybe you weren't really trying to find some way to bring back everyone, but I bet them Pentagon folks could see a whole lot of benefit in being able to bring soldiers back from the dead." Fred tightened his mouth, honing his argument on his lips. He opened his arms, as if to take all of the church into his train of thought. "Can't y'all just see it? You send an army to war and, bam, one of your soldiers gets shot. Then you push a button or you inject him with some needle and he's right back on his feet, gun in hand, running headlong at the son of a bitch what just killed him! It's a damned doomsday weapon!"

People nodded, as though he just might have convinced them or, at the very least, opened the door of suspicion.

Agent Bellamy let the old man's words settle over the crowd. "A doomsday weapon indeed, Mr. Green," he began. "The type of thing nightmares are made of. Think about it—dead one minute, alive the next and getting shot at again. How many of you would sign up for such a thing? I know I wouldn't.

"No, Mr. Green, our government, as large and impressive as it is, doesn't control this event any more than it controls the sun. We're all just trying not to be trampled by it, that's all. We're just trying to make what progress we can."

It was a good word: *progress*. A safe word that you snuggled up against when you were nervous. The kind of word you took home to meet your parents.

The crowd looked at Fred Green again. He hadn't given them anything as comforting as *progress*. He only stood there looking old and small and angry.

Pastor Peters moved his large frame to Agent Bellamy's right side.

Agent Bellamy was the worst kind of government man: an honest one. A government should never tell people that it doesn't know any more than everyone else. If the government didn't have the answers, then who the hell did? The least a government could do was have decency enough to lie about it. Pretend everything was in hand. Pretend that, at any moment, they'd come through with the miracle cure, the decisive military strike or, in the case of the Returned, just a simple news conference where the president sat down fireside, wearing a sweater and smoking a pipe, and said, in a very patient and soft voice, "I have the answers you need and everything will be okay."

But Agent Bellamy didn't know a damned thing more than anyone else and he wasn't ashamed of it.

"Damn fool," Fred said. Then he turned on his heel and left, the dense crowd parting as best they could to allow him through.

With Fred Green gone, things were calmer in that Southern kind of way. Everyone took turns speaking, asking their questions both toward the Bureau man as well as the pastor. The questions were the expected ones; for everyone, everywhere, in every country, in every church and town hall and auditorium and web forum and chat room, the questions were the same. The questions were asked so many times by so many people that they became boring.

And the replies to the questions—*we don't know, give us time, please be patient*—were equally boring. In this effort, the preacher and the man from the Bureau made a perfect team. One appealed to a person's sense of civic duty. The other to a person's sense of spiritual duty. If they hadn't been a perfect team, it's hard to tell exactly what the town would have done when the Wilson family appeared.

They came from the eating hall in back of the church. They'd been living there for a week now. Mostly unseen. Rarely talked about.

Jim and Connie Wilson, along with their two children, Tommy and Hannah, were the greatest shame and sadness the town of Arcadia had ever known.

Murders didn't happen in Arcadia.

But this one had. All those years ago the Wilson family was shot and killed one night in their own home, and the perpetrator never found. Lots of theories floated around. Early on, there was a lot of talk about a drifter by the name of Ben Watson. He had no home to speak of and moved from town to town like some migratory bird. He came through Arcadia usually in the winter and would be found holed up in somebody's barn, trying to get by unnoticed for as long as he could. But no one had ever known him to be the violent type; and when the Wilsons were killed, Ben Watson was two counties away, sitting in a jail cell on charges of public drunkenness.

Other theories came and went with an ever-degrading scope of believability. There was talk of a secret affair—sometimes Jim was to blame, sometimes Connie—but that didn't last very long on account of how Jim was only ever at work, church or home and Connie was only ever at home, church or with her children. More than that, the simple truth was that Jim and Connie had been high school sweethearts, only ever tied to each other.

Straying just wasn't in the DNA of their love.

In life, the Wilsons had spent a great deal of time with Lucille. Jim, who had never really been the type to do as much family research as some others, took Lucille at her word when she told him they were related by way of a great-aunt (the name of whom she could never quite pin down) and came to visit when Lucille asked.

No one turns down the chance to be treated as family.

For Lucille—and this is something she did not allow herself to understand until years after their deaths—watching Jim and Connie live and work and raise their two children was a chance to see the life that she, herself, had almost had. The life that Jacob's death had taken away from her.

How could she not call them family, have them be a part of her world?

In the long years that followed the murder of the Wilson family, it was eventually agreed upon by folks—in that silent, unspoken way small-town people have of consenting to things—that the culprit couldn't have been anyone from Arcadia. It had to be someone else. It had to be the rest of the world that had done it, that had found this special and secret part of the map where these people lived their quiet lives, that had come in and ended all the peace and quiet they'd ever known.

Everyone watched in a pensive silence as the small family emerged, one by one, from the door at the back of the church. Jim and Connie walked in front; little Tommy and Hannah followed quietly. The crowd parted like heavy batter.

Jim Wilson was a young man, barely past thirty-five, blond hair, broad shoulders, a stiff, square chin. He looked like the kind of man who was always building something. Always engaged in some manner of productivity. Always furthering the slow crawl of humanity's progress against the perpetual hunger of entropy. This was why the town had loved him so in life. He had been what the people of Arcadia were supposed to be: polite, hardworking, well mannered, Southern. But now, as one of the Returned, he reminded them all of what they had not known they could be.

"You're all walking up to the big question," Jim said in a low voice, "the one you asked earlier on tonight and left hanging out there. The question about what's to be done with us."

Pastor Peters interrupted. "Now, now. There's nothing 'to be done with you.' You're people. You need a place to live. We've got room for you."

"They can't stay here forever," someone said. Voices in the crowd grumbled in agreement. "Something's got to be done with them."

"I just wanted to say thank you," Jim Wilson said. He had planned to say so much more, but it was all gone now—now that the entirety of Arcadia was staring at him. Some of them staring a bit less friendly than others. "I just...I just wanted to say thank you," Jim Wilson repeated. Then he turned and, taking his family with him, exited the same way he had come.

After that, everyone seemed to have trouble finding what to ask or what to say or what to argue about. Folks milled about for a while, grumbling and whispering now and again, but to no real consequence. Everyone felt suddenly tired and burdened.

Agent Bellamy gave everyone a final round of reassurances as they began trickling out of the church. He shook their hands and smiled as they passed and, when they asked him, he would say that he would do everything he could to understand why all of this was happening. He told them he would stay "until things are sorted out."

The sorting out of things was what people expected from the government, so they put their fears and suspicions away for now.

Eventually there was only the pastor, his wife and the Wilson family, who, not wishing to cause any more problems than they already had, stayed quietly in their room in the back of the church—away from everyone's sight and remembrance— as if they had never returned at all.

"I imagine Fred had a fair amount of things to say," Harold said as Lucille settled into the truck. She wrestled with Jacob's seat belt, huffing and making hard movements with her hands.

"They're just all so...so...irregular!" The click of Jacob's seat belt punctuated her sentence. She turned the knob at the window. After a few hard tugs, it broke free and opened. Lucille folded her arms over her chest.

Harold turned the truck's ignition. It started with a roar. "Your mama's been biting her tongue again, I see, Jacob. Probably sat there that whole meeting not saying nothing, didn't she?"

"Yes, sir," Jacob said, looking up at his father with a smile.

"Don't you do that," Lucille said. "Just don't you two do that!"

"She didn't get a chance to use any of her fancy words, and you know what that does to her, don't you? You remember?"

"Yes, sir."

"I'm not playing with you two," Lucille said, fighting laughter in spite of herself. "I'll get out right now and you'll never see me again."

"Did somebody else get to use a really fancy word?"

"Doomsday."

"Oh...that. It's a fancy way word for sure. 'Doomsday' is what happens when you spend too much time in church. That's why I don't go."

"Harold Hargrave!"

"How's the pastor? He's a good Mississippi boy, in spite of his religion."

"He gave me candy," Jacob said.

"That was nice of him, wasn't it?" Harold asked, wrestling the truck up the dark road toward home. "He's a good man, ain't he?"

The church was quiet now. Pastor Peters came into his small office and settled at the dark, wooden table. In the distance, a truck was gurgling down the street. Everything was simple, and that was a good thing.

The letter lay in the drawer of his desk, beneath stacks of books, assorted papers needing his signature, sermons in various stages of completion and all the general clutter that slowly marches over an office. In the far corner, an old lamp stood throwing a dim, amber glow over the room. Lining the walls of the office were Pastor Peters's bookcases, all of them stacked beyond capacity. His books gave him little comfort these days. A single letter had undone all their work, stripped away all the comfort that words can offer.

The letter read:

Dear Mr. Robert Peters,
The International Bureau of the Returned would like to inform you that you are being actively sought after by one of the Returned by the name of Elizabeth Pinch. As is our policy in this situation, no information outside the family of the Returned is ever given. In most cases, these individuals seek out their families first, but Miss Pinch has expressed a desire to locate you. Per Code 17, Article 21, of Returned Regulations Policy, you are hereby notified.

Pastor Peters stared down at the letter and was, just as he had been upon first reading it, uncertain of everything in his life.

Jean Rideau

"You should be with a young woman," she told Jean. "She would be able to keep up with you during all of this." She settled onto the small, iron-framed bed, huffing. "You're famous now. I'm just an old woman in the way."

The young artist crossed the room and knelt beside her. He rested his head in her lap and kissed the inside of her hand, which only made her aware of the wrinkles and liver spots that had begun showing upon that hand in recent years. "It's all because of you," he said.

He had been a part of her life for over thirty years—since she was fumbling her way through college so long ago and had come across the work of an overlooked artist who died by running into traffic one balmy summer's night in 1921 Paris—and now she had him, had not only his love, but his flesh, as well, completely. And that frightened her.

Outside, the street had finally quieted. The crowd had been scattered by the policemen.

"If I had only been this famous years past," he said. "Perhaps my life would have been different."

"Artists are only ever appreciated posthumously." She smiled, stroking his hair. "Nobody ever expected one would return to redeem his accolades."

She spent years studying his work, his life, never imagining that she would be here with him, like this, smelling the scent of him, feeling the wiry texture of a beard he desperately wanted but had always had poor luck growing. They sat up nights, talking about everything but his art. The press was doing enough of that. *Jean Rideau: Return of the Artists*, one of the more popular headlines had proclaimed.

He was the first of the artistic deluge, the article declared. "A genius sculptor returns! Not long before the masters are back with us!"

So he was famous now. Work he'd made nearly a hundred years ago, work that never sold for more than a few hundred francs, now went for millions. And then there were the fans.

But all Jean wanted was Marissa.

"You kept me alive," he said, nuzzling his head into her lap like a cat. "You kept my work alive when no one else knew me."

"I'm your steward, then," she said. With her wrist, she pushed loose strands of her hair from her face—hair that was a bit more gray and a bit more thin each day. "Is that what I am?"

He looked up at her with calm, blue eyes—even in the grainy, black-and-white photos of him that she had studied for years, she had known they were this particular, beautiful blue. "I do not care about our ages," he said. "I was only an average artist. I know now that my art was meant to lead me to you."

Then he kissed her.

FIVE

It had begun small, as most large things do, with just one government-issue Crown Victoria containing only one government man and a pair of too-young soldiers and a cell phone. But all it had taken was that one phone call and a few days of things being moved around and now Bellamy was entrenched in the school but there were no students, no classes, nothing but the ever-growing numbers of cars and trucks and men and women from the Bureau who had been setting up shop here for the past several days.

The Bureau had developed a plan for Arcadia. The same isolation that had kept the town's economy stifled for all the years of its existence was exactly what the Bureau was looking for. Sure, there were hotels and restaurants and facilities and resources in Whiteville that the Bureau could use for what they were planning, but there were also people. Close to fifteen thousand of them, not to mention the highway and all the various roads that they might have to secure sometime soon.

No. Arcadia was as close to a nonexistent town as they could want, with only a handful of people, none of whom were anyone of note. Just farmers and millworkers, mechanics and laborers and machinists and various other denizens of hardscrabble existences. "No one anybody would miss."

At least, that was how the colonel had put it.

Colonel Willis. The thought of him made Bellamy's stomach tighten. He knew little about the colonel, and that made him uneasy. In an age of information, never trust a person who can't be found on Google. But that was something Bellamy only had time to ponder in the late hours of the night back at the hotel before he nodded off. The day-to-day business of his duties, the interviews in particular, took his full attention.

The schoolroom was small. It smelled of mildew, lead-based paint and time.

"First of all," Bellamy said, leaning back in his chair, his notepad resting on his thigh, "is there anything unusual that either of you would like to talk about?"

"No," Lucille said. "Nothing that I can think of." Jacob nodded in agreement, most of his attention resting squarely on his lollipop. "But I figure," Lucille continued, "you'll be able to ask whatever questions you're supposed to ask that'll help me realize if there maybe was something strange going on. I imagine you're quite the interrogator."

"A bit of a harsh word choice, I think."

"Maybe," Lucille said. "I apologize." She licked the pad of her thumb and wiped a candy smudge from Jacob's face. She'd dressed him handsomely for his interview. New black dress pants. A bright new white, collared shirt. New shoes. Even new socks. And he was doing his part to keep everything clean, like the good boy that he was.

"I just like words, is all," Lucille said. "And, sometimes, they can come across a bit harsh, even if all you're trying to do is add some variety." Lucille finished cleaning Jacob's face, then turned her attention on herself. She straightened her long, silver hair. She checked her pale hands for dirt and found none.

She adjusted her dress, shifting her weight in her seat so that she could nudge her hemline farther down—which is not to say that the hem of her cream-colored dress had been high, gracious, no, but only to say that any respectable woman, Lucille felt, made it a point, when in mixed company, to show that she was going through all manner of effort to conduct herself with modesty and propriety.

Propriety was yet another word not used nearly enough in conversation for Lucille.

"Propriety," she muttered. Then she straightened the collar of her dress.

"One of the things that people have been reporting," Bellamy said, "is trouble sleeping." He took the notepad from his thigh and placed it on the desk. He hadn't expected that a schoolteacher in such a small town would have such a large desk, but such things made sense when you thought about them long enough.

Bellamy sat forward and checked to be sure that the recorder was running. He scribbled in his notebook, waiting for Lucille to respond to his statement, but soon began to realize that no response would be coming without elaboration. He wrote *eggs* on his notepad to look busy.

"It's not that the Returned have trouble sleeping," Bellamy began, once again trying to speak in a slow and non-Yankee tongue. "It's just that they tend to sleep very little. They don't complain of fatigue or exhaustion, but there have been accounts of some of them going for days without sleep, only to rest for a couple of hours and be completely unaffected." He sat back, appreciating the quality of the wooden chair beneath him in the same way he had appreciated the quality of the desk. "But maybe we're just grabbing at straws," he said. "That's the reason we're having all these interviews, to try and see what's an anomaly and what's nothing at all. We want to know as much as we can about the Returned as we do about the non-Returned."

"So is your question about me or Jacob?" Lucille said, looking around the classroom.

"Eventually, both of you. But, for now, just tell me about you, Mrs. Hargrave. Have you been having any trouble sleeping? Any disturbing dreams? Insomnia?"

Lucille shifted in her seat. She glanced toward the window. Bright out today. Everything shiny and smelling of springtime, with the scent of a humid summer not far off. She sighed and rubbed her hands together. Then she folded them and placed them in her lap. But they weren't content there, so she brushed her lap and placed an arm around her son, the type of thing a mother should do, she felt.

"No," she said, finally. "For fifty years I've been awake. Each and every night I've sat up, awake. Each and every day I walked around, awake. It was like I couldn't do anything else but be awake. I was sick with being awake." She smiled. "Now I sleep every night. Peacefully. Deeper and more soundly than I hardly imagined or hardly remembered was possible."

Lucille placed her hands in her lap again. This time they stayed. "Now I sleep the way a person is supposed to sleep," she said. "I close my eyes, and then they open again all on their own and the sun is there. Which, I imagine, is the way it should be."

"And what about Harold? How is he sleeping?"

"Just fine. Sleeps like the dead. Always has and probably always will."

Bellamy made notes on his notepad. *Orange juice. Beef (steak, perhaps).* Then he scratched out the bit about the steak and wrote *ground beef.* He turned to Jacob. "And how are you feeling about all this?"

"Fine, sir. I'm fine."

"This is all pretty weird, isn't it? All these questions, all these tests, all these people fussing about with you."

Jacob shrugged.

"Anything you want to talk about?"

Jacob shrugged again, his shoulders coming up almost to his ears, framing his small, soft face. He looked, briefly, like someone's painting, something created from old oils and technique. His shirt bunched perfectly about his ears. His brown hair seemed to grow down over his eyes. Then, as if anticipating the prod from his mother, he spoke. "I'm okay, sir."

"Can I ask you another question, then? A harder question?"

"*Can* you or *may* you? Mama taught me that." He looked up at his mother; her face was caught somewhere between surprise and approval.

Bellamy grinned. "Indeed," he said. "Okay, *may* I ask you a harder question?"

"I suppose," Jacob said. Then: "Do you want to hear a joke?" A sudden focus and clarity came to his eyes. "I know a lot of good jokes," he said.

Agent Bellamy folded his arms beneath him and sat forward. "Okay, let's hear it."

Again Lucille prayed silently—*Please, Lord, not the one about the beaver.*

"What do you call a chicken crossing the road?"

Lucille held her breath. Any joke involving a chicken had the potential to turn very vulgar very quickly.

"Poultry in motion!" Jacob answered before Bellamy had much time to consider the question. Then he slapped his thigh and laughed like an old man.

"That's funny," Bellamy said. "Did your father teach you that one?"

"You said you had a hard question for me," Jacob said, looking away. He watched the window as if expecting someone.

"Okay. I know you've been asked this before. I know that you've probably been asked this more times than you care to answer. I've even asked you myself, but I have to ask again. What's the first thing you remember?"

Jacob was silent.

"Do you remember being in China?"

Jacob nodded and, somehow, his mother did not reprimand him. She was as interested as everyone else in the memories of the Returned. Out of habit, her hand moved to gently nudge him into talking, but she checked herself. Her hand returned to her lap.

"I remember waking up," he began. "By the water. By the river. I knew I'd get in trouble."

"Why would you get in trouble?"

"Because I knew Mama and Daddy didn't know where I was. When I couldn't find them, I got scared some more. Not scared of getting in trouble anymore, but just scared because they weren't there. I thought Daddy was somewhere around. But he wasn't."

"What happened then?"

"Some people came. Some Chinese people. They spoke Chinese."

"And then?"

"And then these two women came over talking funny, but talking nice. I didn't know what they were saying, but I could tell they were nice."

"Yes," Bellamy said. "I know exactly what you mean. It's like when I hear a doctor or nurse telling me something in all that hospital talk. I don't understand a thing they're saying most of the time but, from the way they're saying it, I can tell they mean it in a nice way. You know, Jacob, it's amazing how much you can tell about a person just by how they say things. Wouldn't you agree?"

"Yes, sir."

They then talked more about what had happened after Jacob was found by the river in that small fishing village just outside Beijing. The boy was delighted to tell it all. He saw himself as an adventurer, a hero on a heroic journey. Yes, it had been painfully terrifying for him, but only in the beginning. After that, it had actually become rather fun. He was in a strange land with strange people and they fed him strange food, which, thankfully, he quickly acclimated to. Even now, as he sat in the office with the man from the Bureau and his lovely mother, his belly rumbled for authentic Chinese food. He had no idea of the names of anything he had been fed. But he knew the scents, the tastes, the essences of them.

Jacob talked at great length about the food in China, about how kind they had been to him. Even when the government men came—and the soldiers with them—they still treated him kindly, as if he were one of their own. They fed him until his stomach simply could not hold any more, all the while watching him with a sense of wonder and mystery.

Then came the long plane ride, which he held no fear of. He'd grown up always wanting to fly somewhere; now he was given almost eighteen hours of it. The flight attendants were nice, but not as nice as Agent Bellamy when they met.

"They smiled a lot," Jacob said, thinking of the flight attendants.

All these things he told his mother and the man from the Bureau. He did not tell them in such an eloquent form, but he said them all by saying, simply, "I liked everyone. And they liked me."

"Sounds like you had yourself quite a good time in China, Jacob."

"Yes, sir. It was fun."

"That's good. That's very good." Agent Bellamy had stopped taking notes. His grocery list was complete. "Are you about tired of these questions, Jacob?"

"No, sir. It's okay."

"I'm going to ask you one last question, then. And I need you to really think about it for me, okay?"

Jacob finished his lollipop. He sat up straight, his small, pale face becoming very serious. He looked like a little, well-dressed politician—in his dark pants and white, collared shirt.

"You're a good boy, Jacob. I know you'll do your best."

"Yes, you are," Lucille added, stroking the boy's head.

"Do you remember anything before China?"

Silence.

Lucille wrapped her arm around Jacob and pulled him close and squeezed him. "Mr. Martin Bellamy isn't trying to make anything difficult and you don't have to answer if you don't want to. He's just curious, is all. And so is your old mama. But I'm less curious and more just plain ol' nosy, I suppose."

She smiled and poked a tickling finger into his armpit.

Jacob giggled.

Lucille and Agent Bellamy waited.

Lucille rubbed Jacob's back, as if her hand against his body might conjure whatever spirits of memory were contained within him. She wished Harold were there. Somehow, she thought this moment could be helped if Jacob had his father rubbing his back and showing his support, as well. But Harold had launched into one of his rants about "the damn fool government" and was being generally disagreeable today—he behaved the way he did when Lucille tried to drag him to church during the holidays—and it was decided he should just stay in the truck while Lucille and Jacob spoke with the man from the Bureau.

Agent Bellamy placed his notepad on the table beside his stool to show the boy that this wasn't simply about the government's need to know. He wanted to show that he was genuinely interested in what the boy had experienced. He liked Jacob, from the first time they'd met, and he felt that Jacob liked him, too.

After the silence had gone on so long as to become uncomfortable, Agent Bellamy spoke. "That's okay, Jacob. You don't have to—"

"I do as I'm told," Jacob said. "I try to do as I'm told."

"I'm sure you do," Agent Bellamy said.

"I wasn't trying to get into trouble. That day at the river."

"In China? Where they found you?"

"No," Jacob said after a pause. He pulled his legs into his chest.

"What do you remember about that day?"

"I wasn't trying to misbehave."

"I know you weren't."

"I really wasn't," Jacob said.

Lucille was weeping now, silently. Her body trembled, expanding and contracting like a willow in March wind. She fumbled in her pocket and found tissues with which she dabbed her eyes. "Go on," she said, her voice choked.

"I remember the water," Jacob said. "There was just water. First it was the river at home, and then it wasn't. Only I didn't know it. It just happened."

"There was nothing in between?"

Jacob shrugged.

Lucille dabbed her eyes again. Something heavy had fallen against her heart, though she did not know what. It was all she could manage not to collapse right there in the too-small chair beneath her. She felt that would be painfully rude, though—for Martin Bellamy to have to help a collapsed old woman. So, as a matter of etiquette, she held herself together, even when she asked the question upon which all of her life seemed to hang. "Wasn't there anything before you woke up, honey? In the time between when you…went to sleep, and when you woke up? Was there a bright, warm light? A voice? Wasn't there anything?"

"What's an owl's favorite subject?" Jacob asked.

In reply to this there was only silence. Silence and a small boy torn between what was he incapable of saying and what he felt his mother wanted.

"Owlgebra," he said when no one answered.

"That's some boy you've got there," Agent Bellamy said. Jacob was gone now—in the adjoining room being kept company by a young soldier from somewhere in the Midwest. Lucille and Agent Bellamy could see them through the window in the door that linked the two rooms together. It was important to Lucille that she didn't lose sight of him.

"He's a blessing," she said after a pause. Her gaze shifted from Jacob to Agent Bellamy to the small, thin hands that sat in her lap.

"I'm glad to hear that everything has been going so well."

"It has," Lucille said. She smiled, still looking down at her hands. Then, as if some small riddle had finally been sorted out in her head, she sat erect and her smile grew so wide and proud that it was only then that Agent Bellamy noticed how thin and frail it had been. "This your first time down this way, Agent Martin Bellamy? Down south, I mean."

"Do airports count?" He sat forward and folded his hands on the grand desk in front of him. He felt a story coming.

"I suppose they wouldn't."

"Are you sure? Because I've been in and out of the Atlanta airport more times than I can count. It's odd, but somehow it feels like every flight I've ever been on has had to go through Atlanta for some reason. I swear I took a flight from New York to Boston once that had a three-hour layover in Atlanta. Not quite sure how that happened."

Lucille barked a little laugh. "How come you aren't married, Agent Martin Bellamy? How come you don't have a family to call your own?"

He shrugged. "Just never really fit in, I suppose."

"You should see about making it fit," Lucille said. She made a motion to stand, then immediately changed her mind. "You seem like a good person. And the world needs more good people. You should find a young woman that makes you happy and the two of you should have children," Lucille said, still smiling, though Agent Bellamy couldn't help but notice that her smile was a little dimmer now.

Then she stood with a groan and walked over to the door and saw that Jacob was still there. "I believe we just missed the Strawberry Festival, Martin Bellamy," she said. Her voice was low and even. "Happens about this time every year over in Whiteville. Been going on as far back as I can remember. Probably wouldn't be all that impressive to a big-city man like yourself, but it's something folks like us like to be a part of.

"Just like it sounds, it's all about strawberries. Most people don't think about it, but there was a time back when a person could have a farm and grow crops and make a living off it. Doesn't happen much nowadays—almost all the farms I knew of as a child been gone for years. Only one or two still around. I think that Skidmore farm up near Lumberton is still running…but I can't say to a certainty."

She came from the door and stood behind her chair and looked down at Agent Bellamy as she spoke. He'd gotten up from his position when she hadn't been looking and that seemed to throw her off. He had looked almost like a child at the desk before, the way he had been sitting. Now he was a grown man again. A grown man from a big, faraway city. A grown man that had not been a child for a great many years.

"It goes on all weekend," she continued. "And it's gotten bigger and bigger over the years, but even back then it was a big event. Jacob was as excited as any child ought to have the right to be. You'd think we'd never taken him anywhere! And Harold, well, even he was excited to be there. He tried to hide it—he hadn't really learned how to be an obstinate old fool just yet, you understand. You could just see how happy he was! And why wouldn't he be? He was a father at the Columbus County Strawberry Festival with his one and only son.

"It was something! Both of them behaving like children. There was a dog show. And there wasn't anything Jacob and Harold liked more than dogs. Now, this wasn't any dog show like you see on the TV these days. This was a good old country dog show. Nothing but working dogs. Blue ticks, walkers, beagles. But Lord, were they beautiful! And Harold and Jacob just ran from one pen to the other. Saying this and saying that about what dog was better than the other and why. This one looked like he might be good for hunting in such and such place in such and such weather on such and such kind of animal."

Lucille was beaming again. She was onstage, proud and wonderfully rooted in 1966.

"Sunlight everywhere," she said. "A sky so bright and blue you could hardly believe it or imagine it these days." She shook her head. "Too much pollution now, I suppose. Can't think of a single thing that's the way it used to be."

Then, quite suddenly, she stopped.

She turned and looked through the window in the door. Her son was still there. Jacob was still alive. Still eight years old. Still beautiful. "Things change," she said after a moment.

"But you should have been there, Martin Bellamy. They were so happy—Jacob and his daddy. Harold carried that boy on his back for half the day. I thought he was gonna pass out. All that walking we did that day. Walking and walking and more walking. And there was Harold carrying that boy slung over his shoulder like a sack of potatoes for most of it.

"The two of them made a game of it. They'd get to some booth or other, take it all in, say whatever they wanted to say about things. Then Jacob would cut off at a run and there was Harold right after him. Running through folks, almost knocking people over. And there I was yelling after them, 'Cut it out, you two! Stop acting like animals!'"

She gazed at Jacob. Her face seemed unsure what stance to take, so it became neutral and waiting. "It really is a blessing from God, Agent Martin Bellamy," she said slowly. "And just because a person don't quite understand the purpose and meaning of a blessing, that doesn't make it any less of a blessing...does it?"

Elizabeth Pinch

She knew he would come. All she had to do was wait and believe. He had always been better than he gave himself credit for, more disciplined, smarter. He was all the things he never told himself he was.

She had come close to finding him. She'd made it as far east as Colorado before they caught her. A local police sheriff saw her at a highway rest stop. She'd been riding with a trucker who was fascinated by the Returned and kept asking her questions about death. And when she didn't answer his questions, he left her at the rest stop where everyone that saw her treated her with uncertainty.

She was transferred first to Texas, where she asked the interviewers from the Bureau, "Can you help me find Robert Peters?" over and over again. After holding her for a while in Texas, they sent her to Mississippi, where she'd lived originally, and placed her in a building with others like her and placed men with guns around them.

"I need to find Robert Peters," she told them at every opportunity.

"He's not here" is the closest thing she ever got to an answer, and that was given with derision.

But he would come for her. She knew that, somehow.

He would find her and everything would be the way it was always meant to be.

SIX

Pastor Peters grumbled in concert with the keystrokes. Only God knew how bitterly he hated typing.

In spite of still being a young man, just forty-three—youngish, at least—he'd never been any good at typing. He had the bad luck of being born into that ill-timed generation of people for whom the epoch of computers was just far enough away that they were never given any reason to learn to type and, yet, the rise of the machines was just close enough that they would be forced to always suffer for their lack of understanding in regard to QWERTY and its arrangement of home keys. He could only wield two fingers at the keyboard, like some huge, computer-dependent mantis.

Peck. Peck-peck. Peck, peck, peck, peck-peck, peck.

He'd begun the letter four times now. And he had deleted it five times—he counted the time he'd deleted everything and turned off the entire computer out of frustration.

The problem with being a poor, mantis-fingered typist was that the words in Pastor Peters's head always ran far, far in front of the words his index fingers took entire eras to construct. If he didn't know any better, he would have sworn on any stack of consecrated tomes that the letters on the keyboard shifted position every few minutes or so, just enough to keep a person guessing. Yes, he could have simply written the letter long-hand and then taken the time to type it through only once, but that wouldn't make him any better a typist.

His wife had come into his office once or twice, offering to type the letter for him, as she oftentimes did, and he had politely declined, as he oftentimes did not.

"I'll never improve if I keep letting you do it for me," he told her.

"A wise man knows his limitations," she replied, not meaning it as an insult, only hoping to start a dialogue, a powwow, as he himself had said to the Arcadia townspeople not long ago. He was distant in the past few weeks, more so in the past few days. And she did not know why.

"I prefer to think of it more as a 'loose boundary' than a limitation," he replied. "If I can ever get the rest of my fingers to play along...well...just you wait and see. I'll be a phenomenon! A miracle unto myself."

When she began walking around the desk, politely asking to see what he was working on, he quickly deleted the few precious words that had taken him so long to assemble. "It's just something I need to get out of my head," he told her. "Nothing important."

"So you don't want to tell me what it is?"

"It's nothing. Really."

"Okay," she said, holding up her hands in submission. She smiled to let him know that she was not angry just yet. "Keep your secrets. I trust you," she said, and left the room.

The pastor's typing was even worse now that his wife had said that she trusted him, thereby implying that there might be something in his writing of the letter that required not only her trust but, even worse, a reminder of that trust.

She was a very skilled spouse.

To Whom It May Concern,

That was how far back he'd gone. All the way to the beginning. He huffed and wiped his furrowed brow with the
back of his hand and continued.
Peck. Peck. Peck. Peck-peck. Peck...

I am writing to inquire

Pastor Peters sat and thought, realizing now that he knew
very little about exactly what he wanted to ask.
Peck-peck-peck...

I am writing to inquire about the status of Miss Elizabeth Pinch. I received your letter stating that Miss Pinch
was trying to find me.

Delete, delete, delete. Then:

I am writing to inquire about the status of Miss Elizabeth Pinch.

That was closer to the truth of it. He thought, then and
there, about simply signing his name and dropping the envelope in the mail. He thought so hard about it that he even
printed the page. Then he sat back in his chair and looked at
the words.

I am writing to inquire about the status of Miss Elizabeth Pinch.

He placed the paper on his desk and picked up a pen and
marked a few things out.

I am writing to ~~inquire~~ about the ~~status~~ of ~~Miss~~ Elizabeth Pinch.

Even if his mind was unsure, his hand knew what he was trying to say. It lifted the pen and launched it at the letter again. Scratching and drawing through until, finally, the truth of everything was there, staring back at the pastor.

I am writing about Elizabeth.

What else could he do then but crumple the paper and toss it into the trash?

The pastor logged on to the internet and pecked Elizabeth Pinch's name into the search bar. All that came back were dozens of other people named Elizabeth Pinch; none of them were the fifteen-year-old girl from Mississippi who had, once upon a time, owned his heart.

He refined the search to display only images.

Pictures of women populated the screen, one after the other. Some smiling, facing the camera. Others not even aware that the camera was there. Some of the images weren't pictures of people at all. Some of them were images from movies or television. (Apparently there was an Elizabeth Pinch in Hollywood who wrote for a very highly rated television crime drama. Images of the crime drama appeared on page after page of the search results.)

Pastor Peters searched on the computer well past when the sun went from gold to auburn, then back to gold just before it slipped beneath the horizon. Though he had not asked for it, his wife brought him a cup of coffee. He thanked her and kissed her and shooed her gently from the room before she could study the computer screen and see the name in the search bar. But, even if she had seen it, what would she have done with it? What good would it have done her? At the very least, seeing the name would have made her suspicious, but she was already suspicious. The name itself would have given her nothing more.

He had never told her about Elizabeth.

Just before bedtime he found it: a newspaper clipping uploaded from the *Water Main,* the small newspaper back in the small Mississippi town that Pastor Peters grew up in not so long ago. He hadn't imagined that technology had made it that far, reached out all the way to a Podunk town in a humid corner of Mississippi where the greatest industry in all the county was poverty. The heading, grainy but legible, read Local Girl Killed in Car Accident.

Pastor Peters's face tightened. A taste of anger rose up in his throat, an anger aimed at ignorance and the incapability of words.

Reading the article he wished for more detail—exactly how Elizabeth Pinch had died in a tangle of metal and sudden inertia. But the media was the last place one should look for truth. A person was lucky to find the facts, let alone the truth.

In spite of what the article lacked, the pastor read the small newspaper clipping over and over again. After all, he had the truth inside him. The facts only served to bring it all back to him in sharp relief.

For the first time all day, the words came easily.

I am writing about Elizabeth. I loved her. She died. Now she is not dead. How do I behave?

Harold and Lucille sat watching the news and very silently fidgeting in their own way. Jacob was upstairs, sleeping, or not sleeping. Harold sat in his favorite comfortable chair and licked his lips and rubbed his mouth and thought of cigarettes. Sometimes he inhaled, held the breath, then pushed it out firmly through lips perfectly shaped to the circumference of a cigarette.

Lucille sat with her hands in the lap of her housecoat. The news was being irrational.

A silver-haired news anchor with perfect and handsome features sat in a dark suit and had only tragic and unfortunate things to say. "In France, there are reports of three dead," he said, a little more unemotionally than Lucille would have liked. "That number is expected to rise as police are still unable to contain the pro-Returned protesters, who seem to have lost the thread of their own protest."

"Sensationalism," Harold spat.

"Lost the thread?" Lucille said. "Why would he say it such a way? He sounds like he's trying to be English."

"I suppose he thinks it sounds better," Harold said.

"So because it's in France he's gotta say something so bad in such a way?"

Then the man with the silver hair disappeared from the television and there were men in uniforms with riot shields and batons taking wide, arcing swings at people beneath the cloudless, sun-filled sky. The crowd responded like water. The mass of people—hundreds of them—rippled back as the men in uniforms surged forward. When the soldiers felt they'd overextended themselves and pulled back, the crowd immediately filled the space left behind. Some of the people ran away, some were hit in the back of the head and fell heavily, like puppets. The people in the mob surged like pack animals, lashing out in groups and slamming against the policemen. Now and again a small flame would suddenly appear at the end of someone's arm. It would reel back, then rise into the air and fall and then there would be a great, shaggy plume of fire.

The newscaster came back. "Frightening," he said, his voice a mixture of excitement and gravitas.

"Just think of it!" Lucille said, shooing the television screen as if it were an ill-behaved house cat. "People should be ashamed of themselves, getting all riled up like that, forgetting about basic, common decency. And what makes it worse is that they're French. I wouldn't expect this kind of behavior from the French! They're supposed to be more refined than that."

"Your great-grandmother wasn't French, Lucille," Harold interjected, if only to distract himself from thinking about the television reports.

"Yes, she was! She was Creole."

"Ain't nobody in your family been able to prove that. I think y'all just want to be French because you're so damned in love with them. Hell if I know why."

The news turned away from Paris and settled comfortably on a broad, flat field in Montana. The field was studded with large, square buildings that looked like barns but were not barns. "Shifting focus closer to home..." the silver-haired man began. "An anti-Returned movement seems to have sprung up right here on American soil," he said. Then there were people on television who looked like soldiers, but were not soldiers.

But they were definitely Americans.

"The French are a sensitive and civilized people," Lucille said, half watching the television and half watching Harold. "And stop cussing. Jacob will hear you."

"When did I cuss?"

"You said 'damn.'"

Harold threw his hands up in mock frustration.

On the television there were pictures of the men in Montana—but there weren't just men; there were women, too—running in their uniforms and jumping over things and crawling under things, all of them carrying military rifles and looking very stern and serious, though failing, painfully sometimes, to look like soldiers.

"And what do you suppose this is about?" Lucille asked.

"Nut jobs."

Lucille huffed. "Now how do you know that? Neither of us heard a word anybody's said about all this."

"Because I know a nut job when I see one. I don't need a newscaster to tell me otherwise."

"Some people are calling them 'nut jobs,'" the silver-haired man on television said.

Harold grunted.

"But officials are saying they aren't to be taken lightly."

Lucille grunted back.

On television, one of the makeshift soldiers squinted down the barrel of a rifle and fired at a paper cutout of a person. A small plume of dust rose up from the ground behind the cutout.

"Some kind of militant fanatics," Harold said.

"How do you know that?"

"What else would they be? Look at 'em." He pointed. "Look at the gut on that one. They're just plain old people who've gone off the deep end. Maybe you should go quote them some scripture."

Then the newscaster was there to say, "It's happening like this all over."

"Jacob!" Lucille called. She didn't want to scare the boy, but she was suddenly very scared for him.

Jacob answered her from his bedroom in a low, soft voice.

"You okay, honey? Just checking on you."

"Yes, ma'am. I'm okay."

There was the light clatter of toys falling down, then the sound of Jacob's laughter.

They called themselves the Montana True Living Movement. Self-made militants formerly preoccupied with overthrowing the U.S. government and preparing for the race wars that would eventually rock America's melting pot to its core. But now there was a greater threat, the man from M.T.L.M. said. "There are those of us out here who aren't afraid to do what needs to be done," he declared.

The television program turned away from the men in Montana and back to the studio where the silver-haired man looked into the camera, then looked down at a sheet of paper, while across the bottom of the screen were the words *Are the Returned a Threat?*

He seemed to find the words he had been waiting for. "After Rochester, it's a question we all have to ask ourselves."

"If there's one thing America will always lead the world in," Harold said, "it's assholes with guns."

In spite of herself, Lucille laughed. It was a short-lived laughter, however, because the television had something very important to say and it was not the patient type. The newscaster's eyes looked uneasy, as though his teleprompter had broken.

"We now go to the president of the United States," he said suddenly.

"Here it is," Harold said.

"Shush! You're just a pessimist."

"I'm a realist."

"You're a misanthrope!"

"You're a Baptist!"

"You're bald!"

They went back and forth this way until they caught what the president was saying. "…stay confined to their homes until further notice." Then the bickering stopped.

"What was that?" Lucille asked.

Then the words were on the bottom of the television screen, just like most information in the modern world. President Orders Returned Confined to Their Homes.

"Dear Lord," Lucille said, going pale.

Outside, far away on the highway, the trucks were coming. Lucille and Harold could not see them, but that did nothing to make them any less real. They carried change and irrevocability, consequence and permanency.

They rumbled like thunder over the asphalt, bringing all these things, rumbling toward Arcadia.

Gov Jun Pei

The soldiers helped him from the back of the van and led him silently into a tall, alabaster-colored building with deep, square windows and an overall impression of seriousness about it. He asked them where he was being taken, but they would not answer him, so he soon quit asking.

Inside the building, the soldiers left him in a small room with what looked like a hospital bed in the center. He paced around the room, still tired of sitting from the long ride to wherever he now was.

Then the doctors came in.

There were two of them, and they asked him to sit on the table and, when he was seated, they took turns poking and prodding him. They took his blood pressure and checked his eyes for whatever it was doctors check one's eyes for. They tested reflexes and drew blood and on and on, all the while refusing to answer his questions when he asked, "Where am I? Who are you? Why do you want my blood? Where is my wife?"

Hours passed before their testing was done and still they had not answered him or even acknowledged anything he said. Even-

tually he found himself naked and cold and tired and sore and feeling like a thing more than a person.

"We're done," one of the doctors said. Then they left.

He stood there, naked and cold and afraid, watching the door shut and being locked into a room whose location he did not know, at the behest of people he did not know.

"What did I do?" he said to no one. But only the sound of the empty cell in which he was now left alone answered him back. It was a loneliness not unlike that of the grave.

SEVEN

Harold and Lucille sat on the porch, just as they usually did. The sun was high and the world was hot, but a breeze rolled up out of the west from time to time to keep things from getting unbearable, which both Harold and Lucille thought was very considerate on the world's part.

Harold sat and puffed quietly on a cigarette, doing what he could to keep the ashes off the new khaki pants and blue work shirt Lucille had bought him. Their usual quarreling and jibing settled into an uneasy silence of hard looks, body language and new pairs of pants.

It started around the time the Returned were ordered confined to their homes and the Wilson family had gone missing from the church. The pastor had said he didn't know what happened to them, but Harold had his own thoughts on that. Fred Green had done a good enough job in the past few weeks of stirring everyone up about the Wilsons staying in the church.

Sometimes Harold thought about who Fred used to be. How, once upon a time, he and Mary came over for Sunday dinner and she would stand in the middle of the living room singing in that high, beautiful voice of hers and Fred would sit there watching her like a child that's come upon a gleaming carnival in the middle of a dark and lonely forest.

But then she died of breast cancer that had developed when she was still so young that no one thought to check for such things. It wasn't anybody's fault, but Fred had taken all the blame on himself and, well, nowadays he wasn't who he had been that day in 1966, when he trudged through the brush at Harold's side, searching for the boy they would both have the horror of finding together.

The wind swept over the earth and there came the sounds of large, heavy trucks grumbling through their gears. Though the construction was all the way over at the school, over in the heart of Arcadia, it was clear and discernible, like a promise intended solely for the couple.

"What do you suppose they're building?" Lucille asked, gently working her hands at fixing a blanket that had gotten torn at some point over the winter. Now was as good a time as any to repair broken things.

Harold only puffed his cigarette and watched Jacob mill about playfully in the dappled sunlight beneath the oak tree. The boy was singing. Harold did not recognize the song.

"What do you suppose they're building?" Lucille asked, raising her voice a little.

"Cages," Harold said, blowing a great, gray cloud of smoke.

"Cages?"

"For the dead."

Lucille stopped sewing. She tossed the blanket to the porch and neatly placed her sewing tools in their containers. "Jacob, honey?"

"Yes, ma'am?"

"Go out farther in the yard and play, baby. Go look over in those bushes by the magnolias and see if you can find us some blackberries. That'll be something tasty for after dinner, won't it?"

"Yes, ma'am."

With the new quest from his mother, the boy's stick became a sword. He shouted a small battle cry and raced off toward the magnolias on the western edge of the property.

"Stay where I can see you!" Lucille yelled. "Do you hear me?"

"Yes, ma'am," Jacob yelled back; already he was assaulting the magnolias with his makeshift cutlass. He didn't often get permission to wander off, even just a little, and it felt good.

Lucille stood and walked to the porch railing. She wore a green dress with white stitching around the collar and safety pins clipped into the sleeves because, at home, she often expected to suddenly need a safety pin. Her silver hair was pulled back in a ponytail. A few strands fell across her brow.

Her hip hurt from sitting so long—that and playing with Jacob. She groaned and rubbed it and sighed a small, frustrated sigh. She placed her hands on the railing and stared down at the ground.

"I won't stand for it."

Harold took a deep pull on his cigarette, then he outed it on the heel of his shoe. He let the last lungful of nicotine slide from his body. "Okay," he said. "I won't use that word. I'll say 'Returned' instead, though I can't say I quite understand exactly how that's any better of a word for them. Would you want to be called 'Returned'? Like some kind of damn package?"

"You could just try calling them people."

"But they're not pe—" He could see in his wife's eyes that now wasn't the best time to say such a thing. "It's just that they're a…unique group of people, is all. It's like saying somebody's a Republican or a Democrat. It's like calling somebody out by their blood type." He rubbed his chin nervously, surprised to find stubble there. How had he forgotten something as basic as shaving? "At the very least," Harold continued, pushing the mystery of the stubble from his mind, "we need to be able to call them something so we know who it is we're talking about."

"They're not dead. They're not 'Returned.' They're people, plain and simple."

"You have to admit they're a special group of people."

"He's your son, Harold."

Harold looked her squarely in the eyes. "My son is dead."

"No. He's not. He's right over there." She raised a finger and pointed.

Silence then. A silence filled only by the sound of the wind and the sound of the construction happening in the distance and the light clatter of Jacob's stick clacking against the trunks of the magnolia trees along the ditch bank.

"They're building cages for them," Harold said.

"They wouldn't do anything like that. Nobody knows what to do with them. There's just too many of them. Everywhere you turn there's more and more of them. As crazy as those fools on the television might be, it's true that we don't know anything about them."

"That's not what you said before. 'Devils.' Remember that?"

"Well, that was before. I've learned since then. The Lord has shown me the error of a closed heart."

Harold huffed. "Hell. You sound like them fanatics on the TV. The ones who want to grant living sainthood to every one of them."

"They're affected by miracles."

"They're not affected. They're infected. By something. Why else you think the government said for them all to stay at home. Why else do you think they're building cages over there in town right now as we speak?

"I seen it with my own eyes, Lucille. Just yesterday when I went into town for groceries. Everywhere you look there's soldiers and guns and Humvees and trucks and fences. Miles upon miles of fences. Stacked on top of trucks. Loaded up in piles. And every able-bodied soldier that wasn't holding a gun was going about the business of putting up that fencing. Ten feet tall. Solid steel. Rolls of razor wire along the top. They got most of it surrounding the school. They done took over the whole building. Ain't been a class held there since the president was on TV. I guess they figure we ain't got all that many children in this little town, anyhow—which is true— so it wouldn't be much harm in having us use some other place as a schoolhouse while they turned the real school into a death camp."

"Was that supposed to be a joke?"

"A pun at least. Want me to try again?"

"Shut up!" Lucille stamped her foot. "You expect the worst out of people. You always have. And that's why your mind is knotted up the way it is. That's why you're not able to see the miracle that's laid out before you."

"August 15, 1966."

Lucille marched across the porch and slapped her husband. The sound of it rang out over the yard like a small-caliber gunshot.

"Mama?"

Jacob was there, suddenly, like a shadow grown out of the earth. Lucille was still trembling, her veins full of adrenaline and anger and grief. Her palm tingled. She clenched and released her hand, not certain, just then, whether or not it still belonged to her.

"What is it, Jacob?"

"I need a bowl."

The boy stood at the bottom of the porch steps, his T-shirt forming a small pouch at the belly, full to bursting with blackberries. His mouth was stained blue-black and bent at a nervous angle.

"Okay, honey," Lucille said.

She opened the screen door and ushered Jacob inside. The two of them went slowly into the kitchen, taking care not to spill any of the precious cargo. Lucille dug through the cabinets and found a bowl she liked and she and her son went about the business of washing the berries.

Harold sat alone on the porch. For the first time in weeks, he didn't want a cigarette. Lucille had only slapped him once before. Years and years and years ago. So long ago that he hardly remembered why she had done it. It had something to do with a comment he'd made about her mother. This was back when they were younger and cared about such comments.

All he knew for certain was that then, just like now, he'd done something very wrong.

He sat in his chair and cleared his throat and looked around for something to distract him. But there was nothing. So he sat and listened.

All he heard was his son.

It was as if there was nothing else in the world but Jacob. And he thought, or perhaps dreamed, that this was the way it had always been. In his mind he watched years pass. Spiraling out from 1966. This vision terrified him. He'd gotten along just fine after Jacob's death, hadn't he? He was proud of himself, proud of his life. There wasn't anything to regret. He hadn't done anything wrong, had he?

His right hand went to his pocket. At the bottom of his right pocket, next to his lighter and some stray coins, Harold's hand found the small, silver cross, the same one that seemed to appear out of nowhere weeks ago, the one rubbed smooth by time and wear.

There was an idea in his mind then. An idea or a feeling so sharp it felt like an idea. It was submerged in the murky depths of his memory, buried somewhere near thoughts of his own father and mother, who had become little more than a grainy still-image buried beneath dim lamplight in his mind.

Perhaps this thing, this idea or feeling that was on his mind, was something else more tangible, like parenting. He thought a lot about parenting these days. Fifty years of being off the job and now he was too old to run the thing properly, but he'd been drafted again by some strange turn of fate—Harold refused to give the credit to any particular deity on account of how he and God still weren't on speaking terms.

Harold thought about what it meant to be a parent. He'd only done it for eight years, but they had been eight years that wouldn't let him go once they had passed. He'd never told Lucille, but in that first decade after Jacob had died Harold had been prone to sudden bouts of indefinable emotion that would come crashing over him like an ocean swell, sometimes when he was driving home from work. Nowadays they called them "panic attacks."

Harold didn't like to think of himself being linked with anything having to do with "panic," but he had to admit that panic is exactly what he felt. His hands would go to trembling and his heart beat like there was a herd of cattle in his rib cage and he would pull over to the side of the road and, body shuddering, light a cigarette and suck on it for all he was worth. His heart thumped between his temples. Even his damn eyes seemed to throb.

And then it would be gone. Sometimes, it left behind some fleeting memory of Jacob, like staring into a full, luminous moon and carrying it with you when your eyes closed and there was supposed to be only darkness.

Just now, with that little silver cross between his fingers, Harold thought he felt one of those attacks coming on. His eyes began to well up. And as any man does when faced with the raw terror of emotion, he surrendered to his wife and buried his thoughts below the anvil of his heart.

"Okay," he said.

The two of them moved across the yard in tandem. Harold stepped slowly and evenly, Jacob circled. "Just spend some time with him," Lucille had finally said. "Just the two of you. Go do something, the way you used to. It's what he needs." Now here they were, Harold and his Returned son, walking the earth, and Harold didn't have the slightest idea what they should do.

So they simply walked.

They walked out over the yard, then past the end of the property and out to the dirt road, which eventually led them to the highway. In spite of the decree that all Returned should stay in their homes, Harold took his son to where the military trucks were passing along the sun-baked asphalt, to where the soldiers would look out from their trucks and Humvees and see the young Returned boy and the withered old man.

Harold was unsure if it was fear or relief he felt when one of the passing Humvees braked, turned in the median and came rumbling back down the highway toward him. For Jacob, it was certainly fear. He held his father's hand and stood behind his leg, peeking around as the vehicle crept to a halt.

"Good afternoon," a square-headed, fortysomething soldier said from the passenger window. He had blond hair, a hard jawline and cold, distant blue eyes.

"Hello," Harold said.

"How are you gentlemen doing today?"

"We're alive."

The soldier laughed. He tilted forward in his seat, looking Jacob over. "And what's your name, sir?"

"Me?"

"Yes, sir," the soldier said. "My name's Colonel Willis. What's your name?"

The boy came out from behind his father. "Jacob."

"How old are you, Jacob?"

"I'm eight, sir."

"Wow. That's a really good age to be! It's been a long time since I was eight. Do you know how old I am? Take a guess."

"Twenty-five?"

"Not even close! But thank you." The colonel grinned, his arm resting in the window of the Humvee. "I'm almost fifty."

"Wow!"

"You're darn right 'wow!' I'm an old, old man." Then the colonel turned to Harold. "How are you today, sir?" His voice was hard now.

"I'm fine."

"Your name, sir?"

"Harold. Harold Hargrave."

Colonel Willis looked over his shoulder at a younger soldier in the truck. The younger soldier wrote something down. "Where are you two gentlemen headed on such a fine day?" the colonel asked. He looked up at the gold sun and the blue sky and the small pods of clouds lazily making their way from one end of the earth to the other.

"Nowhere in particular," Harold said, not looking at the sky, but keeping his eyes trained on the Humvee. "We're just stretching our legs."

"How much longer do you think you'll be out here 'leg-stretching'? Do you gentlemen need a ride home?"

"We found our way out here," Harold replied. "We can find our way back."

"Just offering to help, Mr.—Hargrave, was it? Harold Hargrave?"

Harold took Jacob by the hand and they stood as statues until the colonel understood. Colonel Willis turned and said something to the young soldier in the driver's seat. He nodded at the old man and his Returned son.

The Humvee rattled to life and drove away with a roar.

"He was nice enough," Jacob said, "for a colonel."

Harold's instincts told him to head home again, but Jacob led them in a different direction. The boy turned north and, still holding his father's hand, took them into the underbrush of the forest and then beyond, into the body of the forest itself. They strolled beneath the pines and scattered white oaks. Now and again they could hear some animal bound away in the near distance. Then there would be the sound of birds lifting off from the treetops. Then only the wind, smelling of the earth and the pines and a sky far off in the distance that might, eventually, turn to rain.

"Where are we going?" Harold asked.

"How do mules get out of the barn?" Jacob asked.

"We don't want to get lost," Harold said.

"They use their don-keys."

Harold laughed.

Soon there came the scent of water. The father and son continued on. Harold had a brief memory of the time he, Jacob and Lucille had gone fishing off a bridge near Lake Waccamaw. The bridge wasn't high, which was good because about a half hour into fishing Lucille had decided it would be fun to push Harold off and into the water, but he saw her coming and managed to move aside and nudge her just enough to send her screaming into the water.

When she finally made it out of the water and up the embankment she was a sight to see: her jeans and cotton shirt clinging to her, her hair dripping wet and decorated with a few leaves from the bushes along the bank.

"Did you catch anything, Mama?" Jacob asked, grinning from ear to ear.

And without so much as a word, Harold grabbed Jacob's arms and Lucille grabbed his feet and they threw him, laughing, into the water.

It seemed like just last week, Harold thought to himself.

Then the forest dispersed, leaving only the river standing before Jacob and Harold, dark and slow. "We didn't bring a change of clothes," Harold said, staring. "What'll your mama think? If we show up at the house sopping wet and dirty we'll be in all kinds of trouble." Even as he spoke, Harold was taking off his shoes and rolling up his pants, letting his old, thin legs see the light of day for the first time since he could remember.

He helped Jacob roll his pants up above the knee. Grinning, Jacob removed his shirt and raced down the steep riverbank and into the water until it was up to his waist. Then he ducked below the surface and came up laughing.

Harold shook his head and, in spite of himself, removed his shirt and, as fast as the old man could, ran out into the river to join the boy.

They splashed in the water until both of them were bone tired. Then they trudged slowly out of the river and found a flat, grassy patch on the shore where they lay out like crocodiles and let the sun massage their bodies.

Harold was tired, but happy. He could feel something inside himself clearing.

He opened his eyes and stared up at the sky and the trees. A trio of pines climbed up out of the earth and joined together in a cluster in a low corner of the sky, blotting out the sun, which was on the downside of its day. The way the pines tied together at their apexes was curious to Harold. He lay there on the grass for a very long time staring up at them.

Harold sat up, a dull pain beginning to resonate throughout his body. He was, in fact, an older man than he used to be. He pulled his knees into his chest like a child, wrapping his arms around his legs. He scratched the rogue stubble on his chin and stared out over the river. He had been here before, to this exact place on the river, with its three pine trees pushing lazily out of the earth, joining together in unison in their small pocket of sky.

Jacob slept soundly in the grass, his body drying slowly below the waning sun. In spite of what was being said about how the Returned hardly slept, when they did finally sleep, it seemed to be a wonderful, all-consuming rest. The boy looked as peaceful and content as anyone could ask. As if there were nothing at all going on inside his body except the slow, natural prosody of his heart.

He looks dead, Harold thought. "He is dead," he reminded himself in a low voice.

Jacob's eyes opened. He looked up at the sky, blinked and bolted upright. "Daddy?" he yelled. "Daddy?"

"I'm here."

When he saw his father, the boy's fear faded as suddenly as it had come.

"I had a dream."

Harold's instinct was to tell the boy to come and sit in his lap and tell him about the dream. It's what he would have done all those years ago. But this wasn't his son, he reminded himself. August 15, 1966 had taken Jacob William Hargrave away, irrevocably.

This thing beside him was something else. Death's imitation of life. It walked and talked and smiled and laughed and played like Jacob, but it was not Jacob. It couldn't be. By the laws of the universe, it couldn't be.

And even if by some "miracle" it could be, Harold would not allow it.

Still, even if this was not his son, even if it were only an elaborate construct of light and clockwork, even if it were only his imagination sitting in the grass beside him, it was a child, of sorts, and Harold was not so old and bitter a human being as to be immune to a child's pain. "Tell me about your dream," he said.

"It's hard to remember."

"That's how dreams are sometimes." Harold stood slowly and stretched his muscles and began putting his shirt on again. Jacob did the same. "Was someone chasing you?" Harold asked. "That happens a lot in dreams. At least in my dreams. That can be really scary sometimes, to have somebody chasing you."

Jacob nodded.

Harold took this silence as a cue to continue. "Well, it wasn't a falling dream."

"How do you know?"

"Because you would have been kicking and flailing your arms!" Harold threw his arms up and kicked his legs and made a great, goofy show of it. He looked sillier than he had in decades—half-dressed and still wet—kicking and flailing like that. "And I would have had to throw you out there in the middle of the river just to wake you up!"

Harold remembered then. With a terrible sharpness, he remembered.

This place, here beneath the three trees that threaded together against the cloth of the open sky, this was where they'd
found Jacob all those years ago. This was where he and Lucille
came to know pain. This was where every promise of life that
they had believed in came crumbling apart. This was where
he'd held Jacob in his arms and wept, trembling, as the body
lay lifeless and still.

All Harold could do with the realization of where he now
stood—beneath these familiar trees with a thing that looked
very much like his son—was laugh.

"It's something," he said.

"What is?" Jacob asked.

Harold's only answer was more laughter. Then they were
both laughing. But soon, the sound of it was broken by the
footsteps of soldiers slipping from the forest.

The military men would be polite enough to leave the rifles
back in the Humvee. They would even go so far as to carry
their pistols in their holsters rather than drawn at the ready.
Colonel Willis would be the one to lead the soldiers. He would
walk with his hands behind his back, his chest thrust forward
like a bulldog. Jacob would hide behind his father's leg.

"It's not that I want to do this," Colonel Willis would say.
"I really did try not to. But you both should have gone home."

This would begin a very difficult time for the Harold, Lucille, Jacob and countless others.

But, for now, there was laughter.

Nico Sutil. Erik Bellof. Timo Heidfeld.

This quiet street in Rochester had never seen such excitement. The signs were written in both English and German, but all of the Germans would have understood perfectly well if there had been no signs at all. For days now they encircled the house, shouting, waving their fists. Sometimes a brick or a glass bottle would crash against the side of the house. It had happened so often that the sound did not frighten them anymore.

Nazis, Go Home! many of the signs read. *Back to Hell, Nazi!* read another.

"They're just afraid, Nicolas," Mr. Gershon said, looking out the window with his face knotted up. "It's too much for them." He was a small, thin man with a salt-and-pepper beard and a voice that trembled when he sang.

"I'm sorry," Erik said. He was only a few years older than Nico. Still a boy by Mr. Gershon's standards.

Mr. Gershon squatted to where Nico and Erik were sitting— being sure to stay clear of the windows. He patted Nico's hand. "Whatever happens, it's not your fault. I made this decision— my entire family and I made this decision."

Nico nodded. "It was the decision of my mother for me to join the army," he said. "She worshipped the Führer. I just wanted to go to college and teach English."

"Enough of the past," Timo said. He was Nico's age, but with little of Nico's tenderness. His hair was dark, his face thin and sharp, like his eyes. He looked the way a Nazi was supposed to look, even if he did not act the way they were supposed to act.

Outside, the soldiers worked to part the crowd. They had been keeping the protesters away from the house for the past several days. Then several large, dark trucks rumbled onto the Gershons' front lawn. They came to a halt and soldiers spilled out, their rifles bristling.

Mr. Gershon sighed. "I've got to try talking to them again," he said.

"It is us they want," Erik said, motioning to the six other Nazi soldiers the Gershons had unsuccessfully hidden for the past month. They were mostly boys, all of them caught up in something larger than they could ever hope to understand, much like the first time they had lived. "It is us they want to kill, yes?"

One of the men outside took up a bullhorn and began shouting instructions at the Gershon house. The crowd cheered. "Go back to hell!" they shouted.

"Take your family and leave," Nico said. The other soldiers voiced agreement. "We give up. This has gone on too long. For fighting in war, we deserve arrests."

Mr. Gershon squatted with a grunt, his thin, old body trembling. He placed his hands on Nico's arm. "You've all died once," he said. "Isn't that penance enough? We won't give you over to them. We will prove to them that wars are made of people, and people, outside of those wars, can be reasonable. They can live together—even a silly old Jewish family like mine and lit-tle German boys who a madman dressed in uniforms and said, 'Be horrible or else!'" He looked at his wife. "We have to prove there is forgiveness in this world," he said.

She looked back at him, her face as resolute as his own.

Upstairs there came the sound of a window shattering, followed by a loud hissing sound. Then something thumped against the side of the house near the window. More hissing. A white cloud began to blossom at the window.

"Gas!" Timo said, already placing a hand over his mouth.

"It's okay," Mr. Gershon said, his voice soft. "We will let this happen peacefully." He looked at the German soldiers. "We must all let this happen peacefully," he said to them. "They will only arrest us."

"They'll kill us!" Timo said. "We must fight them!"

"Yes," Erik said, standing. He went to the window, peeked and counted the number of men with guns.

"No," Mr. Gershon said. "We can't let it happen this way. If you fight, then they will kill you, and that is all anyone will remember—the houseful of Nazi soldiers, who, even after being returned from the grave, could only fight and kill!"

There came a banging on the door.

"Thank you," Nico said.

Then the door was breached.

EIGHT

Three weeks ago Lucille's cantankerous husband and previously deceased son were arrested for what Lucille felt amounted to little more than a conflated and inflated charge of Being Ornery and Returned in Public. And while each of them were admittedly guilty of their individual charges, no lawyer in the world could have ever argued that Harold Hargrave was anything other than unlawfully ornery. And Jacob's used-to-be-dead-but-no-longer-dead status was equally unequivocal.

But Lucille soundly believed, in that part of her spirit that subscribed to the notion of certain general and inescapable rights and wrongs, that if there was anybody to blame, it was the Bureau.

Her family had done nothing. Nothing except take a walk on private land—not government land, mind you, but privately owned property—and their walk just happened to take them past where there were Bureau men driving along the highway. Bureau men who followed them back and arrested them.

Since their arrest, hard as she tried, Lucille had yet to manage a full night's sleep. And when sleep did come, it was delivered like a court summons, at only the most unpredictable

and discourteous times. Just now, Lucille was slumped in a
church pew, dressed in her Sunday best with her head hung
at that familiar angle of unconsciousness often times seen in
young children who've missed their nap time. She was sweating a little. It was June now and every day was a sauna.

As she slept, Lucille dreamed of fish. She dreamed she was
standing in a crowd of people, all of them starving. At Lucille's feet was a five-gallon plastic bucket filled with perch
and trout and bass, spots and flounder.

"I'll help you. Here you go," she said. "Here. Take this.
Here. I'm sorry. Yes. Please, take this. Here you go. I'm sorry.
Here. I'm sorry."

The people in her dream were all Returned and she did not
know why she was apologizing, but it seemed vital.

"I'm sorry. Here you go. I'm trying to help. I'm sorry. No,
don't worry. I'll help you. Here." Her lips were moving all
on their own now, as she sat slumped there in the pew. "I'm
sorry," she said aloud. "I'll help you. Don't worry."

In her dream, the crowd pushed in closer, swarming her,
and she could see now that she and the Returned were all
encased in an incredibly large cage—steel fencing and razor
wire—that was getting smaller. "Dear Lord," she said in a
loud voice. "It's okay. I'll help you!"

Then she was awake. Awake and being stared at by almost
the entirety of the Arcadia Baptist Church congregation.

"Amen," Pastor Peters said from the pulpit, smiling. "Even
in her dreams, Sister Hargrave is helping folks. Now why can't
the rest of us manage to do it when we're awake?" Then he
continued on with his sermon—something having to do with
patience from the Book of Job.

Compounding her shame over sleeping in church was a
small degree of shame over distracting the pastor from his sermon. But that, too, was tempered by the fact that Pastor Pe-

ters was always offering distracted sermons these days. There was something on his mind—something on his heart—and while none of his flock could diagnose the exact cause of it, it wasn't difficult to tell that there was something affecting him.

Lucille sat up and wiped the sweat from her forehead and mumbled a mistimed "Amen" under her breath in agreement with an important point in the pastor's sermon. Her eyes were still very itchy and heavy. She found her Bible and opened it and drowsily searched for the verses Pastor Peters was preaching on. The Book of Job wasn't the biggest Gospel, but it was big enough. She fumbled through the pages until she came to what seemed like the appropriate verse. Then she stared down at the page, and immediately fell asleep again.

The next time she awoke, church was over. The air still. The pews all but empty. As if maybe the good Lord himself had up and decided He had somewhere else to be. The pastor was there along with his small wife whose name Lucille still could not quite remember. They sat in the pew ahead, looking back at the old woman with soft, half grins.

Pastor Peters spoke first.

"I've thought a few times about adding fireworks to my sermons, but the fire marshal killed that idea. And, well…" He shrugged. His shoulders rose up like mountains beneath the jacket of his suit.

His brow glimmered with small freckles of sweat, but still, he sat in his dark wool suit jacket looking the way a man of God was supposed to look: willing to endure.

Then his small wife spoke in her small, forgettable voice. "We're worried about you." She wore a light-colored dress with a small, flowered hat. In typical form, even her smile was small. She looked not only ready, but fully willing, to collapse at any moment.

"Don't worry about me," Lucille said. She sat up straight, closed her Bible and held it to her chest. "The Lord will get me through."

"Now, Sister Hargrave, I won't have you stepping on my lines," the pastor said, showing that wide, grand smile of his.

His wife reached over the back of the pew and put her tiny hand on Lucille's arm. "You don't look well. When's the last time you slept?"

"Just a few minutes ago," Lucille said. "Didn't you see?" She chuckled briefly. "I'm sorry. That wasn't me. That was that no-account husband of mine speaking through me—the devil that he is." She gripped her Bible to her chest and huffed. "What better place to rest than in the church? Is there any place on all this earth where I should be so comfortable? I don't think so."

"At home?" the pastor's wife said.

Lucille couldn't quite tell if she meant it as an insult or merely a genuine question. But because of how small the woman was, Lucille decided to give her the benefit of the doubt.

"Home ain't home right now," Lucille said.

Pastor Peters placed his hand on her arm, next to his wife's. "I spoke to Agent Bellamy," he said.

"So did I," Lucille replied. Her face tightened. "And I bet he told you the same thing he told me. 'It's out of my hands.'" Lucille huffed again and adjusted her hair. "What's the point of being a government man if you can't do anything? If you've got no power just like the rest of us?"

"Well, in his defense, the government is still a lot bigger than any of the folks that work for them. I'm sure Agent Bellamy's doing everything he can to help out. He seems like an honorable man. He's not keeping Jacob and Harold there, the law is. Harold chose to stay with Jacob."

"What choice did he have? Jacob is his son!"

"I know. But some people have done less. From what Bellamy told me, it was just supposed to be the Returned who were going to be kept there. But then people like Harold wouldn't leave their loved ones, so now…" The pastor's voice trailed off. Then he began again: "But I believe that's the best thing. We can't let people be segregated, not completely at least, not like what some people want to have done."

"He chose to stay," Lucille said in a low voice, as if reminding herself of something.

"He did," Pastor Peters said. "And Bellamy will take care of them both. Like I said, he's a good man."

"That's what I used to think. Back when I first met him. He seemed good, even if he was from New York. I didn't even judge him on account of him being black." Lucille put a hard stress on that point. Both of her parents had been deeply committed to racism, but she'd learned better—learned from the Word—that people were just people. The color of their skin meant about as much as the color of their underwear. "But when I look at him now," she continued, "I wonder how any decent man—regardless of color—could be a part of such a thing as kidnapping people from their homes—children, no less—and locking them up in prison?" Lucille's voice was like a thunderstorm.

"Now, now, Lucille," the pastor said.

"Now, now," his wife repeated.

Pastor Peters made his way around the pew and settled in beside the old woman and put his large arm around her. "They're not kidnapping people, though I know it can feel that way. The Bureau is just trying to…well, just look like they're helping. There's so many of the Returned now. I think the Bureau is just trying to make people feel safe."

"They make people feel safe by taking an old man and

his child away from their home at gunpoint?" Lucille nearly dropped her Bible as her hands came suddenly to life in front of her. She always spoke with her hands when she was angry. "By holding them for three weeks? By putting them in prison without...without...heck, I don't know, without pressing charges or doing something resembling the Rule of Law?" She looked toward one of the church windows. Even from where she sat she could see the town, in the distance below the hill where the church stood. She could see the school and all of its newly erected buildings and fencing, all the soldiers and Returned buzzing about, the clump of houses not yet within the realm of the fencing. Something in her heart told her that would not last.

Far away, on the other side of the town—hidden by trees and distance, out where the town was ended and the countryside holding sway—was her home, sitting dark, empty. "Lord..." she said.

"Now, now, Lucille," the pastor's wife said, accomplishing nothing.

"I keep talking to that Martin Bellamy," Lucille continued. "I keep telling him that this is wrong and that the Bureau's got no right to do this, but all he says is that there's nothing he can do. He says it's all that Colonel Willis now. It's all about him, Martin Bellamy says. What does he mean there's nothing he can do? He's a human being, ain't he? Ain't a human being full of things they can do?"

Beads of sweat marched down her brow. Both the pastor and his wife had taken their hands from her, as if she were a stove top someone had switched on without warning.

"Lucille," the pastor said, lowering his voice and speaking slowly, something he'd learned calmed people, whether they wanted it to or not. Lucille only looked down at the Bible on her lap. A great question about something settled into the curves of her face.

"God has a plan," Pastor Peters said, "even if Agent Bellamy does not."

"But it's been weeks," Lucille replied.

"And they're both healthy and alive. Aren't they?"

"I suppose so." She opened her Bible to no page in particular. She opened it only to see that the words, and the Word, were still there. "But they're..." She hunted for a good word. She would feel better if she could find a quality word right now. "They're...immured."

"They're in the same school where almost every child in this town learned to read and write," the pastor said. His arm was around Lucille again now. "Yes, I know it looks different now with all those soldiers around, but it's still our school. It's the same building that Jacob went to all those years ago."

"It was a new school back then," Lucille interrupted, her mind falling into memory.

"And I'm sure it was beautiful."

"Oh, it was. Just shining new. It was much smaller back then, though. Back before the additions and renovations that went on after the town got a little older and a little bigger."

"So can't we just think of them still there, in that version of the school?"

Lucille said nothing.

"They're warm and they're being fed."

"Because I take them food!"

"The best food in the county!" The pastor made a show of looking at his wife. "I keep telling my beloved here that she needs to come and spend a few weeks with you and get the secret to that peach cobbler of yours."

Lucille smiled and waved him off. "It's nothing special," she said. "I even take Martin Bellamy food." She paused. "Like I said, I like him. He seems like a good man."

Pastor Peters patted her on the back. "Of course he is. And he and Harold and Jacob and everyone else there at the school who got to taste your cobbler—because I hear you've been taking it over in great quantities and sharing it—they're all indebted to you. They thank you every day, I know it."

"Just because they're prisoners doesn't mean they should have to eat that government slop those soldiers are feeding them."

"I thought they were having their food catered by Mrs. Brown's catering service. What's she calling it now? Gone on to Glory-ous Foods?'"

"Like I said—slop."

They all laughed.

"Things really will settle down," the pastor said when the laughter had trailed off. "Harold and Jacob are going to be just fine."

"Have you been down there?"

"Of course."

"Bless your heart," Lucille said. She patted the pastor's hand. "They need a shepherd. Everyone in that building needs a shepherd."

"I do what I can. I talked to Agent Bellamy—he and I talk quite a bit, actually. As I said, he seems like a decent man. I believe he really is trying to do everything he can. But, with the way things are progressing, with the sheer numbers that the Bureau is having to deal with—"

"They've put that terrible Colonel Willis in charge."

"That's my understanding of it."

Lucille's mouth tightened. "Someone has to do something," she said. Her voice was low, like water whispering from a deep crevice. "He's a cruel man," she said. "You can see it in his eyes. Eyes that seem to get farther away the longer you look into them. You should have seen him when I went over there to get Harold and Jacob back. Cold as December, that's what he was. Like a mountain of apathy."

"God will find a way."

"Yes," Lucille said, even though, for three weeks now, she had been wondering more and more. "God will find a way," she repeated. "But still, I worry."

"We all have our worries," the pastor said.

Fred Green had been coming home to an empty house for several decades now. He was used to the quiet. And while he didn't much care for his own cooking, he'd long since come to grips with frozen meals and the occasional overcooked steak.

Mary had always done the cooking.

When he wasn't tending his fields, he was at the sawmill, trying to pick up any work he could. He rarely made it home until almost dark and his body was a little more tired each day than the day before. But lately he was finding it harder and harder to get jobs on account of the fact that the younger men were always there, waiting in the dim morning light for the day manager to pick out the fellows he wanted to work that day.

And while experience had its merits when it came to manual labor, youth is all but impossible to beat. He felt as if he was starting to wind down. There was just too much to do.

So each evening Fred Green came home, dined on TV dinners, settled in front of the television and turned to the news, where there was only talk of the Returned.

He only half listened to anything the newscasters said. He spent most of his time talking back to them, denouncing them as troublemakers and fools, catching only piecemeal details of the stream of Returned that was growing into more and more of a river with each day.

All any of it did was make him uneasy, possessed by a great sense of foreboding.

But there was something else. Some feeling he could not quite get a handle on. He'd been having trouble sleeping the past few weeks. Each night he went to bed in his empty and silent house—just like he had for decades—and he chased sleep until well after midnight. And when sleep finally did come, it was shallow and restless, devoid of dreams but fitful nonetheless.

Some mornings he awoke with bruises on his hands which he blamed on the wooden headboard. One night he was possessed with the sensation of falling, only to awake the instant before landing on the floor beside the bed with tears streaming down his face and a great, indescribable sadness choking the air around him.

He remained there on the floor, sobbing, angry at things he could not put to words, his head filled with frustration and longing.

He called his wife's name.

It was the first time in longer than he could remember that he had spoken her name. He composed the word on his tongue and launched it into the air and listened to the sound of it resonate through the cluttered, musty house.

He stayed there on the floor, waiting. As if she might suddenly come out from hiding and wrap her arms around him and kiss him and sing for him—in that blessed, resplendent voice that he longed for—bringing music to him after all these years of emptiness.

But no one answered.

Eventually he picked himself up off the floor. He went to the closet and pulled out a trunk which had not seen the light of day in decades. It was black with a thin patina covering the brass hinges. It seemed to sigh when he opened it.

It was filled with books, sheet music, small boxes containing trinkets of jewelry or ceramic knickknacks for which there was no one left in the house to appreciate. Halfway down, buried beneath a small, silk blouse with delicately stitched roses about the collar, was a photo album. Fred lifted it and sat on the bed and brushed it off. It opened with a creak.

And, all of a sudden, there she was, his wife, smiling at him.

He had forgotten how round her face was. How dark her hair was. How perpetually confused she seemed to always look—and how that had been what he loved about her most. Even when they were arguing, she had always seemed confounded, as if she saw the world in a way that no one else did and could not, for the life of her, understand why everyone behaved the way they did.

He sat and turned the pages of the album and tried not to think of the sound of her voice, of the perfect way she would sing for him when the nights were long and he could not sleep. He opened and closed his mouth, as if trying to form some question that, out of stubbornness, would not come out.

Then he came across one photograph that gave him pause. Her smile was not as bright. Her expression no longer confused, but decided. It was from some sun-bathed afternoon not long after her miscarriage.

It had been their secret, that particular tragedy. No sooner than they'd gotten the news from the doctor about her pregnancy, everything came crashing down. Fred awoke one night to the sound of her sobbing softly from the bathroom, the burden of what had happened already weighing on her.

He'd always been a deep sleeper. "Waking you up is like waking the dead," she had told him once. To this day, he wondered if she'd tried to wake him that night, if she had asked for his help and he'd failed her. Surely, he could have done something.

How could a husband sleep through such a thing, he wondered. Lay dreaming like some dumb animal while the small ember of their child's life is snuffed out.

They had planned on telling their friends about the pregnancy at her birthday party, less than a month away. But then there was no need. Only the doctor ever knew what had happened to them.

The only indication that anything had been wrong came in the dimness of her smile after that day, a dimness that he could never forget.

He removed the photograph from the sticky film. It smelled of old glue and mildew. That night, for the first time since her death, he wept.

The next morning Fred went to the sawmill, but the day manager didn't pick him for work. He went home and checked the fields, but they didn't need his attention, either. So he got in his truck and drove over to Marvin Parker's place.

Marvin lived across the street from the entrance gate of the school where they were holding the Returned. Marvin could sit in his front yard and watch the busloads of Returned being brought in. And that's exactly what he did a great many mornings since all of this had begun.

For some reason, Fred felt like this was where he needed to be. He needed to see for himself what the world was coming to. He needed to see the faces of the Returned.

It was almost as if he was searching for someone.

Harold sat quietly at the end of his cot in the center of what was normally Mrs. Johnson's art studio. He wished his back hurt, if only so he could complain about it. Harold had

always found himself better able to ponder deeply profound
or confusing subjects after he'd had a good, solid rant about
the pain in his back. He shuddered to think what might have
happened if, somehow, he'd never been a complainer. Lucille
might have had him sanctified by now.

The cot next to Harold's was where Jacob slept. The boy's
pillow and blanket lay neatly at the head. The blanket was
one Lucille had made. It was full of intricacies and colors and
fancy stitching that would take nothing less than a nuclear as-
sault to unravel. The corners were sharply folded. The pillow
perfectly flat and smooth.

What a tidy boy, Harold thought, trying to remember if it
had always been that way.

"Charles?"

Harold sighed. In the doorway of the art-room-cum-
bedroom stood the old woman. One of the Returned. The
afternoon light came in through the window and fell across
her face and all around the frame of the doorway were paint
splatters in various colors and finishes, remnants of years of
art projects. There were vibrant yellows and fierce reds, all
of them brighter than Harold thought they should have been
considering how old they probably were.

They framed the old woman in a rainbow of color, giving
her an air of magic.

"Yes?" Harold said.

"Charles, what time are we leaving?"

"Soon," Harold said.

"We're going to be late, Charles. And I won't stand for us
being late. It's bad manners."

"It's okay. They'll wait for us."

Harold stood and stretched his arms and walked slowly over
to the old woman, Mrs. Stone, and led her across the room
to her cot in the corner. She was a large black woman, well

into her eighties and senile as could be. But, senile or no, she took care of herself and her cot. She was always clean, her hair always well-kept. What little clothing she had somehow remained spotless.

"Don't you worry none," Harold said. "We won't be late."

"But we're already late."

"We've got plenty of time."

"Are you sure?"

"I'm positive, honey." Harold smiled and patted her hand as she eased down onto the cot. He sat beside her as she stretched out on her side and already was drifting into sleep. It always happened like this for her: a sudden excitement, some inescapable stress, followed by a sudden sleep.

Harold sat with Mrs. Stone—Patricia was her name—until sleep came for her. Then, in spite of the June heat, he covered her with the blanket from Jacob's bed. She mumbled something about not keeping people waiting. Then her lips were still, her breathing slow and even.

He went back to his own cot and sat. Harold wished he had a book. Maybe when Lucille came to visit he'd ask her to bring him one, so long as it wasn't a Bible or some other form of tomfoolery.

No, Harold thought, rubbing his chin. Bellamy had a hand in this somewhere. In spite of his lessening of authority since the Bureau began locking people up, Agent Martin Bellamy was still the most informed person in the area.

In his own way, Bellamy still ran the show. He was in charge of food and room assignments, clothing procurement, making sure everyone got toiletries and whatnot. He oversaw keeping track of both the True Living and the Returned.

He was in charge of it all, though other people actually did the legwork. And Harold was beginning to discover, by way of soldiers who liked to jabber loudly to one another as they patrolled the school, that there was less and less legwork going on these days.

The policy was slowly becoming a policy of simply holding on to the dead, storing them like too much foodstuff. Now and again, if they found one of particular value or notoriety, they went a little above and beyond and bought him a plane ticket home, but mostly the Returned were just being re-planted wherever they happened to sprout up.

It might not be this way everywhere, Harold figured, but it would be soon. As a general rule, it was just becoming easier and cheaper to assign the Returned a number and a case file, punch a few keys on a computer, ask a few questions, punch more keys and forget about them. If a person felt like going the extra mile—which fewer and fewer did—perhaps they would go so far as to run an internet search for the person's name. But that was the length of it. More and more, those few keystrokes—effort barely above doing nothing—was the way of things.

With the old woman sleeping, Harold left the room and made his way through the crowded, old school. Since the very first day they started arresting the Returned, things had been inadequate. And every day since, they were becoming more inadequate. Where there had been open space and room for a body to move here and there among the hallways, now there were only cots and people clinging to them out of fear of having them taken away by whatever newcomers might happen to show up. While things still hadn't devolved to the point of having more bodies than beds, there was a hierar-chy being born.

Those with tenure had their cots set up snugly within the main school building, where everything worked and noth-ing was very far away. New folks—except for the old and/or infirmed; there was still room being kept inside for them—wound up outside, in the parking lot and small sections of street surrounding the school, in an area referred to as Tent Village.

Tent Village was a green, drab assembly. Made from tents so old Harold couldn't look on them without risk of suddenly falling hip-deep into some boyhood memory. A memory so distant it showed up on the movie screen of his mind in black-and-white.

The saving grace thus far had been that the weather was forgiving. Hot and humid, but mostly dry.

Harold crossed Tent Village, headed toward the far side of the camp, near the southern fence, where Jacob's friend, a young boy by the name of Max, stayed. Past the fence, the guards walked their slow paths, rifles at their waists.

"Mindless bastards," Harold barked as he always did.

Harold looked up at the sun. It was still there, obviously, but it seemed warmer all of a sudden. A thread of sweat ran down the center of his forehead and eventually dropped from the tip of his nose.

All at once it seemed to get hotter. Ten degrees at least, like the sun had come down just then and settled upon his shoulders, intent on whispering something very important into his ear.

Harold wiped his face and rubbed the sweat in his hand against the leg of his pants.

"Jacob?" he called out. A tremble began at the base of his spine and moved downward through his legs. It congregated at the knees. "Jacob, where are you?"

Then, suddenly, the earth rose up to meet him.

Jeff Edgeson

If the clock on the wall was to be believed, then Jeff's hour with the colonel was almost over. The colonel had spent the past fifty-five minutes asking the questions they both knew by heart at this point. He would rather be reading. A good cyberpunk novel, or maybe some urban fantasy. He was partial to authors with great imaginations. Imagination was an important and rare thing, he felt.

"What do you think happens when we die?" the colonel asked.

This was a new question, though not a very imaginative one. Jeff thought for a moment, feeling a bit unsettled at the prospect of talking religion with the colonel, whom he'd grown to like. He reminded Jeff of his father.

"Heaven or hell, I guess," Jeff said. "I guess it depends on how much fun you had." He offered a small chuckle.

"Are you sure?"

"No," Jeff said. "I've been an atheist for a long time. Never been sure about much."

"And now?" The colonel sat up straight in his chair and his

hands disappeared beneath the table, as if he were reaching for something.

"Still not sure about much," Jeff said. "Story of my life."

Then Colonel Willis pulled a pack of cigarettes from his pocket and handed them over to the young man.

"Thanks," Jeff said, lighting up.

"This doesn't have to be unbearable," the colonel said. "We've all got our parts to play in this—my kind and yours."

Jeff nodded. He leaned back in his chair and exhaled a long, white plume and he did not mind how uncomfortable the chair was or how bland the walls were or the fact that, somewhere in this world, he had a brother and the colonel and his men would not let him find him.

"I'm not a cruel man," the colonel said then, as if he knew what Jeff was thinking. "I simply have an unsavory role to play." He stood. "But now I have to go. There's another truckload of you due in this evening."

NINE

Harold awoke to a sun that seemed brighter and harder than he ever remembered. Everything was far away and questionable, like coming down from taking too many medications. There was a crowd gathered around him. They all looked taller than they should, stretched out into exaggeration. Harold closed his eyes and breathed deeply. When he opened his eyes again Martin Bellamy was standing over him, looking very dark and official. Still wearing that damned suit, even in all this heat, Harold thought.

Harold sat up. His head hurt. It had been his luck that he'd fallen onto a patch of grass and not the pavement. There was something in his lungs. Something heavy and wet. It sent him coughing.

One cough led to another, and then there was no coughing at all, only outright hacking. Harold folded in half, his body rattling against itself. Little dots appeared before his eyes, fluttering in and out of existence.

When the coughing eventually stopped Harold lay sprawled on the grass with a blanket beneath his head and the sun in his eyes and sweat covering his body.

"What happened?" Harold asked, feeling something sharp and wet in his throat.

"You passed out," Martin Bellamy said. "How are you feeling?"

"Hot."

Agent Bellamy smiled. "It's a hot day."

Harold tried to sit up but the world betrayed him and went to spinning. He closed his eyes and reclined back onto the grass. The smell of the hot grass reminded him of when he was a boy, back when lying out in the grass on a hot June afternoon didn't need to be instigated by passing out.

"Where's Jacob?" Harold asked, eyes still shut.

"I'm here," Jacob said, emerging from the crowd that had gathered. He ran up with his friend Max in silent tow. Jacob kneeled beside his father and took the old man's hand.

"I didn't scare you, did I, boy?"

"No, sir."

Harold sighed. "That's good."

Jacob's friend Max, who had shown himself to be a very tender and concerned boy in general, kneeled at Harold's head and leaned down and removed his shirt and used it to wipe Harold's brow.

"Are you okay, Mr. Harold?" Max asked.

Max was a Returned of the British vintage. Complete with accent and manners. They'd found him over in Bladen County, not far from where that Japanese fellow had been found all those weeks back. Seemed that Bladen County was becoming a nexus for exotic, previously dead individuals.

"Yes, Max."

"Because you looked really sick and if you're sick you should go to hospital, Mr. Harold."

In spite of his calm, stoic Returned nature and refined British accent, Max spoke like a machine gun.

"My uncle got sick a long, long time ago," Max continued, "and he had to go to hospital. Then he got even more sick and he coughed a lot like the way you were coughing only it sounded even worse and, well, Mr. Harold, he died."

Harold was nodding and agreeing to the boy's story even though he'd failed to keep up with anything beyond the initial salvo of "My uncle got sick..."

"That's good, Max," Harold said, his eyes still closed. "That's fine."

Harold lay there on the ground for a very long time with his eyes closed and the warmth of the sun sprawled out across his body. Small conversations came to his ears, even over the sound of the soldiers marching diligently around the fence outside the camp. It hadn't seemed that Harold was this close to the perimeter fence when the coughing fit had first taken over his body, but now he realized how close he was to the edge.

His mind began a chain of imaginings then.

He imagined the land beyond the edge of the fence. He could see the pavement of the school's parking lot. He turned onto Main Street and passed the gas station and the small, old shops that were built along the street so long, long ago. He saw friends and familiar faces, all of them going about their business as they always did. Sometimes they smiled at him and waved and maybe one or two of them shouted hello.

Harold realized then that he was driving the old pickup truck he had owned back in 1966. He hadn't thought about that truck in years, but he remembered it vividly now. The wide, soft seats. The raw strength needed simply to turn the damned thing. Harold wondered then if today's generation could appreciate what a luxury power steering was or if, much the way it was with computers, it was something so common now that there wasn't any more magic to be had in it?

In this small imagining, Harold rode through the entire

town, slowly realizing that there was not a single Returned among its many streets and avenues. He rolled on out beyond the edge of town, along the highway toward home, the truck purring smoothly beneath him.

At home he wrestled the steering wheel into the driveway and found Lucille, young and beautiful. She sat on the porch in the glow of the sunlight with her back perfectly erect, looking regal and important in a way Harold had never seen another woman look in the entirety of his life. Her long, raven hair fell past her shoulders and shimmered in the warm sunlight. She was a creature of grace and importance. She intimidated him, and that was why he loved her so much. Jacob ran small loops around the oak tree in front of the porch, shouting something or other about heroes or villains.

This was the way things were supposed to be.

And then the boy looped behind a tree and did not return from the other side. Gone in an instant.

Agent Bellamy was kneeling in the grass by Harold's side; behind him a duo of eager-looking paramedics cast a shadow over Harold's sweat-soaked face.

"Do you have a history of this?" one of the paramedics asked.

"No," Harold said.

"Are you sure? Do I need to pull your medical records?"

"You can do what you like, I suppose," Harold said. His strength was coming back, riding a low tide of anger. "That's one of the benefits of being a government man, ain't it? Got everybody's information in a damned file somewhere."

"I suppose we can," Bellamy said. "But I think we'd all rather just do this the easy way." He nodded to the paramedics. "See that he's okay. Maybe he'll cooperate with you a little more than he did with me."

"Don't bet on it," Harold muttered. He hated holding a conversation while flat on his back, but there didn't seem to be much choice just now. Every time he thought of sitting up Jacob would press down gently on his shoulder with a look of worry on his small face.

Bellamy stood and brushed the grass from his knees. "I'll see about getting my hands on his medical records. Make a note of all this in the log, of course." He waved his hand, beckoning to someone.

A pair of soldiers came over.

"All this for a tired old man," Harold said loudly, finally sitting up with a grunt.

"Now, now," the paramedic said. He grabbed Harold by the arm with surprising strength. "You should lie down and give us a chance to make sure you're okay, sir."

"Relax," Jacob said.

"Yeah, Mr. Harold. You should lie down," Max inserted. "It's like I was telling you about my uncle. He got sick one day, didn't want any doctors fiddling at him and so he yelled at them whenever they came around. Then he was dead."

"Okay, okay, okay," Harold said. The speed at which the boy spoke was enough to wear down the old man's rebellion. And he was very, very tired all of a sudden. So he just gave in and decided to lie back on the grass and let the paramedics do what they would.

If they did something out of sorts, he figured, he could always sue. This was America, after all.

Then Max raced off into another story about the death of his uncle and Harold was lulled into unconsciousness by the rapid drum of the boy's voice.

"We're going to be late," the old, senile black woman said.

Harold sat up on his cot, not yet certain on how he had

gotten here. He was in his room and it was a little cooler than it had been and the sunlight through the window was all but gone so he figured it was the same day, only later. There was a bandage on his forearm covering up an itch where Harold figured a syringe must have been poked at some point.

"Damned doctors."

"That's a bad word," Jacob said. He and Max were sitting on the floor, playing a game. They leaped up and raced to the bed. "I didn't say anything before," Jacob continued, "but Mama wouldn't want you saying *damn*."

"That is a bad word," Harold said. "What's say we don't tell her?"

"Okay," Jacob said, smiling. "You want to hear a joke?"

"Oh, yes," Max interrupted. "It's a wonderful joke, Mr. Harold. One of the funniest jokes I've heard in a long time. My uncle—"

Harold raised a hand to stop the boy. "What's the joke, son?"

"What is a caterpillar most afraid of?"

"I don't know," Harold said, though he remembered well teaching Jacob this joke, not long before the boy died.

"A dogerpillar!"

They all laughed.

"We can't stay here all day," Patricia said from her cot. "We're already late. Terribly, terribly late. It's bad manners to keep people waiting. They'll start to worry about us!" She reached out a dark hand and placed it on Harold's knee. "Please," she said. "I hate to be rude to anyone. My mother raised me better. Can we go now? I'm all dressed."

"Soon," Harold said, though he didn't know why.

"Is she okay?" Max asked.

The boy usually spoke in paragraphs, so Harold waited for the rest to come. But it never did. Patricia fidgeted with her clothes and watched them as they did not seem to be getting ready to go. This upset her very much.

"She's just confused," Harold finally said.

"I'm not confused!" Patricia said, snatching her hand back.

"No," Harold said to her, and took her hand and patted it gently. "You're not confused. And we won't be late. They called a while ago and said that the time's been changed. They pushed things back."

"They canceled?"

"No. 'Course not. Just moved stuff back a little."

"They did, didn't they? They canceled it because we're so late! They're angry with us! This is terrible."

"That's not the case at all," Harold said. He moved over to her cot, thankful that his body seemed to be getting back to normal; maybe those damned doctors weren't all bad. He put his arm around her large frame and patted her shoulder. "They just changed the time, is all. There was some mix-up with the food, I think. The caterer had some kind of falling out in the kitchen and everything went bad, so they want a little more time, is all."

"Are you sure?"

"I'm positive," Harold said. "In fact, we've got so much time I think you could probably manage a nap. Are you tired?"

"No." She pursed her lips. Then: "Yes." She began crying. "I'm so, so tired."

"I know the feeling."

"Oh," she said. "Oh, Charles. What's wrong with me?"

"Nothing," Harold said, stroking her hair. "You're just tired. That's all."

She looked at him then with a great, deep fear set in her face as if, for an instant, she realized that he was not who he was pretending to be, as if nothing was the way her mind told her it was. Then the moment passed and she was a tired, confused old woman again and he was her Charles. She rested her head on his shoulder and wept, if only because it felt like the right thing to do.

In a little while the woman was asleep. Harold stretched her out on the mat and brushed the stray hairs from her face and looked down at her as if his head were full of puzzles.

"It's a terrible thing," Harold said.

"What is?" Jacob asked in his flat, even voice.

Harold sat on the end of his cot and looked down at his hands. He fixed his index and middle finger as if they held one of those small, wonderful cylinders of nicotine and carcinogenic. He put his empty fingers to his lips. Inhaled. Held his breath. Let it all go—coughing a little when his lungs were out of air.

"You shouldn't do that," Max said.

Jacob nodded in agreement.

"Helps me think," Harold said.

"What are you thinking about?" Max asked.

"My wife."

"Mama's okay," Jacob said.

"Of course she is," Harold said.

"Jacob's right," Max said. "Mommies are always okay because the world couldn't get along without them. That's what my daddy said back before he died. He said that mommies were the reason the whole world worked the way it did and that without mommies everybody would be mean and hungry and people would be fighting all the time and nothing good would ever happen to anybody."

"That sounds about right," Harold said.

"My dad used to say that my mum was the best in the world. He said he'd never trade her in, but I think that's the kind of thing every dad is supposed to say because it sounds good. But I bet Jacob thinks that, too, about his mum—your wife—because that's what you're supposed to think. That's how things are...."

Then the boy stopped talking and only stared blankly at them. Harold welcomed the silence, but was unnerved by its suddenness, as well. Max looked terribly distracted, as if something had suddenly leaped up and snatched away everything in his mind that had been there only seconds before.

Then the Returned boy's eyes rolled white, like a great switch in his mind had been thrown. He fell to the floor and lay there as if sleeping, with only a faint trickle of blood on his upper lip as proof that anything had gone wrong.

Tatiana Rusesa

They were whites, so she knew they would not kill her. More than that, they were Americans, so she knew they would treat her kindly. She did not mind that they would not let her leave; she only wished that she could help them more.

Before they brought her here—wherever she was now—she had been at another place. It was not quite as large as this place, and these people with her now were not the same people, but they were not very different. They all said they worked for something called "the Bureau."

They brought her food. They gave her a cot on which to sleep. She still wore the blue-and-white dress the woman had given her at the other place. Her name was Cara, the girl remembered, and she spoke both English and French and she had been very nice, but Tatiana knew that she was not being very helpful to them, and that weighed heavily on her.

Each morning at 10:00 a.m. the man would come and take her to the room with no windows and he would speak to her—slowly and evenly, as if he was not sure she understood English; but she had done very well in school and English was clean and simple to her. His accent was strange and something told her *that, to him, her accent was possibly equally as strange. So she responded to his questions as slowly and evenly as they were asked, which seemed to please him.*

She thought it important to please him. If she did not please him (or them), perhaps he would tell them to send her home.

So every day for many days now he came for her and brought her here to this room and asked his questions, and she tried, as best she could, to answer them. She had been afraid of him at first. He was large and his eyes were hard and cold, like the ground in winter, but he was always very polite to her, even though—she knew—she was not being very helpful.

She had actually begun to think that he was handsome. In spite of the hardness of his eyes, they were a very pleasing color of blue and his hair was the color of fields of tall, dry grass at sunset and he seemed very, very strong. And strength, she knew, was something that handsome people were supposed to have.

Today when he came for her he seemed more distant than usual. Sometimes he brought her candy, which the two of them would eat on their way to the room with no windows. He did not bring any candy today, and though that had happened before, it felt different now.

He did not make conversation on the way to the room as he often did. He only walked in silence and she stepped quickly to keep pace, which made her feel that things would be different today. More serious than they had been, perhaps.

When they were inside the room, he closed the door as he always did. He paused briefly and looked into the camera that hung in the corner above the door. He had not done that before. Then he began his questions, speaking slowly and evenly as always.

"Before you were found in Michigan, what is the last thing you remember?"

"Soldiers," she said. "And my home—Sierra Leone."

"What were the soldiers doing?"

"Killing."

"Did they kill you?"

"No."

"Are you certain?"

"No."

Even though it had been several days since he asked these particular questions, she knew her answers by heart. She knew them as well as he knew his questions. In the beginning he had asked these same questions every day. Then he stopped and began asking her to tell him stories, and she enjoyed that. She told him how each evening her mother would tell her stories of gods and monsters. "People and events of wonder and magic are the lifeblood of the world," her mother would say.

For almost an hour he asked the questions they both knew by heart. At the end of the hour, which is how long they usually spoke, he asked her a new question.

"What do you think happens when we die?" he asked.

She thought for a moment, feeling unsettled all of a sudden— and slightly afraid. But he was a white—and he was American—so she knew he would not hurt her.

"I do not know," she said.

"Are you sure?" he asked.

"Yes," she said.

She thought then of what her mother had told her once about death. "Death is only the beginning of the reunion you did not know you wanted," she had said. She was about to tell Colonel Willis this when he pulled his pistol and shot her.

Then he sat and watched her and waited to see what would happen next.

Uncertain of what he expected, suddenly he found himself alone with a lifeless, bleeding body that, only a moment before, had been a young girl who had liked him and thought him a decent man.

The air in the room seemed stale to the colonel. He stood and left, pretending all the while that he did not still hear Tatiana's voice—all the conversations the two of them had—replaying in his memory, audible over the sound of the gunshot still ringing in his ears.

TEN

"That poor, poor boy," Lucille said, squeezing Jacob to her chest. "That poor, poor boy." It was all she had managed to say about Max's death, but she said it often and she said it with woe.

What was it about the world, she wondered, that let these kinds of things happen? What was it that made it possible for a child—any child—to be alive and healthy one minute, then gone on to Glory the next? "That poor, poor boy," she said once more.

It was early morning and the visiting room the Bureau established at the Arcadia school was all but empty. Here and there a guard milled about, half nodding or talking with someone about something unimportant. They didn't seem to care very much about the goings-on of the old man who had been arrested with his little Returned son and wouldn't leave him, nor did they care about the old, silver-haired woman who came to visit them.

Nor did they seem to care very much about the Returned boy that died just the other day, and that distressed Lucille. She couldn't say exactly what she thought they should be doing to signify that a life had been lost, that there was mourning to be done and sadness to be reflected upon. Wear a black arm-band or some such. That seemed appropriate. But that idea had seemed foolish as soon as it came to her. People died. Even children. That was just the way of things.

The visiting room was made of corrugated steel fastened to metal posts with large, groaning fans at the entry and exit points trying to make the humid air more manageable. Here and there tables and benches had been set up.

Jacob sat quietly in his mother's lap, suffering that guilt chil-dren suffer at the sight of their mother in tears. Harold sat on the bench next to her with his arm around her. "Come on, now, my old nemesis," he said. His voice was soft, filled with grace and somberness, a tone he'd forgotten himself capable of achieving after all these years of being...well, *disagreeable* wasn't the word he would have chosen but... "It was just, just one of those things," he said. "Doctors said it was an aneurysm."

"Children don't have aneurysms," Lucille replied.

"They do. Sometimes. And maybe that was how it hap-pened the first time with him. Maybe it's just the way it al-ways was."

"They say there's some kind of sickness. I don't believe it, but that's what they say."

"Ain't no sickness other than stupidity," Harold said.

Lucille dabbed her eyes. She adjusted the collar on her dress.

Jacob eased out of his mother's arms. He was wearing the new clothes his mother had brought him. They were clean and soft in that special way that only new clothes ever are.

"Can I tell you a joke, Mama?"

She nodded. "But nothing dirty, right?"

"No problem there," Harold said. "I only ever taught him Christian jokes...."

"I'm just about done with both of you!"

"Don't worry about Max," Harold said. He looked around

the room. "Max went on to, well, wherever it is folks go on to, a long time ago. That was just a shadow that—"

"Stop it," Lucille said softly. "Max was a good boy. You know that."

"Yes," Harold agreed. "Max was a good boy."

"Was he different?" Jacob asked, his face tight with confusion.

"What do you mean?" Harold asked. This was the closest Jacob had come to talking about what everybody on the planet wanted the Returned to talk about: themselves.

"Was he different than he used to be?" Jacob asked.

"I don't know, sweetie," Lucille said. She took her son's hand—the way she'd seen people do in the movies, she couldn't help but think. She'd been watching far too much television lately. "I didn't know Max very well," she said. "You and your father spent more time with him than I did."

"And we hardly knew him," Harold said with only a small amount of unkindness in his voice.

Jacob turned and looked up at the wrinkled face of his father. "But do you think he was different?"

"Different from what? From when?"

Harold let the question hang between them like a fog. He wanted to hear the boy say it. Wanted to hear the boy admit that Max was something that had once been dead. Wanted to hear the boy say that there was something exceptional happening in the world, something strange and frightening and, most of all, unnatural. He wanted to hear Jacob admit that he was not the young boy who had died on August 15, 1966.

Harold needed those words.

"I don't know," Jacob said

"Of course you don't," Lucille interrupted. "Because I'm sure there was nothing different about him. Just like I know there's nothing different about you. There's nothing different about anyone, except that they're a part of a great and beautiful miracle. That's all. It's God's blessing, not His wrath the way some people are saying." Lucille pulled him close and kissed his brow. "You're my beloved boy," she said, her silver hair falling in her face. "The good Lord, God, will take care of you and bring you home again. Or I will."

She drove home in a haze of frustrations and the world seemed full of blurs, as if she were crying. In fact, she was, though she did not realize it until she pulled into the yard and the loud growling of the truck fell silent and there was only the tall, wooden house rising out of the ground, empty and waiting to swallow her. She wiped her eyes and quietly cursed herself for crying.

She crossed the yard with her hands full of the empty plastic containers she used to bring Jacob, Harold and Agent Bellamy food. She kept her focus on the food, on the idea of feeding those three men. She thought about how food softened people and made them stronger at the same time.

If folks only cooked and ate more, the world might not be quite so brusque, she thought.

Lucille Abigail Daniels Hargrave never liked being alone. Even in her childhood, the thing she'd loved most was a houseful of people. Lucille had been raised as the youngest in a family of ten. All of them crammed together in little more than a gray shanty that stood at the outskirts of the small town of Lumberton, North Carolina. Her father worked for the logging company and her mother was a maid for one of the more opulent families and, when the opportunities came about, she was a seamstress to anyone with an out-of-place stitch.

Her father never spoke ill of her mother and her mother never spoke ill of her father. From what Lucille had learned in her marriage to Harold, not speaking badly of each other was the surest sign that a long-term relationship was working. All the kissing and flower-buying and gift-giving didn't mean spit if a husband talked down to his wife or a wife spread gossip about her husband.

Like many people, she had spent most of her adult life trying to recreate her childhood, trying to grow back into it, as if time were not all-powerful. But Jacob had been her one shot at motherhood on account of complications with his birth, a fact about which she did not weep. Not even on the day when the doctors came to deliver the news. She only nodded—because she had known; somehow, she had known—and said that Jacob would be enough.

And for eight years she was a mother with a son. And then for fifty years she was a wife, a Baptist, a lover of words, but not a mother. Too much time passed between her two lives.

But now, Jacob was time beaten into defeat. He was time out of sync, time more perfect than it had been. He was life the way it was supposed to be all those years ago. That's what all the Returned were, she realized just then. And for the rest of the evening she did not cry and her heart was not as heavy and when sleep came for her it found her easily.

That night she dreamed of children. And when morning came she had the urge to cook.

Lucille ran her hands under the faucet. On the stove there was bacon and eggs frying. A pot of grits simmered on one of the back burners. She looked out through the window at the backyard, fighting the nagging sense that she was being watched. Of course, no one was there. She returned her attention to the stove and the too-much food she was preparing.

The most frustrating thing about Harold not being here was that she just didn't know how to cook for one person. It wasn't that she didn't miss him—she missed him terribly—but it was a downright shame that she was always throwing food away these days. Even after wrapping up food to take over to the school, the refrigerator was still full to brimming with leftovers, but leftovers never tasted right to her. Her palette had always been a sensitive one, and something about food that had rested too long in the coolness of a refrigerator made everything taste of copper.

Every day she took food to the school/god-awful-prison-camp-for-the-ornery-and/or-Returned. Even if they were prisoners, Jacob and Harold Hargrave would be very well-fed prisoners. But she couldn't get down there to take them breakfast. For the past twenty years or more Harold had been the one to do all the driving, and now Lucille was rusty behind the wheel and she didn't trust herself to drive up and down the road to deliver three hot meals. So breakfast she ate alone, with only the empty house to sit and watch her. Only the sound of her own voice to speak back to her.

"What's the world coming to?" she asked the empty house. Her voice moved over the hardwood floor, past the front door and small desk where Harold kept his cigarettes, on into the kitchen with its refrigerator full of food and a table where no one was sitting. Her voice reverberated through the other rooms, up the stairs, into the bedrooms where there was no one sleeping.

She cleared her throat, as if to draw someone's attention, but only silence answered her back.

The television might help, she thought. At least with the television on she could pretend. There would be laughter and conversation and words that she could imagine were coming from some grand holiday party being held in the next room—the kind that used to be held all those years ago before Jacob went down to that river and everything in her and Harold's life turned cold.

A part of Lucille wanted to turn on the news to hear if there was any word on that missing French artist—Jean Something-or-Other. The newspeople couldn't stop talking about how he'd come back from the dead, took up his sculpting again, made all the money he'd never even dreamed he would make the first time he was alive and then up and disappeared with the fiftysomething woman who'd helped "rediscover" him.

Lucille had never thought that people would riot over an artist going missing, but there had been riots. It took weeks for the French government to get a handle on things.

But the famous Returned French artist was still nowhere to be found. Some said the fame had gotten to be too much for him. Someone had said that a successful artist is no longer an artist, and that was what had driven Jean away. He wanted to be starving and hungry again, so that he could really find his art.

Lucille laughed at that, too. The sheer notion that a person could want to be starving was plumb foolish.

"Maybe he just wanted to be left alone," she said heavily.

Lucille thought on that for a while but then the silence of the house pressed down on her again like a heavy boot. So she walked into the living room and turned on the news and let the world in.

"Things just seem to be getting worse all over," the newscaster said. It was a Spanish man with dark features and a light-colored suit. Lucille had a brief impression that he was talking about something to do with finances or the global economy or gas prices or any of the other things that seemed to be getting perpetually worse year on year on year. But no, he was commenting on the state of the Returned.

"What's this all about?" Lucille said softly, standing in front of the television with her hands folded in front of her.

"In case you're just joining us," the man on the television said, "lots of debate today about the role and authority of the still new—yet ever-growing—International Bureau of the Returned. At last reports, the Bureau has just secured financial backing from NATO nations as well as several other countries not affiliated with NATO. The exact nature of the funding, or indeed its exact amount, has yet to be disclosed."

Just above the newscaster's shoulder appeared a small emblem—a simple gold standard with the words *International Bureau of the Returned* placed in the center. Then the logo went away and the television screen was consumed by images of soldiers riding in trucks and men with guns running from one side of an airport tarmac into the belly of large, gray airplanes that looked like a whole church could fit inside without the slightest inconvenience to the steeple.

"Lord," Lucille said. She switched off the television, shook her head. "Lord, Lord, Lord. This can't be real."

She wondered then just how much the world knew about what was happening in Arcadia. About whether or not they knew how the school had been taken over, how the Bureau had already become a powerful and terrifying thing.

In her mind she put together an image of the current state of Arcadia. The Returned were everywhere, she realized. There were hundreds of them now, as if they were being drawn to this place, to this town. Even though the president had ordered the Returned confined to their homes, there were just too many of them whose homes were half a world away. Sometimes Lucille would see the soldiers arresting them. History's most ominous reassurance.

Other times Lucille would catch sight of them in hiding. They had enough sense to stay away from the soldiers and keep out of the center of town where the school-cum-camp sat behind its fencing as best they could. But a little bit down the road, just right on Main Street, you could see them peeking out from old buildings and houses nobody was supposed to be living in. Lucille would wave to them as she passed, because that's what she was bred to do, and they would wave back, as if they all knew her and were intrinsically bound to her. As if she were a magnet destined to pull them in, to succor them.

But she was just an old woman who lived alone in a house built for three. There was supposed to be someone else who would come along and put an end to all this. That was how the world worked. Situations this big always hinged upon the actions of big people. People like those in the movies. People who were young and athletic and well-spoken. Not people who lived in a town no one had heard of.

No, she convinced herself, it wasn't her fate to help the Returned. Maybe it wasn't even her fate to help Jacob and Harold. Someone else would do it. Maybe Pastor Peters. More likely it would be Agent Bellamy.

But Bellamy wasn't a parent enduring an empty house. Bellamy wasn't the one the Returned, Lucille felt, seemed to gravitate toward. It was her. It was always her.

"Something has to be done," she said to the empty house.

When the house had quieted and the echo of the television was gone, Lucille returned to her life as though little beyond the realm of her senses had changed. She washed her hands in the kitchen sink and dried them and cracked more eggs into the frying pan and went about the business of lightly scrambling them. The first of the too-much bacon she was cooking was done so she scooped it out of the pan with a spatula and placed it on a paper towel and patted it to take off some of the grease—her doctor was always going on about grease—

and then she plucked a piece from the plate and stood there crunching it as she scrambled the eggs and stirred the grits from time to time.

She thought of Harold and Jacob, locked away inside the belly of that school, behind the soldiers and fencing and razor wire and, worst of all, government bureaucracy. It made her angry to think how those soldiers had just come along and plucked her son and husband up from the river, a river they practically owned considering the history the two of them had there.

As she sat at the kitchen table eating and thinking to herself, Lucille did not hear the footsteps moving over the porch.

The grits Lucille ate were warm and smooth. They slid into her stomach with just a hint of butter left behind. Then came the bacon and the eggs, sharp and salty, smooth and sweet.

"I'd build a church for you," Lucille said aloud, speaking to her plate of food.

Then she laughed and felt guilty. Even a little blasphemous. But God had a sense of humor, Lucille knew—though she would never let Harold know she thought so. And God understood that she was just an old, lonely woman alone in a large, lonely house.

She was halfway through breakfast before Lucille realized the girl was there. She nearly jumped out of her chair when she finally saw her, thin-framed and blonde, standing muddy and unkempt on the other side of the kitchen's screen door.

"Dear Lord, child!" Lucille shouted, covering her mouth with her hand.

It was one of the Wilson children—Hannah, if Lucille's memory served her, which, most times, it did. Lucille hadn't seen them since the town meeting at the church all those weeks ago.

"I'm sorry," the girl said.

Lucille wiped her mouth. "No," she said. "It's okay. I just didn't realize anybody was there." She walked to the door. "Where'd you come from?"

"My name's Hannah. Hannah Wilson."

"I know who you are, honey. Jim Wilson's daughter. We're family!"

"Ma'am."

"Back down the line your father and I are cousins. We share an aunt...I can't quite remember her name, though."

"Yes, ma'am," Hannah said tentatively.

Lucille opened the door and motioned for the girl to come in. "You look half-starved, child. When's the last time you ate?"

The girl stood in the doorway calmly. She smelled of mud and open air, as if she had both fallen from the sky and risen from the earth just that morning. Lucille smiled at her, but still the girl hesitated.

"I'm not going to hurt you, child," Lucille said. "Unless, that is, you don't come in here and eat something. Then I'm going to find the biggest switch I can and whup you until you sit down and eat yourself lazy!"

The Returned girl returned her smile, finally, in that casual, slightly detached way. "Yes, ma'am," she said.

The screen door clattered gently behind her as she entered the house, as if applauding the reprieve in Lucille's loneliness.

The girl ate as much as Lucille would give her, which was a great deal considering all that she had cooked. And when it looked as though the girl would finish off everything that she had made for breakfast, Lucille began rummaging through the refrigerator. "I don't care for any of it. Leftovers. It just ain't right."

"That's okay, Ms. Lucille," the girl said. "I'm full. Thank you, though."

Lucille thrust an arm into the back of the refrigerator. "No," she said. "You're not full yet. I'm not even sure if that stomach of yours has a bottom to it, but I plan to find out. I'm gonna feed you until the grocery store runs out!" She laughed, her voice echoing through the house. "But I don't cook for free," Lucille said, unwrapping the sausage she'd found in back of the refrigerator. "Not for anyone. Even the Lord Jesus would have to earn His keep if He planned to get a meal out of me. So I've got a few things that I need you to do around here." Lucille placed one hand on her back—suddenly looking the part of a very old and very rickety woman—and made a great groaning sound. "I'm not so young as I used to be."

"My mama said I shouldn't beg people," the girl said.

"And your mama's right. But you ain't begging. I'm asking you for help, that's all. And, in return, I'll feed you. That's fair, ain't it?"

Hannah nodded. She swung her feet back and forth as she sat at the table in a chair too large for her.

"Speaking of your mother," Lucille said, still fussing about with the sausage. "She's going to be worried about you. Your daddy, too. Do they know where you are?"

"I think so," the girl said.

"What does that mean?"

The girl shrugged, but since her back was turned and she was busy unwrapping the sausage, Lucille did not see it. After a moment the girl realized this and said, "I don't know."

"Come on now, child." Lucille oiled the cast-iron pan for the sausage. "Don't start behaving that way now. I know about you and your family. Your mother...Returned just like your daddy did. Brother, too. Where are they? Last I heard all of you had disappeared from the church after those soldiers started arresting folks." Lucille placed the sausage in the pan and turned on a low heat.

"I'm not supposed to say," the girl said.

"Oh, my!" Lucille replied. "That sounds very serious. Secrets are always very serious."

"Yes, ma'am."

"I generally don't care for secrets. They can lead to all manner of trouble if you're not careful. In all the time I've been married, little girl, I've never kept a secret from my husband," Lucille said. Then she walked to the girl and whispered softly, "But you want to know what?"

"What?" Hannah whispered back.

"Secretly, that's not true. But don't tell anybody. It's a secret."

Hannah smiled, wide and bright, and her smile was very much like Jacob's smile.

"Did I tell you about my son, Jacob? He's like you. Just like you and your whole family."

"Where is he?" the girl asked.

Lucille sighed. "He's at the school. The soldiers took him."

Hannah's face went pale.

"I know," Lucille said. "It's a frightful thing. He and my husband were both taken. They were down by the river on their own when the soldiers came for them."

"By the river?"

"Yes, child," Lucille said. The sausage was already beginning to sizzle. "The soldiers like the river," she said. "They know there's lots of places for people to hide, so they go through that area a lot, trying to find folks. Oh, they're not bad people, those soldiers. I pray they're not, at least. They never hurt anybody, not other than locking them up away from their families. No. They don't hurt you. They just take you away. Take you away from everyone you love or care about and…"

When she turned, Hannah was gone, with only the clapping of the screen door left in her wake.

"I'll see you when you get back," Lucille said to the empty house, a house which she knew would not be empty much longer.

Just the night before, hadn't she dreamed of children?

Alicia Hulme

"What happened to the boy was just a fluke. There is no sickness. But there have been disappearances." The young girl was
nervous delivering the message to the dark-skinned man in the
well-cut suit on the far side of the desk. "I don't understand any
of this," she said. "But it doesn't sound good, does it?"

"It's okay," Agent Bellamy said. "It's a strange situation."

"What happens now? I don't want to be here any more than
I wanted to be in Utah."

"You won't be here long," Bellamy said. "I'll see to that, just
as Agent Mitchell promised you I would."

She smiled at the memory of Agent Mitchell. "She's a good
woman," she said.

Agent Bellamy stood and walked around the desk. He placed
a small chair next to hers and sat. Then he reached into his sleeve
and retrieved an envelope. "Their address," he said, handing the
envelope to Alicia. "They don't know about you, but from what
I've been able to dig up, they want to. They very much want to."

Alicia took the envelope and opened it with trembling hands.
It was a Kentucky address. "Dad's from Kentucky," she said,
her voice suddenly trembling. "He always hated Boston, but

Mom didn't want to leave. I guess he finally wore her down." She hugged the dark-skinned agent in the well-cut suit and kissed his cheek. "Thank you," she said.

"There's a soldier outside named Harris. He's young, maybe eighteen or nineteen, not much younger than you. Stay with him when you leave my office. Do what he says. Go where he tells you to go. He'll get you out of here." He patted her hand. "It's good that they went to Kentucky. The Bureau is busy in the more populated areas. Lots of places to hide you there."

"What about Agent Mitchell?" she asked. "Are you going to send me back with another message?"

"No," Agent Bellamy said. "That wouldn't be safe for you or her. Just remember to stay with Harris, do what he tells you. He'll get you back to your parents."

"Okay," she said, standing. When she was at the door she hesitated, her curiosity getting the better of her. "The disappearances," she said. "What did she mean by that?"

The agent in the well-cut suit sighed. "Honestly," he said, "I don't know if it's the end or the beginning."

ELEVEN

Fred Green and a handful of other men convened on Marvin Parker's lawn nearly every day now, gathering beneath the sweltering sun, letting their anger boil up as, one after another, buses of Returned came down Main Street into Arcadia.

For the first few days, John Watkins kept count of the Returned on a small piece of wood that he found in his truck. He made tick marks grouped in fives. In that first week his tally was well over two hundred.

"I'm gonna run out of pencil before they run out of Returned," he said to the group at one point.

No one replied.

Now and again Fred would say, "We can't stand for this." He would shake his head and take a gulp of beer. His legs twitched as if they had somewhere they needed to be. "It's happening right here in our own town," he said.

No one was quite able to put a finger on exactly what "it" Fred spoke of but, somehow, they all understood his meaning. They all understood that something larger than anything they had ever imagined possible was happening right in front of them.

"You wouldn't think a volcano could just grow, would

you?" Marvin Parker said one afternoon as they all stood watching another bus being unloaded. He was tall and lanky, with pale skin and hair the color of rust. "But it's true," he continued. "It's the God's honest truth. Heard tell one time about this woman that had a volcano grow up in her back-yard. Started out just a little bump in the lawn, like a gopher hole or something. Then the next day it was a little bigger, and a little bigger the day after that. And so on."

No one spoke. They only listened and constructed the deadly mound of earth and rock and fire in their minds while, across the street, the Returned were off-loaded, counted and processed into Arcadia.

"Then, one day after this hill was about ten feet tall or so, she got scared. You wouldn't think it would take that long before a person got scared of something like that, would you? But that's how it happens. Take your time, let things happen slowly, and it's a long time before you get your wits."

"What could she have done?" someone asked.

The question went unanswered. The story continued: "By the time she called someone, all around her place there was the smell of sulfur. Neighbors got involved then. Finally took their heads out of their asses and decided to look into the molehill that was growing into a mountain right there in their neigh-bor's backyard. But by then it was too late, wasn't it?"

Someone asked, "What could they have done about it?"

But this question, too, went unanswered. The story rolled on:

"Some scientists came out there and took a look at things. Took readings, did tests or whatever it is they do. And you know what they told her? Told her, 'We guess you'd better move.' Can you believe that? That's all they had to say to her. Here she was losing her home, the very thing in this world that every person deserves, the only thing in this world that anybody really has—their God-given home!—and they turn around and tell her, 'Well, tough luck, toots.'

"Not long after that, she up and moved. Packed up her whole life and just lit out. Then other people from the town followed. All of them running from the thing that started growing in her backyard, the thing she and each and every one of them had watched grow." He finished his beer, crushed the can in his hand, tossed it onto his lawn and grunted. "They should have done something at the very beginning. Should have made more of a fuss when they first saw that unnatural lump in her lawn, when their souls told them that something wasn't right about it. But, no, they all hesitated—the woman whose house it was especially. She hesitated and each and every one of them was lost for it."

The buses came and went for the rest of that day with the men watching in silence. They were all gripped with a feeling that something about the world was betraying them, right at this very moment, and perhaps it had been betraying them for years.

They felt that the world had been lying to them for all their lives.

It was on the very next day that Fred Green showed up, carrying his picket sign. It was a square of plywood painted green and, in bright red lettering, was the slogan Returned Out of Arcadia.

Fred Green had no idea exactly what protesting would do. He wasn't sure if it had any merit, what kind of outcome it guaranteed. But it felt like action. It felt like he was giving form to whatever it was that was keeping him up at night, whatever it was that chased sleep away and left him feeling wrung out each morning.

This was his best idea for now, come what may.

***

Agent Bellamy sat at the table with his legs crossed, his suit jacket open and his silk tie half an inch looser than usual. It was the closest Harold had ever seen the man come to relaxed. He wasn't quite sure how he felt about Bellamy, but he figured if he didn't hate the man by now, that meant he probably liked him very much. That was generally how it worked.

Harold slurped at boiled peanuts with a cigarette propped between his fingers, a chalk-white line of cigarette smoke rolling over his face. He chewed and wiped the briny juice from his fingers against the legs of his pants—since Lucille wasn't there to protest—and, when he felt like it, he took a puff of his cigarette and exhaled without coughing—the not-coughing part took effort these days, but he was learning.

This was one of the few chances Agent Bellamy had to speak with Harold alone since things had progressed the way they had in Arcadia. Harold wouldn't often be talked into being away from Jacob. "She'll never forgive me if something happens," Harold had said.

But sometimes he would agree to let Jacob sit with one of the soldiers in another room—so long as he knew which it was—long enough for Bellamy to ask a few of his questions.

"How are you feeling?" Bellamy asked, notebook at the ready.

"I'm alive, I suppose." Harold flicked the end of his cigarette, dropping ashes into a small, metal ashtray. "But who ain't alive these days?" He took a puff of his cigarette. "Elvis make it back yet?"

"I'll see what I can find out."

The old man chuckled.

Bellamy sat back in his chair, shifted his weight and watched the old Southerner curiously. "So how are you feeling?"

"You ever play horseshoes, Bellamy?"

"No. But I've played boccie ball."

"What exactly is that?"

"It's the Italian version."

Harold nodded. "We should play horseshoes sometime. Instead of this." He opened his arms to indicate the small, stuffy room in which they sat.

"I'll see what I can do," Bellamy said with a smile. "How are you feeling?"

"You already asked me that."

"You never answered."

"I did so." Harold looked around the room again.

Bellamy closed his notebook and placed it on the table between the old man and himself. He placed his pen atop the notebook and made a show of patting them both as if to say, "There's only the two of us here, Harold. I promise you. No recorders or cameras or secret microphones or anything else. Only a guard outside the door who can't hear you and wouldn't want to if he could. He's just there because of Colonel Willis."

Harold finished off the bowl of peanuts in silence, then finished his cigarette with Bellamy sitting across the table saying nothing, only waiting. The old man lit another one and took a long, dramatic pull from it. He held the smoke in his lungs until he could not hold it anymore. Then he released it with a cough, a cough that rolled into a string of coughs until he was panting, beads of sweat welled up on his brow.

When the coughing passed and Harold had composed himself, Bellamy finally spoke. "How are you feeling?"

"Just happens more often."

"But you won't let us run any tests."

"No, thank you, Agent Man. I'm old, that's all that's wrong with me. But I'm too much of a bastard to have an aneurism like that boy. And I'm not so stupid as to believe in this 'sickness' your soldiers keep whispering to one another about."

"You're a smart man."

Harold took another drag.

"I've got my suspicions about the cause of your coughing," Bellamy said.

Harold blew out a long, even line of smoke. "You and my wife both."

Harold outed his cigarette and pushed the bowl of peanut hulls to the side. He put his hands together on the table and looked down at them, recognizing then just how old and wrinkled they were—thinner and more frail-looking than he ever remembered seeing them before. "Can we talk, Martin Bellamy?"

Agent Bellamy shifted in his chair. He straightened his back, as if preparing for a great endeavor. "What do you want to know? You frame the questions and I'll answer them to the best of my ability. That's all I can do. That's all you can ask."

"Fair enough, Agent Man. Question number one—are the Returned really people?"

Bellamy paused. His attention seemed to shift, as if some image had sprung up in his mind. Then he answered, as confidently as he could, "They seem to be. They eat—they eat a lot, actually. They sleep—sporadically, but they do sleep. They walk. They talk. They have memories. All the things that people do, they do."

"Oddly, though."

"Yes. They are a bit odd."

Harold popped a laugh. "A bit," he said, nodding his head up and down. "And how long has it been just 'odd' for people to come back from the dead, Agent Man?"

"A few months now," Bellamy said evenly.

"Question two, Agent Man...or is it three?"

"It's three, I believe."

Harold laughed dryly. "You're awake. That's good."

"I try."

"So, question three… People, since as far back as anybody can remember, have never been in the habit of coming back from the dead. Since these individuals are doing just that, can you still call them people?"

"Can we get to the point of this?" Bellamy asked curtly.

"Yankees," Harold grumbled. He shifted in his seat. His leg twitched. All manner of energy seemed to be coursing through his body.

"It's the two of us here," Bellamy said. He leaned forward at the table, as if he might reach out and take Harold's old hands into his own. And, if that had been needed just then, perhaps he would have. But Harold was ready now.

"He shouldn't be here," Harold said finally. "He died. My son died—1966. Drowned in a river. And you know what?"

"What's that?"

"We buried him, that's what. We found his body—because God is cruel—and I scooped him up out of that river myself. He was cold as ice, even if it was the middle of summer. I've felt fish that were warmer than him. He was bloated. Colored all wrong." Harold's eyes shone. "But I carried him out of that water with everybody standing around crying, telling me I didn't have to be the one to pick him up. Everybody offering to take him out of my arms.

"But they didn't understand. I did have to be the one to take him out of that river. I had to be the one to feel how cold and unnatural he was. I had to be the one to know—to be genuinely and truly sure—that he was dead. And that he wasn't ever coming back. We buried him. Because that's what you do to people when they die. You bury them. You dig a place in the earth and you put them there and that's supposed to be it."

"No belief in the afterlife?"

"No, no, no," Harold said. "That's not what I'm talking about. I mean it's an ending for this!" Harold reached across the table and grabbed Bellamy's hands. He squeezed with enough force that it began to hurt the government agent, who tried to pull away when he realized Harold was stronger than he looked. But it was no good by then, Harold's grip was non-negotiable. "All this is supposed to stop and never start again," Harold said. His eyes were wide and sharp. "This is supposed to be over with!" Harold yelled.

"I understand," Bellamy said in his smooth, fast New York voice, disentangling his hands from Harold's. "It's a hard and confusing thing. I know."

"It all stopped," Harold said after a moment. "The feeling. The memories. Everything." He paused. "Now I wake up thinking about the way things used to be. I think about birthdays and Christmases." He chortled and looked at Bellamy with a light in his eyes. "You ever chased a cow, Agent Bellamy?" he asked, smiling.

Bellamy laughed. "No. Can't say that I have."

"There was this muddy Christmas back when Jacob was six. Rained for three days beforehand. By the time Christmas came the roads were so bad almost nobody could get out and go visiting the way they planned, so everybody kind of just kept to themselves and said 'Merry Christmas' over the phone." He sat back in his chair and gesticulated as he spoke. "There used to be this farm out by where I live now. Belonged to Old Man Robinson. I bought the land off his son when he died, but back then, on this Christmas, he had this cow pasture out there. Didn't have much in the way of cows. Just a handful. Maybe once every couple of years he'd take one to slaughter. But, for the most part, he just kept the cows. Not for any particular reason, I don't think. His daddy always kept cows, from what I hear and, honestly, I believe he just didn't know how else to live."

Bellamy nodded. He wasn't sure where the story was going, but he didn't mind riding along.

"So then this muddy Christmas comes along," Harold continued. "Rain was falling like God was angry about something. Coming straight down in buckets. So right there in the middle of the worst of it comes this knock on the door and who is it? None other than Old Man Robinson himself. He was a big bastard. Bald as a newborn and built like a lumberjack. Chest like an oil drum. And he's standing in the doorway covered in mud. 'What's the issue?' I asked him. 'Cows on the run,' he said, and pointed off toward a stretch of fence. I could see where the cows had torn up the ground getting out.

"Before I could say anything, before I could even offer to help, something shot past me. Shot right out the front door and off the porch and out into all that damned rain and mud." Harold smiled wide.

"Jacob?" Bellamy asked.

"I thought about yelling at him. Calling him back to the house. But then I thought, 'What the hell?' And before I could even make it out the front door Lucille was shooting past me nearly as fast as Jacob had—still wearing one of her best dresses. It was covered in mud before she got ten feet off the porch...and all any of us—Old Man Robinson included—did was laugh about it." Harold's hands were finally still. "Maybe everybody was just tired of being cooped up in the house," Harold said finally.

"So?" Bellamy asked.

"So what?"

"Did you get the cows back?"

Harold chuckled. "We did," he said. Then his smile faded and his voice became heavy and serious and conflicted again.

"And then all that was over. And, eventually, it went away. But now...now here I am straddling the chasm." Harold stared down at his hands. When he spoke, there was a tinge of delirium in his voice. "What am I supposed to do? My brain tells me he's not my son. My mind says that Jacob died—drowned to damn death—on a balmy day in August back in 1966.

"But when he speaks, my ears tell me he's mine. My eyes tell me he's mine, just the same as he was all those years ago." Harold slammed a fist on the table. "And what do I do with that? Some nights, when everything is dark and quiet over there, when everyone's bedded down, sometimes he'll get up and come over and lie on the cot beside me—just like he used to do—like he's been having a nightmare or something. Or, worse yet, sometimes it seems like he's just doing it because he misses me.

"He'll come over and curl up beside me and...God damn me...I can't help but put my arm around him just like I used to. And you know what, Bellamy?"

"What, Harold?"

"I feel better than I have in years. I feel whole. Complete. Like everything in my life is the way it's supposed to be." Harold coughed. "What do I do with that?"

"Some people cling to it," Bellamy said.

Harold paused, genuinely surprised by the reply. "He's changing me," Harold said after a moment. "Goddammit, he's changing me."

Bobby Wiles

Bobby had always been good at getting into places he wasn't sup-
posed to. His father had forecast that he would grow up to be a
magician because of all the ways the boy could disappear when
he wanted to. Now Bobby was hidden in the colonel's office,
just inside the school's air vent, peering out through the slats at
the colonel.

There was never anything to do here. Nothing to do but sit
and wait and not go anywhere. But sneaking into places made
things more interesting. The school had lots of places to investi-
gate. He'd already found his way into what used to be the kitchen.
He thought he would find a knife there to play with, but they
were all gone. He'd snuck into the boiler room by way of the air
duct that came in from outside the building. Everything in there
was rusty and hard and fun.

The colonel sat at his desk, staring at a large bank of computer screens. He was tired of Arcadia. He was tired of the Returned. He was tired of this whole unusual condition which had
come and settled over the world. He could see where it was all
going better than anyone else. The hysteria, the riots, whatever
else. People had a hard enough time just getting through the day

when the world spun normally and people died and stayed buried in their graves.

This situation with the Returned, the colonel knew, was a state of being that could never contain itself peacefully. So he did what he was told because that was the only way to help people—to maintain order and trust in the way things were supposed to be.

Unlike so many other people these days, the colonel had no fear of the Returned. Rather, he was afraid of everyone else and how they could react to seeing their loved ones—whether they truly believed them alive or not—standing next to them, breathing air, asking to be remembered.

The colonel had been fortunate. When his father was discovered as one of the Returned, the colonel was informed of it and given the choice of seeing him. He chose not to, but only because it was the best for everyone. It simply wouldn't do for him to get biased, to become swayed by memory and presumptions on a future with someone whose future ended years ago.

The situation with the Returned wasn't the way the world was meant to be, and people would soon enough realize that. Until then, it took men like him to hold the reins as best they could.

So he let the Bureau know that he did not want contact with his father. But he did make sure his father was transferred to one of the better centers. That part of himself, that small action on behalf of this person that might be his father, he could not deny.

In spite of how hard he had to be, in spite of what needed to be done, this one action he could not help. It might have been his father, after all.

On every computer screen in front of the colonel was the same image: an old, large-framed black woman sitting at a desk *across from a clean-cut agent with a square head named Jenkins. Bobby had been interviewed once by Jenkins. But the colonel was something else.*

Bobby breathed slowly, making as little sound as possible as he shifted his weight from one hip to the other. The walls of the air duct were thin and covered in filth.

The colonel sipped coffee from a mug and watched Jenkins and the old black woman talk. There was sound, but Bobby was too far away to hear much of what they were saying on the screen. He repeatedly caught the name "Charles" from the black woman's mouth, and that seemed to frustrate Jenkins.

Probably her husband, Bobby thought.

The colonel continued watching the monitors. Occasionally he would change one of them to a picture of a dark-skinned black man in a well-cut suit. The man sat at his desk, working. The colonel watched him and then looked back at the screen with the old woman.

Soon Agent Jenkins stood and knocked on the door of the interview room. A soldier came in and gently helped the old woman out of the room. Jenkins looked into the camera, as if he knew the colonel had been watching, and shook his head to show his frustration. "Nothing," Bobby heard him say.

The colonel did not speak. He only pushed a button and suddenly all the screens were filled with the dark-skinned agent in the well-cut suit working at his desk. The colonel watched in silence with his face looking very hard and serious until Bobby fell asleep from want of something different.

He awoke to soldiers dragging him from the air duct, shouting questions and handling him roughly. The last he saw of the

colonel was the image of him pointing his finger at a young soldier as they locked him in a room with no windows.

"C'mon, kid," one of the soldiers said.

"I'm sorry," Bobby said. "I won't do it again."

"Just come on," the soldier said. He was young and blond-
haired and acne-scarred and, in spite of the colonel's obvious
anger, he was grinning as he took Bobby from the room. "You
remind me of my brother," he said under his breath when they
were out of the office.

"What's his name?" Bobby asked after a moment. Curiosity was always his strong suit.

"His name was Randy," the young soldier said. And then:
"Don't worry. I'll take care of you."

And Bobby was not as afraid as he had been.

TWELVE

IN another life Lucille would have been a line cook. She would have gone to work every day with a smile on her face. She would have come home every night smelling of grease and all manner of spices and seasonings. Her feet would have been sore. Her legs would have been tired. But she would have loved it. Through and through, she would have loved it.

She stood in a cluttered—but clean—kitchen with the second batch of fried chicken hissing like the ocean on sharp rocks. In the living room the Wilson family was talking and laughing, trying not to turn on the television as they went about their lunch. They sat in a circle on the floor—though why they sat on the floor when there was a perfectly good dinner table not ten feet away, Lucille had no idea—with their plates in their laps, shoveling heaps of rice and gravy, corn, green beans, fried chicken and biscuits into their mouths. Now and again there would be some roar of laughter followed by a long silence of eating.

It went this way until the entire family was full and only a few straggling pieces of chicken remained uneaten on a small plate next to the stove. Lucille placed these in the oven in case someone should get hungry later, then she took stock of the kitchen.

Everything seemed to be getting low, and Lucille liked that.

"Is there anything I can do?" Jim Wilson said as he came in from the living room. Somewhere upstairs his wife chased behind their children, laughing.

"No, thank you," Lucille said, her head halfway in one of the kitchen cabinets. She scratched notes blindly on a shopping list. "I've got everything well in hand," she said.

Jim came over, looked at a pile of dishes and rolled up his sleeves.

"And what are you doing?" Lucille asked, her head finally out of the cabinet.

"I'm helping."

"You leave those right where they are. That's what the children are for." She swatted his hand.

"They're playing," Jim said.

"Well, they can't play all day, can they? You've got to teach them responsibility."

"Yes, ma'am," Jim said.

Lucille buzzed back and forth about the kitchen, stepping around the man who had anchored himself before the sink. In spite of agreeing with her on the proper upbringing of the children, he washed and rinsed and placed the dishes in the rack, doing so one at a time.

One by one.

Wash. Rinse. Rack.

"Honey," Lucille began, "why don't you just put them all in the sink at once? Never seen anybody do dishes one at a time like that."

Jim said nothing, he only carried on.

One by one.

Wash. Rinse. Rack.

"All right, then," Lucille said.

She tried not to blame Jim's strangeness on whatever it was that had brought him back from the grave. Even though they were cousins—as far as she knew—she had never spent as much time with him and his family as she should have. That was a great point of woe for Lucille.

She mostly just remembered Jim as hardworking, which was what most people in Arcadia knew him for up until he and his family was murdered.

It was a terrible thing, that murder. Sometimes Lucille could almost forget that it had happened. Almost. Other times it was all she saw when she looked at any of them. And that was the reason the town had reacted to them the way they had. Nobody likes to be reminded of where they failed, where they went wrong and were never able to make it right. And that's what the Wilsons were.

It was sometime back in the winter of '63, if Lucille's memory served. She remembered it the way a person remembers all tragic news: in scene.

She was in the kitchen grappling with the dishes. It was bone-cold outside. She stared out through the window and watched the oak tree—naked as the day it was born—shudder back and forth when the wind picked up. "Dear Lord," she said.

Harold was out there somewhere, in all that cold, in all that dark, gone for groceries this late in the evening—which didn't make a lick of sense, Lucille thought. Then, as if he'd heard her thought, she suddenly saw his headlights bouncing down the dirt road toward home.

"You'll want to sit down," he said when he'd come in.

"What is it?" she asked, feeling her heart take a sudden, southerly route. It was in Harold's voice, all of it.

"Would you just sit down!" Harold barked. He kept

rubbing his mouth. His lips went back and forth in small, cigarette-size circles. He sat at the kitchen table. Then he stood. Then he sat again.

"Shot," he said finally, almost in a whisper. "All of them. Shot and killed. Jim found dead in the hallway. Shotgun just beyond his reach, like he was going for it but just didn't make it. Wasn't loaded, though, from what I hear, so I doubt he would have even gotten time to use it. He never liked to keep that gun loaded with the children there and whatnot." Harold wiped his eye. "Hannah…they found her under the bed. Guess she was the last one."

"Dear Lord," Lucille said, staring down at her still-soapy hands. "Dear Lord, dear Lord, dear Lord."

Harold grunted some manner of affirmation.

"We should have visited them more," Lucille said, crying.

"What?"

"We should have visited them more. Should have spent more time with them. They were family. I told you Jim and I were related. They were family."

Harold had never been sure if Lucille's claim that she and Jim were kin were true or not. But it was the kind of thing that didn't really matter, he knew. If she believed it, then it was true, which only made what happened to them hurt all the more.

"Who did it?" Lucille asked.

Harold only shook his head and tried not to weep. "Nobody knows."

There would be a lot of that going around Arcadia not only that night, but for years to come. The deaths of the Wilsons, while tragic and terrible in its own right, would have a secret influence on the town of Arcadia and its general sense of place in the world.

It was after the deaths of the Wilsons that people began to

take notice of petty thefts that occurred now and again. Or maybe they noticed that such and such was having marital problems—maybe even having an affair. There was a general sense of violence that rose up around the foundation of Arcadia after the Wilson tragedy. It flourished like mildew, creeping up a little more each year.

By the time Jim Wilson had finished washing the dishes in his strange manner, Lucille was done with her list. She went upstairs and washed up in the sink and dressed and gathered up her list and her purse and stood in the doorway. When she was certain that she was ready, with the truck keys in her hand and Harold's old, blue Ford staring back at her, she inhaled deeply and reflected on how much she hated driving. And to make matters worse, Harold's damned old truck was as biased and temperamental an animal as she'd ever seen. It started when it wanted to. The brakes squealed. The thing was alive, Lucille had told Harold more than once. Alive and full of contempt for women...maybe even for humanity as a whole, just like its owner.

"I'm sorry about all of this," Jim Wilson said, startling Lucille. She still couldn't get used to how quiet and soft-footed he could be.

Lucille nosed through her purse. Her list was there. Her money was there. Her picture of Jacob was there. But still she rifled through her belongings and spoke to the entire Wilson family without looking back. They were all there, standing together behind her like the cover of some Christmas card. She could feel them.

"You sound just like that family of yours," Lucille said. "It makes it easy enough to tell where she gets it from—all that apologizing without cause. I won't hear it." Then Lucille closed her purse, still not feeling settled.

It was like a storm was on the way.

"Sure," Jim said. "I try not to be a bother. I just want you to understand how much we appreciate your help, is all. I just want you to know how grateful we are for all you're doing for us."

Lucille turned with a grin. "Lock up when I'm gone. Tell Connie I'll talk to her when I get back. I got a pie recipe I'd like to give her. Belonged to Great-aunt Gertrude...I think." She paused to think. Then: "Keep those blessed children of yours upstairs. There shouldn't be anyone coming by, but if they do..."

"We'll be upstairs."

"And don't forget—"

"Food's in the oven," Jim interrupted. He saluted.

"Okay, okay," Lucille said, and she marched off to where Harold's old blue Ford was parked, refusing to look back and let them see how suddenly afraid she had become.

The grocery store was one of Arcadia's last holdouts from the town's renovation and reclamation project of 1974—the last time any substantial amount of money had come into the town. The old brick building was one of the last stops on the western edge of town before the town proper came to an end and emptied out into a two-lane road and fields and trees and houses dotting the land here and there. It sat at the end of Main Street, looking square and grand, the way it had been back when it was the town hall.

In fact, all a body had to do was peel back the strategically placed banners and advertisements and City Hall, faded and timeworn, could still be seen in relief against the old stones. On a good day—back before the military set up camp in town—the grocery store was lucky to have thirty customers. And even that was optimistic, even when you counted the old men who sometimes loitered at the store and did nothing but sit in their rocking chairs in the doorway, swapping fictions.

A young soldier offered his arm as Lucille made her way up the stairs. He called her "ma'am" and was gentle and patient—even as so many other young men buzzed past them as if the food might suddenly run out.

Inside a cluster of gossiping men refused to be denied their sitting space. It was Fred Green, Marvin Parker, John Watkins and a few others. The past couple of weeks, she had seen them protesting—if that's what they wanted to call it—over in Marvin Parker's yard. It was a sad sack of protest, she felt. There was hardly a half dozen of them and they still hadn't come up with any kind of decent slogan. One day when she was on her way to see Harold and Jacob she'd heard them shouting, "Arcadia for the living! Not for the giving!"

She had no clue what the heck that was supposed to mean, and she figured they didn't, either. They probably just said it because it rhymed and, as far as they knew, if you were going to protest, you had to rhyme.

When the young soldier escorted her through the door, Lucille stopped in front of the men. "You should all be ashamed of yourselves," she said. She patted the soldier's hand to signal that she would be okay to continue by herself.

"This is shameful," she said.

The men mumbled something among themselves, then Fred Green—that damned instigator, Fred Green!—spoke: "It's a free country."

Lucille clucked her tongue. "And what's that got to do with anything?"

"We're just sitting here minding our own business."

"Shouldn't you be out there on the lawn, shouting that fool slogan of yours?"

"We're on break," Fred said.

Lucille had trouble pinning down Fred's tone. She couldn't quite tell if he was being sarcastic or if they really were all on break. They looked the part—half-sunburned, haggard and exhausted. "I suppose you're doing a sit-in then? Like people used to do back when the Colored wanted equal rights?"

The men looked at one another, feeling the trap but not quite able to catch sight of it. "What do you mean?" Fred asked, erring on the side of caution.

"I just want to know what your demands are, is all. All sit-ins have demands! You have to ask for something when you organize like this." A soldier bumped into her by accident. He paused to apologize, then she continued on. "You've succeeded in disrupting things," Lucille said to Fred. "That's plain. But what's next? What's your platform? What're you standing for?"

Fred's eyes went full of light. He sat erect in his chair and inhaled a deep, dramatic breath. The other men followed his lead and sat straight as tombstones. "We stand for the living," Fred said in a flat, even voice.

It was the slogan of the True Living Movement—those fools that Lucille and Harold had watched on television that day so long ago. The ones who'd gone from promises of race wars to full-on racial integration since the Returned. And now here was Fred Green quoting them.

Without a doubt, Lucille thought, nut jobbery was afoot.

The other men sucked in their breath the way Fred Green had done—seeming to get fatter as they did. Then they all said, "We stand for the living."

"I wasn't aware the living needed someone to stand for them," Lucille said. "But, anyhow, you might try chanting that instead of that 'Arcadia for the living, not for the giving' madness. Giving what? Giving to whom?" She waived her hand dismissively.

Fred looked her over, the wheels in his head turning. "How's your son doing?" he asked.

"Just fine."

"Still over at the school, then?"

"The prison, you mean? Yes," Lucille answered.

"And Harold? I hear he's still at the school, too."

"The prison?" she repeated. "Yep. He's over there."

Lucille adjusted her purse on her shoulder, somehow adjusting her thoughts, as well.

"What are you shopping for today?" Fred asked. The men around him nodded, vouchsafing the question. They all sat inside the doorway in the small area before a person entered into the store proper. The store's owner had tried using it as a place to greet customers—like they did at Wal-Mart—but it wasn't long before the old men took to standing here and watching people enter and exit. Then the standing evolved into sitting when someone made the mistake of leaving a rocking chair near the door one day.

Now there was nothing to do about it. The front of the store—what little store there was—belonged to the gossiping men.

If a person could get past them cleanly, the building was charming only to someone who didn't want much. Along what few aisles the store contained were canned foods and paper towels and toilet tissue and a handful of cleaning supplies. Along the walls of the store near the windows were hardware supplies hung from hooks and dangling from the rafters like a toolshed had exploded somewhere and cast them all asunder. The store owner—an overweight man called "Potato" for some reason Lucille never quite understood—tried to cover all of his bases in a very limited space.

He failed most of the time, but it was good that he tried, Lucille believed. The store wasn't a good place to find what a person wanted, but you could usually find what you really needed.

"I'm shopping for what I need," Lucille said. "How does that grab you?"

Fred grinned. "C'mon now, Lucille." He leaned back in his chair. "I was just asking a friendly question, is all. Didn't mean no harm by it."

"Is that a fact?"

"That's a fact." He put his elbow on the arm of his chair and rested his chin on his fist. "Why would such a simple question make a woman like you so nervous?" Fred laughed. "It's not like you're hiding anybody up there at your place or anything, right, Lucille? I mean, the Wilsons have been missing from the church for a while now. From what I hear, the soldiers came to take them away and the pastor had done set them loose."

"Set them loose?" Lucille huffed. "They're people, not some kind of animals!"

"People?" Fred squinted as if Lucille had suddenly gone out of focus. "No," he said finally. "And I'm sorry you believe that. They *was* people. Once. But that was a long time ago." He shook his head. "No, they ain't people."

"You mean since they were killed?"

"I suppose soldiers would be glad to get a lead on where the Wilsons were hiding."

"I suppose they would," Lucille said, aiming her body toward the interior of the grocery store. "But I wouldn't know anything about it." She was about to walk off, about to quit Fred Green and his contemptible ways, but she paused. "What happened?" she asked.

Fred looked at the other men. "What do you mean?" he replied. "What happened to who?"

"To you, Fred. What happened to you after Mary died? How'd you turn into this? You and she used to come over every Sunday. You helped Harold find Jacob that day, for goodness' sake. When the Wilsons died, you and Mary were at their funeral just like everybody else. Then, when she was gone, so were you. What happened to you? Why do you got so much against them? Against all of them? Who do you blame? God? Yourself?"

When Fred refused to answer her, she walked past him and entered the grocery store proper—quickly to be lost among the tightly spaced aisles—and left the men to gossip or plan or suppose among themselves. Fred Green watched her as she left. Then he stood, slowly, and made his way out of the store. He had something very important to do.

On the way home Lucille's mind was flooded with all the ways in which people weren't dealing with the Returned. She thanked God for granting her the grace and patience she needed to make it through all of this. She thanked Him for directing the small, Returned family to her doorstep in their hour of need—which was also her hour of need—because now the house was not quite so empty and now her heart did not hurt quite so much when she came home in Harold's old truck with the passenger seat full of groceries and a warm house full of living bodies waiting for her at home…the way it was always supposed to be.

The truck loped out of town and onto the two-lane road and out past the fields and trees. Once, she and Harold had talked about living inside the town proper, but decided against it just before Jacob was born. There was something in the idea of the three of them separated from the world—to a small degree, at least—hidden by forest and field, that she fell in love with.

When she reached home she could clearly see the truck treads dug deep in the lawn. The soldiers' boot prints were still clear as day. The front door hung off its hinges and there was mud tracked over the front porch and into the house.

Lucille pulled the old truck to a stop beneath the oak tree and sat behind the wheel with the engine running and the cab full of food and the tears coming to her eyes.

"Where were You?" she asked in a broken voice, knowing full well that, just then, only God could hear her.

Samuel Daniels

Samuel Daniels had been born and raised and taught to pray here, in Arcadia. Then he died. And now he was in Arcadia again. But Arcadia had changed. No longer was it the small, escapable town it had been. The town through which travelers came and went without pause or hesitation, having only a few moments' thought devoted to pondering what it was people did with their lives in such a place. A place of flat, tired-looking houses. A place with two gas stations and only two stoplights. A place of wood and earth and tin. A place where people seemed to be born from the forests that butted up against the fields.

Now Arcadia was no longer the detour, but the destination, Samuel thought, looking out through the fencing, seeing the slow unfurling of the town toward the east. Far off, the church sat, silent and still below the firmament. The two-lane blacktop that led into town was gnarled and chipped where it had, not so long ago, been smooth and even. Each day there was more traffic coming in. Less traffic going out.

The people of Arcadia were not locals anymore, he mused. This was not their town. They were visitors, tourists in their own land. They went about their daily lives uncertain of where they were. When they could, they clustered together—not unlike the way the Returned were rumored to do at times—and they stood, looking out at the world around them with a look of somber confusion on their faces.

Not even their pastor, with all of his faith and understanding in God, was immune. Samuel had gone to him, seeking the Word, seeking comfort and explanation for what was happening in this world, in this town. But the pastor was different than Samuel remembered him. Yes, he was still large and square— a mountain of a man—but he was far away, as well. He and Samuel had stood in the church doorway, talking of how the Returned were brought into Arcadia and transported to the school, which was already becoming too small of a place to hold them. And as the trucks passed and the Returned could be seen, now and then, peeking out—taking stock of this new place in which they found themselves—Pastor Peters would scrutinize them, as if searching for someone.

"Do you think she's alive?" the pastor said after a while, completely ignoring the conversation he and Samuel had been engaged in.

"Who?" Samuel asked.

But Pastor Peters said nothing, as if Samuel were not the one to whom he was speaking.

Arcadia had changed, Samuel thought. The town was surrounded by fencing and walls, caged in and cut off from the world like a castle. Soldiers everywhere. This was not the town he had grown up in, not the small city that squatted on the countryside, open in all directions. This was something else.

Walking away from the fencing, he gripped his Bible. Arcadia, and all within its walls, had been changed, never to go back to the way it was.

THIRTEEN

It was reported that a certain previously dead French artist was found there after weeks of the world community searching for him. He'd married the fiftysomething woman who'd given him a hostel to live in and who'd seen to it that the world knew his name.

When he was discovered, Jean Rideau gave no statements to the press as to the reasons for his disappearance, but that didn't stop the media from trying. The small almost-hut on the outskirts of Rio in which he'd managed to escape the world was overrun by reporters and investigators and, not long after, the soldiers sent to keep the peace. Jean and his wife managed to stay there for almost a week, cordoned off by policemen from the crowds—which were gathering each and every day.

But it wasn't long before the crowd was too large and the policemen too few and the famous French artist and his wife had to be taken out of the city. That was when the riot started. There were almost as many Returned as there were True Living that died that day. The allure of Jean Rideau and the potential of his postdeath art drew all.

If the news reports were to be believed, the death toll for the riot outside Rio numbered in the hundreds. Most of them died as the great, teeming stampede of bodies ran from the gunfire of the policemen. The others were simply killed by the policemen's bullets.

And after everything was settled, after Jean Rideau and his wife were taken from Rio—with the French government screaming for their return—nothing was fixed for them on account of how, at some point in all the madness, Jean's wife had taken a blow to the head and now lay in a coma, with the world still screaming for her and her husband to do some unknown thing, to fill some undisclosed role, to say something secret about life after death via his art.

But all Jean wanted to do was be with the woman he loved.

The pastor and his diminutive wife sat on the couch watching the television with space enough for another adult body between them. He sipped his coffee and stirred it now and again just to hear the sound of the spoon clink against the ceramic.

His wife sat with her small feet tucked beneath her and her hands in her lap and her back erect. She looked very proper and catlike. Now and again she reached up and stroked her hair without really knowing why.

On the television a very famous talk-show host was asking questions to both a minister and a scientist. The scientist's specific discipline was never made quite clear, but he was very famous for a book he had written about the Returned in the early days of their appearance.

"When will this end?" the talk-show host asked, though it was unclear exactly to whom her question was aimed. Perhaps out of modesty, or perhaps because he simply was willing to concede he did not know the answer—at least, this is what the pastor thought—the minister kept quiet.

"Soon," the scientist replied—his name appeared on the bottom of the screen, but Pastor Peters didn't bother remembering it. Then the man said nothing, as if one word would suffice.

"And what do you say to people who claim they need a more specific answer than that?" the talk-show host asked. She looked out at the studio audience and then toward the cameras to convey that she was the everyman.

"This state cannot go on forever," the scientist said. "Simply put, there's a limit to how many people can return."

"What a silly thing for a person to say," the pastor's wife said, pointing to the television. "How can he know how many people can come back?" she said. Then her hands moved nervously in her lap. "How can he pretend to know anything about any of this? This is God's work. And God doesn't need to tell us why He does anything!"

The pastor only sat and watched the television. His wife looked over at him, but he offered nothing. "It's just ridiculous," she finally said.

On the television, the minister finally entered the conversation, but he did so warily. "I believe it would be best if all of us remained patient at this time. None of us should pretend anything. There is a great danger in that."

"Amen," the pastor's wife said.

"What the reverend means to say," the scientist began, adjusting his tie as he spoke, "is that these events are beyond the realm of religion. Perhaps once, when we still dreamed of ghosts and phantasms, this would have been a matter for the church to have dominion over. But that is not the case now. That is not the case with the Returned. These are people. Real and true. They are physical beings. Not ghosts. We can reach out to them. We can speak to them. And they, in turn, can reach back to us, can speak back to us." He shook his head and sat back confidently in his chair, as if all of this were a part of some great design. "This is a scientific matter now."

The pastor's wife sat up straighter on her end of the couch.

"He's just trying to get folks stirred up," her husband said.

"Well, he's doing just that," she replied. "I don't understand why they let people like him on television."

"And what do you have to say to that, Reverend?" the talk-show host asked. She was out in the audience now, with a microphone in one hand and a small stack of powder-blue index cards in the other. She stood next to a tall, burly man dressed as if he'd just come from a very long journey through very cold and hard country.

"To that," the reverend said calmly, "I would argue that, ultimately, everything of the physical world is rooted in the spiritual. God and the supernatural are the roots from which the physical world grows. In spite of all of science's advances, in spite of its many disciplines and theories, the flashing lights and buzzers of its modern phalanx of technology, the biggest questions—how the universe began, what is the ultimate fate and goal of humanity—remain as unanswered now by science as they always have been."

"Well, what's God got to say about all of this?" the burly man shouted, before any applause for the reverend's words could begin within the crowd. He wrapped a large, meaty hand around both the talk-show host's hand and the microphone and barked his question. "If you say the damned scientists don't know anything, then what do you know, Reverend?"

Pastor Peters sighed. He raised a hand to this temple and began rubbing his head. "He's hung himself out to dry now," he said. "They both have."

"What do you mean?" his wife asked.

She did not have to wait long for her answer.

On the television, things were suddenly very loud and very dynamic. The burly man had pried the microphone away from the talk-show host and was yelling about how both the reverend and the famous scientist weren't worth a damn because all they ever did was promise answers while delivering nothing. "When it really comes down to it," the man growled, "both of you are useless."

The audience went into an uproar of applauding and cheering, to which the burly man responded by lunging into a tirade about how no one—not the scientific minds, not the churches, not the government—had an answer for the sea of Returned in which all of the True Living would soon drown. "They're all perfectly content to sit around and keep telling us to wait patiently like children while the undead drag us off to the grave one by one!"

"Turn it off," Pastor Peters said.

"Why?" his wife asked.

"Then leave it on." He stood. "I'm going to my study. I've got a sermon to write."

"I thought you were done with that."

"There's always another one to write."

"Maybe I could help," his wife said, turning off the television. "I don't have to watch this. I'd rather help you." The pastor gathered up his coffee and wiped the table where it had been sitting. He moved his large bulk slowly and with great precision, as he always did. His wife stood and downed the last of her own cup of coffee. "This show gave me an idea about a sermon you could give talking about how people shouldn't be led astray by false prophets."

The pastor grunted a noncommittal response.

"I think that everyone needs to understand that this isn't something happening by accident. They need to know that this is all part of a plan. People need to feel that there's a design on their lives."

"And when they ask me what that design is?" the pastor responded without looking at his wife. He walked quietly into the kitchen. She trailed behind him.

"You tell them the truth—that you don't know, but that you're certain that a plan exists. That's the important part. That's what people need."

"People are tired of waiting. That's the problem every pastor, minister, preacher, shaman, voodoo man and whatever else you want to call them is having. People are tired of being told that there's a plan, but nobody actually telling them what the plan is." He turned and looked at her. She seemed smaller than usual all of a sudden, small and full of failings. *She will always be a picture of failure,* his mind said suddenly. The thought froze him, clipped his train of thought in two and left him standing in silence.

She stood just as silently. Since this all began, her husband had been changing. Something was standing between them these days. Something that he would not tell her about. Something that he didn't dare place into his sermons.

"I need to get started," he said, and made a move to leave the kitchen. She stepped in front of him—a flower standing before a mountain. The mountain stopped at her feet, as it always had.

"Do you still love me?" she asked.

He took her hand in his. Then he leaned down and kissed her gently. He held her face in his hands then and traced his thumb over her lips and kissed her again, long and deep.

"Of course I do," he said softly. And it was the truth he spoke.

Then he lifted her with great gentleness and affection, and moved her aside.

Harold was particularly surly today. It was too hot to do anything but die, he thought, whatever a death was worth these days.

He sat on his cot with his feet drawn up to his body, an unlit cigarette hanging from his lips and a perfectly even layer of sweat glistening on his brow. Out in the hallway the fans droned, moving only enough air through the building to rustle a stray sheet of paper now and again.

Jacob would be back from the bathroom soon and then Harold would be able to leave to go to the bathroom. It wasn't safe to leave the cots unguarded anymore. There were simply too many people about with nowhere to sleep and when a body left a cot unwatched, even for a moment, they invariably returned to discover that, tonight, they would be sleeping on the hard pavement beneath the stars.

The only belongings a person had now were those they could hold on to. Harold had gotten lucky because he'd married a wife that came to visit him and who brought him a change of clothes when he needed it and who brought him food when he was hungry, but even that was beginning to wane. The military simply wasn't allowing visitors the way they had been. "Too many people," they claimed.

They couldn't keep up with the numbers—Returned or True Living—and, more than that, they were afraid that the wrong kind of people might slip inside the school and start a riot—it had happened already out in Utah. Even now they were holed up out there in the desert, with their guns and their demands to be set free.

But the government was still not sure what they wanted to do with the people, so they held them there, surrounded by more soldiers than the small rebels could ever hope to overpower. The standoff was at a week now, and it was only the press coverage and the memories of the Rochester Incident that kept the soldiers at bay.

So the men with guns delivered food and the rebels—led exclusively by True Livings—were in a pattern of shouting demands for freedom and equal rights for the Returned as they came tentatively out from their compound and took the food the soldiers brought them. Then they went back behind their barricades and reentered the life that they and circumstance had manufactured.

But in spite of the fact that, compared to Rochester and the death of the German soldiers and that Jewish family, things were going smooth as butter, the Bureau wasn't about to have things crumble. So, all over the place security levels went up and an iron hand came down and now Lucille could only come to visit her husband and son once a week. Now there were too many people crammed into a space that had never been designed to hold them and word around the camp was that plans were being put into place to give everyone more room, which meant that, somehow, lots of people would be going someplace—and Harold could not ignore how ominous that idea was.

The water was running out in Arcadia, though it hadn't completely gone yet. Everything was on rations. And while having the food on rations was bad enough, having the water on rations seemed to be an unnecessarily draconian fate.

Though no one was dying of thirst, a person was lucky to be able to shower every three or four days. They learned to keep their clothes as clean as they could manage.

In the beginning it had all seemed trivial, maybe even a little fun. Everyone smiled and ate with their pinkies in the air and paper napkins spread out across their laps and tucked into the collars of their shirts and, whenever something did spill, they all took to cleaning it with a flare of drama and importance. In the beginning, everyone was afraid of improperness, afraid of letting the situation make changes to who they were and how they came across.

In the beginning they had dignity. Like this would all end suddenly and they might go home at the end of the day and settle in on the couch and watch whatever reality television show they favored on that particular night.

But then the weeks rolled out into a full month—more than that now—and still no one was at home on the couch watching television. And when the first month passed and the oldest of the prisoners settled into the truth that they were not going home and that things were getting worse by the day, they all started caring less and less about their appearances and how other folks saw them.

The Bureau wasn't any better at cleaning up after so many people than they were at supplying food and water for them. On the west wing of the school the toilets had broken from overuse and that hadn't stopped people from needing to use the bathroom. Some people figured it was better to keep using the out of commission toilets for as long as they could stand them.

Other people just stopped caring. They would piss or shit wherever they could get a moment's privacy. Some didn't even need the privacy.

And somewhere in all this people were getting frustrated. The Returned, just like anyone else, didn't care much for being held against their will. Their lives were spent in longing, wanting to return to those they had loved or, at the very least, wanting to return to the world of life. And while some of them had no idea exactly what they wanted or where they wanted to be, they knew that being held prisoner in Arcadia wasn't it.

All over the camp the Returned were beginning to grumble. Beginning to lose patience.

If someone looked closely, they could foresee what would eventually happen.

★ ★ ★

A little after 5:00 a.m. every morning for the past few weeks, half a dozen or so men in the town of Arcadia received a phone call from Fred Green. There was no small talk, no introduction or apology for the early-morning wake up, just Fred's gruff and abrasive voice shouting, "Be there in an hour! Bring enough food to get you through the day. Arcadia needs us!"

In the first days of their protesting, Fred and his team had kept their distance from the soldiers and the gate where the busloads of Returned were being brought in. Initially, they weren't sure exactly who they were supposed to be mad at: the government or the Returned.

Yes, the Returned were horrible, unnatural things, but wasn't the government, too? After all, it was the government that was taking over Arcadia. It was the government that brought the soldiers and the men in suits and the builders and everyone else.

Protesting was hard work. Harder than they had expected. They went through lulls of energy and their throats were almost constantly sore. But whenever a bus of Returned came chugging down the street, bound for the school, Fred and the others would find their waning spirits renewed. They raised their signs and turned up the volume on their tired voices and they shook their signs and made their hands into fists and waved them.

When the buses came, the slogans went out the window. It was every rebellious man for himself. "Go home!" they shouted. And "You're not wanted here! Leave Arcadia!"

As the days passed, Fred and his crew grew tired of yelling from a distance. So they took to walking out into the path of the buses. They were careful, though. This was about expressing their right to free speech, about letting the world know that there were still decent, good people who wouldn't sit idly by while everything went to pieces. It wasn't about getting run over and becoming martyrs.

So they stayed in control of themselves right up until the moment when the buses stopped at the gate to get clearance before heading into the holding center. Then they speed walked across the street with their signs held up, each of them shouting angrily and waving their fists. Someone even went so far as to grab a rock and throw it once—though, admittedly, they took care not to throw it where it might actually hurt anyone.

But with each day they grew a little bolder.

By the second week there were four soldiers instead of just one at the guard post near Fred and his followers. They stood with their arms behind their backs and their faces stern and expressionless, always watching the protestors but never doing anything to provoke them.

When the buses with the Returned came, the soldiers would walk out from the guardhouse and form a line in front of where the protestors were.

Fred Green and the rest were respectful of this show of authority. So they shouted their slogans and yelled their damnations from behind the soldiers and did not threaten the soldiers in any way. It was a well-behaved civil disobedience.

It was just after six—on the day that would prove to be remarkable—when Fred Green pulled into Marvin's driveway; the sun had barely risen. "Another day at it," John Watkins called. He was sitting in his truck with the door open and one leg dangling out of the cab. The radio was on, its music coming out garbled and tinny from busted speakers. Some song about a no good ex-wife.

"How many did I miss?" Fred asked, his tone hard and sharp. He got out of his truck, clutching his picket sign. He was starting the day in a bad mood. It had been another night of restlessness for him and, as is often the case with certain types of men, he'd decided that being angry in general was the best way to deal with whatever was going on in his heart that he didn't understand.

"What's the matter with you?" John asked. "You feeling okay?"

"I'm fine," Fred said. He tightened his face and wiped his brow—not sure exactly when he had begun sweating. "Many buses this morning?"

"None so far," Marvin Parker said, walking up behind Fred. Fred turned quickly, his face flush. "Fred, you all right?" Marvin asked.

"I'm fine," he spat.

"I asked him the same thing," John said. "He looks off, don't he?"

"Dammit!" Fred shouted. "Let's just get to it."

They made their way out into the street just as they had on all the other mornings. This was all any of them did now, this minor civil disobedience. Fred's fields were getting overgrown, the corn beginning to rot on the stalk. He hadn't made it down to the sawmill in weeks.

None of that seemed to matter anymore. The normality of the way his life had been for years was gone, and he blamed all of it on his restless nights, and those he blamed on the Returned.

The buses eventually came, and each time they passed, Fred screamed, "To hell with you freaks!" Everyone else took their cue from Fred. He was wound a little more tightly than usual today, so they became edgy, as well. They all screamed that much louder and shook their picket signs that much more fervently and many of them went to looking for more than small rocks to throw.

Eventually the soldiers on duty called for backup, beginning to feel that things were taking a southward turn. One of the soldiers warned Fred and the others to settle down.

"To hell with the Returned!" Fred yelled in reply.

The soldier repeated his warning, in a sterner voice.

"To hell with the Bureau!" Fred yelled.

"This is the last time I'm going to tell you," the soldier said, raising a pepper spray canister.

"To hell with you!" Fred shouted. Then he spit in the man's face and diplomacy fell apart.

It started with Marvin Parker running out in front of one of the buses that was coming down the street. It was probably the most damned fool thing he had ever done in his life, but there he was, in the middle of the street, screaming and waving his sign and refusing to move. Two soldiers jumped on Marvin and wrestled him to the ground, but he was surprisingly nimble for a man his age and scuttled to his feet. The busload of Returned squealed to a stop in front of the melee.

Fred and the rest—nearly a dozen of them—charged up to the bus and pounded on it, waving their signs and shouting and cursing. The soldiers were grabbing and pulling at them, but still uneasy about using the pepper spray and throwing a genuine punch at anybody. After all, Fred and his bunch had been harmless for weeks now. The soldiers were still trying to figure out what the hell had changed today.

But then Marvin Parker landed a right hook square across the jaw of one of the soldiers, knocking him unconscious. Marvin was thin and lanky, but he'd done more than his fair share of boxing back when he was young enough for that type of thing.

Everything became a blur of flailing and shouting after that.

A pair of strong arms wrapped around Fred's waist and lifted him off his feet. He tried to pull the person off him but they were too strong. He kicked wildly and connected with the back of someone's head. The grip around his waist was broken and Fred tumbled into the legs of a soldier, who bowled him over.

Somebody was yelling, "Fascists!" over and over, making the whole kerfuffle even more surreal. The busload of Returned watched through their windows, not certain of exactly how frightened they should be by it all. For most of them, it wasn't the first time they'd come across these types of protests, but that did little to make it more bearable.

"Don't worry," the bus driver told them. "I've seen these guys out here for weeks now." He furrowed his brow. "They're mostly harmless," he finished.

Fred was cursing and scuffling with one of the young soldiers he'd tumbled into at some point when another pair of hands began grabbing at him, accompanied by the shouting voice of Marvin Parker. "Come on, Fred! Move your ass!" In spite of their passion, Fred and the rest of his fellows lacked the training—and, more relevantly, the youth—of the soldiers.

Fred stumbled to his feet and started running. Even with all the adrenaline, he was exhausted. He was just too old for this, and it hadn't been the confrontation he'd thought it would be. Nothing was decided. Nothing was settled.

Everything had happened so quickly, and with nothing to actually show for it, it all felt anticlimactic.

Marvin was laughing as they ran. He obviously didn't share Fred's exhaustion and frustration. There was a line of sweat running down his temple, but his long, thin face was bright with excitement. "Woo!" he hollered. "Goddamn, that felt good."

Fred looked back over his shoulder to see if the soldiers were giving chase. They weren't. They had wrestled a couple of his cohorts to the ground and were holding them down on the asphalt. Everyone else in Fred's gang was running behind him—some of them with small bruises already appearing on their faces but, all in all, none the worse for wear.

They made it back to their trucks, everyone scrambling to get into their vehicles and get the engines started. Marvin jumped in with Fred and the two of them lit out from Marvin's driveway with the tires squealing.

"They probably figure we've learned our lesson," Fred said, looking in the rearview mirror. No one was coming after them.

Marvin laughed. "Well, they don't know us then, do they? We'll be back at it tomorrow!"

"We'll see" was all that Fred would say. His mind was working. "I think I might have something better," he said. "Something you might like even better, seeing as you seem to be in the best shape out of all of us."

"Woo!" Marvin shouted.

"How are you at cutting through fencing?" Fred asked.

Harold's feet hurt. Still sitting on his cot, he removed his shoes and socks and looked at his toes. Something looked very odd about them. They itched and they smelled, particularly between the toes. Athlete's foot, most likely. He rubbed his toes and dug a finger between them and scratched and scratched and scratched until they began to burn and he could feel that there was a raw spot between them.

Definitely athlete's foot.

"Charles?" Patricia called out from her cot beside him as she awoke from her dream.

"Yes?" Harold answered. He put his socks on again but decided against the shoes.

"Charles, is that you?"

"It's me," Harold said. He moved to the edge of the cot and patted her shoulder to fully wake her. "Get up," he said. "You're dreaming."

"Oh, Charles," she said, a single tear streaking down her

face as she sat up. "It was terrible. Just terrible. Everyone was dead."

"Now, now," Harold said. He got up from his cot and settled beside her. A young, scruffy-looking boy that happened to be passing by the doorway peeked in and saw Harold's empty cot and made a move toward it. "It's mine," Harold said. "And the one beside it is mine, too."

"You can't have two cots, mister," the boy said.

"I don't," Harold replied. "But these three cots belong to my family here. That cot's mine and the one beside it is my son's."

The boy eyed Harold and the old black woman suspiciously. "So that's your wife?"

"Yes," Harold said.

The boy stood his ground.

"Charles, Charles, Charles," Patricia said, patting Harold's thigh. "You know how much I love you, don't you? Of course you do. How's Martin?" She looked over at the boy in the doorway. "Martin, honey, where have you been? Come here, baby, and let me give you a hug. You've been gone for so long. Come give your mother a kiss." She spoke in a slow, even manner, with no accent to speak of, which made her words sound all the more unsettling.

Harold smiled and held Patricia's hand. He wasn't sure exactly how lucid she was just then, but it didn't matter.

"I'm here, honey," Harold said. He kissed her hand gently. Then he looked at the boy. "Now get out of here," he said. "Just because they've got us locked up here like animals doesn't mean we have to behave that way!"

The boy turned on his heel and darted from the door, his head turning left and right as he walked, already searching for another empty cot to misappropriate.

Harold huffed.

"How did I do?" Patricia asked with a soft chuckle.

He squeezed her hand. "Wonderful."

He moved back to his cot—still looking over his shoulder now and again to be sure no one would creep in and take Jacob's cot.

"You don't ever have to thank me, Charles."

Harold tried to smile.

"Do you want some candy?" she asked, suddenly patting the pockets of her dress. "I'll see what I can find here for you," she said.

"Don't worry about it," Harold said. "You don't have any."

"I might," she said, looking disappointed as she was proven wrong. Nothing but empty pockets surrounded her.

Harold stretched out on his cot and wiped sweat from his face. This was the most miserable August in recent memory. "You never do," he said.

The woman moved over and sat on the cot beside him with a groan.

"I'm Marty again now," Harold said.

"Don't you start pouting. I'll pick up some candy for you when I go back into town. But you can't be misbehaving like this. Your father and I taught you better than this. You're behaving like a spoiled child, and I won't stand for it."

Harold had gotten used to this newest senility of hers. Most times Jacob played the role of her Marty. But, now and again, the wiring in her head went more akimbo than usual and, without warning, Harold found himself cast into the stage play of her mind as her child—who, by his estimate, was somewhere around the age of seven or so.

But there was no harm—or alternative. So Harold only closed his eyes—even with his disagreeable temperament— and let the woman coo gently to him about how he should learn to be better behaved.

Harold tried for a while to become comfortable but had

trouble on account of the fact that he couldn't stop thinking of Jacob. Jacob had left to go to the bathroom quite some time ago and still hadn't come back. He told himself that it was nothing to be worried about. He came up with all the reasons why he shouldn't be upset.

Reasons such as the fact that it probably hadn't been as long as he thought. Time was a hard thing to keep up with these days and since he hadn't worn a watch in years—he rarely had any place he needed to be—he was ill prepared to measure how long his son had been gone, so his mind went about the business of deciding, of its own accord, how long was too long.

It was quickly approaching that point.

He sat up on his cot and looked in the direction of the door, as if by staring at the door intently enough Jacob would come walking through. The staring went on for a few moments and, still, the boy had not appeared.

Even though he was fifty years out of practice, Harold was still a parent. His mind went to all the places a parent's mind goes. His imagination began with Jacob simply using the bathroom—even if most of them were broken, it was still where people went when they had to go—and stopping off along the way to talk to someone. Then the scenario reset in Harold's mind and Jacob left the bathroom and was stopped by one of the soldiers. The soldier asked the boy to come with him. Jacob protested and the soldier grabbed the boy by the waist and lifted him and slung him over his shoulder—all the while with Jacob screaming and calling for his father.

"No," Harold said to himself. He shook his head and reminded himself that this was not the case. It couldn't be, could it?

He stepped into the hallway, looking left and right at the people coming and going. There were more today than yesterday, he thought. He looked back at Mrs. Stone still sleeping on the cot. Then he looked at the two empty cots.

If he left, they might not be here when he came back.

But then there was the image in his mind of Jacob being hauled away by some soldier and Harold decided it was a risk worth taking.

He moved quickly out into the hallway, hoping that no one would see exactly what room he had come out of. He bumped into people here and there along the way and could not help but marvel at the amount of diversity in the camp at this point. While nearly all of them were Americans, they seemed to be from everywhere. Harold couldn't remember the last time he'd traveled such a little distance and come across so many different accents.

When he neared the bathroom Harold saw a soldier walking past. He walked with his back erect and his eyes focused intently ahead, as if something serious were occurring in front of him.

"Hey!" Harold called out. "Hey!"

The soldier—a young, redheaded boy with an unfortunate case of acne—did not hear. Harold managed to reach out and grab the soldier's arm before he passed.

"Can I help you?" the soldier said in a hurried tone. The name on his uniform said "Smith."

"Hey, Smith," Harold said, trying to sound both pleasant and concerned. There was no need in being too disagreeable just now. "I'm sorry about that," Harold said. "I didn't mean to grab on you like that."

"I'm late for a meeting, sir," Smith said. "What can I do for you?"

"I'm looking for my son."

"And you're probably not the only one," Smith said, taking none of the edge out of his voice. "Talk to the MPs. They can help you."

"Goddammit, why can't you help me?" He straightened

his back. Smith was tall and wide and muscular—youth in its most refined and virile state.

Smith squinted at the old man, sizing him up.

"I just need some help finding him," Harold said. "He went to the bathroom a while back and—"

"So he wasn't in the bathroom?"

"Well." Harold paused. It was a long time since he behaved this irrationally, he realized. "I haven't actually made it that far," he said finally.

Smith sighed with irritation.

"Just go about your business," Harold said. "I'll find him."

Smith did not wait around for Harold to change his mind. He turned and darted off down the hallway, making his way swiftly between the crowds of people as if they weren't there.

"Young bastard," Harold said to himself. Even though he knew Smith had done nothing wrong, it felt better to curse him.

When he reached the bathroom Jacob was just coming out. His clothes and hair were a bit out of order and his face was red. "Jacob, what happened?" Harold asked.

Jacob's eyes went wide. He began tucking his shirt into his pants and trying to straighten his hair. "Nothing," he said.

Harold squatted onto his haunches and lifted Jacob's chin, taking a good long look at his face.

"You've been fighting," Harold said.

"They started it."

"Who did?"

Jacob shrugged his shoulders.

"Are they still in there?" Harold asked, looking toward the bathroom.

"No," Jacob said. "They left."

Harold sighed. "What happened?"

"It was because we have a room of our own."

Harold stood and looked around, hoping that whatever boys had been involved were still around. He was angry at himself for missing it, even though a part of him was strangely proud that his son had been fighting. (It had happened this way once before when Jacob had just turned seven and got into a fist-fight with the Adams boy. Harold had been there for that one. He'd even been the one to break it up. And to this day he felt a little twinge of guilt at the fact that Jacob had won the fight.)

"I won," Jacob said, smiling.

Harold turned to keep Jacob from seeing his grin. "C'mon," Harold said. "That's enough adventure for both of us today."

No one had taken their cots when they made it back to the art room, luckily. The old woman was asleep on her cot.

"Is Mama coming today?"

"No," Harold said.

"Tomorrow?"

"Probably not."

"The day after tomorrow?"

"Yes."

"Two days, then?"

"Yes."

"Okay," Jacob said. He stood on his cot and pulled a small nub of a pencil from his pocket and made two scratches on the wall above his cot.

"Is there anything you want her to bring?"

"You mean for food?"

"I mean for anything."

The boy thought for a moment. "Another pencil. And some paper."

"Okay, that sounds reasonable. Looking to draw something, I suppose."

"I want to write some jokes."

"What?"

"Everyone's already heard the ones I know."

"Ah. Well—" Harold sighed gently "—that happens to the best of us."

"Do you have any new ones you can teach me?"

Harold shook his head. This was the eighth time the boy had asked him for this pittance, and it was about the eighth time Harold had refused him.

"Marty?" the old woman said, dreaming again.

"What's wrong with her?" Jacob asked, watching Patricia.

"She's a little confused. That happens sometimes when people get old."

Jacob looked at the woman, then to his father, then back to the woman.

"It won't happen to me," Harold said.

That was what the boy had wanted to hear. He moved down to the end of his cot and sat with his feet hanging from the edge, almost touching the floor. He straightened his back and sat staring out the doorway as the overcrowding of people came and went in a great, disheveled mass.

In recent weeks Agent Bellamy was looking more and more overcome by his situation in life, whatever that situation was exactly. He and Harold had gotten away from doing their interviews in the sweltering heat of the schoolhouse where there was no air-conditioning and no breeze and only the stench of too many people confined to a too-small space.

Now they conducted their interviews outside, playing horseshoes in the sweltering heat of August where there was no air-conditioning and no breeze and only the burden of humidity that was like a fist clenching around the lungs.

Progress.

But Bellamy was changing, Harold had noticed. A patchy beard was trying to find ground on the man's face and his eyes were unusually tired and reddened, like the eyes of someone who has recently been crying or, at the very least, not sleeping for great stretches of time. But Harold wasn't the type of man to ask another man about such things.

"So how's life between you and Jacob these days?" Bellamy asked. The question ended with a small grunt and he swung his arm and let the horseshoe fly. It hung in the air, then hit the ground with a thud, missing the stake and scoring him no points.

It wasn't a bad horseshoe field. Just a stretch of open ground carved out on the back side of the school between the walkways the Bureau had erected to bring in the newest arrivals to the camp.

Things were crowding up again, even with things expanding out from the school to take in the town itself. Just when people got settled into the rhythm of life, just when they carved out a place within the city for themselves—whether it be in a tent planted in one of the lawns or, if they were lucky, bunked in one of the town's houses that the Bureau was using to fill the need—more people came in. Things got tighter. More complicated. Just a week ago one of the soldiers had gotten into a fight with one of the Returned. Nobody was ever able to get a clear answer on what it was over—something trivial was the only thing everyone agreed on—but it had resulted in a bloodied nose for the soldier and a black eye for the Returned.

Some people were sure that this was just the start.

But Harold and Agent Bellamy steered clear of such things. They only watched it happening around them and tried not to get carried away by it. Playing horseshoes helped.

Often, as the two men stood alone playing at their game, they would see Returned and True Living being marched in, one after the other, looking sullen and afraid.

"We're doing okay," Harold replied. He took a pull on his

cigarette, planted his feet and took his turn. The horseshoe clinked against the metal stake.

Up above, the sun was bright, the sky clear and blue. It was beautiful enough, Harold sometimes thought, to let him believe he and the young Bureau man were nothing more than a pair of friends winding away a summer afternoon. Then the wind would shift and the stench of the camp would wash over them and would bring with it thoughts of the sad state of their environment, thoughts of the sad state of the world.

Bellamy took his turn. He missed the stake again, scoring no points. He removed his tie just as a small group of Returned were being led through the walkway from Processing into the main part of the school. "You wouldn't believe some of the stuff that's going on out there," he said after the procession had passed.

"I can hardly believe what's going on in here," Harold said. "As for what's going on out there, I might believe it more if we actually had a television and were allowed to watch it." Harold took a drag on his cigarette. "Spending your life on nothing but gossip and hearsay isn't any way to stay informed." He threw his horseshoe. It landed perfectly.

"That wasn't my decision," Bellamy said in that New Yorker speed of his. The two men began the walk to collect their horseshoes. Harold was ahead by seven points. "The colonel made the call," Bellamy said. "And, quite frankly, I can't even say it was his decision. It was those elected officials in Washington that decided to take the television and newspapers out of the centers. It didn't have anything to do with me. It's all above my pay grade."

"Well, now," Harold replied. He collected his horseshoes, turned on his heel and took his throw. It landed perfectly. "Isn't that convenient?" he said. "And I suppose that next you'll say that it wasn't even the politicians' fault, either. It was the American people. After all, they elected them into office. They're the ones who put them there to make those types of decisions. It doesn't have any bearing on you, right? You're just a part of a much larger machine."

"Yes," Bellamy said with no commitment. "Something like that." He took his turn, finally hooking the stake. He grunted some modest celebration.

Harold shook his head. "This is all heading toward trouble," he said.

Bellamy did not reply.

"And how's that colonel getting along?"

"He's fine. Just fine."

"Terrible shame about what happened to him. What almost happened to him, I mean." Harold took his throw. Another perfect one. More points.

"Yeah," Bellamy said. "Still can't quite figure out how that snake got into his room." He tossed and missed, but partly because he wanted to laugh.

They continued their game in silence for a while, just living below the sun like the rest of the world. Even though there were more people in Arcadia now than there ever should have been, more people than Agent Bellamy could ever hope to interview or counsel—which had become his primary job now that the colonel was in charge of the security and overall running of the camp—he always kept his appointments with Harold. He had given up interviewing Jacob.

"So tell me about the woman," Harold said after a while. He took his throw. Not a bad one, but not perfect, either.

"I'm afraid you'll have to be more specific."

"The old woman."

"I'm still a little unclear." Bellamy tossed and missed the stake by leagues. "Turns out there are a lot of old women in this world. There's a theory floating around that, over a long enough timeline, all women will become old women. It's really a revolutionary thought."

Harold laughed.

Bellamy tossed, hissing when it went even more terribly wide than his previous one. Then he walked down to the other end of the horseshoe pit without waiting for his opponent. He rolled up his sleeves. Still, somehow, in spite of all the heat and humidity, he was not sweating.

After watching him for a moment, Harold finally followed.

"Okay," Bellamy said. "What would you like to know?"

"Well, you told me that you had a mother once. Tell me about her."

"She was a very good woman. I loved her. What else is there to tell?"

"I think you said she hadn't returned."

"That's right. My mother is still dead."

Bellamy looked down at his legs. He brushed a patch of dust from his pants and looked at the heavy horseshoes clutched in his hand. They were filthy. His hands were filthy. Then he saw that it wasn't just that one spot of dirt on his suit pants; they were covered in dust and grime. How had he not noticed that?

"She died slowly," he said after a moment.

Harold puffed quietly on his cigarette. Another group of Returned were led through the corridor near where the men were going about their game. They watched the old man and the agent.

"Any other questions for me?" Bellamy eventually said. He straightened his back—ignoring the grimy state of his suit—and his arm went stiff as he swung and took his toss. It missed the mark completely.

John Hamilton

John sat in handcuffs between a pair of imposing soldiers the entire time the two men in the office argued.

The black man in the well-cut suit—"Bellamy" was his name, John suddenly remembered—had been ending one of their interviews when Colonel Willis entered the room with the two large soldiers who promptly handcuffed John. The entire group marched through the building toward the colonel's office as if someone had just been caught cheating on their math test.

"What's this about?" John asked one of the soldiers. They politely ignored him.

Bellamy came out of the colonel's office, walking fast with his chest pushed out in front of him. "Let him go," he barked to the soldiers. They looked at each other. "Now," he added.

"Do as he says," the colonel said.

When John was uncuffed, Bellamy helped him up and led him away from the colonel's office.

"Be sure we understand each other," the colonel said before they turned the corner.

Bellamy said something under his breath.

"Was it something I did?" John asked.

"No. Just come with me."

They passed out of the building and into the sunlight. People buzzed about like ants below the clouds and wind. "What's this all about? What did I do?" John asked.

Before long they came to a tall, lanky soldier with red hair and freckles. "No!" the man said in a hard, low voice when he saw Bellamy and John approaching.

"Last one," Bellamy said. "You've got my word on it, Harris."

"I don't give a shit about your word," Harris replied. "We can't keep doing this. We're going to get caught."

"We already have."

"What?"

"We've been caught, but nothing can be proven. So this is the last one." He motioned to John.

"Can I ask what we're talking about?" John said.

"Just go with Harris," Bellamy replied. "He'll get you out of here." He reached into his pocket and extracted a large fold of money. "It's all I've got left, anyhow," he said. "This is the last one whether I like it or not."

"Shit," Harris said. He obviously did not want to do it, but he also obviously did not want to turn down the sweaty pile of money, either. He looked at John. "Last one?"

"Last one," Bellamy said, stuffing the money into Harris's hand. Then he patted John on the shoulder. "Just go with him," he said. "I would have done more, if I'd had more time," Bellamy said. "For now, all I can do is get you out of here. Try Kentucky if you can. It's safer than most places." Then he left and the light of the summer sun fell around him.

"What was that all about?" John asked Harris.

"He probably just saved your life," Harris said. "The colonel thinks you were about to be propositioned."

"Propositioned by whom? To do what?"

"At least this way," Harris said, counting the wad of money in his hand, "you're not around, but you'll still be alive."

FOURTEEN

Harold sat on his cot looking down at his feet and generally being grumpy.

Damned August.

Damned cough.

Jacob and Patricia Stone slept on their cots. Jacob's brow was shiny with sweat, the old woman's dry—she was always complaining of being cold, somehow, in spite of the way the humidity smothered everything like a wet towel.

Through the window above his cot, Harold could hear people talking and moving about. Some of them were soldiers, but most of them weren't. The inmates of this particular prison had long ago come to outnumber the keepers. The number of people at the school was probably in the thousands by now, Harold thought. It was hard to keep track.

Outside Harold's window a pair of men talked in hushed tones. Harold held his breath and thought of standing to hear better, but decided against it, not trusting the sturdiness of the cot. So he only listened and caught little other than the sounds of frustration and whispering.

Harold shifted on his cot. He placed his feet on the floor and stretched quietly. Then he stood and stared up at the window, hoping to catch more of the conversation—but those damned fans were still droning like a bushel of giant bees in the hallway.

He slipped his itchy feet into his shoes and started out into the school.

"What's wrong?" a voice asked from the dimness behind him. It was Jacob.

"I'm just going out for a walk," Harold said softly. "Lie down and get some rest."

"Can I come?"

"I'll be right back," Harold said. "Besides, I need you to take care of our friend." He nodded at Patricia. "She can't be left alone. And neither can you."

"She won't know," Jacob said.

"What if she wakes up?"

"Can I go?" the boy repeated.

"No," Harold said. "I need you to stay here."

"But why?"

From outside the school there came the sound of heavy vehicles moving along the road, the sound of soldiers, their guns rattling.

"Marty?" the old woman said, pawing at the air as she woke. "Marty, where are you? Marty!" she called out.

Jacob looked over at her. Then he looked back at his father. Harold wiped his mouth with his hand and licked his lips. He patted his pocket but could find no cigarette. "Okay," he said, coughing a little. "I guess if we're all destined to be up we may as well head out as a team. Take whatever you don't want stolen," Harold said. "More than likely this is the last time we'll be able to sleep in here. By the time we come back, we'll be homeless. Or cotless, I suppose."

"Oh, Charles," the old woman said. She sat up on her cot and slid her arms into a thin jacket.

Before they turned the first corner, a group of people made their way into the now-vacant art room and began settling in.

Being able to live in the art room and not be crowded in quite as badly as everyone else was the best thing Bellamy had been able to do for Harold, Jacob and Mrs. Stone. Bellamy and Harold had never talked about it, but Harold was smart enough that he knew who to thank.

Now that they were walking away from it, into the unknown, Harold couldn't help but wonder if he was committing a betrayal of some sort.

But there was nothing to be done about it now.

The air outside was humid and dense. Off in the east the sky was beginning to break into the dawn. Harold looked down at his watch and realized that it was morning now. He'd stayed awake the entire night.

There were trucks and soldiers shouting instructions. Jacob reached up and took his father's hand. The old woman stepped closer to him, as well. "What's going on, Marty?"

"I don't know, love," Harold said. She put her arm around his and trembled slightly. "Don't worry," Harold said. "I'll take care of you both."

When the soldier came over Harold could make out how young he was, even in the dim glow of the early morning. Barely eighteen. "Come with me," the boy-soldier said.

"Why? What's going on?"

Harold was worried that there might have been a riot breaking out. There was a pressure that had been building in Arcadia in the past few weeks. Too many people held against their will in too tight of a space. Too many of the Returned wanted to get back to their lives. Too many of the True Living sick of seeing the Returned treated like creatures instead of people. Too many soldiers caught up in the middle of something bigger than they were. To Harold, it seemed a foregone conclusion that this might all suddenly end badly.

People can only be expected to endure a thing for so long.

"Please," the soldier said, "just come with me. We're moving everyone."

"Moving us where?"

"Greener pastures," the soldier said.

Just then, from the direction of the gate leading into the school, came the sound of someone yelling. Harold thought he recognized the voice. They all turned and, even though it was some distance away and the light of the morning was still dim, Harold could make out Fred Green standing chest to chest with one of the guards at the front gate. He was shouting and pointing his finger like a madman, getting all the attention he could, it seemed.

"What the hell is that?" the soldier standing with Harold said.

Harold sighed. "Fred Green," he said. "Most likely trouble."

The words had hardly been said when what sounded like a mob came barreling out from the interior of the schoolhouse. There were twenty-five to thirty people, Harold guessed, running and shouting, some of them shoving to get soldiers out of their way. They were coughing and screaming. A thick, white smoke was beginning to billow out of the doorway and out of some of the windows.

At the back of the crowd, in the direction of the smoke and shouting, coming closer to the door through which everyone was scrambling, was a muffled voice shouting, "We stand for the living!"

"Holy hell," Harold said. He looked back in the direction of the front gate. All the soldiers were racing about, everyone trying to understand what was happening.

Fred Green had disappeared.

Likely as not, Harold thought, this was all his doing to begin with.

All of a sudden Marvin Parker emerged from the school, from the cloud of smoke. He wore work boots, a gas mask, and a T-shirt that said LEAVE ARCADIA written in what looked like Magic Marker ink. He tossed a small, green metal canister onto the ground back toward the door of the school. After a second, it made a popping sound and white smoke began shooting out. "We stand for the living!" he shouted again, his voice somewhat garbled by the gas mask.

"What's going on?" Mrs. Stone asked.

"Come on here," Harold replied, pulling her away from the mass of people.

The young soldier he'd just been speaking to had already dashed off toward the crowd—his rifle at the ready—shouting for everyone to get back.

A pair of soldiers tackled Marvin Parker. Whatever gentleness they might have normally shown the old man was gone. He swung at them, even got in a solid punch on one of them, but that was the extent of it. They caught him around the legs and he landed with a gruesome crunch, followed by a muffled bellow of pain.

But it was too late to stop what was happening. Everyone was already riled up. The pressure in the school had built up for too long for the Returned. They were tired of being held here, away from their loved ones. They were tired of being treated like Returned and not like people.

Rocks and what looked like glass bottles began to fly. Harold saw a chair—probably pulled from one of the classrooms—sail through the early-morning sky and land squarely against a soldier's head. He crumbled to the ground, clutching his helmet.

"Dear Lord!" Mrs. Stone exclaimed.

The three of them managed to get behind one of the trucks on the other side of the courtyard. Harold heard only yelling and cursing behind them as they ran. He waited for the sound of gunfire, waited for screams to break out.

Harold lifted Jacob and held him wrapped tightly in one arm. He held Mrs. Stone next to his body with the other. She was weeping gently, saying, "Dear Lord," over and over again.

"What's going on?" Jacob asked, his breath hot on Harold's neck. There was terror in his voice.

"It's okay," Harold said. "It'll be over soon. People are just scared. Scared and frustrated." His eyes began to burn and he felt a tickle in his throat. "Close your eyes and try to hold your breath," Harold said.

"Why?" Jacob asked.

"Just do what I told you to, son," Harold replied, his voice full of anger only to mask the fear. He looked around for somewhere he could take them, somewhere they would be safe, but he feared what might happen if one of the soldiers mistook them for one of the rioters. That's what it was, after all, a riot. Something he never would have believed could happen here, something that only happened on television in crowded cities where too many people had been wronged.

The smell of tear gas grew stronger. It stung bad. His nose was beginning to run and he couldn't help but cough. "Daddy?" Jacob said, frightened.

"It's okay," Harold said. "It's nothing to be afraid of. It'll be okay." He looked around the corner of the truck behind which they were hiding. A wide, fat pillar of marshmallow-white smoke was billowing out of the school and rising into the morning sky. The sound of fighting had begun to quiet, though. Mostly there was only the sound of dozens of people coughing. Now and then, inside the cloud, someone could be heard crying.

People emerged from the smoke, walking blindly, their arms extended in front of them as they coughed. The soldiers stayed just outside the reach of the smoke, seemingly content to let it do the legwork of settling everyone down.

"It's almost over," Harold said. He caught sight of Marvin Parker. He was on his belly on the ground. His gas mask had been removed.

He didn't look at all the way Harold remembered him. Yes, he was still tall and pale and thin, with deep-set wrinkles around his eyes and that fire-red hair of his, but he looked harder, colder. He was even grinning as they cuffed his wrists behind his back. "This isn't over," he shouted, his face tight and cruel, his eyes watering from the tear gas.

"Dear Lord," Mrs. Stone repeated yet again. She clutched at Harold's arm. "What's gotten into people?" she asked.

"It'll be okay," Harold replied. "I'll keep us safe." He searched his memory, reviewed all that he knew—or thought he knew—about Marvin Parker. None of it—apart from the fact that Marvin used to be a bit of a boxer once—made this moment make sense.

"Where did Fred Green get to?" Harold wondered aloud, his eyes searching. But he did not find him.

Pastor Peters's wife rarely interrupted him once he cordoned himself off in his study. Unless he invited her in to help him with a particular point in the writing, she kept her distance and let him do what he needed to create his sermons. But now there was a very upset old woman at the door begging to speak with her pastor.

The pastor's wife led Lucille through the house slowly, holding her by the hand as they went, with Lucille leaning her weight on the small woman. "You're so sweet," Lucille said, moving slower than she wanted to. In her free hand she clutched her worn leather Bible. Its pages were beginning to tear. The spine was broken. The front cover was torn and soiled. It looked exhausted now, much like its owner.

"I need a blessing, Pastor," Lucille said when she was seated in his study and his small, nameless wife had left.

Lucille dabbed her brow with a handkerchief and pawed at the cover of her Bible as if it might give her luck. "I'm lost," she said. "Lost and wandering the wilderness of a questioning soul!"

The pastor smiled. "That's very eloquent," he said, hoping he did not sound as condescending as he thought he did.

"It's just the truth of things," Lucille said. She dabbed the corners of her eyes with the handkerchief and sniffled. The tears would be coming soon.

"What's the matter, Lucille?"

"Everything," she said. Her voice caught in her throat. She grunted to clear it. "The whole world's gone and lost their minds. People can just come and take folks from a home like prisoners. They even knocked the damned door off its hinges, Pastor. Took me an hour to fix it back. Who does a thing like that? It's the End Times, Pastor! God help us all."

"Now, Ms. Lucille. I never thought of you as the end-of-the-world type."

"Neither did I, but look around you. Look at how things have become. It's just horrible. It makes me believe that maybe Satan isn't to blame for our current condition, not the way they say, at least. Maybe he never even came into the garden. Maybe Adam and Eve plucked the fruit all on their own and then chose to throw the blame on Satan. Would have never even thought such a thing was possible before. But now, after seeing the way things are..."

She let her sentence fade.

"Can I get you something to drink, Ms. Lucille?"

"Who can drink at a time like this?" she replied. Then: "Well, I suppose I could use a glass of tea."

The pastor clapped his large hands together. "Now that's what I like to hear."

When he returned with her tea, she was much calmer. She had finally released her Bible and placed it on the table next to her chair. Her hands were in her lap and her eyes less puffy and less red than they had been.

"Here you go," the pastor said.

"Thank you." She sipped. "How's your wife? She seems distracted."

"She's just a little concerned about things, is all."

"Well, there's plenty to be concerned about."

"Like the End Times?" He smiled.

She sighed. "They've been locked up in that place for weeks now."

The pastor nodded. "You've been able to visit them, haven't you?"

"Early on, I could visit them every day. I took them food and washed their clothes and made sure my son knew his mother loved him and hadn't forgotten him. It was bad, but it was at least bearable back then. But now...now things have gotten abhorrent."

"I heard that they weren't allowing visitations anymore," Pastor Peters said.

"They're not. Not since even before they took over the town. I never would have imagined they could cut off a whole town like that. Never would have imagined it in my entire life. But I guess just because I can't imagine something doesn't mean it can't happen—that's the solipsist's flaw! The truth of things is right out there. All you have to do is open the door and there it is, all of it, everything I can't imagine, right there for you to reach out and shake hands with." Her voice broke.

The pastor sat forward in his chair. "You make it sound like it's all your fault, Ms. Lucille."

"How could it be my fault?" she said. "What could I have done to make any of this possible? Did I make the world the way it is? Did I make people small and timid like they are? Did I make people jealous and violent and envious? Did I do any of that?" Her hands were shaking again. "Did I?"

Pastor Peters took her hand and patted it. "Of course you didn't. Now, when's the last time you spoke with Harold and Jacob? How are they?"

"How are they? They're prisoners. How should they be?" She dabbed her eyes and threw her Bible to the floor and stood and began walking back and forth in front of the pastor. "There has to be a pattern to this. There has to be some kind of plan. Doesn't there, Pastor?"

"I hope so," the pastor said gingerly.

She huffed. "You young preachers. Didn't anyone teach you to give your flock the illusion that you had all the answers?"

The pastor laughed. "I've given up on illusions these days," he said.

"I just don't know what to do about anything."

"Things will change," he said. "That's all I'm genuinely sure of. But how that change will come and what that change will be is beyond me."

Lucille picked up her Bible. "Then what do we do?" she asked.

"We do what we can."

For a very long time Lucille sat and said nothing. She only stared down at her Bible and thought to herself about what the pastor had said and what it meant for her to "do what she could." She had always been the type to do as she was told, and the Bible had been the best at telling her what to do in the situations of her life. It told her how to behave as a child. It told her how to behave when she was done with childish things and blossoming into adolescence. Admittedly, she'd had trouble listening to what it had to say and had engaged in certain behaviors that, while not explicitly forbidden by the Bible, were most definitely frowned upon. But they had been good times and, all in all, had caused no lasting harm to anyone, including herself.

After marriage, her Bible had still been there and was full of answers. Answers on how to be a good wife, though some parts of that she'd had to pick and choose from. There were some parts of the rules for a wife that just didn't make sense in this day and age. Frankly, Lucille had thought, they probably didn't make much sense back in biblical times, either. And if she'd acted the way those women in the Bible acted...well, let's just say that the world would be a quite different place, and Harold, most likely, would have drunk and smoked and ate himself into an early grave and not been here to see the miracle of his son returning from the dead.

Jacob. That was the focus of it. That was what all of her tears were about. They were killing the Returned now. Killing them just to be rid of them.

It wasn't happening everywhere, but it was happening.

There had been reports of it coming in on the television for over a week now. Some countries—countries notorious for their brutality—had begun killing them on sight. Killing them and burning the bodies as if they were diseased, somehow contagious. Every evening now, more and more reports were coming, more pictures and videos and web broadcasts.

Just this morning Lucille had come downstairs—her lonely footfalls drifting through the dark, empty house—to find the television in the living room switched on and whispering to the empty room. She wasn't sure how it had been left on.

She was certain she'd turned it off before bed. But she wasn't above admitting that she might have been mistaken. She was a seventy-three-year-old woman now, and such things as thinking you'd turned something off when you actually had not weren't above possibility.

It was early still, and a bald-headed black man with a thin, perfectly manicured mustache mumbled something in a low voice. Over the man's shoulder, in the studio behind him, Lucille could see people buzzing about. They were all young-looking, all dressed in white shirts and conservatively colored ties. They were probably the up-and-comers, Lucille thought. All of them hoping to one day come out of the background and take the bald-headed man's seat.

She turned up the volume and sat on the couch and listened to what the man had to say, even though she knew she would not care for it.

"Good morning," the man on the television said, apparently returning to the beginning of whatever cycle he was trapped in. "Our top story today coming out of Romania, where the government has ruled that the Returned are not inherently afforded civil rights, declaring that they are simply 'unique' and therefore not subject to the same protections as others."

Lucille sighed. She could not think of what else she could do.

The television cut away from the bald-headed black newscaster and turned to what Lucille assumed was Romania. A pale, gaunt-looking Returned man was being led from his home by a pair of soldiers. The soldiers were clean-shaven and thin, with small features and a certain gait of awkwardness, as if they were still too young to fully understand how the mechanics of their bodies worked.

"The fate of the children..." Lucille said to the empty house. Her chest tightened as the thought of the Wilsons and of Jacob and Harold came rushing in to fill the emptiness of the house. Her hands trembled and the television became a blurry haze. This confused her for a moment, and then she felt the tears trailing down her cheeks and pooling at the corners of her mouth.

Somewhere along the line—though she was not quite sure when exactly—she had promised herself that she wouldn't let herself be brought to tears by any of this. She was too old for tears, she felt. There reached a point in a lifetime when everything that could be done to make a person cry should have come and gone. And while she still felt things, she didn't care for crying—maybe she had just spent too many years with Harold, whom she had never seen cry. Not once.

But now it was too late. She was crying and there was nothing to be done about it and, for the first time in a great many years, she felt alive.

The newscaster carried on over the images of the man being handcuffed and placed in the back of a large military truck alongside other Returned. "No word yet from NATO, the UN or the Bureau of the Returned on Romania's initiative yet, but while the official comments from other governments have been slim, those comments have been split equally between those who favor the Romanian initiative and others who believe the government's actions violate basic human rights."

Lucille shook her head, her face still wet with tears. "The fate of the children..." she repeated.

It wasn't just confined to "those other countries." Not at all. Right here in America it was happening. Those damned fools, the True Living Movement, had spread, cropped up in all manner of offshoot from one side of the country to the other. For the most part, they did nothing but mouth off about things. But, now and again, someone turned up dead and some group that claimed to be "standing up for the living" claimed responsibility.

It had happened in Arcadia, though no one talked about it. Some Returned foreigner found dead in a ditch along the highway. Killed by a 30-06 rifle shot.

Everything seemed to be falling apart with each passing day. And all Lucille could think of was Jacob.

Poor, poor Jacob.

After Lucille was gone and his wife had finally drifted off to sleep, Pastor Peters sat alone in his study rereading the letter he'd received from the Bureau of the Returned.

In the interest of public safety, Elizabeth Pinch, and all other Returned in that particular part of Mississippi, was being held at the facility in Meridian. The letter gave very few details apart from that. It only went on to reassure the pastor that the Returned were all being treated in a manner befitting the situation and that all human rights were being expressly upheld. It all sounded very formal and proper, in a bureaucratic type of way.

Outside his study the house was quiet. Only the rhythmic, heavy clicking of his wife's old grandfather clock at the end of the hallway. It had been a gift from her father—a gift given only a few short months before his cancer would take him. She had grown up with the sound of that great, old clock thumping rhythmically through the nights of her childhood. When she and her husband first got married, she was so unsettled by the missing drumming of the clock that they'd been forced to purchase a metronome to count the time away or else she couldn't sleep.

The pastor walked out into the hallway and stood in front of the clock. It was just over six feet tall and ornately carved. The pendulum was as large as a fist. It clucked back and forth as smoothly as if the clock had only just been crafted and was not, in actuality, over a hundred years old.

It was the closest thing her family had to an heirloom. When her father died she'd fought viciously with her sisters and brother—not about the cost of the funeral or what to do with their father's home, land or meager savings, but rather about the grandfather clock. To this day the relationship between the siblings was strained on account of that clock.

But where was their father now? Pastor Peters wondered.

He had noticed how much more care his wife had given the grandfather clock since the Returned started showing up. It smelled of cleaning oil and polish.

The pastor left the old clock and continued on through the house. He went into the living room and stood for a while looking at things, cataloging them to his memory.

The table in the center of the room they had found during their long move from Mississippi. The couch they'd picked out while on a church visit to Wilmington. Not nearly as far away as Tennessee, but it was one of the few purchases they had both agreed on. It was patterned in blue and white—"Carolina Blue!" the salesman had declared with pride—with alternating blue and white piping along the cushions. The arms curled outward and the pillows were large and soft and plentiful.

It was the complete opposite of the table she'd picked up in Tennessee. He'd hated that table when they first came across it. It was too skinny and the wood was too dark and the trim was flat. It just wasn't worthwhile, he felt.

Pastor Peters walked the living room, picking up any of his books that were piled together in places they did not belong. He did this slowly and carefully, wiping off each book as he handled it. Then he slid it into its place on the bookshelf. Now and then he cracked the cover of one and slipped a finger between its pages and rubbed back and forth, taking in the scent and the texture for himself, as if he might never see another book again, as if the inevitable march of time had finally won.

This cleaning went on for a very long time, though the pastor did not realize it just then. It was only when the crickets were beginning to quiet outside and, far out somewhere in the world, there came the sound of a dog barking at the coming sun.

He had waited too long.

But in spite of his mistake—in spite of his fear—he moved quietly and slowly through the house.

First he went to his study and retrieved the letter from the Bureau of the Returned. Then he took his notebook and, yes, his Bible. He loaded them all into the messenger bag his wife bought for him last Christmas.

Then he went and retrieved his bag of clothes from behind the computer desk. He'd packed the bag only the day before— his wife did the laundry all the time. She would have noticed the clothes missing from his closet if he'd packed too soon. And he wanted to leave with as little trouble as possible, as cowardly as that was.

The pastor crept through the house and out the front door and placed the clothes and the messenger bag in the backseat of his car. The sun was finding its home in the sky now. It sat just beyond the trees, but definitely up, and rising higher by the second.

He entered the house and walked slowly to his bedroom. His wife lay sleeping in a small ball in the center of the bed.

This will hurt her terribly, he thought.

She would be awake soon. She always awoke early. He placed a small note on the bedside stand and thought briefly of kissing her.

He decided against it and left.

★ ★ ★

She awoke to an empty house. Out in the hallway the grandfather clock was keeping time. The sun pushed in through the blinds. It was already a warm morning. It would be a hot day, she thought.

She called out to her husband and he did not answer her back.

He must have fallen asleep in the study again, she thought. He was falling asleep in his study a lot lately and that worried her. She was about to call out to him again when she saw the note on the bedside stand. Very simply written in his rough handwriting was her name.

He wasn't the type to leave notes.

She did not cry when she read it. She only cleared her throat, as if she could say something back to the words. Then she sat there listening only to the sound of her own breathing and the mechanical heartbeat of the grandfather clock in the hallway. She thought of her father. Her eyes were wrapped with tears, but still she would not cry.

The words looked blurry and far away, seeming to rise up through a heavy mist. But still, she read them again:

"I love you," the letter said. And then, below that, he had written, "But I have to know."

Jim Wilson

Jim didn't understand any of it. Not the soldiers, not the role Fred Green had played in everything. In Jim's memory, Fred Green had always been likable enough. The two of them hadn't been friends per se, but only because they'd never worked together and they spent their time in different circles. They'd just never had time to become friends, Jim thought. But how could that cause this current state of things? Jim wondered.

He was a prisoner now. Soldiers had come for him and taken him and his family away at gunpoint and, somehow, Fred Green had been there, watching. He pulled up behind the soldiers in his old pickup truck and just sat there in the cab while Jim and Connie and the kids were led from the house in handcuffs.

What had changed in Fred? The question kept Jim up at night. If he'd thought far enough ahead to answer that question sooner, maybe they wouldn't all be imprisoned now.

Jim stood in the crowded school with his family huddled around him, all of them waiting in line for the lunch that would fail to satiate, as it always did. "What happened to him?" Jim asked his wife. It was something he'd asked her before, but all the answers she had given him thus far hadn't done much to solve the riddle. And Jim had come to find that a riddle—even a dark one like Fred Green—was a good way to take his mind off what was happening to his family. "He wasn't always this way."

"Who?" Connie replied. She wiped Hannah's mouth, which was perpetually chewing on things since they'd been arrested... detained...whatever the word for it was. Fear manifested itself in strange ways, she knew. "You're too old to be acting like a toddler," she scolded.

Tommy wasn't as much trouble, fortunately. He was still frightened over how they were taken from the Hargraves's house. He didn't have the energy to misbehave. Mostly he just sat quietly, not speaking much and seeming very far away.

"I don't think he used to be this way," Jim said. "What changed? Did he change? Did we? He seems dangerous."

"Who are you talking about?" Connie asked, frustrated.

"Fred. Fred Green."

"I heard his wife died," Connie said flatly. "I hear he wasn't the same after that."

Jim paused. When he thought hard enough, he was able to find a handful of memories of Fred's wife. She was a singer, and a damned good one. He remembered her as tall and slender, like some grand and beautiful bird.

Jim took stock of his family. He looked them over, suddenly aware of all they were, suddenly aware of all they meant, all that anyone could mean to someone else. "I suppose that can happen," he said. Then he leaned over and kissed his wife, holding his breath as if it could hold the moment, as well, as if this single kiss could keep his wife and family and everything he loved from ever coming to harm, from ever leaving him alone.

"What was that for?" Connie asked when their lips finally
separated. *She was flush and felt a little dazed, the way she
had felt when they were younger and kissing each other was still
new to them.*

"For everything I don't know how to say with words."

FIFTEEN

Harold was not so bold to say that he had taken a liking to the young soldier, but he was willing to go so far as to say that he saw something of merit in the boy. Or, if not merit, something familiar. And in a world in which the dead did not stay dead, familiarity in any form was a blessing.

It was the same young man he had met on the morning of the riot—just over a week ago now—and that had bonded them. When the dust settled that day, somehow, no one had been seriously injured. Just a fair amount of scrapes and bruises from where the soldiers went in and wrestled people to the ground. One person, Harold had heard, needed to be taken to the hospital due to an allergic reaction to the tear gas. But even they had been okay.

It all seemed distant now, as if it had happened years ago. But just like many things that happened in the South, Harold knew that the wounds hadn't really healed. They had only been covered up by the heat and perpetual "Sirs" and "Ma'ams" of the locals.

People were still wound too tightly.

* * *

Harold sat on a wooden stool beside the barbed-wire-adorned fencing called "the Barricade."

The Barricade had grown at a hideous and terrifying rate. It snaked out from the south end of town where Long's Gas, Guns and Gear sat, old and decrepit, and it kept going, cutting through yards, butting up against houses now and again that were no longer houses, but outposts for soldiers. It wrapped around the entire town—encompassing the stinking, ruined school, encircling a great many houses and stores, encapsulating the fire department building and the sheriff's office, which were one and the same. The Barricade, propped up by the soldiers and their guns, took in everything.

Only those houses beyond the town proper—those people who were farmers or simply leery of living in cities like Harold and Lucille, the preacher and a few others—lay beyond the reach of the fences. Inside the town, people were living in the houses like dormitories. The school had just been pressed too hard, so the townspeople were moved out of their homes and set up in hotels over in Whiteville. Then the soldiers went into their homes and set up cots and made it generally livable for the Returned that would be sleeping there. There was all manner of uproar put on by the townspeople forced to move, but Arcadia wasn't the only town this was happening in and America wasn't the only country.

There were just too many people in the world all of a sudden. Concessions for life had to be made.

So now the town and houses of Arcadia were completely consumed by the event, by the fencing and the soldiers and the Returned and all the complexity and promise of tension that came with it.

But the town of Arcadia was never meant to hold many. Whatever small relief that came with expanding outward from the school dissipated as quickly as it materialized. Even with the whole town being consumed, there was no peace.

For his part, Harold was just happy he and Lucille had made the decision so long ago to live outside of town. He couldn't imagine having his house taken over and dished out to strangers, even if it was the right thing to do.

Beyond the Barricade surrounding Arcadia proper lay a twenty-foot swath of open space that ended at the exterior fencing. Soldiers were placed at hundred-yard intervals. Sometimes they actually went about the business of patrolling both the Barricade and Arcadia. When they did walk through the town, they clustered together into groups, carrying their guns along the same streets where children once played. They were stopped by people and asked about the general state of things— not only in Arcadia, but in the world—and when they might change.

They did not often answer these questions.

But mostly the soldiers only stood—or sometimes even sat—at the Barricade, looking either very detached or very bored, depending on the lighting at that particular moment.

The young soldier that had caught Harold's interest was called "Junior." The name, expectedly, was a bit of a mystery because the boy, from what he told Harold, had never known his father and they didn't share a name. His real name was Quinton, the boy said, but as far back as he could remember, he had been called "Junior" and that seemed to him just as fair a name as any other.

Junior was clean-cut and eager to please, all that the military could want from a recruit. He had made it to the end of his teenage years and into a soldier's uniform without ever having pierced his ear or gotten a tattoo or done anything else particularly rebellious with his life. His joining the military was done at the behest of his mother. She had told him that the military was the place that all true men eventually went. So when he was seventeen and a half and had skated through high school, his mother drove Junior down to the recruiter's office and signed him up.

His test scores hadn't impressed anyone. But he could stand and he could hold a gun and he could do as he was told, which is what he did most of the day now as he stood guard in a town swollen with Returned. And now, of late, he'd found himself more and more in the company of a bitter old Southerner and his previously deceased son. The Southerner Junior could tolerate; it was the boy, always at his father's heels, that Junior didn't care for.

"How much longer they going to keep you here?" Harold asked from his wooden stool behind the Barricade. He spoke to Junior's back, which was how most of their conversations were conducted. In the distance behind Harold, just beyond earshot, Jacob sat and watched his father speak to the soldier.

"Not sure," Junior said. "I suppose as long as they keep you here."

"Well," Harold said in a tired drawl, "I reckon it won't be as long as it has been. There's only so long these types of conditions can persist. Somebody'll figure out a plan, if only for the grace of the roosters."

Harold had been making up expressions for Junior's sake for days now, the more bizarre the better. It was surprisingly easy, just a matter of tossing some reference to farm animals, weather or landscape into an enigmatic arrangement. And if Junior ever asked what the strange expression meant, Harold would make up the meaning right there on the spot. The game, for Harold, was remembering which expressions he had already made up and what they meant, and then trying not to duplicate them.

"What the hell does that mean, sir?"

"Well, good Lord! Ain't you never heard 'grace of the roosters' before?"

Junior turned to face him. "No, sir, I haven't."

"Well, I can't hardly believe that! If I live to grow potato roots from m' feet I won't hardly ever believe that, son!"

"Yes, sir," Junior said.

Harold killed his cigarette on the heel of his shoe and slapped the half-empty pack for another. Junior watched him. "You smoke, son?"

"Not on duty, sir."

"I'll save one for ya," Harold said in a whisper. He lit his cigarette with flair and pulled in long and slow. In spite of the pain, he made it look easy.

Junior looked up at the sun. It was hotter here than he had expected when his orders came in. He'd heard all the stories about the South and, for certain, it got hot enough in Topeka. But here, in this town, in this place, the heat seemed well-settled. It was hot every day.

"Can I ask you something?" Harold asked.

He hated it here. That much Junior was sure of. But at least the old man was fun.

"Ask away," Junior said.

"What's it like out there?"

"It's hot. Same as it is in there."

Harold smiled. "No," he said. "The TVs and computers are all gone in here. What's it like out there?"

"That's not our fault," Junior said before he could even be accused. "It's just orders," he said.

There was a small patrol coming. Just a pair of soldiers from California who seemed to always wind up on duty at the same time. They came marching up the way they usually did and nodded and passed without taking much notice of Junior and the old man.

"It's strange," Junior said.

"What's strange?"

"Stuff."

Harold smiled. "We gotta work on your words, son."

"It's just...it's just that everyone's confused."

Harold nodded.

"Confused and afraid."

"Imagine how it is in here."

"It's different," Junior said. "In there, things are more controlled. People are getting fed. You've got clean water."

"Finally," Harold said.

"Okay," Junior said. "I'll admit it took us a while, but we got the logistics worked out. But it's still better in there than it is out here. After all, everyone that's inside there chose to be in there."

"I didn't."

"You chose to stay with it," Junior said, nodding at Jacob—the boy was still sitting quietly just beyond earshot as Harold had told him to do. He wore a striped cotton shirt and jeans that Lucille had brought him weeks ago. He only watched his father, now and again stopping to look off at the shimmering steel of the Barricade. His eyes followed it, as if not able to fully understand how it came to be there around the town and exactly what it meant.

Junior looked over Jacob. "They offered to take it away from you," he murmured, "but you chose to stay with it, just like all the rest of the True Living in there. It was a decision you all made, so you don't have any reason to be scared or nervous or confused. You've all got it easy."

"You must not have seen the toilets in here."

"There's a whole town in there." He returned his attention to Harold. "Plenty of food, water—everything you people could need. There's even a baseball field."

"Baseball field's full up with people. Camped out in tents. It's a shantytown."

"And then there's the Renta-Johns." He pointed back behind Harold into the direction of a string of blue-and-white standing rectangles.

Harold sighed.

"You think this is bad," Junior said. "This is nothing compared to what's happening in some other places. A buddy of mine is stationed in Korea. It's the small countries that have it the worst. Big countries have places to put them. But Korea—Korea and Japan—they're having it hard. There's just not enough room to put everyone.

"There are these tankers," Junior said in a low voice. He spread his arms wide, with his pale hands as bookends, indicating something of very great size. "They're almost as big as oil tankers. They're just full of them." He looked away. "There's just so many."

Harold watched his cigarette burn away.

"There's just too many of them and everybody's catching hell for it," Junior said. "Nobody can keep up. Nobody wants them back. A lot of the time nobody even calls to say they've found a new one. People just let them wander the streets." Junior spoke through the fencing. Even with the seriousness of what he was saying, he seemed indifferent to it all. "We call them 'dead barges.' The newspeople call them something else. But they're really just dead barges. Cargo holds full of the dead."

Junior kept talking, but Harold was not listening. He saw in his mind a large, dark ship drifting unguided over a flat, unreflecting ocean. The hull grew up from the water, as much liquid as steel and rivets and welds. It was something out of a horror movie, this doomed ship traversing this doomed sea. Aboard the ship, stacked one atop the other, each one darker and heavier than the one below it, all of them pressing down upon one another like anvils, were cargo containers. Each one cluttered with the Returned. Now and then the ship would move, tilted forward or backward by some unseen swelling of ocean. Still the Returned remained unmoved and unconcerned. Harold could see thousands of them. Tens of thousands. Crowded into these dark, hard shipping containers, being shoved over the earth.

In his mind Harold looked down upon them from a great distance, able to take in the sight of each and every one of them in a wholeness and completeness that only the world of dreams can afford. He saw everyone he had ever known somewhere in this Fleet of the Dead, including his son.

A chill struck him.

"You should see them," Junior said.

Before Harold could reply the coughing began. He was not aware of much after that. He only knew that he was in a great deal of pain and, very suddenly—just like before—the sun was standing above his face and the earth had come and nuzzled up gently against his back.

Harold awoke with that same feeling of distance and unease he had the last time this happened. His chest hurt. There was something wet and heavy inside his lungs. He tried to inhale but his lungs would not work as they should. Jacob was there beside him. Junior, as well.

"Mr. Harold?" Junior said, kneeling.

"I'm fine," Harold said. "I just need a minute, is all." He wondered how long he'd been unconscious. Long enough for Junior to make it to one of the gates and get inside the fencing to try and help. His rifle was still slung over his shoulder.

"Dad?" Jacob asked, his face tight with unease.

"Yes?" Harold said in an exhausted croak.

"Don't die, Dad," Jacob said.

* * *

There were plenty of bad dreams to go around these days. Lucille had all but given up on sleeping. She had gotten so far removed from normal nights that she hardly missed them. She remembered sleep in a vague and distant way, the way one misses the sound of the car they rode in during their child-hood—sometimes hearing its timbre in the murmur of distant highways.

When she did sleep, it was only by accident. She would awaken all of a sudden with her body in uncomfortable positions. Most times there would be a book in her lap, staring up at her, holding its place diligently, waiting for her to return. Sometimes her eyeglasses would be crumpled in the pages of her book, having leaped from her nose as she slept.

Some nights she would go into the kitchen and simply stand, listening to the emptiness around her. In her mind, memories would come smoking up out of the darkness. She remembered Jacob and Harold throughout the house. She remembered, most often, one October night in Jacob's youth, a night that had been nothing special but, by that same token, had become very special to her.

When the world was as full of magic as it was these days, it reminded Lucille that the normal moments were the ones that had mattered all along in life.

She remembered Harold in the living room, plucking clumsily at the strings of his guitar. He was always a terrible musician, but he had a great deal of energy and passion for it—at least, he once did, back when he was a father—and he practiced whenever he wasn't at work or working on something around the house or spending time with Jacob.

Lucille remembered Jacob in his bedroom, thumping about, lifting toys from his toy box and placing them not so gently upon the hardwood floor. She remembered him sliding furniture around in his room, which, in spite of being repeatedly warned not to do it, he still did, anyway. When she and Harold would ask him about it Jacob simply said, "Sometimes the toys demand it."

In this memory, while Harold maimed music with his guitar and Jacob went about the business of playing, Lucille was in the kitchen, in the throes of cooking some holiday dinner. There was a ham in the oven. Mustard greens and chicken cooking on the stove. Gravy, mashed potatoes, white rice flavored with thyme, corn and red pepper, butter beans, green beans, chocolate cake, pound cake, gingersnap cookies, roast turkey.

"Don't make your bedroom into a mess, Jacob!" Lucille called. "It'll be time to eat soon."

"Yes, ma'am," the boy answered back. Then: "I want to build something," Jacob yelled from his room.

"What do you want to build?" Lucille yelled back.

Harold sat in the living room plucking at his guitar, killing the one Hank Williams song he had been trying for weeks to teach himself.

"I don't know," Jacob said.

"Well, that's the first thing you have to figure out."

Lucille looked out through the window and watched the clouds pass before the pale, perfect moon. "Can you build a house?"

"A house?" the boy said contemplatively.

"A great, big house with vaulted ceilings and a dozen bedrooms."

"But there's only three of us. And you and Daddy sleep in the same bed. So we only need two bedrooms."

"But what about when people come to visit?"

"Then they can use my bed." Something in Jacob's bedroom fell and crashed against the floor.

"What was that?"

"Nothing."

There came the broken chords of Harold abusing his guitar.

"It sounded like a lot of something."

"It's okay," Jacob said.

Lucille checked the food. Everything was cooking perfectly. The smell of it wafted over the entire house. It seeped through the gaps in the walls, out into the world.

Satisfied, Lucille left the kitchen and went to check on Jacob.

His room was everything she imagined it would be. The bed was turned on its side and pushed up against the far wall so that the mattress stuck out like a barricade and the headboard and footboards were magnificent buttresses. Trailing out from behind the makeshift barrier was a wasteland of fallen and scattered Lincoln Logs.

Lucille stood in the doorway wiping her hands dry with a dishcloth. Now and again the boy reached out from behind the fort and plucked a particular log to contribute to some unseen construction project.

Lucille sighed, though not in frustration.

"He's going to be an architect," she said, coming into the living room and easing down exhaustedly into the couch. She made a show of wiping her brow with the dishcloth.

Harold banged away at his guitar. "Maybe," he managed, though the break in concentration threw his fingers into even worse disarray. He flexed his digits and began the song again.

Lucille stretched out. She turned onto her side and pulled her legs into her body and tucked her hands beneath her chin and watched, sleepily, as her husband battled on against his musical ineptness.

He was beautiful, Lucille thought, most beautiful when he was failing.

His hands, though they did not enjoy the guitar, were thick

and nimble. His fingers smooth and strangely plump. He wore the flannel shirt Lucille had bought him when the frost first came this year. It was red and blue and he had protested against how tightly the shirt fit, but the very next day he wore it to work and came home to tell her how much he loved it. "It stayed out of my way," he said. It was a small thing, but small things mattered.

Harold wore jeans—faded, but clean—which she liked. She had grown up with a father who'd spent most of his life preaching sermons to people who hardly cared to listen. He wore extravagant suits that he and his family could not afford, but it was desperately important to Lucille's mother that her husband look the part of Salvationist, no matter what the costs.

So when Harold had come along all those years ago dressed in his jeans and stained shirt with that soft, suspicious-looking smile, she fell in love with his wardrobe and, eventually, with the man that wore it. "You're distracting me," Harold said, adjusting the tune of the sixth guitar string.

Lucille yawned, drowsiness falling on her like a hammer. "I didn't mean to," she said.

"I'm getting better," he said.

She laughed a little. "Just keep practicing. You've got thick fingers. That's always a little more challenging."

"Is that what it is? My thick fingers?"

"Yes," she said, looking very, very sleepy. "But I like thick fingers."

Harold raised an eyebrow.

"Dad?" Jacob yelled from the bedroom. "What are bridges made of?"

"He's going to be an architect," Lucille whispered.

"They're made of stuff," Harold yelled.

"What kind of stuff?"

"Depends on what kind of stuff you have."

"Oh, Harold," Lucille said.

Both of them waited for the next question, but it never came. There came only the clattering of a few stray Lincoln Logs tumbling across the hardwood floor as some construction project was undone and begun anew.

"He's going to build houses one day," Lucille said.

"He might change his mind in a week."

"He won't," she said.

"How do you know?"

"Because a mother knows these things."

Harold placed the guitar on the floor beside his leg. Lucille was all but asleep. He got a small blanket from the hall closet and placed it over her. "Is there anything I need to do to the food?" Harold asked.

Lucille only replied, "He's going to build things." And then she was asleep, both in memory and in the empty, lonely house.

Lucille woke on the living room couch, lying on her side with her hands tucked beneath her head and her legs pulled up into her body. In the chair where Harold should have been sitting and plucking away at his guitar, there was only emptiness. She listened for the sound of Jacob and his logs playing in the bedroom.

More emptiness.

Lucille sat up on the couch, still drowsy, with her eyes stinging from exhaustion. She didn't remember lying on the couch or falling to sleep. The last thing she remembered was standing by the kitchen sink, looking out the window and getting ready to wash the dishes.

It was very late or very early now. There was a chill in the air like that of autumn beginning to awaken. The crickets rattled on outside the house. Upstairs, one of their numbers had found its way inside and it sat in some dusty corner, trilling.

Lucille's body hurt and, more than that, she was very frightened.

It was not the realism of the dream that had frightened her. Nor was it the fact that it was her first dream in weeks and her mind told her that there was something very unhealthy about that. What frightened her the most was the way she had been so suddenly thrust back into her old, tired body.

In her dream, her legs had been strong; now her knees ached and her ankles were swollen. In her dream there was a firmness all about her, the impression that any task could, in time, be overcome. And that had made the foreboding she felt in the dream more bearable. Even if it had suddenly turned into a nightmare, she would be able to handle it so long as she had her youth, which, in her dream, was guaranteed.

Now she was an old woman again. Worse than that, she was an old woman alone. Loneliness terrified her. It always had and, most likely, it always would.

"He was going to be a builder," she said to no one. And then she began crying.

It was sometime later when the crying stopped. She felt better then, as if a valve somewhere had been opened and some invisible pressure released. When Lucille went to stand, arthritis pain struck her bones. She inhaled sharply and fell back onto the couch. "Dear Lord," she said.

She stood more easily the next time. The pain was still there, but it was lessened by her expectation of it. Her feet shuffled as she walked, making a light, swishing sound as she moved through the house. She made her way to the kitchen.

Lucille managed a cup of coffee and stood in the porch doorway listening to the crickets. Soon they were quieting softly and the question of whether it was very late or very early was answered. Off to the east there was the dim glow of what would, eventually, become the sun. "Praise God," she said.

There were things that she needed to do, plans she needed to make if she was really going to do this. And she didn't need to be thinking about how quiet and empty the house was if she was going to be doing the hard work of planning. So the television, in spite of its babbles about nothing, was a welcome friend.

"It'll be okay," she told herself as she sat writing in a small notebook.

In the beginning she only wrote simple things, the things she knew, the things that were without question. "The world is a strange place," she wrote. That was at the top of the list. She laughed at that a little. "I've been married to you too long," she said to her absent husband. The television babbled back some reply about the dangers of erections lasting for four or more hours.

Then she wrote, "The just have been unjustly imprisoned." Then: "My husband and son are prisoners."

She looked down at the paper. It all looked as simple as it did imposing. The facts were a good enough thing to have, but the facts seldom pointed the way to salvation, she thought. The facts did nothing but sit there and stare out of the darkness of possibility and look into the soul to see what it would do when it faced them.

"Should I do this?" she wrote. "Does any person in this world really try to save people? Does it really happen that way? Will going there do anything other than make me out to be a crazy old woman and get me arrested, or maybe worse? Will I be killed? Will Harold? Will Jacob?"

"Oh, Lord," she said.

The television laughed at her. But still she continued.

She wrote that the town was a horror, in violation of all civility. She wrote that the Bureau was a tyrannical evil—then she erased that and wrote, instead, only that the government was in the wrong. Rebellion was new to her, new and hot enough to scald her if she let it. She needed to ease into it.

She thought of David and Goliath and every other Bible story she had ever heard of God's chosen people battling against a powerful oppressor. She thought of the Jews and Egypt and the Pharaohs.

"Let my people go," she said, and laughed a little when the television said, in a child's voice, "Okay."

"It's a sign," she said. "Isn't it?"

She wrote for a very long time. She wrote until her list could not be held on a single sheet of paper and her hand began to cramp and the sun was well above the horizon and the television had gone to talking about the current news of the day.

She half listened as she went on with her writing. There was nothing new happening anywhere. More Returned were returning. No one knew how or why. The detention centers were growing larger and larger. Entire towns were being taken over, and no longer just in rural areas such as Arcadia, but in larger cities. The True Living were being usurped, or so one of the announcers said.

Lucille thought the news announcer was overreacting.

A woman in Los Angeles who was being interviewed thought that he wasn't reacting strongly enough.

When Lucille had finished her list, she sat and stared at it. Most of it didn't matter, she decided upon review, but those first things, those things in the beginning of the list, they were still important, even in the light of day. Something needed to be done about those things and, as much as she had prayed, she had to admit that nothing had been done about them.

"Dear Lord," she said.

Then she stood and went to the bedroom. Her feet did not shuffle now. They marched. In the bedroom closet, far, far in the back, beneath a stack of boxes and old shoes that neither she nor Harold could fit anymore, beneath tax paperwork and unread books and dust and mildew and cobwebs, was Harold's pistol.

The last time she remembered seeing that pistol was fifty years ago, on the night when Harold had hit that dog on the highway and they'd brought it home and, in the end, had to put it down. The memory came in a sudden flash and then was gone again, as if some part of her didn't want to be associated with the details of it just now.

The pistol was heavier than Lucille remembered. She had only held it once in her entire life—the day Harold brought it home. He'd been so proud of it, for whatever reason. Lucille, at the time, had difficulty understanding exactly what it was about a gun that anyone would have reason to be proud of.

The barrel was a smooth, hard blue-black rectangle that mated perfectly with the handle of steel and wood. The grip was, at the core, solid steel—Lucille could tell by the heft and weight of it—but with wooden sections on each side that fit comfortably in her hand. It looked like a movie gun.

Lucille thought about all the movies she had seen and all the things that guns had done in those movies. Killing, making things explode, threatening, killing, saving, giving confidence and a sense of safety, killing.

It felt like death, she thought. Cold. Hard. Immutable.

Was this what it had come to? she mused.

The True Living Movement was all Fred Green had anymore.

The fields were overgrown. The house hadn't been cleaned. He hadn't gone to the sawmill and searched for work in weeks.

Marvin Parker was being held without bail and charged with a felony after the ruckus at the school. He'd come out of it with a dislocated shoulder and a cracked rib and, while they had both known the risks, Fred still felt bad about it. It had been a fool idea to begin with, Fred thought, looking back on it. At the time, he'd told Marvin, "It'll teach them a lesson. Make them think about moving all those Returned to someplace else. Make them think about taking over somebody else's town." And Marvin had agreed wholeheartedly. But now Marvin was hurt up and behind bars and that didn't sit well with his conscience.

There was nothing Fred could do for him just now. And, more than that, Fred felt that maybe what had happened—even with all its consequences—wasn't enough.

Maybe they'd both been thinking too small. There was plenty still to do.

Other men had come and found Fred after that night. Locals who understood what Fred and Marvin had tried to accomplish and who wanted to do what they could to help out. There weren't many of them—and most of them were only good for talking—but there were two or three that Fred felt confident would do what needed to be done when the time came.

And the time was quickly coming. The whole town had been taken over. Everybody forced to either move out of their homes or live with the Returned. Hell, Marvin Parker's very own house was a part of it now! Taken over by the Bureau and the damned Returned.

It was happening like this in other places, Fred knew: people being pushed too far by the Bureau and the Returned. Someone had to put an end to all this. Someone had to make a statement, for the sake of Arcadia, for the sake of the living. If the people of Arcadia had all made a fuss, had all come together against the Returned like they should have in the beginning, things wouldn't have gotten this far. It was like Marvin had said about the volcano in that woman's backyard. Too many people had sat idly by and watched it happen. Fred couldn't let that happen. It was up to him now.

Later that night, after he had made his plans for what would come next, Fred Green went to bed and, for the first time in months, he dreamed. When he awoke, it was still very late in the night and his voice was hoarse, his throat sore. He could not say why. He remembered few details of the dream—mostly he remembered being alone in a darkened house. He remembered music, the sound of a woman's voice singing.

Fred reached a hand into the empty space in the bed beside him, the space where no one slept. "Mary?" he called.

The house did not answer.

He rose from the bed and went into the bathroom. He switched on the light and lingered there, staring at the bare bathroom tiles where Mary once wept for the loss of their child, wondering what she would think of him if she were here now.

Eventually, he turned out the light and left the bathroom. He made his way to what, over the years, he had come to call his "Project Room." It was a large room that smelled of mildew and dust, cluttered with tools, abandoned woodworking projects, all manner of unfulfilled endeavors. He stood in the door of the room, staring at all the things he had begun and not finished: a chess set made from redwood (he'd never learned to play, but he respected the intricacy of the pieces), an ornate podium made from rotted oak (he had never given a speech in his life, but admired the site of a speaker on a well-made podium), a small, half-finished rocking horse.

He couldn't remember, just then, why he'd begun building it, or why he'd stopped. But there it was, in the corner of his project room, buried under boxes and quilts stored until winter.

Why had he started building something so foolish?

He made his way through the clutter and dust to where the thing sat. He rubbed a hand over the rough wood. It was unsanded and rough but, somehow, pleasing to the touch. The years of neglect had softened its edges.

While it wasn't the best thing he'd ever started working on, Fred didn't think it was hideous. Amateurish maybe. The mouth was wrong—something about the size of the horse's teeth was wrong—but he liked the look of the animal's ears. He remembered, suddenly, how much attention he had given them when working on them. They were the only part of the creature he thought he might actually have a chance of getting right. They had been difficult and had left his hands sore and full of cramps for days. But, looking at them now, the effort seemed worth it.

It was just behind the ears, above where the mane began, where only the rider—as small as they would have to be to ride the animal—could see, that Fred noticed the letters carved into the wood.

H-E-A-T-H-E-R.

Wasn't that the name he and Mary had picked out for their child?

"Mary," Fred called one last time.

When no one answered, it was as if the universe had, with finality, confirmed everything that he was planning to do, everything that he knew had to happen. He had given the universe a chance to change his mind, and it had given him only silence and an empty house in return.

Nathaniel Schumacher

It was two months now since he returned and his family loved him no less than they had in the long, shining days of his life. His wife, though she was older now, welcomed him by throwing her arms around him and weeping and clinging tightly to him. His children, though they were no longer children, huddled around him as they had all the days of his life. They were still the type of siblings that fought each other for their parents' attention and none of that had changed in the twenty years of time between when their father had died and when he had become one of the Returned.

Bill, his oldest, even though he had a family of his own now, still trailed his father and called his sister, Helen, "foolish" and "impossible" the way he had for the entirety of their childhood.

Both of them moved home, as if sensing that time would be frail and fleeting, and they spent their days orbiting him and all that he represented to them. They were drawn in by the gravity of him. They sat up late into the night sometimes, explaining to him all of the threads of life that had frayed outward since his leaving. He smiled at their news and there were arguments now and again, when he did not approve, but even those were greeted with a sense of appropriateness, a type of reassurance that, indeed, he was who he appeared to be.

He was their father, and he was Returned.

And then one day he was gone again.

No one could say just when he disappeared, only that he was not there. They searched for him, but with great uncertainty, as they were forced to admit to themselves that his returning from the grave had been an uncertain and unexpected thing to begin with, so why would his disappearance be anything else?

For a brief while they lamented. They wept and made a great fuss and Bill and Helen argued with each other, each saying the other had done such and such to cause his leaving, and their mother would have to intercede on behalf of decency. Then they would apologize without meaning it and grumble to each other about what needed to be done. They went and filed a missing person's report. They even went to the soldiers from the Bureau and told them that their father was gone. "He just disappeared," they said.

The soldiers only took notes and seemed unsurprised.

In the end there was nothing to be done. He simply was not there anymore. They thought of visiting his grave, digging the coffin up from its hallowed vault, only to assure themselves that everything had been returned to the way it was supposed to be and that he was not simply somewhere in the world without them.

But their mother did not approve, saying only, "We had our time."

SIXTEEN

she was thinner. Apart from that, she had not changed at all. "How are you?" he said. She stroked his hand and nuzzled against his shoulder.

"I'm fine."

"Have you been eating? Are they feeding you, I mean?"

She nodded and raked her nails gently along his forearm. "I've missed you."

The detention center of Meridian, Mississippi, allowed some mingling between the True Living and the Returned. Things were bad here, but not quite as bad as Arcadia. The living and the Returned met in a fenced-in patio area between the larger holding facility and the security zone where the living were checked for weapons and bad intentions in general.

"I've missed you, too," he finally said.

"I tried to find you," she said.

"They sent me a letter."

"What kind of letter?"

"It just said that you were looking for me." She nodded.

"This was before they started locking everyone up," he said. "How's your mother?"

"Dead," he said, more flatly than he had planned. "Or maybe she isn't. It's hard to be sure these days."

She was still rubbing his hand in that slow, hypnotic way a familiar love sometimes does. Sitting this close to her—smelling her, feeling her hand, hearing the sound of life moving in and out of her lungs—Pastor Robert Peters forgot all the years, all the mistakes, all the failures, all the grief, all the loneliness.

She leaned in across the table. "We can leave," she said, quietly.

"No, we can't."

"Yes, we can. We'll leave together just like we did last time."

He patted her hand with an almost fatherly tenderness. "That was a mistake," he said. "We should have just waited."

"Waited for what?"

"I don't know. We should have just waited. Time has a way of fixing things. I've learned that. I'm an old man now." He thought for a moment, then corrected himself. "Well, maybe I'm not an old man, but I'm definitely not a young man. And one thing I've learned is that nothing is unbearable with enough time."

But wasn't that his greatest lie? Wasn't the unbearableness of not being with her every day the very thing that drove him here? He had never gotten over her, had never forgiven himself for what he had done to her. He had married and lived and turned his life to God and done everything else that a person is supposed to, and still he had not gotten over her. He had loved her more than he loved his father, more than he loved his mother, more than he had loved God. But still he had left her. And then she had gone off. Gone ahead and did what she promised she would do. Left on her own and gotten herself killed.

And every day he remembered that.

The marriage to his wife had only been a concession of his soul. It was the thing that seemed logical. So he had done it, with all the enthusiasm and levelheadedness of buying a house or investing in a 401(k). And the fact that, later, he and his wife would come to find out that children would not be a part of their lives, even that had seemed apropos.

Truth was, he had never imagined having children with her. Truth was, as much as he believed in the institution of marriage, as many sermons as he had preached on it over the years, as many marriages as he had personally helped repair, as many times as he had told sullen-eyed couples in his office, "God and divorce just don't get along," as much as he had done all these things, he had always been looking for a way out.

It had only taken the dead to begin returning from the grave to give him the motivation he needed.

Now he was with her and, while everything did not seem perfect, he felt better than he had in years. Her hand was in his. He could feel her. He could touch her. He could smell the familiar scent of her—a scent that had not changed in all these years. Yes, this was the way things were intended to be.

Here and there across the visiting area, the guards were separating the dead from the living. Visiting time was over.

"They can't keep you here like this. It's not humane." He gripped her hand.

"I'm okay," she said.

"No. You're not."

He wrapped his arm around her and took a deep breath and the smell of her filled him up inside. "Do they come to visit you?" he asked.

"No."

"I'm sorry."

"Don't be."

"They love you."

"I know."

"You're still their daughter. They know that. They have to know that."

She nodded.

The guards were making their rounds. When they had to, they were pulling people apart. "Time to go" was all they said.

"I'll get you out of here," he said.

"Okay," she said. "But if you don't, that's okay, too. I understand."

Then the guards came and put their time to an end.

It was fitful sleep for the pastor that night, the same dream over and over again.

He was sixteen and sitting alone in his bedroom. Somewhere in the house his father and mother were asleep. The silence of the house was filled with heaviness. The heat of their arguing still hung about the eaves like a dark-fallen snow.

He stood and dressed as quietly and secretly as he could manage. He crept barefoot over the hardwood floor of the house. It was summer and the humid night was full of the songs of crickets.

He had expected a very dramatic departure. He had expected that his father or mother would awaken as he made his way from the house and there would be some sort of confrontation, but none came. Perhaps he'd read too many bad novels or seen too many movies. In the movies, leavings were always full of spectacle. Someone was always yelling. Sometimes there was violence. There was always some foreboding final statement made in the exit—"I hope I never see you again!" or some such—which eventually sealed the fate of all characters involved.

But in his own life, he had left while everyone slept, and

all that would happen is that they would awaken and find him not there and that would be the end of it. They would know where he went and why. They would not come after him because that was not his father's way. His father's love was an open door. It would never close—neither to keep you out nor to keep you in.

It was almost an hour of walking before he met her. The moonlight turned her face pale and gaunt-looking. She had always been a skinny girl, but just now, in this light, she looked dying.

"I hope he dies," she said.

The pastor—who was not a pastor yet, but just a boy—stared at her face. Her eye was swollen and a dark line of blood was smeared in the gap between her lip and nose. It was hard to tell which was bleeding.

She had lived the dramatic leaving that Robert had imagined for himself.

"Don't say things like that," he said.

"Fuck him! I hope he gets hit by a fucking bus! I hope a dog rips out his throat! I hope he gets some disease that takes weeks to kill him and every day is more fucked than the last." She spoke through clenched teeth and her hands were fists swinging at the ends of her arms.

"Lizzy," he said.

She screamed. Anger and pain and fear.

"Liz, please!"

More screaming.

More of the things Robert Peters, in the years of memory that had settled between who Elizabeth Pinch really was and who he remembered her being, had forgotten.

Pastor Peters woke to the sound of a large truck rumbling along the highway outside. The motel had thin walls and always there were trucks moving back and forth to and from the detention center. Large, dark trucks that looked like some exaggerated, prehistoric beetles. Sometimes they were so full that soldiers dangled from the sides.

The pastor wondered if they'd traveled along the length of the highway like that, hanging from the side. It was a dangerous way to travel. But, then again, with Death being a bit ambivalent these days, perhaps it was not as dangerous as it had once been.

On the way back from the detention center, the radio said that a group of Returned had been killed outside Atlanta. They were hiding in a small house in a small town—all of the bad things seemed to be happening in the small towns first—when a group of supporters of the True Living Movement found out and showed up demanding the Returned surrender and go peacefully.

Some sympathizers had been caught up in the middle of things, as well—caught hiding the Returned. The Rochester Incident seemed far away now.

And when the True Living fanatics showed up at the front door, things went very bad very quickly. In the end, the house caught fire, and everyone inside, living and Returned alike, was killed.

The radio said that arrests were made, but no official charges had been pressed just yet.

Pastor Peters stood for a long time in that motel window, watching things happen around him and thinking of Elizabeth. He called her "Elizabeth" in his mind.

"Liz" is what he once called her.

Tomorrow he would go see her again—provided the soldiers didn't cause any trouble. He'd talk to whomever he needed to talk to about having her released into his custody. He could throw his spiritual weight around when he needed to. Apply a little emotional guilt, as all men of the cloth are trained to do.

It would be difficult, but it would all work out. He would have her back, finally.

By God's grace, it would all work out. All Pastor Robert Peters had to do was commit to it.

"By God's grace," Robert said, "it will all work out. All we have to do is commit to it."

She laughed. "When did you get all religious, Bertie?"

He squeezed her hand. No one had called him by that name in years. No one had ever called him "Bertie" but her.

Her head was leaning against his shoulder again, as if they were sitting in that old oak tree on her father's farm all those years ago, and not sitting in the visitor's room of the Meridian Detention Center. He stroked her hair—he had forgotten how honey-colored it was and how it slid through his fingers like water. Every day with her was a rediscovery. "They just need a little more convincing," he said.

"You'll do your best," she said.

"I will."

"It'll all work out," she said.

He kissed her brow—something which earned him disapproving glances from some of those around them. After all, she was only sixteen. Sixteen and small for her age. And he was so large and so much older than sixteen. Even if she was Returned, she was still a child.

"When did you become so patient?" he asked.

"What do you mean?"

"Your temper's gone."

She shrugged. "What's the point? Rage against the world and the world remains."

He looked at her with wide eyes. "That's very profound," he said.

She laughed.

"What's so funny?"

"You! You're so serious!"

"I suppose I am," he said. "I've gotten old."

She returned her head to his shoulder. "Where are we going to go?" she asked. "Once we're out of here, I mean."

"I've gotten old," he repeated.

"We could go to New York," she said. "Broadway. I've always wanted to see Broadway."

He nodded and looked down at the young, small hand that he held in his own. Time had done nothing to that hand. It was still as small and smooth as it always had been. This should not have surprised Robert Peters. After all, this is what the Returned had always been: a refusal of nature's laws. So why should her hand, as clean and smooth as it was, unsettle him so?

"Do you think I'm old?" he asked.

"Or maybe we could go to New Orleans," she said. She sat up with excitement. "Oh, yes! New Orleans!"

"Perhaps," he said.

She stood and looked down at him, the corners of her eyes turned up happily. "Can't you just imagine it?" she said. "You and me on Bourbon Street. Jazz music everywhere. And the food! Don't get me started on the food!"

"That sounds nice," he said.

She took his hands and pulled his large mass to its feet. "Dance with me," she said.

He obliged her, in spite of the stares and whispers it drew. They turned slowly. Her head barely reached his chest, and she was so small—almost as small as the pastor's wife.

"It's all going to work out," she said, her head lying against his wide chest.

"But what if they refuse to let you go?"

"It'll work out," she repeated.

They swayed in silence. The soldiers watched. *This is the way it will be from now on,* Pastor Peters thought.

"Do you remember that I left you?" he asked.

"I can hear your heart beating," she said in reply.

"Okay," he said. Then, after a moment: "Okay."

This was not the conversation he had imagined having with her. The Elizabeth Pinch of his memories—the one who had hung above the altar of his marriage all these years—was not one to sidestep any argument. No. She was a fighter, even in the places and times that neither warranted nor accepted a fight. She cursed, she swore, she threw things. She was like her father: a creature of anger. And that was why he had loved her so much.

"I'll get you out of here somehow," Pastor Peters said— even as, in his mind, he had already left her dancing alone in this prison.

Robert Peters knew what he would do: he would leave her and not come back in the same way he had done before. This was not his Elizabeth. That would make this time easier.

But even if it had been her—even if it had been his "Liz"— it would not have mattered. He had left her before because he had known, he had always known, that she would leave him. She would grow tired of him, his religion, his large, slow frame, his utter normalness.

Liz had been the type of person to dance without music, and he was the type of person to dance only when forced to. All those years ago, if he had not left her and gone back home, she would have left him and gone on to New Orleans, just like this specter of Liz wanted to do now.

That much of her lingered in this Returned young girl—

just enough of Lizzy to remind Robert of all that was grand and terrible about himself. It was enough to make him see the truth: that no matter how much he had loved her, no matter how much he had wanted her, their romance would not have worked. And in spite of how it turned out for her, even if he had stayed with her all those years ago, if he'd gone off with her and, perhaps, been able to keep her from dying, it wouldn't have changed anything. The thing that he loved about her would have died the longer she stayed with him until, eventually, she would be gone. Maybe not physically, but all that he loved about her would be gone.

And they would both lament it.

So Pastor Robert Peters stood in the Meridian Detention Center and danced with the sixteen-year-old girl who he had once loved, and he lied and told her he would take her away from here. And she lied back to him and told him she would be waiting for him and that she would never leave him.

They danced together this last time and told each other these things.

It was happening like this all over.

Connie Wilson

Everything was moving toward the coming terror. She felt it. It was inevitable now, like when the earth is dry and barren, the trees gray and brittle, the grass brown and parched—something must change. All those in the town of Arcadia could feel it, she believed, though none knew exactly what the feeling was. She tried to ignore her fears, bury them in the day to day of taking care of her husband and keeping her children fed and clean, but she was worried about Ms. Lucille. They'd come across her husband, Harold, once since coming here, and she had intended to stay with him and Jacob, to keep tabs on them, for Ms. Lucille's sake.

But then things had gotten away from her and now she didn't know where either of them were.

"It will be okay," she said often.

The Returned were still prisoners of the small town, still prisoners of the Bureau and a world unsure. And the True Living of

*Arcadia were victims in their own right, their entire town stolen
away from them, its very identity absconded.*

*"None of this will be okay," Connie said, seeing all of this
before her.*

*Then she took her children in her arms and, still, the fear
would not release her shoulders.*

SEVENTEEN

Harold and Bellamy stood together beneath the oppressive summer heat of Arcadia for what would be their final interview—a fact that didn't particularly bother Harold. The New Yorker was getting good at horseshoes. Too good.

Bellamy was being transferred, finally, in spite of his many protests. The colonel had seen to it, citing the overcrowding and general lack of time at the Arcadia Detention Center for Bellamy's interviews to be conducted. There were other jobs for Bureau agents to do, much more urgent jobs, but they weren't the type of jobs Bellamy would agree to being involved in, so the colonel was sending him away.

Bellamy tried not to think about it. Tried not to think about what it would mean for his mother. He tossed his horseshoe and hoped for the best. It landed solidly.

Klink.

"I suppose you know that I'm leaving," Bellamy said in his smooth, direct way.

"I'd heard something about it," Harold said. "Or, rather, I'd figured as much." He took his shot.

Klink.

Neither man kept score anymore.

They still played in the small strip of grass in the middle of the school, as if there weren't other places to choose from. But there was something about this particular place that they had both gotten used to. It was slightly more private now that the whole town was available for the rest of the prisoners. People had gone about the business of spreading outward, migrating out from the school and the few other interim buildings the Bureau had set up. Now the town of Arcadia was full. All the buildings that had been left empty by years of a town existing and failing and people moving away were transformed into places where people could live. Even the streets—what few there were in Arcadia—had become places where people could pitch tents or set up areas for the distribution of necessities by the Bureau. The consumption of Arcadia was complete now.

But even without all that, this place, this small stretch of town, was where they had both spent the past few weeks chipping away at each other.

Bellamy smiled. "Of course you did." He looked around. Up above, the sky was a sharp, hard blue, punctuated here and there with rainless white clouds. Off in the distance, the wind was blowing, rustling through the trees in the forests, swinging back through the heat and humidity and drumming up against the buildings of the town.

When the breeze hit Harold and Bellamy, it was only an exhalation of heat and mugginess. It smelled of sweat and urine and too many people kept too long in poor conditions. Nearly everything in Arcadia smelled that way these days. It was stuck on everything, that smell. So much so that everyone, including Agent Bellamy, hardly noticed it anymore.

"Are you going to ask me or not?" Harold said. He and Bellamy walked together through the heat and stink to retrieve their horseshoes. Jacob was not far away, just inside the schoolhouse, with Mrs. Stone—someone who had been on Harold's mind for a while now. "And before we spend too much time playing games—pun intended—let's just both agree to skip all the dancing, if you don't mind. We both know who she is."

"When did you know?"

"Not long after she got here. I didn't think it was coincidence that she wound up in our room."

"I suppose I'm not as clever as I think, huh?"

"Nothing like that. Your judgment was clouded, is all. I'll try not to hold it against you."

They both took their turn. *Klink. Klink.* The wind picked up again and, for a moment, the air smelled fresh, as if some change were slowly coming. Then it was gone and the air was hot again and the sun crossed the sky.

"How is she?" Agent Bellamy asked.

Klink.

"She's fine. You know that."

"Does she ask about me?"

"All the time."

Klink.

Bellamy thought for a moment, but Harold was not finished. "She wouldn't know you if you sat down in front of her and kissed her on the forehead. Half the time she thinks I'm you. The rest of the time she thinks I'm your daddy."

"I'm sorry," Bellamy said.

"For what?"

"For getting you involved in all this."

Harold straightened his back and fixed his feet and took aim. He tossed a good, solid shot and missed the stake completely. He smiled. "I would have done the same. In fact," he continued, "I plan to."

"Quid pro quo, I suppose."

"An eye for an eye sounds better."

"Whatever you say."

"How's Lucille?"

Bellamy sighed and scratched the top of his head. "Good, from what I hear. Doesn't leave the house much, but honestly there isn't much in this town to come out for."

"They've done a number on us," Harold said.

Bellamy took his shot. It landed perfectly.

"She's started carrying a gun," he said.

"What?" The image of his old handgun flashed in his mind, followed by the memory of the night before Jacob's death and the dog he'd been forced to put down.

"That's what they tell me, at least. She stopped at one of the checkpoints on the highway. Had it in the seat of your truck. When they asked her about it she gave some speech about 'the Right of Safety' or some such. Then she threatened to shoot. Not sure how serious she was about that, though."

As Bellamy went to the other end of the track, dust rising beneath his footfalls, Harold stood and looked up at the sky and wiped the sweat from his face. "That doesn't sound like the woman I married," he said. "The woman I married would have shot first and made her speech second."

"I always thought of her as more of the 'let God handle it' type," Bellamy said.

"That came later," Harold said. "Early on, she was a hell-raiser. You wouldn't believe some of the things we got into when we were younger."

"Nothing that showed up on a record. I've run files on you both."

"Just because you don't get caught doesn't mean you ain't breaking the law."

Bellamy smiled.

Klink.

"You asked about my mother once before," Bellamy began.

"I did," Harold said.

"She, eventually, died of pneumonia. But that was at the end. It was the dementia that really took her, piece by piece."

"And she came back the same way."

Bellamy nodded.

"And now you're leaving her."

"It's not her," Bellamy said, shaking his head. "She's a photocopy of someone, that's all. You know that as well as I do."

"Ah," Harold said coldly. "You're talking about the boy."

"You and I," Bellamy said, "we're alike in that. We both know that the dead are dead and that's the end of it."

"Then why'd you bring her to me? Why go through so much trouble?"

"For the same reason you stay with your son."

The air stayed hot and the sky a hard, impenetrable blue for the rest of that day. The two men went around and around, game after game, neither tallying the points, neither sure exactly how many games they'd played or what the point of it all was. They only orbited each other in the middle of a town that was not the way it had been, in a world that was not the way it had been, and they let the world turn, with all their words buzzing in the air around them.

When the evening came, it found Lucille hunched at her writing desk and the Hargrave house filled with the scent of gun oil. Reverberating throughout the house was the sound of a wire brush worrying steel.

Beneath the gun Lucille had found the small cleaning kit that had only occasionally been used in all these years of ownership. There were instructions next to the supplies. The only hard part had been disassembling the gun.

It was unsettling, having to point the barrel one way while applying a tool to turn some bushing; there were springs to mind and small, hard bits that couldn't be lost when the time came to put everything back together again. All of this she struggled with while reminding herself, every single second, that the gun wasn't loaded and that she wouldn't mess around and shoot herself like some kind of fool.

She removed the bullets and they now stood in a line on the far end of the desk. She'd cleaned them, as well, using only the wire brush and keeping clear of the cleaning solvent on account of fearing some mysterious chemical reaction should the turpentine-smelling solvent mingle with the gunpowder inside.

Maybe she was being overly cautious, but she was okay with that.

When she was unloading the bullets, she found something harmonic in the sound they made, one after the other, as they popped from the slender, steel magazine.

Click.

Click.

Click.

Click.

Click.

Click.

Click.

She held seven lives in her hand. An image came to her then of herself, Harold, Jacob and the Wilson family all dead. Seven deaths.

She rolled the small, heavy projectiles in her palm. She made a fist and concentrated on the feeling they gave her hand—the smooth, round tips digging into her palm. She squeezed them so tightly she thought, for a second, that she might hurt herself.

Then she lined them up along the desk with care and gentleness, like little mysteries. She placed the gun in her lap and read the instructions.

The paper showed an image of the top of the gun sliding back to reveal the inside of the barrel. She picked up the gun and examined it. She placed her hands near the back of the slide the way the picture showed her and pressed. Nothing happened. She pressed harder. Still nothing. She examined the photo again. She seemed to be doing everything right.

She gave it one final try, pressing so hard that she could feel the veins of her body rising. She gritted her teeth and gave a little groan and, all of a sudden, the slide flew back and a bullet leaped from the gun and clattered to the floor.

"Lord," she said, her hands beginning to shake. For a very long time she let the bullet rest there on the floor and she only stared at it, thinking about what might have been. "I may have to be ready for that," she said.

Then she retrieved the bullet and placed it on the desk and went about the business of cleaning the weapon and thinking on exactly what the evening might bring.

When the time came to leave the house, Lucille made her way out front and stood next to Harold's tired old truck and looked back, and for a very long time she said nothing. From far enough away, she imagined, she could be seen orbiting the weathered old house where she had been married and loved and raised a son and grappled with a husband—a husband who, now that she was apart from him, she realized had never been quite so ornery and contemptible as she often thought; he loved her, for every day of their fifty-some years together, he loved her—and now, as the evening rose up around her, she was leaving.

For her part in things, Lucille breathed in, held the image of the house and all that it meant to her in the universe of her lungs until she thought she might faint. Then she held it longer, clawing at this moment, this image, this life, this single breath, though she knew she would have to let it go.

The guard on duty that night was a young, skittish boy from Kansas. Junior was his name and he'd come to not mind guarding the town quite so much on account of the crotchety, funny old man he'd made friends with.

And Junior, like all participants in a tragedy, had the sense that unfortunate things were in the works. He'd spent the evening compulsively checking his phone for new messages, worried by a feeling that there was something important he was destined to say to someone.

From inside the guardhouse, he cleared his throat at the sound of an old Ford rumbling up out of the distance. It was a little strange to him, sometimes, the way the fencing around the town ended so suddenly and the single, two-lane road emptied so suddenly into the countryside. It was as if all that was going on inside the fencing, inside the Barricade, inside the entirety of the town that was now contained, was meant to all end suddenly.

The engine loped and chugged and the headlights skittered a little over the road as if whoever it was behind the wheel was having trouble. He thought it might have been some kid out joyriding—he had memories of stealing his father's old truck one fall evening back when he was of the age when such things were what a person did.

Kansas and North Carolina weren't so different, Junior thought. This part of North Carolina wasn't so different, at least. Flatlands. Farms. Regular, hardworking folks. If it wasn't for the damned humidity that hung in the air like a specter, then maybe, just maybe, he could think about settling down here. They hardly ever had tornadoes, and the people, with all that Southern hospitality he'd heard about, were friendly enough.

The truck's squealing brakes brought Junior's attention back where it belonged. The blue pickup chugged for a moment and then the engine went silent. The headlights still burned, bright and hard. He remembered a training he'd had once about such things. Headlights were supposed to blind everyone so that the person inside could get out and move around and pick their shots without ever being seen.

Junior had never cared for guns—which was a good thing because, as it happened, he was a terrible shot. Just now the high beams went low and he was able to make out, finally, the seventysomething-year-old woman behind the wheel— her face tight and filled with rage—and he was struck with the impression that, more than anything, there should be no guns anywhere in the area just now. But he was a guard, so he had his gun. And when Lucille finally stepped out of the truck he was able to see that she had her gun, as well.

"Ma'am!" Junior shouted, moving quickly from the makeshift guardhouse. "Ma'am, you're going to have to put down the weapon!" His voice was shaky, but his voice was always shaky.

"This ain't about you, child," Lucille said. She came around and stood in front of the truck, the headlights still turned on, glaring behind her. She was dressed in an old, blue cotton dress that came down, flat and even and with no flourishes, almost to her ankles. It was the dress she wore for doctors' appointments when she wanted to let the doctor know, right from the beginning, that she wasn't about to accept any news she didn't particularly like.

A crowd of Returned filed out of the truck bed and out of the cab. So many of them that Junior had memories of the circus that used to come through every fall.

The Returned clustered together behind Lucille, forming a small, silent crowd. "It's a matter of decency and proper behavior," Lucille said, not necessarily speaking to the young soldier. "Just basic, human decency."

"Sir!" Junior called out, not quite sure exactly who he was calling for, knowing only that whatever was happening now was something he didn't particularly care to be a part of. "Sir! We've got a situation here! Sir!"

There was the *clump, clump, clump* of booted feet approaching.

"Thy rod and thy staff comfort me," Lucille said.

"Ma'am," Junior said. "You're going to need to put down that weapon, ma'am."

"I'm not here to have trouble with you, child," Lucille said. She made sure to keep her pistol pointed down.

"Yes, ma'am," he said. "But you're going to have to put the gun down before we can talk about whatever it is you came here to talk about." The other night guards were all there now, guns drawn—though something in them, perhaps some old lesson of upbringing, kept them from pointing their guns directly at Lucille.

"What the hell's going on, Junior?" one of the soldiers whispered.

"Fuck if I know," he whispered back. "She just showed up here with them—a whole group of Returned—and that damned pistol. Started out there was just her and this truck full of them, but..."

As they all could plainly see, there were others. Many others. Even if the handful of soldiers couldn't tell exactly how many there were, they knew they were outnumbered. That much they were sure of.

"I'm here to see about the liberation of everybody locked up in there," Lucille shouted. "I don't have anything in particular against you boys. I suppose you're just doing what you been ordered to do. And that's what you're trained to do. So, because of that, I don't feel any kind of way toward you. But I will say that you should remember you've got a moral responsibility to do right, to be just and fair individuals, even if you are supposed to be following orders."

She wanted to pace back and forth, the way the pastor sometimes did when he needed to get his thoughts together. She'd had it all planned out in her head on the drive over, but now, standing here, actually doing this thing that she was doing—all these guns—she was scared.

But this wasn't a time to be scared.

"I shouldn't even be talking to you," Lucille yelled. "You're not the cause, none of you are. You're just mostly the symptom. I gotta get to the cause. I want to see Colonel Willis."

"Ma'am," Junior said. "Please put the weapon down. If you want to see the colonel, we'll let you see the colonel. But you're going to have to put down that weapon." The soldier next to him whispered something. "Put down the weapon and surrender those Returned individuals for processing."

"I will do no such thing," she barked, and her grip tightened on the pistol. "Processing," she growled. The soldiers still hesitated to point their guns at her so they aimed their guns at those that had come with her. The Returned that were gathered behind and around Lucille made no sudden movements. They only stood and let Lucille and her pistol act on their behalf. "I want to see the colonel," she repeated.

In spite of feeling suddenly guilty about what she was doing, she wasn't about to be talked out of anything. Satan was a subtle tempter, she knew, and he worked his evil works by convincing us to make those small concessions that, eventually, lead to great sins. And she was tired of standing idly by.

"Colonel Willis!" Lucille said, calling the man's name like shouting for a tax auditor. "I want to see Colonel Willis!"

Junior wasn't cut out for this level of tension. "Get somebody," he said in a low voice to the soldier next to him.

"What? She's just an old woman. She's not going to do anything."

Lucille heard them and, to prove that they'd judged the situation all wrong, she raised her gun and fired a shot into the air. Everyone jumped. "I'll see him now," she said, her ears ringing just a little.

"Get somebody!" Junior said.

"Get somebody," the soldier next to him said.

"Get somebody," that soldier said.

And on down the line it went.

Somebody finally came and, as Lucille had expected, it was not Colonel Willis but Agent Martin Bellamy. He came through the gate in something that was partly a run and partly a walk. As always, he was wearing his suit, but his tie was missing. A sure sign, Lucille thought, that the whole situation was doomed.

"Nice night for a drive," Bellamy said, coming out past the soldiers—partly to keep her attention focused on him and partly to step in front of as many gun barrels that might be aimed at the old woman as possible. "What's going on, Ms. Lucille?"

"I didn't send for you, Agent Martin Bellamy."

"No, ma'am, you most certainly didn't. But they came and got me and here I am nonetheless. Now what's all this about?"

"You know what this is all about. You know as well as anyone." Her gun hand trembled. "I'm angry," she said flatly. "And I won't stand for the way things are anymore."

"Yes, ma'am," Bellamy said. "You've got a right to be angry. If anybody does, it's you."

"Don't you do that, Agent Martin Bellamy. Don't you try to make this all about me, because it ain't. I just want to talk to Colonel Willis. Now go get him for me. Or send somebody else to get him. I don't particularly care which."

"I've got no doubt in my mind that he's on his way here right now," Bellamy said. "And, frankly, that's what I'm afraid of."

"Well, I'm not afraid," Lucille said.

"That gun only makes things worse."

"Gun? You think I'm not afraid because I got a gun?" Lucille sighed. "This ain't got nothing at all to do with the gun. I'm not afraid because I'm resolved to my path." She stood erect, like a hard flower dug into hard soil. "Too many people in this world are afraid of things—myself included. And I'm still afraid of a lot of things. Terrified of some of the stuff I see on the television. Even before all this began, and even after it all ends, I'll be afraid of things.

"But I'm not afraid of this. I'm not afraid of what's happening here right now or what might soon happen here. I'm okay with it, because it's the right thing. Good people have got to stop being afraid of doing the right thing."

"But there will be consequences," Bellamy said, trying not to make it sound like a threat. "That's just the way the world works. For everything, there's a consequence, and it's not always the consequence we can see. Sometimes it's things we can't even imagine. However things end tonight—and I'm hoping, more than you could know, that it ends peacefully—there are going to be real consequences."

He took a small step toward Lucille. Up above him, as if there was nothing amiss in the world, the stars shone and clouds moved in their silent, complex patterns.

Bellamy planted his feet and continued.

"I know what you're trying to do. You're trying to make a point. You don't like the way things have played out, and I can relate to that. I'm not fond of the current state of things, either. You think I'd have taken over a whole town and packed it full of people like objects or cargo if I had anything at all to say about it?"

"That's why I don't want to talk to you, Agent Martin Bellamy. You're not in charge of anything anymore. This ain't about you. It's about that Colonel Willis."

"Yes, ma'am," Bellamy said. "But Colonel Willis isn't in charge of anything, either. He's just doing what he's been ordered to do. He works under somebody else, just like these young soldiers here."

"Stop that," Lucille said.

"You've got to go above him if you want any satisfaction, Ms. Lucille. You've got to go on up the chain."

"Don't treat me like a fool, Agent Martin Bellamy."

"After the colonel there's a general or some such that's above him. I'm not a hundred percent sure of the chain of command. I've never served in the military, so a lot of what I know comes from what I see on TV. But I do know that no soldier does anything that they're not either ordered to do or held responsible for. It's all just a great chain that, eventually, leads up to the president and, Ms. Lucille, I know that you know very well that the president doesn't run anything. It's the voters, the private industry lobbyists and on and on. There's no end to it."

He took another step forward. He was almost close enough to reach her. Just a few yards away.

"Stop right there," Lucille said.

"Is Colonel Willis the man I would have put in charge of all this?" Bellamy asked, turning a little at "all this" to aim his words toward the sleepy, dark town that was no longer a town, but a great, bloated gulag. "No, ma'am. I would never have put him in charge of anything this important, anything this sensitive. Because this is most definitely a sensitive situation."

Another step forward.

"Martin Bellamy."

"But here we are—you, me, Colonel Willis, Harold, Jacob."

A gunshot rang out.

Then another shot, into the air from the dark, heavy pistol in Lucille's hand. Then she lowered the weapon and leveled it at Bellamy. "I got nothing against you, Agent Martin Bellamy," she said. "You know that. But I won't be led astray. I want my son."

"No, ma'am," a voice said from behind Agent Bellamy, who was retreating, step by step. It was the colonel. Next to him were Harold and Jacob. "You won't be led astray at all," Colonel Willis said. "We're going to see about getting things on the path, I'd be willing to say."

The sight of Harold and Jacob next to the colonel caught Lucille flat-footed—though, now that she saw it, she knew it was the very thing she should have expected. She immediately turned the gun on the colonel. The soldiers bristled, but the colonel motioned for them to stay calm.

Jacob's eyes were wide. He'd never seen his mother with a gun before.

"Lucille," Harold called.

"Don't give me that tone, Harold Hargrave."

"What the hell are you doing, woman?"

"I'm doing what needs to be done. That's all."

"Lucille!"

"Hush up! I'm doing what you would have done if things were switched around. Tell me that ain't true."

Harold looked at Lucille's gun. "Maybe," he said, "but that just means that now I gotta do what you would have done, if things was switched around like you said. Here you are with a goddamn pistol!"

"Don't blaspheme!"

"Listen to your husband, Mrs. Hargrave," Colonel Willis said, looking very distinguished and relaxed, even with Lucille's gun aimed at him. "This won't end well if it ends in anything other than you and these things giving up peacefully."

"You hush up," Lucille barked.

"Listen to the man, Lucille," Harold said. "Look at all these boys with guns."

There were at least twenty of them—somehow both more and less than she expected. All of them looked unsettled— guns and soldiers, opportunities for it all to end so horribly. And here she was: just an old woman in an old dress standing in the street trying not to be afraid.

Then she remembered that she was not alone. She turned her head and looked behind her. What she saw was a heaving mass of them, the Returned, all standing side by side, watching her, waiting for her to decide their fate.

She hadn't planned this. None of it. She'd only intended to drive to the gates and make her case to the colonel and, somehow, he would release everyone.

But then she was driving in and she saw them here and there along the outskirts of the town. Sometimes half-hidden, looking sullen and afraid. Other times, standing clustered together, only watching her. Perhaps they had no more fear of the Bureau. Perhaps they had resigned themselves to being taken prisoner. Or, perhaps they had been sent by God.

She stopped and asked them to come help her. And they got into the truck, one by one. But there hadn't been as many then—only a truckload. Now, there seemed to be dozens of them, as if some great call had gone up, sent from one to another in some secret, quiet way, and they had all responded.

They must have all been hiding, she thought. Or maybe it really was a miracle.

"Lucille."

It was Harold.

She came back from her musing on miracles and looked at her husband.

"You remember that time back in…well, back in '58, the day before Jacob's birthday, the day before he went away, when we were driving back from Charlotte? It was nighttime and raining, coming down so hard we talked about pulling over and sitting until it passed. You remember that?"

"Yes," Lucille said, "I remember it."

"Damn dog come shooting out there in front of the truck," Harold continued. "You remember that? Didn't even have time to swerve. Just *whump!* The sound of all that metal smacking into that damned dog."

"That don't have anything to do with this," Lucille said.

"You were crying as soon as it happened, before I'd even put two and two together and come up with any clue as to what the hell it was. You just sat there, weeping like it was a child I'd hit, saying, 'Lord, Lord, Lord,' again and again. Scared the hell out of me. I thought I actually might have hit somebody's child, even though it didn't make a lick of sense for any child to be out there in weather like that, at that time of night. But all I could think about was Jacob lying out there, dead and run over."

"Hush," Lucille said, her voice wavering.

"But there it was—that damned dog. Somebody's coon dog. Probably on the scent of something and all confused by the rain. I got out in all that damned rain and found him, all busted up like he was. I put him up in the truck and we brought him home."

"Harold."

"We took him home and brought him in the house and, well, there it was—everything we couldn't fix. Already dead. Body just hadn't figured it out yet. So I went into the room there and got that gun, that same damned gun you're holding right now. Told you to stay in the house, but you wouldn't, Lord only knows why." Harold paused and cleared something that had become lumped in his throat. "Last time I used that gun," he said. "You remember what it looked like when I used it, Lucille, I know you do." Harold looked around the soldiers, the soldiers and their guns.

He lifted Jacob and stood there holding him. The gun took on a new weight in her hand then. A trembling began at her shoulder and walked down past her elbow, down to her wrist and hand and, having no other choice, she lowered the weapon.

"That's very good," Colonel Willis said. "Very, very good."

"We need to talk about the way things are," Lucille said, feeling very tired all of a sudden.

"We can have all manner of talks."

"Things have got to change," she said. "They just can't go on the way they've been going on. They just can't." Even though the gun was lowered, it was still clutched in her hand.

"You might be right," Colonel Willis said. He looked over at a group of soldiers—among which was the boy from To-peka—and nodded toward Lucille. Then he turned back to her. "I'm not going to stand here and pretend as if everything is the way it should be. Things are out of accord, to say the least."

"Out of accord," Lucille echoed. She'd always liked that word: *accord*. She looked over her shoulder. They were all still there, the wide, sweeping body of Returned. They still looked to her: the only thing standing between the soldiers and themselves.

"What'll become of them?" Lucille asked, turning back just

in time to see Junior almost close enough to reach out and take her pistol. The boy froze—his own pistol still in its holster. He loathed violence, that boy. All he really wanted was to get home safely, just like everyone else.

"What was that, Mrs. Hargrave?" Colonel Willis asked, the glare of the floodlights along the southern gate still shining behind him.

"I asked what'll become of them." Lucille's fingers flexed around the pistol. "Assuming abdication…"

"Oh, hell," Harold said. He lowered Jacob to the ground and took him by the hand.

Lucille's voice was hard and controlled. "What will become of them?" She motioned to indicate the Returned.

Junior had never heard the word *abdication* before. But he had a feeling it was a precursor to something not very good, so he took a step back from the gun-wielding old woman. "Don't you move!" Colonel Willis barked.

Junior did as he was told.

"You have not answered," Lucille said, each word perfectly enunciated. She took a small step to her left, only to clearly look past the young soldier that had been sent to take her gun away.

"They'll be processed," Colonel Willis said. He straightened his posture and placed his hands behind his back in a very military fashion.

"Unacceptable," Lucille said, her voice harder than it had been.

"Hell," Harold cursed under his breath. Jacob looked up at him with fear in his eyes. He understood what his father understood. Harold looked over at Bellamy, trying to get some manner of eye contact. Bellamy needed to know that Lucille was past the point of being calmed.

But Agent Bellamy was as engaged in what was happening as everyone else.

"Abominable," Lucille said. "Irresolvable."

Harold trembled. The worst argument he and Lucille had ever had came not long after the word *irresolvable*. It was her war cry. He stepped back toward the open gate, away from where the bullets might fly if everything went south—which he was pretty damned sure it was about to.

"We're leaving," Lucille said, her voice deadly and steady. "My family and the Wilsons are coming with us."

Colonel Willis's face was unchanged. He looked stern and hard. "I don't believe that's going to happen," he said.

"I'll have the Wilsons," Lucille said. "I'll have them back."

"Mrs. Hargrave."

"I understand that you've got appearances to maintain. Your men need to respect you as their leader and having a seventy-three-year-old woman come here with one little gun and her group of rabble and walk out of here with all those locked within the walls of that entire town, well, I don't need to be a military strategist to know that's not the light you want to be seen in."

"Mrs. Hargrave," Colonel Willis repeated.

"I won't demand nothing less than what's owed, nothing less than what's mine—my family and those under my protection. I've got God's work to do."

"God's work?"

Harold pulled Jacob closer. It seemed like every prisoner in the town of Arcadia had assembled at the fence. He searched the crowd, hoping to catch sight of the Wilsons. It would be his job to take care of them once things went the way they were obviously going to go.

"God's work," Lucille repeated. "Not the Old Testament God that parted the sea for Moses and crushed the pharaoh's armies. No, not that God anymore. Maybe we drove that God off."

Junior took another step back.

"Stay where you are, soldier!" Colonel Willis yelled.

"Harold, get Jacob somewhere safe," Lucille said. Then, to Colonel Willis, "Things have got to stop. We've got to stop waiting for someone else, even God, to help us out of the things that we should be helping ourselves out of."

"Don't you move a step, Private!" Colonel Willis barked. "You will relieve Mrs. Hargrave of that weapon so that we can all go about our night peacefully."

Junior was shaking. He stared into Lucille's eyes, asking what to do.

"Run away, child," she repeated in a voice she normally reserved for Jacob.

"Private!"

He reached for the gun.

Then Lucille shot him.

Lucille's not-so-small army of Returned wasn't as frightened by the shooting as the soldiers expected. Maybe it was because the vast majority of them had already died once in life and proven that, ultimately, death couldn't contain them forever.

That was one possibility. But not a likely one.

They were still people, after all.

When Junior crumpled to the pavement, clutching his leg and wailing in pain, Lucille didn't pause to tend to him as she once would have. Instead, she stepped over him and began walking directly toward Colonel Willis. Willis shouted for the soldiers at their posts to open fire. He placed his hand on the pistol on his hip but, much like Junior, was reluctant to draw on the old woman. She wasn't like the Returned. She was alive.

So the gunshots rang out from the soldiers. Some of them found homes in the bodies of people, but most of them only in the empty air and the summer-warmed earth. Lucille marched toward Colonel Willis, gun leveled.

Before Junior was shot, Harold had scooped Jacob up into his arms and was dashing off away from the gunfire. Bellamy wasn't far behind. He caught up to Harold and the boy shortly and, without asking, reached out and took Jacob from Harold's arms.

"Let's get to your mama," Harold said.

"Yes, sir," Jacob said.

"I wasn't talking to you, son."

"Yes, sir," Bellamy said.

And the three of them raced off into the enclosed city.

What the Returned lacked in artillery, they made up for in sheer number. Even without the ones that had come to Lucille's aid, there were still the thousands on the other side of the southern fence, still held within Arcadia. There were too many of them there watching things play out to be counted.

The soldiers seemed so few.

The Returned charged—silently, as if the whole event was not their ultimate purpose, only a scene to be performed—and the soldiers knew that ultimately their guns amounted to little more than posturing against such a crowd. As a result, the gunfire did not last very long. The Returned swelled around the knot of soldiers, consuming them like a tide.

Lucille's army billowed ahead, quickly opening the distance between where she stood with her gun aimed at the colonel. There was the sound of yelling, the sound of people fighting and wrestling one another. It was an orchestra of chaos—passion for life on both sides of the divide.

Windows of buildings were broken. Fights raged on front lawns and in doorways as soldiers retreated in small groups. Sometimes they might gain some small advantage on account of the fact that the Returned were not soldiers, only people, and so they were afraid as people often are when faced with men with guns.

But life motivated them. They surged forward.

"You could have killed that boy," Colonel Willis said, looking past Lucille to Junior. He had stopped yelling—resigned to the fact that he had been shot but was still alive and, for the most part, well. He only moaned and clutched his leg.

"He'll be fine," Lucille said. "My daddy taught me how to shoot almost before he taught me how to walk. I know how to hit what I'm aiming at."

"This won't work."

"I figure it's already worked."

"They'll send more soldiers."

"That won't undo the fact that the right thing was done today." Lucille lowered her gun, finally. "They'll come for you," she said. "They're people. And they know what you've done. They'll come for you."

Colonel Willis wiped his hands clean. Then he turned on his heel and walked away, saying nothing, headed toward town where the soldiers were scattered and, here and there, still shooting, still trying to claw back control, even as they failed at it. The Returned would not be held much longer.

Colonel Willis said nothing.

It was not long before the Wilsons arrived. They came the way a family should: Jim and Connie standing like bookends, with their beautiful children between them, protected from the world. Jim nodded at her. "I hope this wasn't all on our account," he said.

Then Lucille hugged him tightly. He smelled musty, as if he needed a shower, and Lucille thought that smell appropriate. It validated her. Indeed, he and his family had been mistreated. "This was the right thing," she said to herself.

Jim Wilson was about to ask her what she meant. And she would have only waved him away and joked about the dishes he needed to do when they returned to the house. Perhaps she would have lectured him on child-rearing—playfully, of course, meaning no harm, only as the beginning of a running joke.

But a gunshot rang out in the distance and Jim Wilson trembled suddenly.

Then he fell, dead.

Chris Davis

They found him in his office, staring at a wall of monitors. He did not speak. He did not run, as Chris thought he would. He only straightened his back when they entered the room and stared them all down and said, "I did my part, nothing more." Chris could not tell if he was asking them for forgiveness, or making some manner of excuse. The colonel didn't seem like the type of man to make excuses.

"I don't know what you are any more than you do," the colonel said. "Maybe you're like the ones in Rochester, ready to fight until you die a second time. But I don't believe that." He shook his head. "You're something else. This can't last. None of it can." Then: "I did my part. Nothing more."

For a moment Chris expected Colonel Willis to kill himself. It seemed dramatic enough for the moment. But when they took him, they found his gun empty and placed harmlessly atop his desk. On the monitors on the wall—where he had, for so many weeks, watched the lives and, sometimes, deaths of the Returned—there was only the image of an old black woman sitting alone on her cot.

The colonel inhaled sharply when they lifted him and began carrying him through the halls of the school. Chris wondered what the man's imagination was doing to him.

When the door to the room opened, the boy inside—in dirty, soiled clothes—covered his eyes from the light with a trembling hand. "I'm hungry," he said weakly.

Two of them entered the room and helped the boy out. They lifted him in their arms and carried him away from his prison. Then they placed Colonel Willis inside the room where the boy had been held for days. Before they closed the door and locked it, Chris could see the colonel looking out at the mass of Returned. The colonel's eyes were large and filled with wonder, as if the Returned before him were spreading out to cover the entire world, filling its empty places, forever rooted in this world, this life, even after their deaths.

"Okay, then," Chris heard the colonel say, though it was not clear to whom he was speaking.

Then they shut the door and locked it.

EIGHTEEN

"WE'VE got to stop," Harold huffed, his lungs burning.

Even though every instinct in him told Bellamy that they should keep going—his mother was out there somewhere, in all this madness—he gave no protest. He needed only look at Harold's state to know that there was no choice. He placed Jacob on the ground. The boy went to his father. "Are you okay?" he asked.

Between coughs, Harold gasped for air.

"Sit down," Bellamy said, putting his arm around the old man. They were near a small house on Third Street. It was far enough away from the gate to keep them out of trouble. This particular part of town was quiet, as so many other people were back at the gate where everything was happening. Likely as not by now, Bellamy figured, everyone that could escape Arcadia was doing just that. *Eventually this might all be empty,* he thought.

The house belonged to the Daniels family, if Bellamy's memory served him correctly. He'd made it a point of remembering as much about the town as possible, not because he ever expected any of this to happen, but only because his mother had always taught him to be a man of details.

In the direction of the gate, a single gunshot cracked.

"Thank you for helping me get him out of there," Harold said. He looked down at his hands. "I wasn't fast enough."

"We shouldn't have left Lucille," Bellamy replied.

"What was the alternative? Stay and get Jacob shot?" He groaned and cleared his throat.

Bellamy nodded. "Good logic, I guess. It'll be over soon, though." He placed his hand on Harold's shoulder.

"He'll be okay?" Jacob asked, wiping his father's brow as Harold went on coughing and gasping.

"Don't worry about him," Bellamy said. "He's one of the meanest men I've ever met in my life. Don't you know the mean ones live forever?"

Bellamy and Jacob led Harold up to the porch steps of the Daniels's house. The house was lonely looking, squatting beneath a broken streetlight next to an abandoned lot.

Harold coughed until his hands knotted into fists.

Jacob rubbed his back.

Bellamy was standing with his eyes aimed toward the heart of town, toward the school.

"You should go tend to her," Harold said. "Nobody's going to bother us. The only people that had guns were the soldiers and, well, they're a mite outnumbered." He punctuated the promise by clearing his throat.

Bellamy continued staring in the direction of the school.

"Nobody's concerned with an old man and a young boy right now. We don't need you standing over us." He reached over and put his arm around Jacob. "Ain't that right, son? You'll keep me safe, won't you?"

"Yes, sir," Jacob said sternly.

"You know where we live," Harold said. "I reckon we'll head back to find Lucille. Things sound quiet up that way now. It's all moved past the gate but Lucille will stay there, I imagine. She'll wait for us."

Bellamy turned his head sharply. He squinted in the direction of the southern gate.

"Don't you worry about Lucille. Nothing'll happen to that woman." Harold laughed, but it came out heavy and filled with tension.

"We just left her," Bellamy said.

"We didn't leave her. We got Jacob to safety. And if we hadn't done that, she would have shot us herself. I can guarantee that." He pulled Jacob closer.

Off in the distance there was the sound of shouting, then silence.

Bellamy rubbed his brow. Harold noticed then that, for the first time since he'd met the man, Bellamy was sweating. "She'll be fine," Harold said.

"I know," he replied.

"She's alive," Harold said.

Bellamy chuckled. "That's still the question, isn't it?"

Harold reached out and shook Agent Bellamy's hand. "Thank you," he said, coughing a little.

Bellamy grinned. "You're going soft on me now?"

"Just say you're welcome, Agent Man."

"Oh, no," Bellamy said. "I'm dragging this one out. If you're going to get all soft and cuddly on me, I want to take a picture. Where's my cell phone?"

"You're an ass," Harold replied, suppressing his laughter.

"You're welcome," he said brightly after a pause.

With that the two men parted ways.

Harold sat with his eyes closed, focusing on opening the distance between himself and that damned cough that didn't seem to want to let go. He needed to figure out what to do next. He could feel that something else was left to take care of before it was all over, something horrible.

All his talk about knowing Lucille was okay was just that: talk. He wanted very much to see for himself that she was okay. He felt guiltier than Bellamy about leaving her there. He was her husband, after all. But he reminded himself that it was for Jacob's safety. Lucille herself had told him to do it. It made sense. With all those guns and all those people and all that fear, there was no way to tell what might have happened. That was no place to stand holding your child.

If things had been reversed, if he'd been the one standing out there and it had been Lucille standing on the other side of those soldiers, he would have wanted her to grab the boy and take off running.

"Dad?"

"Yes, Jacob? What is it?" Harold still desperately wanted a cigarette, but his pockets were bare. He folded his hands between his knees and stared out at the city of Arcadia, which had grown deathly quiet.

"You love me, don't you?"

Harold flinched. "What kind of fool question is that, son?"

Jacob pulled his knees to his chest and wrapped his arms around his legs and said nothing.

They made their way through the town carefully, slowly heading back to the gate. They passed other Returned now and again. There were still so many people within the walls of the town, even though many had escaped into the countryside.

Harold tried to move surely, without sending his lungs into a panic. Now and then, Harold talked of whatever stray thing crossed his mind. Mostly he talked of Arcadia. Of how it was "back then"—when Jacob had been alive. It seemed very important to him just now to take notice of how much things had changed over the years.

The empty lot next to the Daniels's place hadn't always

been empty. Back then, when Jacob was alive, it was where the old ice-cream shop stood, until sometime in the seventies, when it finally went under around the time of the oil crisis.

"Tell me a joke," Harold said, squeezing Jacob's hand.

"You've heard them all," Jacob replied.

"How do you know?"

"Because you're the one who told them to me."

Harold's shortness of breath was gone now and he was beginning to feel better. "But I'm sure you've got some new ones."

Jacob shook his head.

"What about some you've seen on TV? Maybe some you heard somebody else tell?"

More head shaking.

"What about the kids back when we were staying in that art room with Mrs. Stone? Kids always have jokes to tell. They must have told you a few before things got all crowded over and whatnot—and before you had to beat them up." He smirked.

"Nobody's taught me any new jokes," Jacob said flatly. "Not even you."

He released Jacob's hand and the two of them walked with their arms swinging. "Okay, then," Harold said. "I suppose we need to try."

Jacob smiled.

"So what should our joke be about?"

"Animals. I like jokes about animals."

"Any particular animal in mind?"

Jacob thought for a moment. "A chicken."

Harold nodded. "Good, good. Lots of rich territory with chicken jokes. Male chicken jokes in particular—but don't let those get back to your mother."

Jacob laughed.

"What did the mittens say to the hand?"

"What?"

"I'll always glove you."

By the time they neared Arcadia's southern gate, the father and his son had their joke—and a working philosophy of joke-telling—together.

"So what's the secret to it?" Jacob asked.

"Delivery," Harold answered.

"What about delivery?"

"Tell the joke like you know it."

"Why?"

"Because if you sound like you're making the joke up, then nobody wants to hear it. Because people always think a joke is funnier if they think it's been told before. People want to be a part of something," Harold finished. "When people hear a joke—and we're talking about prepared jokes—they want to feel like they're getting ushered into something bigger than they are. They want to be able to take it home with them and tell their friends about it and bring them into the joke, too. They want to make those around them a part of it."

"Yes, sir," Jacob said happily.

"And if it's really good?"

"If it's really good, it can keep going."

"That's right," Harold said. "Good things never die." Then, with a suddenness, without even time enough to tell their joke once more, they were at the southern gate, as if they had been wandering aimlessly—just a father and a son sharing time alone—and not headed back to where everything had happened, back to where Lucille was, and to where Jim Wilson lay.

Harold made his way through the scrum of Returned surrounding Jim Wilson with Jacob in tow.

Jim looked peaceful in death.

Lucille was kneeled beside him, weeping and weeping and weeping. Someone had stuffed a jacket or some such thing beneath his head and placed another over his chest. Lucille held one of his hands. His wife, Connie, held the other. Thankfully, someone had taken the children away.

Here and there, small pockets of soldiers sat together, unarmed and surrounded by Returned. Some had been tied with makeshift restraints. Others, knowing a lost cause when they saw one, sat without restraint and only watched in silence, offering no further resistance.

"Lucille?" Harold called, squatting down beside her with a grunt.

"He was family," she said. "It's all on me."

Somehow Harold did not see the blood until he was kneeling in it.

"Harold Hargrave," Lucille said in a thin voice. "Where's my boy?"

"He's here," Harold replied.

Jacob walked behind Lucille and wrapped his arms around her. "I'm here, Mama," Jacob said.

"Good," Lucille said, but Harold was not sure if she really registered that the boy was there. Then she grabbed Jacob and pulled him close. "I've done something terrible," she said, clutching him. "God forgive me."

"What happened?" Harold asked.

"Someone was behind us," Connie Wilson said, pausing to wipe the tears from her face.

Harold stood, slowly. His legs were heavy with pain. "Was it one of the soldiers? Was it that damned colonel?"

"No," Connie replied calmly. "He'd gone already. It wasn't him."

"Which direction was Jim facing? Looking over into town

or back that way?" He pointed in the direction of the road heading out of Arcadia. He could see where the city ended and the fields and trees began.

"Toward town," Connie said.

Harold turned in the other direction. He looked off into the countryside. He saw only the long, dark road that stretched out of Arcadia, between the empty fields of corn. Along the edges of the cornfields there were grand, dark pines jutting up against the starry night.

"Damn you," Harold said.

"What is it?" Connie asked, hearing a certain recognition in his voice.

"You damned son of a bitch," Harold said, his hands balled into tight fists.

"What is it?" she asked again, suddenly expecting to be shot down herself. She looked off in the direction of the forest, but saw only trees and darkness.

"Get the children," Harold said. He looked at his old pickup truck. "Put Jim into the back. You, too, Connie. Get in there and lie down and don't get back up until I tell you!"

"What's wrong, Daddy?" Jacob asked.

"Never you mind," Harold said. Then, to Lucille: "Where's the gun?"

"Here," she said. She passed it to him with disgust. "Throw it away."

Harold stuffed the gun into his waistband and went around to the driver's side of the truck. "Daddy, what's going on?" Jacob asked. He was still holding his mother. She patted his hand now, as if finally admitting that he was there.

"Just hush up, now," Harold said sternly. "Come over here and get in the truck. Get in and duck your head down into the seat.

"But what about Mama?"

"Jacob, son, just do as you're told!" Harold barked. "We need to get away from here. Get back to the house where we can get Connie and the kids safe."

Jacob lay down on the seat in the truck and Harold, to let him know that this was for his own good, reached in and patted the boy on the head. He did not apologize—because he knew he had not been wrong to yell at the boy just then, and Harold had always believed that a person shouldn't apologize when there was nothing done wrong. But there was nothing in his beliefs that prohibited a person from affectionately rubbing a child on the head.

When the boy was settled in, Harold came around to help with Jim Wilson's body. Lucille watched them lift the man and a sudden quote of scripture came to mind.

"My God sent His angel, and He shut the mouths of the lions. They have not hurt me, because I was found innocent in His sight."

Harold offered no rebuttal. The words sounded right.

"Careful," Harold said as they carried the body, speaking to no one in particular.

"Penitently," Lucille said, still kneeling. "Penitently," she said again. "It's all on me."

When the body was safely in the bed of the truck, Harold told Connie to get in, as well. "Put the children up front, if need be," he said. Then he apologized, though he couldn't have said why.

"What's going on?" Connie asked. "I don't understand any of this. Where are we going?"

"I'd rather the children sat in the cab," Harold replied.

Connie followed Harold's instructions. The children squeezed into the cab beside Lucille, Jacob and Harold. Harold told all three of the children to put their heads down. They did as they were told, whimpering now and again as the truck roared to life and headed out of town.

Lucille only looked into the distance, her mind elsewhere.

In the bed of the truck, Connie lay beside her husband's body—in much the way she must have lain beside him for all those years of life and marriage. She held his hand. She did not seem afraid or uneasy about being so close to the dead, or perhaps she simply did not want to leave her husband.

As they drove, Harold's eyes scanned the darkness along the edge of the headlights, looking for the barrel of a rifle to poke out and sound off and send him on to the grave. When they were not very far from home, with the town dropping away into darkness behind them, he reached over and placed a hand on Lucille's.

"Why are we going home?" Jacob asked.

"When you were in China by yourself and scared, what did you want to do?"

"I wanted to go home," Jacob said.

"That's what a person does," Harold said, "even if they know hell might find them there."

When they pulled off the highway and onto the dirt road that led home, Harold told his wife, "First thing we do is get Connie and the children inside. No questions asked. Don't worry about Jim. You just hustle these children inside. You hear me?"

"Yes," Lucille answered.

"Once you're inside, get upstairs. Don't stop for nothing."

Harold stopped the truck at the end of the driveway, turned the headlights on high and let the glare wash everything of its color. The house was dark and empty-looking in a way Harold could hardly remember ever seeing it.

He pressed the accelerator and started forward. He gained speed coming up the driveway and swung the truck around in the yard and backed it up to the porch steps as if he were planning to unload a Christmas tree or a bed full of firewood and not the body of Jim Wilson.

He was possessed of a sense of being followed, a feeling that things had not been settled just yet and so he did everything in a hurry. When he listened, he could hear the low rumble of truck engines in the air—probably at the end of the dirt road now, Harold figured by the sound.

He opened the truck door and stepped out. "Get inside," he said. He pulled the children from the cab, plopped them onto their feet like foals, and pointed them toward the porch. "Come on, now," he said. "Hurry up and get in there."

"That was fun," Jacob said.

"You just get inside," Harold said.

Suddenly the glare of headlights bounced up the driveway. Harold shielded his eyes and pulled the pistol from his waistband.

Jacob and Lucille and the Wilsons were scuttling through the door when the first truck slid to a stop in the yard just below the old oak tree. The three trucks that followed parked beside one another, all of them with their headlights on high.

But Harold already knew who they were.

He turned and climbed onto the porch as the truck doors opened and the drivers stepped out. "Harold!" a voice called out from behind the wall of lights. "Come on now, Harold!" the voice said.

"Turn those damned lights off, Fred!" Harold shouted back. "And you can tell your friends to do the same thing." He stepped in front of the door and switched the safety off the pistol. Inside the house he could hear the sound of everyone scrambling upstairs the way he'd told them to. "I can hear that Clarence still ain't got that belt tightened on that truck of his."

"Don't you worry none about that," Fred Green replied. Then the lights on his truck went out. Shortly after, the lights on the other trucks went out, as well.

"I imagine you still got that rifle with you," Harold said.

Fred walked around to the front of his truck as Harold's eyes were adjusting. Fred carried the rifle cradled in his arms.

"I didn't want to do it," Fred said. "You got to know that, Harold."

"Oh, come on now," Harold said. "You just saw a chance to do something you always wanted to do, and you did it. You always been a hothead, and with the world the way it is now, you finally get to be the hothead you've always wanted to be."

Harold took another step back toward the door and raised his pistol. The old men who'd come with Fred raised their rifles and shotguns, but Fred didn't raise his rifle.

"Harold," Fred said, shaking his head, "just send them out and let's put an end to all this."

"By killing them?"

"Harold!"

"Why's it so important that they stay dead?" Harold stepped back again. He hated leaving Jim's body there in the bed of the truck, but there was little choice. "How did you get like this?" he asked. "I thought I knew you better." Harold was almost inside the house.

"It's just not right," Fred said. "None of it."

Harold entered the house and slammed the door. A silence settled in around everyone for a moment. The oak tree at the front of the house rustled beneath a sudden wind that came up out of the south like a promise of misfortune.

"Get the gas cans," Fred Green said.

Patricia Bellamy

He found his mother alone in the schoolroom sitting at the end of her cot—waiting and waiting and waiting—with her hands in her lap and her eyes aimed straight ahead without commitment to any one particular thing. When she saw him at the door, there came the sudden light of recognition to her eyes. "Oh, Charles," she said.

"Yes," he said. "I'm here."

She smiled then, brighter and with more vibrancy than she ever did in Bellamy's memories of her. "I was so worried," she said. "I thought that you had forgotten me. We've got to make that party on time. I won't stand us being late. It's rude. It's downright unkind."

"Yes," Bellamy said, easing down onto the cot beside her. He sat with her and took her hands into his own. She smiled more and rested her head on his shoulder. "I've missed you," she said.

"I've missed you, too," he said.

"I thought you'd forgotten me," she said. "Ain't that the silliest thing?"

"It is."

"But I knew you would come back to me," she said.

"Of course you knew," Bellamy said, his eyes slick with tears. "You know I can never get away from you."

"Oh, Charles," the old woman said. "I'm so proud of him."

"I know," Bellamy said.

"That's why we can't be late," she said. "This is his big night. The night when he becomes a fancy government man... our son. He needs to know that we're proud of him. He needs to know that we love him and that we'll always be here for him."

"I'm sure he knows," Bellamy said, the words catching in his throat.

For a very long time, they sat like this. Now and again there was the sound of some commotion coming from outside, small battles being fought here and there—as is the nature of things. Some soldiers were still loyal to Colonel Willis—or, at the very least, still loyal to what he represented. They couldn't quite put it together that everything he'd said and done, all of his opinions about the Returned, could have been wrong. So they fought a little longer than others, but that was fading, moment by moment, and soon it would all be over. Soon there would only be Martin Bellamy and his mother, trying to live through things one more time, until death—or whatever it was that took the Returned away like whispers in the night—came for her, or for him.

He would not repeat his mistakes.

"Oh, Marty," his mother said then. "I love you so much, son." She began searching her pockets, the way she had done when trying to find candy for him when he was a boy.

Martin Bellamy squeezed his mother's hand. "I love you, too," he said. "I won't forget that again."

NINETEEN

"YOU don't suppose I'm foolish enough to come in there, do you?" Fred yelled, his voice barreling through the thin front door and thin walls of the house like the ringing of a bell.

"I'd hoped as much," Harold replied. He'd just about finished dragging the couch to block the front door.

"C'mon, now, Harold. Let's not do all this. Me and the boys will burn you out if we have to."

"You might try," Harold said, turning off the house lights, "but that'll involve coming close to the house. And I'm not too sure you'll want to do that, what with me having this pistol and all."

When all the lights were out and the doors all locked, Harold settled in behind the couch in front of the door. He heard them at the back of the house already, splashing gasoline against the walls. He thought about heading back that way, maybe firing off a round but if things went as bad as he thought they might, he'd hate himself for wasting an opportunity to shoot one of them.

"I don't want to do this, Harold."

Try as he might, Harold couldn't help but hear something that sounded like sincerity in Fred's voice, though he wasn't certain how much he could trust it. "It's just something that has to be done."

"I guess we all got things we have to do, huh?"

Harold looked in the direction of the stairs. Above him he heard the sound of someone moving about. "Stay away from the damned windows!" he yelled. Lucille came to the stairs and shuffled her way down in an awkward, slightly arthritic-looking crouch. "Get the hell back upstairs," Harold barked.

"I've got to do something," Lucille replied. "This is all my fault. It's all on me!"

"Gracious, woman!" Harold huffed. "Don't that book of yours say that greed's a sin? Stop being stingy and share some of that guilt. Just imagine how our marriage would have gone if you'd been so prone to taking all the blame as you are now? You would have bored the hell out of me!" He thrust his chest out at her. "Now get back upstairs!"

"Why? Because I'm a woman?"

"No. Because I told you to!"

In spite of herself, Lucille laughed at that.

"That goes for me, too," Connie said, working her way down the stairs.

"Aw, hell," Harold groaned.

"What are you doing down here, Connie?" Lucille asked. "Get back upstairs."

"See how it feels?" Harold said to Lucille.

"What are we going to do?" Lucille asked.

"I'm sorting that out," Harold said. "Don't you worry."

Connie low-walked into the kitchen, avoiding the windows as best she could, and plucked the largest knife she could find from the carving block.

"What is it with women and knives?" Harold asked. "Remember that Bobbitt woman?" He shook his head. Then: "Let's just put a stop to all this, Fred."

"This can't end well," Lucille said.

"That's just what I was going to say," Fred yelled. From the sound of his voice, he was almost on the porch. "Harold," he called. "Harold, come to the window."

Harold stood with a groan.

"Please, Harold," Lucille said, reaching for him.

"It's okay."

"Let's talk about this," Fred Green said. He stood on the porch in front of the window. Harold could have shot him clean through the gut if he'd been inclined to. And, with the sight of Jim Wilson's body lying there in the bed of the truck—so perfectly performing its rendition of death—Harold felt a strong and undeniable urge to pull the trigger. But Fred was standing there without his gun, looking genuinely upset. "Harold," he said. "I really am sorry."

"I want to believe that, Fred."

"Do you mean that?"

"I do."

"Then you got to understand that I don't want any more bloodshed."

"Not from the True Living, right?"

"That's right," Fred said.

"You just want me to hand over this family to you, these children."

"That's right, but you got to understand that we're not out for a killing. It's nothing like that at all."

"Then what do you suppose it is?"

"It's a reckoning, a repairing of things."

"Repairing?"

"We're just putting things back the way they're supposed to be."

"The way they were supposed to be? Since when was killing one another the way they were supposed to be? Ain't it bad enough they been killed once already? Now they got to die again?"

"We didn't kill them!" Fred yelled.

"We who?"

"I don't know who did it," Fred continued. "Some stranger. Some crazy fool passing through town. They just happened to be the ones who got the bad luck that day. That's all. It wasn't us. It wasn't Arcadia. We don't kill people here!"

"I didn't say you did," Harold replied.

"But it happened," Fred said. "And this town ain't never been the same." He paused. "They don't belong here," he said. "And if we have to root them out one family at a time, then that's what we're gonna do."

Neither Harold nor Fred had to look over at Jim Wilson's body. Simply by being there and being dead, Jim Wilson seemed to say too much about the state of Arcadia, too much about the state of both Harold's and Fred's lives. "Do you remember what it was like before everything happened?" Harold asked finally. "Remember Jacob's birthday party? The sunlight. Everybody buzzing around, smiling and whatnot. Mary was going to sing that evening." He sighed. "Then, well, then everything just went a different way, I suppose. We all did."

"That's what I'm talking about," Fred began. "Certain things are supposed to happen in certain places. Muggings, rape, people getting shot and killed, people dying before their due. Those things don't happen here," he said.

"But it did happen," Harold said. "It happened to the Wilsons, to Mary. And then, from looking at how we are right now, I guess it happened to us. The world found us, Fred. Found Arcadia. Seeing Jim and Connie dead a second time won't change that."

There was a silence then, a silence of potential and possibility. Fred Green shook his head, as if declining some argument in his mind.

"We got to put an end to this," Harold said after a moment. "They didn't do anything wrong," he said. "Jim was born and bred here. Connie, too. Her folks were from over in Bladen County, not far from where Lucille's family lived. It's not like she's a damned Yankee or anything. Lord knows if she was a New Yorker I would have shot her myself!"

The two men laughed, somehow.

Fred looked over his shoulder at Jim's body. "I might burn for it," he continued. "I know that. But it had to be done. I tried to do the right thing the first time, tried to play by the rules. I told the soldiers they were staying here, and they came and took them away peacefully. It was over. I was willing to let that be the end of it. But, well..."

"All he was ever trying to do was live. Live and protect his family like anybody else in this world."

Fred nodded.

"Now, Lucille, Jacob and I are protecting them."

"Don't make this happen, Harold," Fred said. "I'm begging you."

"I don't suppose I really have a say in any of it," Harold replied. Then he, too, looked over at Jim's body. "Can you imagine the explaining I'd have to do if he suddenly sat up right now and asked me how the hell I just handed them over to you? I imagine if it was Lucille lying there..." He looked at his wife. "No," he said, shaking his head. He used the gun to motion for Fred to leave the porch. "Whatever this is about with you, Fred," Harold said, "I'd rather we just get on with it."

Fred raised his hands and slowly worked his way down from the porch. "You got an extinguisher?" he asked.

"I do," he said.

"I won't shoot on you so long as you don't shoot on me or

my men here," Fred said. "You can just send them out and put a stop to this whenever you want. It's all up to you. I swear, we'll do everything we can to save the house. You just send them out and we'll call it all off."

Then he was gone from the porch. Harold called upstairs for the children. At the same time Fred Green could be heard outside yelling something. Then there was a muffled sound of combustion at the back of the house, followed by a low crackle.

"How did it come to this," Harold said, not sure exactly whom he was asking.

It felt as though the room was spinning. Nothing made sense. He looked over at Connie. "Connie?" Harold called.

"Yes?" she answered, holding her children in her arms.

Harold paused. His head was full of questions.

"Harold…" Lucille interrupted. Two people couldn't live together for all their lives and not know each other's mind. She knew what he was about to ask. She felt it was wrong of him to ask, yet she couldn't bring herself to stop him. She wanted to know as much as anyone.

"What happened?" Harold asked.

"What?" Connie replied, her face wrapped in confusion.

"All those years ago." Harold looked at the floor as he spoke. "This town… It was never the same after that. And just look at where we are now. All these years of not knowing, all these years of wondering, being afraid that it was somebody from our own town—one of our own neighbors—that might have done it." He shook his head. "I just can't help but feel that if folks could have gone to bed knowing what really happened that night, maybe things would never have gotten this bad." Finally, he looked Connie in the eyes. "Who was it?"

For a long time Connie did not reply. She looked at her children, who were afraid and uncertain. She held them to her breasts and covered their ears. "I..." she began. "I don't know who it was." She swallowed hard, as if something were suddenly stuck in her throat.

Harold, Lucille and Jacob said nothing.

"I can't really remember," Connie continued, her voice sounding far away. "It was late. I woke up all of a sudden, thinking I'd heard something. You know how it is sometimes when you're not sure if what you heard was a part of a dream you were having or something from the real world."

Lucille nodded in affirmation, but did not dare speak.

"I was just about to try and go back to sleep when I heard footsteps in the kitchen." She looked at Harold and Lucille. She smiled. "A parent knows the sound of their children's footsteps." Her smile faded. "I knew it wasn't them. That's when I got scared. I woke up Jim. He was groggy at first, but then he heard it, too.

"He looked for something to use, but all he found was my old guitar by the bed. He thought about taking it, but I think he was afraid it would get broken. My father had given it to me just before Jim and I got married.

"It was a foolish thing for Jim to think about something like that, but that's the kind of man he was."

Connie wiped a tear from the corner of her eyes. Then she continued.

"I ran into the children's room and Jim ran into the kitchen. He yelled for whoever it was to get out of the house. They scuffled. It sounded like they were tearing the whole kitchen down. Then came the gunshot. Then came the silence. That was the longest silence of my life. I kept waiting for Jim to say something. To scream or yell out, anything. But he never did. I could hear whoever it was going through the house, like he was searching for something. Taking whatever was worth anything, most likely. Then I heard footsteps coming toward the children's bedroom.

"I got the kids and hid under the bed. I could only see to the doorway. All I saw of whoever it was were a pair of old work boots. They were stained with paint." Connie paused and thought, sniffling as she spoke. "I remember there had been these painters in town around that time. They were working over at the Johnson Farm. Never saw much of them, but Jim had helped out with the painting—we always needed a few extra dollars. I took Jim to lunch one day and I think I remember seeing a man with boots like the ones I saw from the children's room that night.

"I can't remember much about the man who wore them. Red hair, pale. That's about it. He was just a stranger. Someone I never thought I'd see again." She thought for a moment. Then, "He had a bad look about him," she said. She shook her head. "Or maybe I'm imagining he did because I want to believe it.

"But the truth is I don't know who did it. We didn't do anything to deserve what happened. But, then again, I can't imagine any family deserving to have something like that happen to them." Finally, she uncovered her children's ears. Her voice was not shaking anymore. "The world is cruel sometimes," she said. "All you need to do is look at the news any day of the week to know that. But my family loved one another up until the last moment. That's all that really matters."

Lucille was crying. She reached over and took Jacob in her arms and kissed him and whispered that she loved him.

Harold put his arm around them both. Then, to Connie, he said, "I'll take care of you. I promise."

"What are we going to do?" Jacob asked.

"We're gonna do what we have to do, son."

"Are you going to send them out, Daddy?"

"No," Lucille said.

"We're going to do what we have to do," Harold said.

The fire worked faster than Harold had expected.

Perhaps because it was an old house and had always been in his life, he imagined it could not be destroyed or, at the very least, would be a difficult thing to take from this world. But the fire proved it to be simply a house, nothing more than an assemblage of wood and memories—both very destructible things.

So when the fire climbed the back wall, the smoke rolled forward in great, sudden streaks, pushing the Hargraves and the Wilsons through the living room toward the front door of the house, toward Fred Green and his waiting gun.

"I should have stalled more," Harold said, coughing, praying that this was not one of those coughs that ended in unconsciousness. "I should have stalled more and got more bullets," he said.

"Lord, Lord, Lord," Lucille said. She wrung her hands and counted in her mind all the ways in which this was all her fault. She saw Jim Wilson. He stood tall and handsome and alive, with a wife and a daughter and a son wrapped around him, hugging him, clinging to him. Then she saw him shot in the streets of Arcadia, shot and falling stiff and dead.

"Daddy?" Jacob said.

"It's going to be okay," Harold said.

"This is wrong," Lucille said.

Connie held her children to her chest, her right hand still gripping that butcher's knife. "What did we ever do?" she asked.

"This is just wrong," Lucille said.

The children were crying.

Harold ejected the magazine from the pistol again, checked

it to be sure that the four bullets were still there, then he placed
it back into the gun. "Come here, Jacob," he called.

Jacob came over—coughing through the smoke—and Harold took the boy by the arm and began pushing the couch
from in front of the door. Lucille watched for a moment then,
without questioning, helped and trusted that there was a plan
in this, trusted in the way she trusted in all of God's plans.

"What are we going to do?" Jacob asked his father.

"We're getting out of here," Harold said.

"But what about them?"

"Just do what you're told, son. I'm not going to let you die."

"But what about them?" the boy asked.

"I got enough bullets," Harold said.

The gunshots rang out evenly and clearly over the dim,
moonless countryside. Three shots.

Then the front door was opened and out came the pistol,
tumbling through the air. It fell into the bed of the truck next
to Jim's body. "All right!" Harold yelled, walking out the front
door with both hands held high. Lucille followed with Jacob
tucked safely behind her. "You won, goddammit," Harold
yelled. His face was dark and somber. "At least I know you
won't get the satisfaction. I put them out of the misery you
would have made for them, you bastard."

He coughed.

"Lord, Lord, Lord," Lucille repeated under her breath.

"I'll reckon I need to see that," Fred Green said. "The boys
are still at the back of the house, just to be sure this ain't some
game you're playing, Harold."

Harold worked his way down the porch steps, leaning on
the truck for support. "What about my house?"

"We'll get to it. I just need to check to be sure you did what
you say you did."

Harold was coughing again. A long, hard, continuous cough that buckled him in half and dropped him to the ground next to his truck. Lucille held his hand, squatting next to him. "What have you done, Fred Green?" she asked, her face glowing in the rising firelight.

"I'm sorry, Lucille," he said.

"It's burning down," Harold wheezed.

"And I aim to take care of it," Fred said. He walked from his truck to Harold's side, his rifle held low on his hip, aimed at the doorway just in case the dead were not dead.

Harold coughed until he saw small points of light flashing before his eyes. Lucille wiped his face. "Damn you, Fred Green! Do something!" she yelled.

"At least get my damned truck away from the house," Harold managed. "If anything happens to Jim's body I'll kill every last one of you!" Jacob kneeled down and took his father's hand—partly to help him through his coughing, and partly to be sure that his parents stayed between himself and Fred Green's rifle.

Fred Green walked past Harold and Lucille and even Jacob. He went up the stairs toward the open door. Smoke rolled out in great, white plumes. From where he stood he could see the light of the flames burning their way forward from the rear of the house. He hesitated on going into the house when he did not see the bodies of the Wilsons. "Where are they?"

"Heaven, I hope," Harold said. He laughed, but only a little. His coughing had passed, though he was still light-headed and the small points of light were dogged about staying before his eyes, no matter how much he swatted at them. He squeezed Lucille's hand. "It'll be okay," he said. "Just keep to Jacob."

"Don't play games with me, Harold," Fred yelled, still up on the porch. "I'll let it all burn if I have to." He peered into the house, listening for the sound of coughing or moaning or crying, but heard only the crackle of the fire. "If you sent them out the back, I suppose the boys'll get them. And if they come through the front, I'll get them. And, well, there's the fire." He stepped back away from the growing heat. "You've got insurance, Harold. You'll get a great big check out of all this. I'm sorry."

"You and me both," Harold said, rising to his feet.

With a swiftness that surprised even himself, Harold was on his feet and up the porch steps while Fred Green still stood there staring into the burning house. Fred could hardly hear Harold bounding up the steps over the sound of the fire, and by the time he heard him, the butcher's knife was already running through his right kidney.

Harold's face was waist-high when the knife went in and Fred Green spun in pain and his finger squeezed around the trigger. The butt of the rifle leaped back and the nasal bone of Harold's nose split in two.

At the very least, he was no longer in any condition to kill the Wilsons.

"Get out here!" Harold coughed. "Hurry up!" The gun lay on the porch beside him, neither man thinking clearly enough just now to scramble for it. "Lucille?" Harold called out. "Help 'em!" He gasped for air. "Help 'em…"

She did not answer him back.

Connie and the kids, barely able to hear Harold over the sound of the fire, came from the house beneath the blanket they'd hastily managed to wet and hide beneath when the house started burning. As soon as they made it out into the fresh air the children went to coughing, but Connie led them past where Fred Green lay writhing with the knife sticking out of him.

"Get in the truck!" Harold yelled. "Those other assholes will be around here any second now."

The family scrambled down the porch steps past Harold and Fred and went to the driver's side of the truck. Connie checked to be sure the keys were still in the ignition. They were.

It was luck mostly that she was standing where she happened to be standing when the first shotgun blast came. The old truck proved a damned good barrier against buckshot. It was a '72 Ford, after all, made in that bygone era before fiberglass was deemed worthy of transporting a man and his family from one point in the universe to another. And that was why Harold had clung to the old truck for all these years, because they didn't make trucks that stood their ground against double-ought buckshot anymore.

But, unlike Connie and her children, the Hargraves were on the killing side of the truck. Lucille was on the ground, her body huddled over Jacob in the trembling glower of the burning house. Jacob had his hands over his ears.

"Stop shooting, dammit!" Harold yelled. His back was to the men with the guns, so he knew there was a very good chance they would not hear him. And, even if they did, there was a very good chance they would not listen. He covered his wife and son and hoped.

"God help us," he said, for the first time in fifty years.

Harold found Fred's rifle. He still hadn't managed to get himself onto his feet just yet, but that didn't mean he couldn't draw some attention. He sat on his behind with his legs spread out in front of him and his head throbbing and his nose bleeding, but he managed to draw back the rifle's bolt and chambered the 30-06 and fired one shot into the air, bringing everything to a sudden pause.

In the glow of his burning house, with Fred Green right

there on the porch beside him wrapping his shirt around his knife wound, Harold tried to get a handle on things.

"That's enough, I reckon," Harold said when the report of the rifle was gone.

"Fred? Fred, you all right?" one of the gunmen yelled. It sounded like Clarence Brown.

"No, I'm not all right!" Fred yelled. "I been stabbed!"

"He brought it on himself," Harold rebutted. The blood from his nose covered his mouth, but he couldn't wipe it on account of needing his hands as dry as they could be to handle the rifle, and he already had Fred Green's blood on his hands. "Now why don't ya'll just go on home?"

"Fred?" Clarence yelled. It was hard to hear over the sound of the house burning down. The smoke billowed from every crack and crevice of the house and rose up in a great, dark plume in the direction of the moon. "Tell us what to do, Fred!"

"Connie?" Harold called.

"Yeah?" came the reply from the cab of the truck. Her voice was low, as if speaking through the old truck's seat cushions.

"Take the truck and get on out of here," Harold said. He did not take his eyes away from the men with the guns as he spoke.

After a moment, the truck started with a roar. "What about you?" Connie called back.

"We'll be okay."

Connie Wilson took her children and her dead husband and rumbled off into the night, saying nothing else, not even looking back that Harold could tell.

"Good," Harold said softly. "Good." Harold wanted to say something to them about taking care of Jim, but it seemed implied. Plus, his broken nose was hurting like hell and the heat from his house burning down was getting unbearable. So he simply huffed and wiped the blood from his mouth with the back of his hand.

Clarence and the other men with guns watched the truck leave but kept their guns trained on Harold. If Fred had told them to do otherwise, then they would have, but their leader was silent as he shakily rose to his feet.

Harold turned the rifle on him as he stood.

"Damn you, Harold," Fred said. He made a move toward Harold and the rifle.

"I wish you would," Harold said, leveling the gun barrel at his throat. "Lucille?" he called. "Jacob?" They both lay motionless, a round, smooth hump atop the earth. Lucille still covering the boy.

Harold had something else to say, something maybe to bring sense to all this, even if it was too late for sense, but his lungs would not participate. They were too full of the razor-bladed cough that had been trying to take hold of him ever since his scuffle. It was a great, dark bubble rising up inside him.

"This house is gonna burn down around you," Fred said.

The heat from the flames was unbearable. Harold knew that he would have to move soon if he planned on living, but there was that damned cough inside him, waiting to come roaring out and fold him into an unconscious ball on the ground.

And what would become of Jacob then?

"Lucille?" Harold called yet again. And again she did not answer him. If he could just hear her voice, he thought, he could believe that all of this was going to be okay. "Just leave," Harold said, and he poked the end of the gun barrel at Fred.

Fred took his cue and backed away, slowly.

Everything hurt when Harold went to stand. "Jesus," he groaned.

"I've got you," Jacob said, suddenly there, suddenly returned to him. He helped his father to his feet.

"Where's your mama?" Harold whispered. "Is she okay?"

"No," Jacob said.

To be safe, Harold kept the gun trained on Fred and he kept Jacob behind him, just in case Clarence and the rest of the boys out by their trucks should decide to get excited with those shotguns of theirs.

"Lucille?" Harold called.

Jacob and Harold and Fred Green and Fred Green's rifle all limped down from the porch together and out into the yard. Fred walked with his hands around his abdomen. Harold just stepped sideways, like a crab, with Jacob in his shadow.

"Okay," Harold said when they were far enough away from the house. Then he lowered the gun. "I suppose we're done here." The gun fell then, but not because Harold had given it up, but because the cough—that damned rock slide of pain inside him—finally broke free. The razor blades in his lungs were as bad as he knew they would be. The pinpricks of light reappeared before his eyes. The earth came up and slapped him across the face. There was lightning everywhere, lightning and the thunder of the cough that seemed to tear Harold's body apart with every tremor. He didn't even have the energy to curse. And of all things he could do, cursing was the one that probably would have made him feel better.

Fred gathered the gun from the ground. He cycled the bolt to be sure there was a round in the chamber.

"I suppose what happens next is your fault," Fred said.

"Let the boy stay a miracle," Harold managed.

Death was there. And Harold Hargrave was ready for it.

"I don't know why she didn't come back," Jacob said, and both Harold and Fred Green blinked, as if he had only just appeared before them. "Your wife," Jacob said to Fred, "I remember her. She was pretty and she could sing." The eight-year-old boy's face blushed beneath his brown mop of hair.

"I liked her," he said. "I liked you, too, Mr. Green. Y'all gave me a BB gun and she promised to sing for me before you went home on my birthday." The light from the burning house washed over his face. His eyes seemed to sparkle. "I don't know why she didn't return like me," Jacob said. "People go away and don't come back sometimes."

Fred took a breath; he held it in his lungs and his entire body tightened, as if that one breath would burst him, as if it was his last and it held everything. Then he made a wet, choking sound as he lowered the rifle with a sigh and he wept, right there in front of the boy who, by some miracle, had returned from the dead and not brought his wife with him.

He sank to his knees in an awkward, twisted heap. "Get out of here. Just...just go," he said. "Just let me be, Jacob."

Then there was only the sound of the house burning down. Only the sound of Fred crying. Only the sound of Harold gently wheezing below the dark plume of ashes and smoke, which had grown so grand it was like a long, dark arm, reaching, the way a parent reaches for a child, a husband for a wife.

She gazed up at the sky. The moon was off in the corner of her eye, as if leaving her, or leading her perhaps. It was impossible to tell which.

Harold came and knelt beside her. He was thankful that the ground was soft and that here the blood did not seem to show as red as he knew it actually was. In the twisted light of the burning house, the blood was only a dark stain that he could imagine was anything other than what it was.

She breathed, but only barely.

"Lucille?" Harold whispered, his mouth almost at her ear.

"Jacob," she called.

"He's here," Harold said.

She nodded her head. Her eyes closed.

"None of that," Harold said. He wiped the blood from his face, suddenly realizing how he must look, covered in blood and soot and grime.

"Mama?" Jacob called.

Her eyes opened.

"Yes, baby?" Lucille whispered. There was a light rattle in her lungs.

"It's okay," Jacob said. He leaned in and kissed her cheek. Then he lay beside her and nuzzled his head against her shoulder, as if she were not dying, only nodding off beneath the stars.

She smiled. "It is okay," she said.

Harold wiped his eyes. "Damn you, woman," he said. "I told you people weren't worth anything."

She was still smiling.

The words came so low that Harold had to strain to hear them. "You're a pessimist," she said.

"I'm a realist."

"You're a misanthrope."

"You're a Baptist."

She laughed. And the moment lingered for as long as it could with the three of them connected, held together, just as they had been all those years ago. Harold squeezed her hand.

"I love you, Mama," Jacob said.

Lucille heard her son. Then she was gone.

Jacob Hargrave

In the moments after his mother's death, he wasn't sure if he had said the right thing. He hoped he had. Or at least, he hoped that he had said enough. His mother always knew what to say. Words were her method of magic—words and dreams.

In the glow of the burning house, kneeling at his mother's side, Jacob thought back to the way things had once been, back before the day he went down to the river. He remembered the times he had spent with his mother, when his father would travel for work for a few days at a time, leaving them alone together. She was always sadder when he was away, Jacob knew, but a part of him could not help but enjoy the moments they shared when it was only the two of them. Each morning they would sit across from each other at the breakfast table talking of dreams and omens and their expectations for the day. While Jacob was the type who awoke in the mornings unable to remember what he had dreamed during the night, his mother could recall everything in vivid detail. There was always magic in her dreams: impossibly tall mountains, speaking animals, oddly colored moonrises.

Each dream had a meaning for her. Dreams of mountains were omens of adversity. Talking animals were old friends soon to reenter her life. The color of each moonrise a portent of the mood of the day to come.

Jacob loved hearing her explanations of these wondrous things. He recalled one morning in particular, during one of those weeks his father was away. The wind rustled the oak in the front yard and the sun peeked up from the treetops. The two of them made breakfast together. He kept watch over the bacon and the sausage sizzling on the stove top while she tended to the eggs and silver-dollar pancakes. All the while, she told him of a dream.

She had gone down to the river, alone, not knowing why. When she reached the banks, the water was as calm as glass. "Dappled in that impossible blue you can find only in oil paintings left too long in a damp attic," she said. She paused and looked at him. They were sitting at the table now, starting in on breakfast. "Do you know what I mean, Jacob?"

He nodded, even though he did not know exactly what she meant.

"A blue that was less of a color and more of a feeling," she continued. "And as I stood there, I could hear music playing far off downriver."

"What kind of music?" Jacob interrupted. He had been so focused on his mother's story that he had eaten very little of his food.

Lucille thought for a moment. "It's hard to describe," she said. "It was operatic. Like a voice singing far off across a wide-open field." She closed her eyes and held her breath and seemed to be resurrecting the wonderful sound in her mind. After a moment she opened her eyes. She looked dazed and happy. "It was just music," she said. "Pure music."

Jacob nodded. He shifted in his seat and scratched his ear. "Then what happened?"

"I followed the river for what seemed like miles," Lucille said. "The banks were filled with orchids. Beautiful, delicate orchids— nothing like anything that could ever grow around here. Flowers more beautiful than I've ever seen in any book."

Jacob put down his fork and pushed his plate forward. He folded his arms on the kitchen table and rested his chin on his arms. His hair fell down over his eyes. Lucille reached over, grinning, and moved the strands away from his face. "I need to give you a haircut," she said.

"What did you find, Mama?" Jacob asked.

Lucille continued. "Eventually the sun was setting and, even though I had gone miles, the music was still no nearer. It was when the sun was beginning to set that I realized that the sound wasn't coming from downriver, but from the middle of it. It was like the music of the sirens, calling me out into the water. But I wasn't afraid," Lucille said. "And do you know why?"

"Why?" Jacob replied, hanging on her every word.

"Because back in the direction of the forest and all those orchids blooming along the riverbank, I could hear you and your daddy, playing and laughing."

Jacob's eyes grew wide at his mother's mention of him and his father.

"Then the music got louder. Or maybe not louder exactly, but stronger somehow. I could feel it more, like a nice hot bath after I've been working all day in the yard. A soft, warm bed. All I wanted was to go toward the music."

"And Daddy and I were still playing?"

"Yes," Lucille said with a sigh. "And the two of you were get-ting louder, too. Like you were competing with the river, trying to hold my attention, trying to call me back." She shrugged. "I'll admit—there was a moment when I didn't know where to go."

"So what did you decide? How did you figure it out?"

Lucille reached over and rubbed Jacob's hand. "I just followed my heart," she said. "I turned my back and started off toward you and your daddy. And then, just like that, the music from the river did not sound as sweet. Nothing is as sweet as the sound of my husband and son laughing."

Jacob blushed. "Wow," he said. His voice was far away, the spell of his mother's story finally broken. "You have the best dreams," he said.

They ate the rest of breakfast in silence, with Jacob now and again staring across the table, marveling at the mysterious and magical woman who was his mother.

As he knelt over her in those final moments of her life, he won-dered what she thought of all that had happened in the world. All that had led them both to that moment when she lay dying in the glow of their burning house, on the very same earth where she had raised her son and loved her husband. He wanted to explain to her how things had gotten this way, how he had re-turned to her after being gone for so long. He wanted to do for her what she had done for him on those gentle mornings when they were alone: explain all the wondrous things.

But their time was short together, as life always is, and he did not know how any of this had happened. He knew that the whole world was frightened, that the whole world was wondering

*how the dead had returned, how confusing it was for everyone.
He remembered Agent Bellamy asking him what he remembered
from before he woke up in China—what he remembered about
the in-between time.*

*But the truth of it was that all he remembered was a soft, far-
away sound, like music. And that was all. A memory so delicate that he wasn't sure it was real. He had heard the music for
every second of his life since his return. A whisper, seeming to
call him. And hadn't it been growing slightly louder recently?
As if summoning him. He wondered if it was the same music
from his mother's dream. He wondered if she heard that music
now, as she passed away, that thin, fragile music that sounded
at times like that of a family laughing together.*

*All Jacob knew for certain was that in this very moment he
was alive, and that he was with his mother and, more than anything, he did not want her to be afraid when her eyes closed, their
time together finally ended.*

*"I'm alive for now," he almost said as she lay dying, but he
could see that she was already unafraid. In the end, "I love you,
Mama" was all that he told her. And it was all that mattered.*

Then he wept with his father.

EPILOGUE

The old truck bucked back and forth over the highway. The engine coughed. The brakes squealed. Every turn sent the whole thing to shuddering. But, still, it was alive.

"A few more miles yet," Harold said, wrestling the steering wheel as he entered a curve.

Jacob stared silently out of the window.

"Glad to be out of that church," Harold said. "Too much more time in there and I swear I'll convert...convert or start shooting." He chuckled to himself. "Or maybe one will lead to the other."

Still the boy said nothing.

They were almost at the house now. The truck chugged along the dirt road, sputtering blue smoke from time to time. Harold wanted to blame the bad condition of the truck on being shot, but that didn't hold water. The truck was just old and tired and about ready to give it all up. Just too many miles. He wondered how Lucille managed to drive it all those months, how Connie had made do with it that night. He would apologize to her if he could. But Connie and her children were gone now. None of them seen since the night Lucille died. Harold's truck had been found along the interstate the next day, pitched at an awkward angle, as if it had come to a rest unguided, as if there had been no one at the wheel.

It was like the Wilson family had up and disappeared, which wasn't unheard of these days.

"It'll get better," Harold said when they finally pulled into the yard. Where the house had been, there was only a skeletal wooden frame. The foundation had proved itself strong enough. When the insurance money came in and Harold had hired the men to rebuild, they'd managed to keep almost all of the foundation. "It'll be the way it was," Harold said. He parked the truck at the end of the driveway and switched off the ignition. The old Ford sighed.

Jacob said nothing as he and his father walked up the dusty driveway. It was October now. The heat and humidity had moved on. His father seemed very old and very tired since Lucille's death, Jacob thought, even though he tried very hard to not seem old and tired.

Beneath the oak tree in front of where the porch had been was where Lucille was buried. Harold had wanted to bury her at the church graveyard, but he needed to be near her. He hoped she would forgive him for that.

The boy and his father stopped at the grave. Harold squatted and raked his fingers over the earth. Then he mumbled something under his breath and walked on.

Jacob lingered.

The house was coming along better than Harold wanted to admit. In spite of being little more than a skeleton just now, he could already see the kitchen, the living room, the bedroom at the top of the stairs. The wood would be new, but the foundation was still as old as it always had been.

Things would not be the way they were, as he had told Jacob, but they would be however they were meant to be.

He left the boy standing at Lucille's grave and continued on to the debris pile in back of the house. Debris and the stone foundation was all the fire had left. The men building the new house had offered to haul off the rubbish, but Harold had stopped them. Almost every day he came here and sifted through the ash and rubble. He did not know what he was looking for, only that he would know it when he found it.

Almost two months now and still he had not found it. But at least he had stopped smoking.

An hour later, nothing new had been found. Jacob was still at Lucille's grave, sitting in the grass with his legs pulled to his chest and his chin tucked between his knees. He did not move when Agent Bellamy came driving up. Nor did he respond when Bellamy walked past him, saying, "Hello," and moving on without stopping—he knew the boy would not reply. This was how it had been every time he came to see Harold.

"Find what you're looking for?" Bellamy said.

Harold stood from kneeling. He shook his head.

"Want some help?"

"I'd like to know what I'm looking for," Harold grumbled.

"I know the feeling," Bellamy said. "For me it's photographs. Pictures from my childhood."

Harold grunted.

"They're still not sure exactly what it means or why it's happening."

"Of course not," Harold said. He looked up at the sky. Blue. Open. Cool.

He brushed his sooty hands against his pants legs.

"I hear it was pneumonia," Harold said.

"It was," Bellamy replied. "Just like the first time. She went peacefully enough in the end. Just like she did the first time."

"Is it the same all around?"

"No," Bellamy said. He adjusted his tie. Harold was glad to

see Bellamy back to wearing his suits properly. He still hadn't quite figured out how the man had made it all through the summer wearing those damned things and looking no worse for the wear, but toward the end Bellamy had started looking disheveled. Now his tie was tight about his neck again. His suit sharply pressed and immaculately clean. Things were getting back to the way they should be, he felt.

"It was okay this time," Bellamy said.

"Hmph," Harold grunted.

"How are things at the church?" Bellamy walked around the debris.

"Good enough," Harold said. He squatted again and went back to sifting the ashes.

"I hear the pastor's back."

"I reckon. Him and the wife are talking about adopting some kids. Finally getting in on a tried and true family," Harold replied. His legs were sore. He quit squatting and kneeled, dirtying his knees just as he'd done yesterday and the day before and the day before that.

Bellamy looked over at Jacob—still sitting at his mother's grave. "I'm sorry about all this," Bellamy said.

"Wasn't your fault."

"Doesn't mean I can't be sorry."

"In that case I guess I'll have to say I'm sorry, too."

"Sorry for what?"

"For whatever."

Bellamy nodded. "He'll leave soon."

"I know," Harold said.

"They get distant like that. At least, that's what the Bureau has been seeing. It's not always the case. Sometimes they just up and disappear, but usually they become withdrawn, silent, in the days before they vanish."

"That's what the television's been saying."

Harold was up to his elbows in the remains of the house. His forearms were black and gray with soot. "If it's any consolation," Bellamy began, "they're usually found in their graves. They're put back…whatever that means." Harold did not reply. His hands moved of their own accord, as if they were getting closer to the thing he was desperately seeking. His fingers were cut from loose nails and splinters of wood, but still he did not stop. Bellamy watched him dig.

It went on this way for what seemed like a very long time.

Finally, Bellamy removed his suit jacket and kneeled in the ashes and dug his hands in. The two men said nothing. They only dug for some unknown thing.

When Harold found it, he immediately knew why he had been looking for it. It was a small, metal box, burned to black by the heat of the flames and the soot of the destroyed house. His hands trembled.

The sun was setting in the west. It was growing cool. Winter would come early this year.

Harold opened the box, reached in, and removed Lucille's letter. A small, silver cross fell out into the ashes. Harold sighed and tried to keep his hands still. The letter was half-burned by the fire, but most of the words were still there, written in Lucille's long, elegant hand.

…world in madness? How's a mother supposed to react? How's a father supposed to deal with it? I know it seems like too much for you, Harold. There are times when I think it's too much for me. Times when I want to run him off, back to that river where our boy died.

A long time ago, I was afraid I'd forget everything. And then I hoped I could forget everything. Neither seemed much better than the other, but both of them seemed better than the loneliness, God forgive me. I know He's got a plan. He's always got a plan. And I know it's too big for me. I know it's too big for you, Harold.

It's worse for you. I know that. This cross, it winds up all over the place. This time I found it out on the porch by your chair. You probably fell asleep with it in your hand the way you always do. You probably never even knew it. I think you're afraid of it. You shouldn't be.

It wasn't your fault, Harold.

Whatever it is in you that makes your head go all screwy around the cross, it's not your fault. Ever since Jacob went on to Glory, you've carried this cross, the same way Jesus carried His. But even He was released from it.

Let it go, Harold. Let him go.

He's not our son. I know that. Our son died in that river, hunting for little trinkets like this here cross. He died playing a game his father had taught him to play, and you can't let that go. I remember how happy he was when you and he went down to the river and came back with this. It was like something magical. You sat there on the porch with him and told him that the world was full of secret things like this. You told him all a soul had to do was search for them and they would always be there.

You were still in your twenties then, Harold. He was your first child. You couldn't have known he would believe you. You couldn't have known he'd go back down there on his own and drown.

I don't know how this child, this second Jacob, came to be. But honestly, I don't care. He's given us something we never thought we could have again: a chance to remember what love is. A chance to forgive ourselves. A chance to find out if we are still the people we were when we were a pair of young parents hoping and praying that nothing bad would ever happen to our child. A chance to love without fear. A chance to forgive ourselves.

Let it go, Harold.

Love him. Then let him go.

Everything was blurry. Harold squeezed the small, silver cross in the palm of his hand and laughed.

"Are you okay?" Bellamy asked.

Harold answered only with more laughter. He crumpled the letter and held it to his chest. When he turned to look on Lucille's grave, Jacob was gone. Harold stood and looked out over the yard, but the boy was not there. Neither was he by the frame of the house. Nor was he at the truck.

Harold wiped his eyes and turned to the south, in the direction of the forest that led to the river. Perhaps it was only chance, or perhaps it was the way things were meant to be. Either way, for an instant, he caught a glimpse of the boy below the glare of the setting sun.

Months ago, when the Returned began being confined to their homes, Harold had told his wife how things would begin to hurt after that. He had been right. He knew that this would hurt, as well. All the while, Lucille had never believed Jacob to be her son. But, all the while, Harold knew that he was. Maybe that's the way it was for everyone. Some folks locked the doors of their hearts when they lost someone. Others kept the doors and the windows open, letting memory and love pass through freely. And maybe that was the way it was supposed to be, Harold thought.

Things were happening like this all over.

★ ★ ★ ★ ★

AUTHOR'S NOTE

TWELVE years after my mother passed away, I can hardly remember the sound of her voice. Six years after my father's death, the only visions of him I am able to recall are those last few months leading up to his final breath. These memories I wish I could forget.

Those are the rules with memory, with losing someone. Certain parts remain while others eventually disappear completely.

But fiction is something else.

In July 2010, a couple of weeks after the anniversary of my mother's death, I dreamed of her. The dream was a simple one: I came home from work and she was there, at the dinner table, waiting for me. For the course of the entire dream, we simply talked. I told her about grad school and life in general since her death. She asked me why I still hadn't settled down and started a family. Even after death, my mother was trying to marry me off.

We shared something that, for me, is only possible within the dreamscape: a conversation between a mother and son.

That dream stayed with me for months. Some nights, as I fell asleep, I hoped to recreate it—but I never did. Not long after that, I cornered a friend over lunch and told him about my emotional unease. The conversation went the way it does with old friends: meandering, mocking at times but, ultimately, restorative. Sometime later in our lunch, as conversation was running low, my friend asked: "Can you imagine if she actually did come back, just for one night? And what if it wasn't just her? What if it happened to other people, too?"

The Returned was born that day.

What *The Returned* became for me is difficult to explain. Each day that I worked on the manuscript, I struggled to resolve certain questions. Questions of general physics, questions of minute details and final outcomes. I grappled with even the most basic fundamentals: Where did the Returned come from? What are they? Are they even real? Some of these questions were easily answered, but others were paralyzingly elusive, and there reached a point in the process where I very nearly gave up and stopped writing.

But what kept me going was the character of Agent Bellamy. I began to see myself in him. His tale of his mother's death—her stroke, the illness that followed—is the tale of my mother's death. His constant desire to distance himself from her is my own attempt to flee from some of the more painful memories of my mother's final days. And, ultimately, his reconciliation became my reconciliation.

The Returned became more than just a manuscript for me; it was also an opportunity. An opportunity for me to sit with my mother again. An opportunity to see her smile, to hear her voice, a chance to stay with her in those last days of her life, rather than hide from her the way I did in the real world.

I eventually realized what I wanted this novel to be—what it *could* be. I wanted *The Returned* to be an opportunity for my readers to feel what I felt in that dream back in 2010, to find their own stories here. I wanted it to be a place where—

through methods and magic unknown even to me—the hard, uncaring rules of life and death do not exist and people can be with those they loved once more. A place where a parent can once again hold their children. A place where lovers can find one another after being lost. A place where a boy can, finally, tell his mother goodbye.

A good friend once described *The Returned* as "time out of sync." I think that fits. My hope is that the reader can enter this world and find the unsaid words and unreconciled emotions of their own lives played out within these pages. Perhaps even find their own debts forgiven. Burdens, finally, left behind.

ACKNOWLEDGMENTS

NO man is an island, and no writer writes alone. "Thank you" feels insufficient, but until I can raise a glass with each of you, here goes:

To my agent, Michelle Brower (and to Charlotte Knott), who took a clumsy, knock-kneed, cow-eyed writer and his manuscript, cleaned them both off, whipped them into shape and made them believe in one another.

To my editor, Erika Imranyi, who steered me past the pitfalls, and cheered me on the entire way. I didn't know what having my first editor would be like, but I couldn't have imagined it being as wonderful as it has been.

To Maurice Benson and Zach Stowell, the best pair of Rybacks a Ryback could ask for. Thanks for all the steaks, video games, cream sodas, '80s action movies and, more importantly, for keeping my feet grounded and keeping me about the business of staying busy. For freedom!

To Randy Skidmore and Jeff Carney, who took time out of their lives and endured the Dune-like wasteland that was the original draft of this novel. Your bravery and courage have undoubtedly secured your places in Valhalla.

To my brother-in-writing, Justin Edge, for all the planning sessions that were the foundation for this novel. Without those long hours spent vetting plot, characters and all manner of other ideas, none of this would have been possible.

To my other sister, Angela Chapman Jeter, for giving me "the talk" that day in the parking lot at work. I've got many, many moments to thank you for, but I was on the edge that particular day. You talked me down, and then all the wonderful things began happening.

To Cara Williams, for years of cheering me on and believing that this was possible. There aren't enough ways in the English language for me to thank you for your support. You're too wonderful for the likes of me.

To the many other friends, supporters and fellow writers who have helped make this possible: Michelle White, Daniel Nathan Terry, Lavonne Adams, Philip Gerard, the Creative Writing department of UNC Wilmington, Bill Shipman, Chris Moreland, Dan Bonne and his wonderful ILY troupe (imleavingyoutheshow.com), Mama & Papa Skidmore (Brenda and Nolan aka "Mr. Skid") for making me feel like family, Mama & Papa Edge (Cecelia & Paul) for adopting me as well, Samantha, Haydn and Marcus Edge, William Coppage, Ashley Shivar, Anna Lee, Jacqueline Bort, Ashleigh Kenyon, Ben Billingsley, Kate Sweeney, Andy Wiles, Dave Rappaport, Margo Williams, Clem Doniere and William Crawford.

To everyone at MIRA and Harlequin for making this all feel like some wonderful dream. Your support, excitement and encouragement have been overwhelming and I will be forever grateful. I hope to make you all proud.

To my family: Sweetie, Sonya, Justin, Jeremy, Diamond, Aja and Zion, for a lifetime of love and support.

Most of all, to my mother and father: Vaniece Daniels Mott and Nathaniel Mott Jr. Even though you are gone, you are always with me.

THE RETURNED

JASON MOTT

Reader's Guide

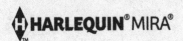

THE
RETURNED

JASON MOTT

Reader's Guide

HARLEQUIN MIRA

In the Author's Note, you indicate that the novel was inspired by a dream you had in which your mother, who passed away in 2001, returned to your life. How else has your life experience informed the novel?

In the years since my mother's passing, I've learned to appreciate the connections I have with the people in my life. I have what I've come to call my "adoptive family"—people who came into my life after the deaths of my parents and, in their own way, provided me with that connection of unconditional love and support that I once received from my mother and father. With *The Returned*, I wanted to bring some of that into the book. I wanted the book to be about connections and the bonds formed between people. Hopefully readers will feel I was successful.

Are there any characters in the novel to whom you particularly relate?

There are parts of myself in each of the characters, but Agent Bellamy was most directly my proxy character. His story of coming to terms with his mother's death is very much akin to the reckoning I experienced with my own mother's passing. At times his story was a tough one to write, but, in the end, it was very cathartic for me.

The Returned is set in a fictional small Southern town. Why did you choose to set the novel here, and is Arcadia based on any real towns?

I've lived nearly my entire life in a very small Southern town. I'm fascinated by small towns. They're special places full of connections and internal dynamics that you don't get in larger cities. I think I'll always write about them in some context.

The fictional Arcadia is an amalgamation of several small, southeastern North Carolina towns. It combines my hometown of Bolton with the towns of Whiteville, Wilmington, and my mother's hometown of East Arcadia. I borrowed the name of that town as an homage to my mother.

In addition to being a novelist, you are also a published poet. How has being a poet impacted your longer-form writing?

It keeps me from meandering. Before I started writing poetry, I was notoriously long-winded as a fiction writer. I overwrote scenes and never really knew when to stop. Poetry taught me to be more precise (and concise) with my words. It taught me how to use an image or a single turn of phrase to encapsulate something larger, rather than rolling on for page after page.

When you began the novel, did you have Lucille and Harold's journey already mapped out? How did they surprise you along the way? Were there any interesting surprises from other characters?

At the start of the project, I had the majority of Harold and Lucille's journey planned out. I'm a big fan of outlines and planning ahead. But I have to admit that their best moments came later, after the first draft was completed and I was able to focus on the nuances of the story. In my opinion, that's where the best writing moments always occur.

The character that surprised me the most was Fred Green. He was a character that, in the initial drafts, existed primarily in the background of the story. But during revisions my editor saw potential in him that I hadn't considered. She forced me to take a long, hard look at his character and what he truly could be. And, in the end, I think he became a wonderful and inimitable addition to the story.

What was your greatest challenge while writing _The Returned_, and what was your greatest pleasure?

I think the greatest challenge was keeping the focus of the story on the personal connections rather than the event itself. I didn't want readers to get hung up on the how and why of the dead returning to life. I wanted them to suspend their disbelief and just think about abstract ideas such as life, loss and personal relationships. So there was great difficulty in finding the middle ground between the magical elements and the realistic components. Hopefully readers will feel that I managed to strike the appropriate balance.

The greatest pleasure was, ironically, grappling with the challenges of the story. Writing is a journey we commit to each and every day. It's never easy—never ever. But when you find some aspect of writing that presents a new challenge, yes, it can be frustrating and exhausting and terrifying. But in the end it's also exhilarating. It forces you to be creative and to grow as not only a writer, but as a person. There's nothing else like it. It's why I write.

Can you describe your writing process? Do you write scenes consecutively or jump around? Do you have a schedule or routine? A lucky charm?

My process can vary depending on the genre I'm writing in and the stage of the writing, but I'll try to give a general view of how I work:

For a novel, once I have what I think is a good idea, I always start with an outline. I draw up the major plot points of the story and try to see where the story might go. Once I've completed that, I launch into a first draft. During that draft, I write freely, without stopping to edit. It's all about getting the words out. After that I go back and begin revising and editing, trying to get a sense of what I should keep and what should be discarded. This process is slower than writing the initial draft, but it's equally rewarding.

I always write first thing in the morning. I've found that if I don't, it becomes very easy to not write at all that day, and that's not what I want. So I start writing at about 7:00 a.m. and work until about 1:00 or 2:00 p.m. That's my workday. After that I step away from the computer and let my brain decompress.

What can you tell us about the book you're working on now?

I don't want to say too much about the next book just now. But I will say that it is another novel centered around a small, Southern town in which a miraculous event has occurred and the ramifications of that event become far-reaching.

1. In *The Returned,* the Hargraves find themselves at the center of a worldwide phenomenon where people's loved ones are returning from the dead. If a deceased loved one returned to you, how would you react? Would you be scared? Grateful?

2. Despite constant questioning, Jacob can't recall what happened to him between the time he passed away in the river and when he awoke again in China. What do you believe happens to us when we die?

3. In Arcadia, and around the world, there are various strong reactions to the Returned. Which side did you identify with—those who believed it was a miracle, or those who thought it was a harbinger of the end times? Did your reaction change over the course of the novel?

4. Several vignettes feature emotional reconnections between loved ones. Does love—either romantic or familial—transcend death? If so, how?

5. Jason Mott includes an extremely touching author's note at the end of the text explaining his inspiration for the novel. How does his sense of longing for closure—for one more chance to speak to his mother—inform his treatment of the characters in *The Returned*?

6. Fred Green is perhaps the most vocal opponent to the existence of the Returned in Arcadia. Why? Can you sympathize with him? Would his reaction have been different had his wife also Returned?

7. Near the end of the novel we learn that, in fact, Lucille never believed the Returned Jacob was her son. Meanwhile, Harold believed that he was. Were you surprised by this revelation? Do you think it could be a metaphor for different methods of grieving?

8. The government intervention in Arcadia quickly escalates from peacekeeping to near military governance. Could you imagine such a takeover happening in your town? Were you reminded of any other moments in history?

9. What is the role of religion in the novel?

10. Discuss the significance of the cross and Harold's search for closure after Lucille's death.

11. Do you believe in miracles? If so, what kind?

12. Harold often recalls the jokes he used to tell with his son. What are some of your favorite memories of a loved one you've lost?